Johanna Lindsey is world renowned for her 'mastery of historical romance' (*Entertainment Weekly*), with more than sixty million copies of her novels sold. She is the author of over fifty previous bestselling novels, many of which reached the number one spot on the *New York Times* bestseller list. Johanna lives in New Hampshire with her family.

Praise for Johanna Lindsey's legendary novels:

'If readers need to remember why they are Lindsey fans, she delivers every reason in this spinoff of *One Heart to Win*. She incorporates her signature captive/captor plotline with sassy dialogue, plenty of verbal sparring, lots of heat and a bit of humor, all in perfect proportions' *Romantic Times*

'Many wonderful heroes have been created by Johanna Lindsey, and those who live in the Old West are always a favorite' *Single Titles*

'You could feel the sexual attraction between these two . . . Lindsey allowed their relationship to develop slowly increasing the tension and making unexpected kisses sizzle . . . If you are looking for strong characters and a slow burning romance wrapped in suspense and surrounded by tumbleweeds look no further' *Caffeinated Book Reviewer*

'There is action, romance and suspense which make for a perfect escape from reality . . . I enjoyed this book so much' *My Nook, Books And More*

'This is a wonderful historical western romance with some twists that make this story totally unique. Ms Lindsey is known for her awesome historical novels . . . I was immediately hooked and stayed that way until the end of this story. I absolutely loved the characters, the settings and the interactions . . . Fantastic story from beginning to end that has Ms Lindsey's storytelling talent shining' *Night Owl Romance*

'Johanna Lindsey still has a knack of creating fun and unforgettable characters who remain in a reader's thoughts and heart years after finishing a book . . . I adore Johanna Lindsey's brand of storytelling' *Romance Junkies*

'One thing is for sure, Johanna Lindsey has a remarkable ability to pen characters w   riguing, loving, admi   o much more, all at

By Johanna Lindsey

Stormy Persuasion
One Heart To Win
Let Love Find You
When Passion Rules
That Perfect Someone
A Rogue Of My Own
No Choice But Seduction
The Devil Who Tamed Her
Captive Of My Desires
Marriage Most Scandalous
A Loving Scoundrel
Wildfire In His Arms
Make Me Love You
Beautiful Tempest
Marry Me By Sundown

JOHANNA LINDSEY

MARRY ME BY SUNDOWN

HEADLINE
ETERNAL

Published by arrangement with Gallery Books,
An imprint of Simon & Schuster, Inc.

First published in Great Britain in 2018
by HEADLINE ETERNAL
An imprint of HEADLINE PUBLISHING GROUP

First published in paperback in Great Britain in 2019
by HEADLINE ETERNAL
An imprint of HEADLINE PUBLISHING GROUP

1

Cataloguing in Publication Data is available from the British Library

ISBN 978 1 4722 5053 7

Offset in 11.38/15.5 pt Adobe Garamond Pro by Jouve (UK), Milton Keynes

Printed and bound in Great Britain by CPI Group (UK) Ltd, Croydon, CR0 4YY

MIX
Paper from
responsible sources
FSC® C104740

Headline's policy is to use papers that are natural, renewable and recyclable
products and made from wood grown in well-managed forests and other
controlled sources. The logging and manufacturing processes are expected
to conform to the environmental regulations of the country of origin.

HEADLINE PUBLISHING GROUP
An Hachette UK Company
Carmelite House
50 Victoria Embankment
London EC4Y 0DZ

www.headlineeternal.com
www.headline.co.uk
www.hachette.co.uk

MARRY ME
BY SUNDOWN

Chapter One

"I DON'T THINK SHE'S GOING to stop crying, even for this party," Sophie warned Violet as she returned to the bedroom the two girls shared.

Violet Mitchell sighed, knowing Sophie was talking about her aunt Elizabeth, Sophie's mother. But then Violet put her arm around her cousin's shoulders and squeezed gently. She was good at consoling, good at mothering, too, having tried to be a mother to her two brothers when they were all still children.

"She doesn't want me to go," Violet remarked.

"None of us want you to go!"

"She shouldn't have arranged this party, which is just going to remind her that I'm sailing back to America in the morning."

"If only that letter hadn't arrived four days ago," Sophie said in a grouchy tone. "If it had come next week, you would at least have been here for the first ball of the Season. I can't believe you're going to miss them all!"

Violet was going to start crying herself in a moment. She had so looked forward to the festivities this summer and sharing them with Sophie. She and her cousin had both turned eighteen this year, Violet last month, Sophie in early spring. Violet had continued to grow this year, ending up at five feet seven inches, while Sophie was quite petite at only five foot three. And Elizabeth had spared no expense in having beautiful wardrobes made for both of them.

Violet had lived with her aunt and uncle and their large brood of children these last nine years, ever since Aunt Elizabeth had come to America and visited Philadelphia, where she and Violet's mother had been born, and swooped into the Mitchell household insisting that Violet was returning to London with her to live with her and her husband, Lord Edmund Faulkner, and their six daughters. Violet's father, Charles, hadn't protested too much.

Violet actually understood why her father was relieved to have her taken off his hands. Raising a daughter without his wife, who had died of consumption a few years after Violet was born, had probably been a bit much for him. Her brothers, Daniel and Evan, hadn't protested either. They didn't exactly enjoy her bossing them around, but with no mother to guide the rambunctious boys, Violet had taken it upon herself to assume a motherly role toward her brothers, even though they were two years older than she. But there had been no one to mother her, and by the age of nine, she'd definitely felt that lack. So she hadn't protested much either when she'd been told she would be leaving her immediate family and moving to London. It had been hard trying to be a mother. Yet the behavior had been ingrained in her by then, and she'd done her fair share of bossing her cousins in England, too. But at least they didn't mind. They called it her being American!

"You should be happy for me," Violet remarked. "It will be

wonderful to see Papa and my brothers again. You don't think
I've missed them?"

"You never mentioned it, so, no, it's not something I gave
much thought to."

Violet tried teasing: "If I've learned anything from you
Brits, it's to keep unpleasant emotions under wraps."

"As my mother is currently doing, flooding her bedroom
with tears?"

They both smiled before Violet continued, "You know what
I mean. And you, my girl, have kept me too busy and enter-
tained to darken your moods by sharing those occasional
twinges of sadness I've felt when thinking about my brothers
and father. But I wrote to them weekly, and while the boys
aren't as good about replying as I would have liked, I understand that they have other things on their minds besides writing letters. And I know my father hates writing. I was lucky to
get eight letters from him in all the years I've been here, but he
always had the boys include a few lines from him in their letters. And at least they all visited twice."

"They should have come more often."

"I'm surprised there was even a second visit five years ago,
considering how terribly Papa and Evan suffered with seasickness on the first voyage."

"Oh, I forgot about that. Still, they should have braved it
for your come-out. If you hadn't sent them that portrait of you
last year, they probably would have, just to see for themselves
how you turned out, seasickness or no."

"Stop being annoyed for my sake when I'm not. I told them
not to come again, that I would visit them instead. They might
have enjoyed touring London, but they already did that
twice—and while they would never say so, I don't think they

were all that comfortable with the formality of British society. But mainly, I felt too guilty that my father and Evan had to suffer like that both coming here and returning home. And I did plan to visit them this year, just not this soon. I probably shouldn't have mentioned that I hoped to bring a fiancé with me. They weren't very happy about that."

"Did you really tell them that?" Sophie squealed happily.

"Why wouldn't I? Your mother has been talking to us both about this particular Season for years, so, yes, I thought it was something that might happen, and I shared that with my family. After all, your mother expected us both to get engaged this Season."

"What exactly did your father say about it?"

"Nothing yet. There were no lines from Papa in that reply, or in this last vague letter. But Papa will want me to be happy, so I expect to receive his permission to marry an Englishman when the time comes. In any case, it will be sorted out when I get home."

Sophie suddenly gasped. "Is *that* why they want you home immediately? They are afraid to lose you to an English husband?"

Violet frowned for a moment as she considered that possibility, but then shook her head. "No, they wouldn't dare try to pull a ruse like that. Daniel just wrote that it was urgent and sounded desperate about it."

"Yet failed to mention what is so urgent," Sophie reminded her in pique.

Violet sighed. "I'm sure he meant to explain, but he did mention that Evan had warned him not to write me about whatever is going on, so Daniel probably rushed the letter off so Evan wouldn't find out about it. He might have thought he did explain better than simply saying, *It's urgent, Vi. Only you can fix this.*"

"But you will return soon, won't you? You're good at fixing things, so it shouldn't take you long a'tall to fix whatever is wrong and be on the next ship back to us. Then you won't miss *all* of the Season. And bring your brothers back with you, your father, too. It's been five years, and we're their family, too!"

"I'll ask them, but there's no guarantee I'll be back before the end of this Season, not when it takes three to four weeks just to cross the ocean. Tonight I should be finishing my packing, not socializing. Shall we see if your mother is ready to go downstairs? I hope she didn't invite many people to this bon voyage party."

"I wouldn't count on that, Cousin. The Season does start next week. Besides, a lot of the *ton* lives in London as we do and others come early to make sure the hostesses know they are in town. At least you will meet a few of them tonight."

Violet laughed. "I'm going to meet them just to say good-bye?"

"No, no, you can assure them you'll be back soon. Or not tell them a'tall. Mama didn't exactly mention this is a good-bye party in the invitations, she just so wanted you to enjoy at least one party before you sail off tomorrow. And you're so pretty, Vi. You were destined to break some hearts this summer. And no, I'm not the least bit jealous. You can only have one, after all. There will be plenty of young gentlemen to go around. And maybe you'll meet the one you want tonight. Wouldn't that be splendid! You'll be yearning to return quickly," Sophie ended with a laugh.

"But the packing—"

"Is mostly done and the servants will finish that while we're downstairs. There's no help for it, Cousin. You're destined to simply enjoy yourself tonight."

Enjoy herself? Violet thought. Maybe if she hadn't been worried about her brothers and her father since Daniel's letter had arrived four days ago. And maybe if she didn't feel like crying herself because she had to say good-bye to her family here whom she'd come to love so much. But she'd been keeping these feelings to herself, mostly. If she'd learned anything during her stay with the Faulkners, it was how to put on a good face for all occasions.

Aunt Elizabeth did that now. She'd dried her tears before Sophie knocked on her door and offered a brilliant smile as she looked over her two favorite girls. Sophie was blond and blue-eyed and wearing an evening gown of palest aqua. Violet was also blond but favored lilac, the color of many of her new gowns, since it went so well with her dark-violet eyes. Tonight's gown was trimmed in white satin and she was wearing her mother's cameo on a ribbon about her neck. She hadn't had much occasion to wear any baubles until now.

Her father had sent her all of her mother's jewelry for her sixteenth birthday. She had hoped he would surprise her with a third visit to London that year, but he didn't. Her father actually expected her to return home about this time, now that her schooling was done and she no longer needed Elizabeth's mothering. He'd said as much the day she'd left home. But he hadn't mentioned it again in those few letters that he actually wrote himself, merely saying that he loved and missed her. She really was going to give all three of them a good scolding when she got home for not writing more often, particularly Daniel for not explaining what required her to rush back to Philadelphia. She'd hoped he had immediately sent off another letter with a full accounting, but no further missives had arrived in the last four days. And while she had come up with all sorts of reasons, she could never, ever have guessed what awaited her at the home where she was born.

Chapter Two

HIS NAME WAS ELLIOTT Palmer—actually, Lord Elliott Palmer. And Violet decided that very night in the Faulkners' elegant parlor that she was going to marry him one day. Instantly smitten, she gushed, she giggled, she blushed repeatedly, which was so not like her, but she couldn't seem to control her emotions in his presence. And he proceeded to monopolize her at the party, more than was proper, so she was quite sure he was smitten with her as well.

Blond with green eyes, and three or four inches taller than she, Lord Elliott was charming, debonair, and humorous. He regaled her with tales about his previous three Seasons, which accounted for all her silly giggling, even though she wouldn't normally have found some of the tales amusing as they focused on other people's stumbles, mishaps, and mismatches. But he seemed to find these *faux pas* so funny that she laughed with him. She simply couldn't help herself!

"I'll be turning twenty-one this summer," Elliott confided

at one point, then leaned closer to whisper, "I suppose it's time I start looking for a wife."

She nearly swooned in delight at such a provocative hint as that!

Sophie tried to keep her circulating among the guests. More people had come than either of them expected. Violet met all the other young gentlemen present, but Lord Elliott never left her alone for long.

"You're breaking every rule, you know," Sophie whispered as she dragged her away from Elliott yet again.

"I know, but no one will remember it by the time I get back," Violet replied.

"He is handsome, I suppose," Sophie said grudgingly.

"Incredibly."

"I wouldn't go that far—good grief, Vi, you weren't supposed to fall in love at your very first party!"

"I haven't—well, I don't think I have." But she soon amended, "So what if I have?"

"It simply isn't done." But at Violet's smile, Sophie threw up her hands, conceding, "Well, at least it shall get you back here posthaste, agreed?"

"Absolutely."

Her aunt, having noticed Elliott's attention, confided to Violet, "I know his mother well. She has complained quite often that she despairs of her boy ever settling down. I will be happy to inform her that might not be the case after all."

And her uncle also whispered an aside to her: "Good choice, m'dear. He's going to be a viscount one day."

Elliott stole a kiss, but it was a chaste one on the cheek as he was leaving. And it made him blush. Perhaps he'd finally realized that he'd broken more than one rule of etiquette that night. But he left not knowing that she was sailing in the morning. After meeting him, she so wished she weren't. She'd nearly confided that she was leaving London for a while, but decided not to say anything that might deter his interest in her. She intended to quickly settle whatever needed fixing in America and be on another ship back to London within the week.

ELLIOTT PALMER DOMINATED HER thoughts on the voyage home. Her thrilling memories of him kept her from worrying so much about what she might find when she reached Philadelphia. And Jane Alford, her new maid, provided distraction as well.

Talkative once she relaxed, the portly, middle-aged woman had been hired by Elizabeth to accompany her. Violet wished the maid she knew so well could have come with her instead, but she'd shared Joan with Sophie all these years and couldn't ask her cousin to relinquish her, even if only for a couple months—not that Joan would have agreed. Her aunt had complained that most of the women she'd interviewed for the position had refused to travel to America. Jane was the only one willing—and only when Elizabeth, desperate by then, had agreed to provide her with money for her own return passage in case she got homesick by the time they reached Philadelphia. Violet had to repeatedly assure the maid that America was a civilized land and Philadelphia was as fine a city as London. Despite Jane's trepidation, Violet found it hard to contain her excitement about seeing her family again after all these years.

The day finally arrived when she was standing outside the home she'd been born in, her trunks piled on either side of her. She didn't immediately go to the door, just stood there smiling as the memories flooded back. The large house had been her brothers' playground. How often she'd had to chase after them to keep them from breaking things! Boys that age could be quite rambunctious. She'd never told her father about their wild antics unless something did actually break. Charles hadn't often been at home during the day, and the servants had been afraid to scold the sons of the house.

Her father was wealthy, had received a substantial inheritance from his father, including the house. He was able to live a life of leisure and pursue his own amusements and interests. She wasn't sure what those were, could only remember that he liked betting at the racetrack and finding promising investments that he could brag about to his friends.

Violet finally noticed that all the draperies were drawn shut on the windows on either side of the front door, which was odd for such a beautiful Sunday in June. Even if the family wasn't at home, the servants should have opened the drapes. She moved to the front door, but found it locked. She knocked, but no one answered. Where the deuce was the butler? She knocked louder, pounding on it with her fist, quite worried now. A locked house was definitely not what she'd expected to find at the end of her journey.

She turned around but was daunted by the sight of her four large trunks. She'd dismissed the hired carriage and had no idea how long it would take to find another. Was she supposed to sit on her trunks all day waiting for her family to come home? If they were coming home. Again she wondered why no servant had answered the door.

"Will we need to break into the house, Miss Violet?" Jane asked.

Such a pragmatic solution! "Let's hope not."

Violet glanced to the side at the windows. She didn't relish crawling through one in her fancy traveling ensemble, but if they were open that would at least indicate someone was in the house. But the windows were shut, too. The drapes on the other side of the glass were utterly still.

"Is it an American holiday then, and everyone's gone off to celebrate?"

Violet didn't know what to think, except that someone, even if not the butler, should be manning the door.

Looking worried, Jane added, "Shall I go to the corner and hail a carriage? We can go to a hotel and wait there for your family to return."

Violet was about to agree when she heard the door open. She turned back to it, but it had opened barely a crack, and all she could see was an eye peering out at her; then: "Violet?"

She let out a relieved sigh. "Of course!"

The door opened wide to admit her. Both brothers were standing there, and while she used to have no trouble telling the twins apart, today she couldn't. Dark-blond hair like hers, sapphire-blue eyes, strapping instead of slim like their father, very handsome, they looked nothing like the boys she'd last seen five years ago. They were men now, twenty years old, and as tall as their father, which was a half foot taller than she! She leapt forward exuberantly to hug them, only to be grabbed by the one on the left who said, "I'm Daniel." He lifted her high in the air, then passed her to Evan, who swung her around in a full circle. By the time her feet were on the floor again she was laughing, and finally managed to put her arms around their waists and hug them both at the same time.

She'd missed so much these last five years. She'd asked them to have portraits done when she'd sat for hers, and to send them to her so she could see how they'd turned out, but they hadn't done it. They'd turned out splendidly indeed. And she felt something like motherly pride as she looked them up and down. It was hard to imagine she'd ever bossed and scolded these two, or that they'd let her!

But they had much to account for, and recalling that, she stepped back to say, "One of you let Father know I've arrived, then have someone bring in my trunks. We'll talk in the parlor. You've much to explain, Brothers."

They both walked past her to bring in her luggage themselves, Daniel only saying, "Father isn't home."

"Twin brothers?" Jane whispered as she joined Violet in the hallway. "And no butler?"

Violet sighed. "I will have a private word with my brothers. Wait here in the hall. I shouldn't be long."

"I'll find the kitchen, miss, and order you some tea."

"Thank you."

Violet headed to the parlor, the first room on the left of the long hallway. She intended to open a few windows. The house smelled more than a little musty. But she stopped short just inside the parlor and didn't take another step. This had been such a beautifully appointed room the last time she was in it, but nothing remained except the sofa. All the other furniture was gone. All the paintings that had been on the walls were gone. Were the boys waiting for her here so they could take her to their new home?

At the sound of footsteps behind her, she said, "I hope you didn't make me cross an ocean just to tell me Father has sold this house and moved to a bigger one."

"No," one of them answered. "You might want to sit down, Vi."

Without turning, she snapped, "No, *you* sit down, Evan on

the right, Daniel on the left. I want to know who I'm shouting at."

She was glaring at their backs as they moved past her. She saw them wincing as they turned to sit down on the sofa.

Abashed, Daniel said, "It's as bad as it looks."

"Really?" Her tone was sarcastic, but the added screech wasn't. "If you haven't moved, where's all the bloody furniture?!"

"We had to sell it to make payments on Father's loan and to keep up appearances," Daniel explained. "The paintings sold well, but the furniture didn't. A nasty amount of money is due every month."

Her eyes were wide by then. "Why would he—*where* is Father?"

"Not here. He left seven months ago to make a new fortune," Evan said. "He didn't want us to tell you he was broke, so we didn't. But if we can't pay the loan, Mr. Perry, the banker, is going to take the house."

"Broke? How is that possible?"

"Three bad investments in as many months," Evan went on. "Father didn't even realize his funds had gotten so low until he went to the bank to withdraw for the monthly household account and the clerk warned him he couldn't do that for much longer. He came home and dismissed some of the staff but not all, because he didn't want our neighbors and friends to know he's fallen on hard times. Then he got drunk for a week. Perfectly understandable, now that we know why, but we didn't find out until after he sobered up."

"When he did, he went to the bank and got a loan, using the house as collateral," Daniel put in.

"He wanted us to be able to live our lives as usual while he made more money," Evan continued. "He showed us a flier touting the discovery of more gold out west. We don't know why he fell for that nonsense. We've seen fliers like that since we were children. No one ever comes back rich. But he was so sure that gold mining would be the solution to our sudden dilemma."

"Believe me, Vi, we both tried to talk him out of it. We warned that he was gambling on a one-in-a-million chance of finding gold, that he should come up with a more realistic plan. But he wouldn't be dissuaded."

She glanced around the empty room again, and her shoulders slumped a little. "I suppose you're going to tell me next that after seven months, he hasn't found any gold?"

"Worse," Evan replied.

"What could be worse?" And then she paled. "Don't tell me he's—he's—?"

She couldn't say the word *dead*, but Daniel jumped in, "No, not that. Of course not. But he was writing regularly, and then the letters stopped. And we ran out of money. Both happened two months ago, which is why we sent for you."

"You should just let us tell you the whole of it, Vi, and then you might not have so many questions," Evan suggested.

She doubted it, which was why she was tapping her foot even as she nodded. "Go ahead."

"Father gave us half the loan money he received to use for the monthly payments and our own expenses, and took the other half to finance his mining venture." Daniel grimaced. "But the payments on the loan escalated after four months, and the entire loan has to be paid off in one year. Father assured us he'd be back in three to five months, so he told us not to worry about it. But with these higher payments, we had to start selling things."

"And we still haven't had another letter from Father. But he seemed optimistic in the last one he wrote."

"More like excited," Daniel corrected his twin. "He tried his luck in two towns out west, but they turned out to be a pure waste of time. But in that last letter, he mentioned he'd just staked a claim in Butte, Montana, near a known silver mine."

"That sounds promising," she remarked. "He's no doubt too busy mining to write."

"For more than two months? It's been about that long since we got his last letter." Evan sounded somber.

Her shoulders slumped again. Either their father was dead—*no*, she refused to believe that when there were too many other possibilities to account for his silence, including his hating to write letters. She knew firsthand what a terrible correspondent he was.

And then she realized how dire the situation was. "Then you've already lost the house? Should you even be here? Why did you tell me to come here? How am I supposed to fix this?"

Daniel held up his hand to halt her questions. "The banker—Mr. Perry—did come pounding at the door. And he appeared to relish the fact that most of the furniture had been sold off, as if that meant the house would soon become the bank's property. The only painting we hadn't sold was your portrait. We couldn't bear to part with it. He saw it hanging above the mantel in here and seemed mesmerized by it."

Her eyes went to the fireplace, but the portrait wasn't there. "Where is it?"

"He took it as last month's payment and—and—" Daniel couldn't finish.

Evan snorted and insisted, "Tell her."

"*You* tell her."

"One of you better tell me, and quickly," she snapped.

Evan looked down at her feet before saying, "He wants to marry you. He said he'd cancel the loan if you agree. We told him you weren't even in the country, that it would take time to get you here. He said he would extend the loan until you arrived."

It was too much to take in. In fact, she was having a hard time believing any of it. No money? Good God, were they actually paupers now? "I don't suppose he's reasonably young and personable?"

Daniel's eyes widened. "You'd consider it?!"

"No, but I do want to know my options."

Evan quickly said, "Not young, not nice, even fat, if you must know."

And Daniel added, "But many women in our social circle make arranged marriages. And at least Perry is rich, lives here in Philadelphia, and is already willing. If you married him, we'd have you back with us, Violet. Our family would be together again, and the house problem would be solved!"

"So this is why you summoned me home, to toss me to a fat wolf? Now I know why your letter was so bloody vague!"

Daniel winced. "It's not like that. We missed you! And we always assumed you'd make an arranged marriage—here in America. So you can't imagine how distressing it was when you wrote in the spring that you hoped to marry over in England. It meant we'd never see you again! If Father had been here to read that letter, we would have convinced him to forbid it."

Her eyes narrowed on Daniel. "Oh, you would, would you?"

Evan elbowed his brother. "I told you she wouldn't agree to it." Then he smiled at Violet. "But I'm happy that you came back, Vi, even if it is to such a desperate mess."

"Thank you, but the Perry option is crossed off the list."

"We have others?"

"Of course," she said, though a bit prematurely. "Give me a moment to gather my thoughts."

She started pacing in front of them. Obviously, they could return to England with her, even if they didn't like it there, but that would mean they would lose this house, the house they'd all spent their childhoods in, the house the boys had lived in all their lives. Maybe her uncle would pay off the loan for them, but sending a letter to London and waiting for a reply would take time.

She stared at the ceiling in exasperation. "You do realize that if you had mentioned any of this in your letter to me, I could have come here with enough money to pay off that loan so you could at least stop worrying about losing the house?"

"We did discuss it," Daniel said, "and agreed that Father would be furious if we asked the Faulkners for money. That's why I wrote to you in the hope you'd be interested in Mr. Perry's . . ." At Violet's glare, his voice trailed off. Then he added, "But there's a glimmer of hope now that Father's got a mine. We just don't know exactly where it—or he—is."

A mine that wasn't paying off yet, but still could, though it might not happen in time. Maybe she could make the next loan payment with the money her father had given her when she first sailed off with Aunt Elizabeth. She'd never needed to spend any of it. But if she used that to make the payment, she wouldn't have enough to solve their other problem: finding their father.

Chapter Three

Tʜᴇʏ ᴍᴏᴠᴇᴅ ᴛᴏ ᴛʜᴇ kitchen to continue their talk because the dinner hour was approaching. They, or rather she, had come up with a reasonable plan of action. At least, it struck Violet as the most reasonable option she could think of. It was amazing she could think at all, considering how unsettled she felt after learning she was no longer an heiress but a pauper. But then Jane put a dent in her plan when she stopped in the hall to explain to the maid where they were going tomorrow. And was met with a flat refusal.

"I wouldn't have come here if I didn't have money to return to London, and a good thing I insisted on that," Jane said, her expression quite bullish. "So I'm returning. You'll be needing to hire a new maid, miss."

There wasn't time for that! "Jane, it will take just a few days traveling by train to reach Montana. It will be interesting! Don't you want to see—"

"I've read me a few dime novels about that wild place west of here. There's Indians and bears and duels on every corner.

No, miss, I most certainly am not going anywhere except back home."

The woman grabbed her bag and marched out of the house. Violet gave her brothers an exasperated look, which warned them not to laugh. But she had a brief respite from their dilemma when they reached the kitchen and her brothers paused, looking at her expectantly. They were hoping she'd cook for them, she realized.

She laughed. "D'you really think Aunt Elizabeth would let me near her kitchen? I can't cook, but if you've been on your own all these months, surely you've learned how to by now."

"Not really," Evan said. "But at least the meal will be filling."

"If very bland," Daniel warned. "And eating standing up doesn't make the food taste any better."

They really had sold everything, even the kitchen table, which was why she suggested, "I could take us to dinner at a restaurant."

"You can't, not if we're keeping your arrival a secret," Daniel pointed out. "What if we ran into Mr. Perry?"

That wasn't likely, but if it did happen, then her plan would be over before it started. So she just nodded and said, "My maid's defection doesn't alter my plan—well, it does, it just means one of you will have to accompany me to find Father, while the other stays here to stall Mr. Perry for another month's extension. D'you need to draw straws?"

They'd already discussed this part. Perry was to be told that she'd sent them a letter explaining that she needed time to think about marriage to him. She was even going to write that letter tonight, in case he demanded to see it. But she was confident she would be back from Montana in less than a month, either with enough money from their father to save the house, or with their father himself, who would talk the banker into modifying the loan.

Daniel spoke up first. "Evan has to stay. He's courting a rich heiress and can't lose momentum on that. His marrying her would solve our dilemma—but he has to hurry it up."

"There are three others courting her as well, so it's not a sure solution, though I am hopeful. But these things can't be hurried."

"You love her?" Violet asked Evan.

"No, not yet, but at least she's pretty, so I'm willing to make the sacrifice, even if you aren't. And she likes me," he added with a rakish grin.

She rolled her eyes at him. Of course the young woman would like him. He and Daniel were both so handsome. But they were never supposed to have to sacrifice when choosing a wife. Then again, they were never supposed to end up poor either. She was going to give her father a blistering tongue-lashing for thoughtlessly squandering his inheritance and putting them in this dilemma.

She turned to Daniel who, by default, had become her traveling partner, but he winced and admitted, "I hate to say it, but I'm also committed. I would have gone to look for Father myself if I weren't. Although I'm sure he's fine. You know how charismatic he is. He makes friends and charms people into helping him wherever he goes."

"Committed how?" she asked, daunted by the thought of traveling to Montana without at least one of her brothers.

"It's a debt to a friend," Daniel said, then blushed. "We gambled. I really thought I could win, but I didn't, and I didn't have the money to pay him. If he weren't a friend, he probably would have had me tossed in jail. He was willing to wait for payment, but then his sister came to town and he offered to cancel the debt if I would agree to escort her during her visit. It was worth it to him to get out of the task himself. And I was delighted that I wouldn't have to admit that I couldn't afford to pay him back. It was only supposed to be for a few weeks, but she decided to extend her stay."

"How much do you owe him?" Violet asked.

Evan glanced up from chopping carrots. "Don't be annoyed with him, Vi. Had he gotten lucky, he could have turned that first bet into our next loan payment. Besides, Father told us to go on as if nothing had changed. It hasn't been easy, keeping our reduced circumstances from our friends."

She repeated more sternly, "How much?"

Daniel sighed. "Only fifty dollars, but that's a damn lot now that our pockets are empty."

She hated to see her brothers pinching pennies like this, but was relieved by the amount. "I can pay that off, so you can come with me to Montana." When he started to grin, she added, "Don't look so pleased. You may end up having to help work Father's mine."

He groaned. Evan laughed as he put the slab of beef in the oven to roast with the carrots. But Violet continued giving orders. "Evan, while you stay here to continue your courtship and deal with Mr. Perry, you might want to discreetly find out if anyone you know is interested in buying this house, just in case we have to lose it. Selling it will allow you to pay off the bank loan as well as any other debts you have and still end up with a profit."

"You know you actually sound British now?" Daniel suddenly said.

She raised a brow. "What did you expect? I've lived in London for as many years as I lived here, so of course I picked up an accent and a few expressions you aren't familiar with."

"You sound exactly like Aunt Elizabeth did when she came for you, furious that Father had let you turn into a tomboy," Evan added.

She laughed. "No, I wasn't a tomboy. And if I were to stay here for a few months, I might start sounding American again."

"You won't stay? Even if we drag Father home and all is as it should be again?"

Daniel looked so hopeful she almost told him what he wanted to hear. But if all could be as it should be, her life wouldn't change and she could go back to London and enjoy the Season, so she gently said, "No, but I will start visiting every few years now that my schooling is done. I won't ask Father and Evan to make that trip again, but you could, you know. In either case, I won't let another five years pass without us seeing each other, I promise you that."

"But why go back?" Daniel protested.

"Right before I sailed, I met the man I'm going to marry, Elliott Palmer, an English lord. And I intend to be back in England sooner rather than later so I don't lose him to some other debutante. So let's focus on our plan. Evan, you convince Mr. Perry to hold off on foreclosing on the house. The letter I write tonight should help with that. And Daniel and I will return from Montana with good news—or bring Father with us."

"Send word to me immediately," Evan said. "I want to know that he's well."

He *was* worried, Violet realized, and Daniel probably was, too; they just didn't want her to know it and start worrying as well. She said staunchly, "Someone would have notified you if anything bad happened to Father, particularly since he owns property in Montana, if a mining claim can be called that. So it's a good thing that you've heard nothing. He's probably too busy mining so he can get us out of this pickle, and too far from a town to post a letter. Now, is there a bed left in this house for me to sleep in tonight?"

Chapter Four

V IOLET WAS A LITTLE excited when she and Daniel left for
the train station the next morning. She'd had him buy her a
valise yesterday when he'd gone to pay off his friendly wager,
because it would be a nuisance to take one of her trunks on this
journey when she didn't expect to be in Montana more than a
few days. And he'd come back with good news. His friend had
refused to take the money, assuring him that putting up with
his sister for as long as Daniel had sufficed as payment in full.

She was more worried about the other creditors her brothers had mentioned, but both assured her their credit was still
good because none of those merchants were aware of their financial straits. Still, she left Evan with a little money, wishing it
could be more, but she needed to make sure there would be
enough left for the whole family to live on if their father hadn't
been successful out west. But she was hopeful and so looking
forward to seeing her father again.

They just managed to buy tickets for a train that was about
to depart. She boarded ahead of her brother and found them a

seat, setting down her valise. She thought he was right behind her until she glanced out and saw him on the platform being led away by a policeman! He was shouting, trying to tell her something, but she couldn't hear him clearly through the closed windows. She rushed to the boarding stairs and would have stepped off onto the platform, but the train started to move.

She heard Daniel yelling, "It's my tailor. He thinks I'm skipping town without paying him. I'll straighten this out and follow you tomorrow. Don't waste your ticket to stay and wait for me!"

She couldn't get off the train now even if she wanted to. She *did* want to and considered jumping off, but was afraid she'd break one of her limbs, and then she wouldn't be going anywhere. But she really didn't want to travel alone even for just one day. At least she would have had a maid with her if Jane hadn't been so afraid of going on this trip—good God, now she was just as afraid as Jane. Daniel might follow her tomorrow, if he could get a refund for his ticket to buy another, but he would still be a day behind her for the entire trip, unless she went no farther than the first layover. But time was of the essence, time during which a loan payment was rapidly coming due again.

She finally pushed her fears aside when she looked around the train car and noticed that the other passengers were all well-dressed, respectable-looking people like her. She took her seat and stared numbly out the window. At the first stop, she sent Evan a telegram telling him she would wait for Daniel in Butte. But she nearly changed her mind later in the week when the train crossed into what was considered the West.

She hadn't expected it would take her six days to reach her destination, especially after her brothers had bragged that she'd be riding most of the way on the fastest train in the world. They were misinformed. The transcontinental railroad used the same trains as the other railroads; it was touted as being the fastest way to cross the entire country simply because it didn't stop in every town for passengers. But she'd had to change trains twice before getting on the express train. Then she'd had to change again in Utah for the branch train that continued north to Montana—and each of those stops had required a sleepover while waiting for the new train, which amounted to a day wasted at each stop and funds wasted at hotels. She would have to start counting every penny.

Violet felt as if she'd entered a different world after the last change of trains. The easterners who had traveled with her this far and had kept her nervousness at bay were continuing on to California, while she was traveling north. When she looked out the window, she saw wide-open spaces, untouched forests, lakes so big she couldn't see the opposite shores. Fascinated by the landscape, she might have enjoyed this trip if she weren't making it alone and hadn't become such a curiosity to the new passengers, who appeared to be cowboys, farmers, and ragtag men who talked excitedly about getting rich in Butte. Had her father felt as excited and optimistic as these men when he'd come west? He would have been confident of success, so maybe he had.

Arriving at last, Violet could never have imagined a town like Butte, Montana. Her schooling hadn't prepared her for the American frontier. She'd studied European history and the wars that Britain had fought against America, but the English weren't interested in the western half of America, which they considered primitive and uncivilized. She'd learned from one of her fellow passengers that Montana wasn't even a state, merely a U.S. territory.

But for a frontier town, Butte was larger than she'd expected, filled with all manner of businesses and numerous hotels, even entertainment halls, though most of those appeared to be saloons. It was nothing like the two cities in which she'd grown up. The buildings were mostly made of wood and no higher than two stories. Late on a Saturday afternoon, it was incredibly crowded and, even worse, incredibly dusty, with so many people walking and riding through the streets. Most of the men were in work clothes. She saw only a few sporting derby hats, but the men weren't wearing suit coats. The women were plainly dressed, except for a few she was shocked to see in gaudy, low-cut gowns. There was too much to take in, so she didn't try. She just made her way to the nearest respectable-looking hotel, paid for a room, and, bone-weary, went right to sleep.

The next morning she was anxious to start searching for her father. After finishing a small breakfast in the hotel restaurant, she asked the attendant in the lobby whom she should talk to about finding a missing person. He gave her directions to the sheriff's office. She stopped at the telegraph office first to see if there was word from her brothers. There wasn't, so she sent a telegram to let them know she had arrived in Butte, and told the clerk where she was staying so any replies could be delivered to her.

The streets weren't as crowded this early in the morning. There were only a few wagons delivering goods. The miners who had filled the streets yesterday must have left town or were sleeping off their revelries. Twice last night she'd been woken by gunshots.

How on earth had her father managed in this town? Charles Mitchell was a gentleman born and bred, always meticulously dressed. She hadn't seen a single man in a suit yesterday and not one today either. The only men she saw were in work clothes or in pants, shirts, wide-brimmed hats, and gun belts. It was the gun belts that made this place so foreign to her, and made her so eager to leave it. She hoped she'd find her father today and could be on a train back to Philadelphia tomorrow with good news for her brothers.

A man was sitting in a chair on the porch of the sheriff's office. He appeared to be sleeping with his head resting back against the wall and his hat pulled down low over his face. She tried not to disturb him as she stepped past him and went inside.

"Sheriff?" she said to the man seated behind the desk. He was middle-aged and clean-shaven, neatly dressed in a leather vest worn over a shirt with rolled-up sleeves.

The man glanced up from the newspaper he'd been reading and set it aside. "No, ma'am. The sheriff's gone fishing with his brother, does every weekend. I'm Deputy Barnes. What can I help you with?"

"My father, Charles Mitchell, is missing. He came here a few months ago. The information I have is that he staked a claim in this area. Is that how you say it?"

"Good enough." The deputy grinned. "And what makes you think he's missing?"

"Because his habit was to write home often, but he hasn't sent another letter since he informed us he arrived here and began mining. Too much time has passed since then. We fear he may be hurt—or worse."

He looked solemn now as he said, "That I can find out immediately."

He opened a drawer in the desk and pulled out a ledger. He

turned a few pages in it before he glanced up at her again. His new expression made her heart sink.

"The sheriff usually deals with bad news, but obviously this won't wait till he's back," he said in extreme discomfort. "I'm sorry, ma'am. Your pa died two weeks ago. He was known in these parts as Charley, not that anyone knew him all that well. I recall now that Dr. Wilson let us know about it. He fills in when Dr. Cantry goes away. Your father had been Doc Cantry's patient for more'n a month and never regained consciousness after an accident that happened at his mine. Another mine owner brought him to the doctor. He's the one who found him. I think their mines are in the same area."

Violet started to feel faint, and the deputy helped her to a chair. She heard his words; they just weren't sinking in yet. Dead? Her brothers were going to be as crushed as she felt. She'd been so sure she would see her father today. She couldn't believe she'd never see him again! He was really dead?

A handkerchief was being waved in front of her face. She realized she was crying. It had been so long since she'd seen her father, yet she still had so many memories of him, walks and picnics in the parks, him teaching her and her brothers to swim in Springton Lake, boat rides on the Delaware River, and the four of them gathered in the parlor where he would read stories to them with her leaning against his shoulder and the boys sitting at his feet. The memories overwhelmed her. This news overwhelmed her. What was she to do now?

"Callahan, the man who brought your father to town, was checking on his condition whenever he came down from the hills," the deputy was saying. "Even left money for a funeral if it was needed. He got back to town a few days after your father died and was buried in the graveyard on the edge of town."

She was so numb! He couldn't really be dead. It could be a mistake, some other man with the same name. . . .

"Dr. Cantry might be able to tell you more. And Morgan Callahan—well, never mind him.."

"Why?"

"Callahan is something of a hermit, abides up in the hills where no one else lives and doesn't come to town often. Most folks figured he was just a mountain man when he showed up in a bear coat last winter, complete with the fur and looking as shaggy as one. Acts like a bear, too, if you ask me. Turns out he's been mining all this time and just tried to keep it a secret, which is not surprising, with the big mine owners around here buying up the little mines pretty fast. But the news got out that Morgan had found a pretty rich silver vein, and only your father managed to figure out where. Anyways, Morgan's just too gruff and surly for a lady such as yourself to speak to."

She nodded her agreement. "My father's belongings? Where might they be?"

"Probably still at his mine. And you might want to close out your father's bank account here, too, if he had one, but that will have to wait until tomorrow when the bank's open."

"Where is the doctor?"

He helped her to her feet to escort her out, saying, "I can take you to him now. He might have something to recommend for your shock, too."

"And my father's mine, where it is?"

"You would need to check with the claims office tomorrow, though that won't be helpful other than to confirm he staked a claim. They might give you the general direction in which it lies, but not much more. You'll need a guide to take you to it in any case, if it is indeed near Callahan's, though I doubt anyone knows where that is. Morgan seems a mite obsessive about keeping the location of his mine a secret, always leaving town in a different direction."

Despite the warnings, she had to ask, "But Mr. Callahan could show me?"

The deputy sighed. "He might be the only one who knows exactly where it is, but honestly, ma'am, you won't want to deal with him."

"Is he in town?"

He appeared glad to say, "No, least, I haven't heard that he is, and I would've heard. He stirs up gossip when he does show up, but that's not often. And when he does, he only spends one night in a hotel, then is gone the next day. But I can point you to the hotel he usually stays at. You could leave a message there for him if you've a mind to. Maybe he'll draw you a map and you can hire someone not as ornery to show you the way."

The last was said without any conviction. If Morgan Callahan was still keeping the location of his mine a secret, he would never draw a map to it, not even for his friend's daughter. Had he and her father been friends? Or just passing acquaintances? No, they must have been friends if Callahan had paid for the funeral, so maybe he would actually draw her a map—if it came to that. And just in case it did . . .

"Could you show me the hotel first?" she asked.

"Certainly."

The desk clerk at the hotel, which was in a newer section of town than where Violet was staying, told her Callahan hadn't been there for weeks.

"Kinda expected to hear that," Deputy Barnes said; then, noticing her crestfallen look, he added, "That's good news if you're determined to meet him. Means he's due to show up, maybe in the next week or two. I'll ask around, but I'm pretty sure Morgan's location is still a well-kept secret, and with reason. Used to be competition was cutthroat and claim jumping a major problem around here until the big mine owners bought up all the small mines. All the miners you see in town work for them. There aren't many small mines left near town, which is why I figure Morgan's mine is a long distance from Butte and why he doesn't show up often. But come along, the doc's office is in the next block and he lives upstairs from it, so he should still be there even if the office is closed."

Violet was daunted by how long she would have to wait for that Callahan fellow just to find out whether her father had found metal worth selling. But she might get the answer tomorrow at the bank, if there was a decent amount in her father's account.

"It's incredible that you know the comings and goings of all the miners in this town," she remarked on the way to Dr. Cantry's office. "How is that possible?"

The deputy chuckled. "It's not. People have come here from all over the world, Irish, Welsh, Germans, Chinese, heck, even Serbians, just to name a few. And many of the migrants who gave up mining have opened businesses instead."

"Then why do you know so much about Mr. Callahan?" she asked.

"That's because we know his family. The Callahans have a large ranch over in Nashart to the east. They used to herd cattle to us before the Northern Pacific Railway reached their town and new ranchers moved in closer to us over in Bozeman. When Morgan came here last year, the rumor was that he's the black sheep of the family and finally got booted from it. But it's just a rumor, and Morgan's temperament is bad enough as it is, so don't mention it if you meet him."

If? Yes, she might not have to wait for him if there was a substantial amount in Charles's bank account. She could then let her brothers decide what to do with their father's mine while she returned to England.

The doctor wasn't available when they reached his residence, he was out on a call. She decided to wait there for him to return, since she didn't have anything else to do other than let her brothers know that what none of them had wanted to consider even a remote possibility was true—their father was dead.

Chapter Five

THE DILEMMAS VIOLET ENCOUNTERED kept getting worse. Why had she thought she could deal with all of this alone? She didn't even realize just how deep her despair was because she was also grieving.

The brief conversation she'd had with the good doctor had revealed what her brothers didn't know: Charles had left home with a bad heart. He'd visited Dr. Cantry soon after he reached town because he'd been having chest pains. The doctor had warned him to avoid any strenuous activity because it could bring on a heart attack—yet Charles had gone from that visit up into the hills to mine? Something so utterly strenuous? Cantry said a heart attack had likely caused a fall and the resultant head trauma that Charles had never woken from.

She went to the claims office first thing the next morning. The man there confirmed that Charles Mitchell had staked a claim, but it was against their policy to show their maps to anyone, even relatives of claim holders. However, he did confide as she was leaving that the map wouldn't be helpful since it included no landmarks. "Not many do. If the miner is there, his mine is there, his stakes are there, therefore it's his place. If there's a fight over it, whoever holds the claim with the earlier date tends to win." She must have looked as confused as she felt, because he added, "It's not as shoddy a system as it sounds, ma'am. We have a large map of the area, but again, it's not for public viewing. We're not here to help men find ore, only to record it when they do."

She thought she understood, although she wondered how her father had managed to find ore. But at least she'd confirmed that he did have a mine in the area.

She decided to wait to send a telegram to her brothers until after she'd gone to the bank, which was where she headed next. She wanted to be able to add some good news along with the bad. But she wasn't able to do that. Her father had no bank account in this town.

She found out a possible reason why when she asked the bank clerk to check his records twice. The man complained, "We were robbed three months ago, so I'm not surprised that your father wouldn't trust us with his money. The miners are sending their money straight home or hiding it, and businesses are keeping their money in their own safes. It might be years before the bank recovers if that money isn't found."

So she had no good news to tell her brothers, but she couldn't hold off sharing the bad any longer. And she asked in that telegram why Daniel hadn't yet arrived in Butte as he'd promised, and stressed that she still needed him there to help find their father's money. Then she sat in her room for two days waiting for their reply. When some of the numbness wore off, she realized she should have switched to Callahan's preferred hotel to be absolutely sure she didn't miss him when he came to town. After she accomplished that, she took flowers to her father's grave and wept some more. Afterward she tried exploring the town to pass the time, but gave up that notion when she drew too many whistles and rudely inappropriate remarks from men she passed on the boardwalks.

She stayed in her new room mostly during the days, going down to the hotel dining room only for dinner. That first night in the new hotel, she met Katie Sullivan, a kindred spirit. Katie was a lively girl, red-haired, green-eyed, quite pretty. She lived with her family in Chicago and was only in Butte for a visit with her father and to introduce him to her fiancé, Thomas, who had just arrived and was staying at the hotel.

Violet guessed that Katie had invited her to sit with her and Thomas because of the way she was dressed. So little high fashion was seen in this town that she stood out, as did Katie, and they were naturally drawn to each other by apparent shared interests—at least in fashion.

But there was more when Violet introduced herself and mentioned her father's name. "Morgan Callahan's friend?" Katie asked.

"So you've met Morgan Callahan?"

"Goodness, no, I wouldn't get anywhere near such an uncouth fellow. But everyone knows *of* him by now. They say he's a former cowboy turned trapper, then a miner, and now he's just crazy from so much solitude—but in any case, he's very unsociable, by all accounts. And my father doesn't like the man, says that he's the most stubborn jack—er, mule he's ever met. My father, Shawn Sullivan, will be joining us shortly. He's always late. And we might not want to mention that you know Mr. Callahan."

That sounded ominous. Violet assured the girl, "But I don't, and apparently, I don't want to. However, I've been informed that he might be the only one who can show me to my father's mine. I am hoping that he will simply draw me a map to the location instead."

"A map? Yes, that would be ideal, wouldn't it? The less time you must spend with him, the better."

Following Katie's advice, Violet didn't mention Callahan's name after Shawn Sullivan arrived. He was a gregarious fellow once he relaxed, middle-aged, astute, portly, with a very distinct Irish brogue. Most of the dinner was spent with the parent grilling the possible future son-in-law about his family, his connections, his means. But once he gave his blessing, laughing that there still might be stipulations, both Thomas and Shawn relaxed to enjoy the last of the dinner agreeably.

Which was when Mr. Sullivan turned his green eyes to Violet and remarked, "A Mitchell, eh? The name sounds familiar."

"My father was in the area for a few months before he died," she explained, then added hopefully, "Perhaps you met him?"

"He might have worked for me if he was a miner."

"No, he had his own mine, I just don't know where it is yet."

"Well, that's too bad."

He did briefly look sad on her behalf, as if he didn't think she would have any luck in finding it, which left her feeling quite crestfallen. So she only vaguely listened to the rest of the conversation that centered on his family in Chicago.

But apparently Katie must have told her father later that night that Violet intended to have words with Morgan Callahan and why. She actually got a note from Shawn Sullivan the next day, saying if she did get a map to her father's mine, he would be pleased to supply her with an armed escort to take her there. So nice of him!

With Katie leaving the next day to return to Chicago to plan her wedding, Violet kept mostly to her room again, plying her needle. The little embroidery frame and kit of threads were the only nonessential items she'd stuffed into her valise, because needlepoint was one of her favorite hobbies. She didn't leave the hotel except to visit her father's grave, where she did most of her crying, and to stop by the telegraph office twice a day, even though she'd been assured any telegrams for her would be delivered to her hotel.

She didn't get her brothers' response until later in the week, and it wasn't what she was hoping for. They said it was impossible for them to join her but they were counting on her to find their father's mine, which was likely where he'd hidden his money. She'd already concluded that if Charles had any money, that's where it would be, so she ought to make every effort to find out, but she hadn't expected to continue this mission alone! How could she? And how much longer could they stall Mr. Perry? It was nearly two weeks since she'd left Philadelphia, and she'd already been waiting a week for Callahan to arrive. She couldn't wait for him indefinitely, or the next telegram she got from her brothers would inform her that they'd lost the house. Another week at the most, then she was leaving. But she started waiting in the hotel lobby. She couldn't afford to miss the man if he did finally show up.

A few people checked in that day, including another fashionably dressed lady. Someone else from back east? Violet considered introducing herself until she saw the young woman speak angrily to one of the gentlemen escorting her and march up the stairs.

The next morning Violet went straight to the desk to ask after Callahan again, which was what she should have been doing all week. She could no longer leave this to chance or depend on the hotel employees to remember to give him her note when he arrived. There was a new attendant today, one she didn't recognize, so she had to explain once more who she was and that it was imperative that she speak with Morgan Callahan when he checked in and that her note for him was being kept there at the desk. He opened a few drawers until he found it.

"You do know who I'm talking about?" she asked the new clerk.

"Everyone knows him, ma'am. The mountain man, least that's what we thought he was, a gruff hermit of few words, and in fact, he looks mean as hell, beg your pardon. But then word spread that he has a rich silver mine somewhere in the area. That didn't make him any friendlier. Are you sure you want to speak to a man like that?"

She wondered how many times she would be asked that question. "I don't really have a choice," she replied. "So tell me what he looks like. I would like to recognize him when I see him. Or will his identity be very obvious because he still looks like a bear?"

The man grinned. "No, ma'am, he won't be wearing that smelly bear coat in this warm weather. The man's tall, black-haired, in his midtwenties, and he usually wears a gun on his hip no matter the weather."

Everyone in this town except the miners seemed to do that, but the clerk's description was helpful and she thanked him. She joined an elderly man on the sofa across from the desk so she could keep an eye on it. He turned to her excitedly and said, "He's the fastest gun in the West."

She glanced at the elderly gentleman. "Who is?"

"The notorious gunfighter Degan Grant. I heard he's staying in this very hotel."

She lost interest as he droned on about the amazing gunfighter and glanced around the lobby again. Two men came out of the dining room walking briskly toward the hotel's front door, one short, wearing a long tan coat and a wide-brimmed hat pulled low, and the other tall, black-haired, and with a gun on his hip. Was that Callahan? Had he checked in last night and the new desk man didn't know it? She certainly hoped not. The man was quite intimidating, dressed all in black from hat to boots and looking very angry. And it appeared that he was leaving again?!

She stood up to stop him. The old man pulled her back down, whispering, "That must be him! And don't gawk. He'll shoot you if you stare too long."

Shot for gawking? What utter nonsense. And the old fellow was only guessing that this was the gunfighter, when he could in fact be the very man she was waiting for. Who was leaving without talking to her.

She followed the pair out of the hotel and saw them walking briskly down the middle of the street. But they were already the length of three shops away. She'd have to yell to stop him now, which simply wasn't done. She couldn't bring herself to break that golden rule of etiquette. At least, not in public. Instead she hurried along the boardwalk after him.

She was almost abreast of the duo and about to ask the man in black if he was Morgan Callahan when she heard a woman shout, "Degan Grant, come back here!"

Eyes wide, Violet looked back at the hotel and saw the same woman she'd almost approached yesterday, dressed just as finely. This time she wore an outfit that was three shades of blue; even the little hat she wore, which was just like Violet's bonnet, was blue. The pretty lady had actually walked out into the street to yell at the gunfighter. Thank goodness this wasn't Morgan Callahan, Violet thought.

The gunfighter didn't halt for the lady, didn't even look back, which prompted her to yell even louder, "Degan, stop! You *have* to hear me out!"

He did stop then, but not for the lady. A man had stepped into the street ahead of the gunfighter and was slowly walking straight toward him. Violet didn't need to be from the West to realize a gunfight was about to take place, especially when people quickly vacated the shops nearby and ran down the boardwalks away from the two men in the street. She knew she ought to do the same, but she was rooted to the spot, too shocked by what was happening to move.

She was close enough to hear Grant's companion warn him, "There's a man on the roof up ahead with a rifle pointed at you. This is an ambush."

"I know. I've already spotted two others."

"But that one is out of your range, while you're not out of his."

"It might not matter if I kill Jacob first. This is his fight, not theirs."

"The better idea would be to take cover, don't you think?" the shorter man suggested.

"You are," Degan Grant replied. "Get back in the hotel and do it fast."

Violet was amazed that he could talk so calmly about killing people. And the short man, or boy—she hadn't actually seen his face—ran back to the hotel, stopping to say something to the lady, who seemed more concerned about not stepping in the horse droppings in the street than the imminent gunfight. But the lady did at that point hurry back to the hotel herself. Which was what Violet started to do, but was suddenly yanked inside the shop behind her.

"What the hell, lady!" the shopkeeper said disparagingly. "Don't you realize what's happening out there?"

"Yes."

"Then maybe you don't know bullets can fly astray in fights like that? And kill innocents who aren't involved?"

She blanched a little. "No, I wasn't aware of that. Thank you."

"Just get down below the window. Mine's been broken before in fights like this. Gunfights don't tend to happen up in this section of Butte anymore, usually only in the rowdier part of town."

Even as he spoke, he was staring out the corner of the shop window. Violet glanced down at the dirty floor; refusing to sit on it, she took shelter behind the shopkeeper instead and peeked around his shoulder, his broad back providing good cover. Degan Grant and the man he'd called Jacob were both in view from that angle. She was surprised to see the boy in the long coat on the boardwalk, hurrying past the shop window, not staying out of harm's way after all.

The shopkeeper hadn't closed the door when he dragged her inside, and Degan Grant was close enough for her to hear him say to the other gunfighter, "I didn't kill you last time because you were grieving the loss of your brother. You've had enough time for that grief."

That brought a confident laugh from Jacob, but he was too far away for her to hear his reply if he made one. And then

Degan Grant drew his gun and fired. Unbelievable, how fast he did that. The other man's gun fired moments later, but his bullet must have gone astray since he was already falling to the ground as he pulled the trigger. If that bullet hit anything, it wasn't obvious. And Jacob lay unmoving in the street now, dead or badly wounded.

Then more shots were fired farther down the street. That must be the ambush that she'd overheard the companion mention. The gunfighter had disappeared and must have gone to deal with it.

She heard more shots, followed by several minutes of silence. Finally she asked, "Is it safe for me to return to my hotel now?"

The shopkeeper turned around and gave her a long look before smiling. "Aren't you the brave little lass. The last time a woman hid in my shop was the time the window broke, and she was in tears for a good hour after the last shot was fired, wouldn't leave until all the bodies in the street had been carried to the undertaker."

There was nothing brave about Violet's reaction to the violence; she just couldn't afford to miss Callahan and was afraid he might have arrived at the hotel while all the drama was taking place in the street. He could be there checking in right now!

"I'll be fine," she replied. "I'm staying at the hotel a few doors down."

"Suit yourself, lady."

He left the shop first—in fact, everyone along the street was leaving their cover to view the body that had been left there. There were enough people gathered around it that she couldn't see it now, for which she was grateful. But she did notice Dr. Cantry running up the boardwalk toward the crowd, so perhaps the man wasn't dead yet. She turned her back on the macabre scene and started back to the hotel to resume her vigil.

VIOLET BECAME A FIXTURE in the hotel lobby as the days dragged by. She began to recognize all of the hotel guests, saw them check in, saw them check out. And despite the assurances she received that she would be notified as soon as Morgan Callahan arrived, she still checked at the desk twice a day. She even politely declined the invitation she received to dine with Shawn Sullivan and his sister at his home in Butte because she was afraid to be away from the hotel for that long a time and risk missing Morgan. But, desperate to stretch her legs and get out of the hotel for a few minutes, she did actually walk past his house and found it quite impressive.

In the middle of her second week in Butte she received another telegram from her brothers, informing her that they'd stalled Mr. Perry for another month. That was a relief, though they still insisted they couldn't join her yet. She was annoyed that they didn't explain why, which made her assume the worst, that Daniel was in jail and they had no money to get him out, and Evan thought his marriage to that heiress was their only hope now. Which didn't say much for their confidence in their sister's saving them. And maybe they were right. Charles's mine could be worthless, which would mean there was no money hidden there and she was putting herself through this hellish wait for nothing.

And then, at the end of her second week in Butte, he showed up. She'd just finished a quick lunch in the dining room and returned to the lobby when the clerk at the desk waved her over to tell her Morgan Callahan had checked in and immediately left again.

"He's probably gone out for some fun, ma'am, like he usually does when he first arrives in town."

"Where?"

The question embarrassed the fellow and his reply was vague. "To places you can't follow him to. Best to wait until morning to speak with him, before he checks out again—if he'll talk to you."

"I've waited two weeks," she reminded the man. "I can't afford to miss him. Did you give him my note?"

"Tried to, along with all the other notes piled up here for him, but he wouldn't take any of them."

"Please tell me that you at least told him it's imperative that I speak with him?"

"In so many words, I did. He didn't appear curious, didn't even ask why, just nodded, got his key, and left."

His eyes wouldn't meet hers. He was keeping something from her, she was sure of it. Even his posture seemed guilty now.

"There's something you aren't telling me, isn't there?" she demanded. "And what did you mean, *if* he'll talk to me? Why wouldn't he?"

"There's nothing further I can tell you," the man said stiffly, but then actually did, adding, "But if you need Mr. Callahan's help with something, then you probably shouldn't have dined with his worst enemy."

Katie? No, of course not Katie—her father. "Mr. Sullivan?"

"I'm done talking, ma'am. Go away or I'll summon my manager."

She sucked in her breath indignantly and marched away to

retake her seat in the lobby. What the deuce had just happened? She recalled Katie saying her father didn't like Morgan. Well, it appeared Morgan didn't like Katie's father either.

None of which explained why Morgan might not talk to her. If he recognized her name, and had known her father, why wouldn't he?

Chapter Six

Before the dinner hour, the manager of the hotel approached Violet in the lobby. He introduced himself with a slight bow, but his tone was firm when he said, "I must ask you to leave the lobby, Miss Mitchell."

She frowned at him. "Why?"

"Because you have been disturbing my guests."

She was doing no such thing, but his expression warned he wouldn't argue about it. She was mortified when he added, "I also expect you to vacate your room in the morning. I won't have you harassing my employees any longer either. They've filed complaints. And in this town, good employees are harder to obtain than guests, so I have no choice but to insist you go."

She was furious as she went upstairs to her room and even slammed the door shut, hoping that awful manager could hear it downstairs. She didn't doubt that Morgan Callahan had somehow arranged for her eviction. And obviously, there would be no waiting for him comfortably in the lobby tomorrow. He'd seen to that. But she could wait outside the hotel for him to come out. She refused to be undone by these despicable she-nanigans of his.

She packed her valise that night. If she couldn't find Morgan as he left town tomorrow, she'd have no choice but to return to Philadelphia. She couldn't afford to wait weeks more for the man to come again to Butte on one of his infrequent visits. Leaving meant her brothers would lose the family home, and she knew they wouldn't want to go to England with her—actually, she couldn't return there either if she failed here. The Faulkners loved her, but she simply couldn't live there as their poor relation. And she certainly couldn't ask her uncle for a dowry when he had six daughters to provide for.

She sat on the bed quite shocked by the circumstances before her. She had to find her father's mine! She fervently hoped he'd hidden a fortune there. If not, she and her brothers would have to figure out a way to exploit the mine to make their own fortune. Otherwise, she would have to become a schoolteacher in Philadelphia and her brothers would have to get jobs. They would live dreary lives as genteel poor people. Or she could marry Mr. Perry. . . . She blanched at that thought.

But dare she stay in Butte any longer and risk running out of money? No, the thought of working in this particular town was appalling. She had enough money to send one of her brothers back here to continue the search. They owned a mine somewhere in this territory, and she had the name of the man who could show them to it. Perhaps Daniel or Evan would have better luck than she was having. But whichever brother came, he was going to have to work here in order to stay here.

Her anger returned when she realized that her future and theirs depended on a single man who wouldn't even take the time to find out what she wanted of him! But she still had one last chance to corner him in the morning and hoped she wouldn't be so furious with him that it would put him off dealing with her. If he didn't sneak out of the hotel by a rear exit. If he didn't simply leave town tonight. And she wouldn't even know if he'd managed to escape her notice!

More fuel for the fire. She was so angry that it took a while to get to sleep that night, hours actually. Fury just wouldn't let her mind rest. But exhaustion finally won out, she had no idea how late.

Being disturbed from that hard-won slumber brought the fury back—but only for a moment.

The gag was the first clue that she was in trouble. It tasted salty—from sweat?! She screamed under it, a pathetic mewling sound even to her ears. And then she was yanked out of the bed, only to be tossed back down on top of the covers. She screamed again when a very large shadow loomed over her. Violation came horribly to mind and suddenly terrified her. But she wasn't being accosted—she was being rolled up in the bloody blanket! And hefted over a shoulder to be carried out of there.

She understood then. She wasn't being allowed to leave the hotel of her own volition. She was being tossed out! Well, she had glared at the manager a bit, no, a lot. He might have thought that she would refuse to vacate the room and this was his only option. Or Morgan Callahan had paid for her to be evicted. This way? Like throwing out the trash? And in the middle of the night so no one would notice such a despicable deed?

She expected to be unrolled on the boardwalk outside the hotel and at least given her belongings, even if they didn't want her payment for the room. But that didn't actually happen. She was on that shoulder for too long. Was she being taken to a different hotel? Had it all been prearranged?

When the man carrying her finally stopped, she hoped she could actually stand upright in her tight cocoon. But she didn't get a chance to find out because her feet never touched the ground. She was dragged off his shoulder simply to be tossed on the back of a horse, stomach down, still bundled tightly in that blanket.

Her new position was what alerted her to the possibility that she was being abducted. She was even being tied to the horse, felt straps tighten across her back to keep her on it! So utterly ignoble. But one frightful thought led to another, until she finally concluded that this was the fault of her clothes! Someone in this town thought she was rich because of them and that a hefty ransom might be forthcoming. And how long would she have to wait to disabuse her captor of that notion? Would he even believe her when she told him that she wasn't rich? Well, her immediate family wasn't, but her uncle in England was. But it would take two months to obtain money from him! And another possibility loomed, that she might be killed instead if her captor chose not to wait months for a ransom.

It was excruciating waiting to get any answers, and time dragged because the ride was so uncomfortable. Her stomach ached even though the horse wasn't moving fast. Her back ached from trying to work loose of the straps so she could slide off the horse and run. And every so often she felt something press down on her back. Her abductor's hand, so he could assure himself she was still there?

It could have been an hour or less, or even two or three, for all she knew, before the horse finally stopped, the straps were undone, and her feet touched the ground. The blanket was unwrapped from her and tossed aside, then the gag was removed. She was extremely thirsty and her body ached and, wearing only a thin nightgown, she felt the chill in the air. But she kept her eyes on the man. She thought he might be tying the gag around his neck, but she couldn't be sure since he was just a huge shadow standing next to her.

Nonetheless, she demanded, "Who are you and why have you abducted me? I insist you return me immediately to my hotel!" He heard her, was looking right at her, but didn't answer, making her point out, "You've somehow gotten the wrong idea about me. I'm not rich. I warn you, no one will offer a ransom for me."

"I didn't think anyone would pay to get you back, and I'm not after money."

She was jarred by that rude reply, but he turned, apparently not intending to say more. With the eastern sky beginning to brighten behind him, making him just a dark shape, she carefully moved around him to make use of dawn's light to see who had abducted her.

He was a big bear of a man with a full black beard and mustache, long unkempt hair of the same color beneath a cowboy hat, and feral, light-blue eyes. He wore a tan coat with the sleeves cut off so it resembled a long vest; it was held down by his gun belt, no shirt under it. He was excessively tall, excessively broad of chest, too, and his bare arms were thick with muscles. His pants were dark blue, his boots brown, scuffed, and spurred. There might be a handsome man under all that facial hair or a grotesque one, she simply couldn't tell in the meager dawn light. But from the desk clerk and Deputy Barnes's descriptions, she had no doubt that she was staring at Morgan Callahan.

Thinking of the deputy, she realized Morgan might have found out from him yesterday exactly what she needed from him. The hotel employees didn't know about her mission. He must have decided to help her but didn't want anyone to see him leaving town with her. He could have knocked on her bloody door to say so!

Her valise was suddenly tossed by her feet. "Change your clothes if you've a mind to. Don't matter to me unless you take too long doing it."

She was so pleased that he'd grabbed her valise from her room, she almost thanked him. She quickly bent to open it and saw that her purse was in it, thank God. All the money she had was in that purse. And everything that she'd left out to wear today had been stuffed in the bag. She carried the valise around one of the six pack mules that were tethered to Morgan's horse to have some privacy while she changed clothes. But first she quickly moved to the stream nearby and cupped a handful of water, then another. She assumed it was drinkable, since the animals were helping themselves to it. But she was really too thirsty to care.

"Here's the deal," she heard him say on the other side of the mule. "You can ride upright without the blanket, but if you make any noise, it's back on your stomach. Try to run and it's back on your stomach."

"It's you, isn't it?" she said stiffly. "Don't try to deny it. I know you're Morgan Callahan."

"Stomach again it is."

"Don't be absurd!" she snapped. "At least tell me why you've done this."

"You cozied up to the wrong people, lady. How much did they pay you to impersonate Charley's daughter?"

Impersonate? Was he serious? "I *am* Charles Mitchell's daughter."

"No, you aren't, but I suppose Shawn wouldn't know that I know that."

He was making no sense. Maybe he really was as crazy as Katie had suggested.

Then he added, "And you were warned about noise."

She sucked in her breath before blurting out, "I'll be quiet!"

"Smart choice," he said. "'Sides, nothing you say changes my mind, and we'll both have the truth when we get to where we're going."

"Where is that?" Instead of answering, he took a step toward her. She quickly held up a hand. "All right!"

She really couldn't bear any more riding on her stomach. And where he was taking her would be obvious enough when they got there. But she was nervously aware that he hadn't confirmed that he was Morgan Callahan. What if he wasn't? But he had to be! There couldn't be two men who looked and behaved so similarly. And he knew Shawn Sullivan and her father. Didn't that confirm it?

She got her skirt and blouse on before she thought to mention, "If you will at least tell me you're taking me to my father's mine, I won't say another word. That is why I wanted to speak to you, all I was going to ask of you."

"You bargaining with me, lady?" he asked in an ominous tone.

She frowned. "I asked one simple question."

"And said a whole lot more. But the fact is, I'm not going to believe anything you say until you tell the truth and admit you're working for Sullivan, so don't bother."

"Then why did you abduct me?!"

"To find out exactly what you and Sullivan are up to—and you're out of words and time."

"Wait! I haven't finished dressing."

"Then stop talking and get to it," he growled.

It wasn't easy getting her socks and boots on without sitting down, but she managed it by leaning a little against the mule's side. She pulled her jacket out of the valise, shook it out, and donned it, since the morning was still chilly. Then she saw that her hat had been smashed under the jacket and gasped. It was utterly flattened! Did he know no better, putting a beautiful hat under a pile of clothes and boots? She tried to reshape it before tying it on.

There was nothing she could do for her hair. She'd braided it for bed as usual, but it was already starting to unravel. And it was too dark yet to see if he'd tossed her hairpins into the bag, not that she could fix her hair properly without a mirror. He might have grabbed them if he wanted no trace of her left in the room so it would appear she'd left on her own. Then no questions would be asked. But the sheriff might be notified that she'd skipped out without paying her bill—unless Morgan had paid it.

For all she knew, he might have left her key along with payment on the desk for the sleeping attendant to find when he woke; then, indeed, no questions would be asked, no sheriff would search for her.

She came out from behind the mule with the scathing complaint, "You've ruined my hat."

He stared at her. If he smiled or frowned, she realized she wouldn't be able to see it because his long mustache blended into his beard.

But he obviously couldn't care less about her hat, because all he said was, "You'll ride with me."

The devil she would. Ride in close proximity to him for however long it took to reach his mine, which could be days, for all she knew?

"That's out of the question. A lady doesn't ride with a gentleman who is not her fiancé or a member of her family, let alone a stranger who has abducted her."

"Spare me the etiquette lesson, lady. If you don't want to sit behind me, I suppose you can ride on one of the pack mules, though it'll be a tight fit."

Tight? He had six mules in assorted colors, but all six of them were heavily burdened with sacks, crates, small barrels, baskets, even hay bales. There was no room left on any of them where she could sit even if she would deign to do so. Actually ride a mule? Good God, her options were intolerable. But it was better than riding touching him.

He didn't wait for her answer. He went to one of the mules and began moving the three hay bales strapped to it farther back toward its rump to make room for her to sit up front. Then he retrieved the blanket he'd tossed aside and folded it for her to sit on. But she could see no way to get onto the mule's back. It didn't have a normal saddle, a pommel, or stirrups, just some sort of apparatus on its back with a lot of straps attached to secure whatever it was carrying. Could she pull herself up by gripping that?

"They're all sweet gals as long as they're well-fed, and they currently are," Morgan said when she moved to stand beside him. "You won't get bucked off. Carla here has the lightest load, so she won't mind your weight. And being at the front of the team, you'll taste less dust."

"How wonderful," she said sarcastically.

"You could always walk," was his terse reply.

But then his hands suddenly circled her waist and she was lifted high to be plopped down on the mule. Having had no warning, she screeched when he did it. And he just stood there watching her, his thumbs hooked in his belt.

She felt herself blushing because of the way he'd touched her, no matter that he'd done it to help her. And he seemed to be waiting for something. "D'you expect me to thank you? That will not be happening!"

But all he said was, "You did notice there's no horn on that pack saddle to help you keep your balance if you're going to sit sideways like that?"

"I'll manage," she said primly.

He shook his head. "I doubt it. And Carla probably won't like the uneven distribution of weight, might even do some bucking to fix it."

"But you assured me—"

"That was before I saw the silly way you intend to ride her," he cut in. "Besides, no one will notice if you sit properly."

"Your idea of what is proper is different from mine. I'll manage," she repeated.

"Suit yourself," he replied. "Just don't say I didn't warn you."

She glared at his back as he turned to mount his black horse. And as soon as he urged the animal forward with the mule string following, she was sure she was going to slide to the ground. It was a long way down. Unlike donkeys, the mules were nearly as big as normal-sized horses, just not as big as Morgan's mount.

She gripped Carla's mane on one side and the edge of the hay bale on the other and tried to scoot back just a little to gain a steadier perch—and appease the mule. But then her valise started to slide off her lap, so she let go of the hay and grabbed the valise and wiggled a little more until her lap was flat enough to keep the valise from sliding off again.

She felt like laughing hysterically. Good grief, this was ridiculous. And she kept having the urge to bend her right leg for the hook that wasn't there. She'd learned to ride in England with Sophie. Ladies there only rode sidesaddle, perfectly comfortable, perfectly proper. This wasn't comfortable at all and the only thing she could be grateful for at this point was that it wasn't happening in town where it might have created a spectacle, her slowly moving through the streets on the back of a mule. Good Lord, she would have been utterly mortified.

Chapter Seven

NOW THAT IT WAS daylight and she was sitting upright, Violet could see the landscape clearly. She found it interesting because it was so very different from England and the eastern half of the United States that she was familiar with. Green and golden grass of different lengths swayed and bent in the breeze. There were trees of different shapes and sizes, hills on either side of the road, and lovely mountains in the far distance. There were also a lot of yellow and purple wildflowers. She wanted to inhale deeply to find out if the air was redolent with their fragrance, but she didn't dare with Morgan's large horse kicking up dust in front of her.

The morning grew steadily hotter, but then every day since she'd arrived in Montana had been excessively warm. She was thirsty again. She was sweating, too. She wanted to take off her jacket, but she was afraid to let go of Carla's mane long enough to slip it off her arms.

She began to regret mightily the decisions she'd made since returning to America. And she was angry at her brothers for not checking on their father sooner, and especially angry at Daniel for not following her to Montana as he'd promised. And she was angry at herself for thinking this would be just a quick trip, here and back, that would fix everything for all three of them. She was even angry at her father for frittering away his inheritance and her dowry along with it, and dying before he could recover from that disaster. She shouldn't be the one here riding on this bloody mule!

It had already sunk in how much her own future depended on finding the money her father had made from mining, that she was no longer an heiress. And worse, going to her father's mine might not solve anything. It might not have rich ore in it, it might not be where he'd stored his money, it might not even be worth selling.

She should at least risk asking Morgan about the value of the mine, but could she trust his answer if he deigned to give her one? Probably not. He'd kept his mine a secret, and if her father's was near it, he'd want to keep her father's a secret, too. Yet he was taking her there, wasn't he? She suddenly froze, wondering if he'd spirited her out of town because he intended for her never to return. Was he planning on killing her to keep his secret? But if so, wouldn't he already have done it when they'd stopped at the stream?

She was finding it difficult to see any hope in this situation, but she supposed there was a glimmer of hope in his not having killed her yet. She clung to that until he suddenly stopped in the middle of the road, and her whole body stiffened. He'd had an afterthought! He'd remembered that he ought to kill her!

He dismounted and glanced at her as he untied something from his saddle. "You're going to be in the sun all day," he said. "You sure you want to wear that silly hat?"

She let out the breath she'd been holding; that certainly didn't sound like a death threat. And the fright she'd just had made her sound a little more indignant than she would have otherwise. "There's nothing silly about this exquisite bonnet."

"Other than it's useless in keeping the sun off your face?" he countered.

That was true, but she did have a solution, and with Carla standing still for the moment, she would show him. But first, while the mule wasn't moving, she swiftly shrugged out of her traveling jacket, but didn't try to pull the jacket's bustled train out from under her. She didn't try to get down from Carla, either, which would necessitate Morgan's having to lift her back up. He wouldn't like that any more than she would. Instead, she dug into her valise and took out the one parasol she'd brought with her, slipped her hand through the strap at its base, and opened it. Morgan laughed as she positioned it to block the sun. She bristled. Truly, she didn't like this burly bear one bit.

He sauntered her way and took the valise from her. "No need for you to hold that in your lap all day, but you'll need this."

He handed her his water canteen. She reached for it so fast, her fingers touched his. Blushing with embarrassment, she almost let go of the canteen, but he didn't appear to notice and proceeded to tie her valise to one of the straps on Carla's pack saddle.

Violet took a long drink of the warm water, then asked, "What about you? Will you halt this journey to get your canteen every time you want a drink?"

"Won't need to." He moved to a different mule, opened one of the baskets it was carrying, and took out another canteen for himself. "I always carry two in the summer, and you're here smack in the middle of the hottest weather this territory sees."

He came back to stand beside her, but he was looking straight ahead at the long stretch of road before them as he said, "The stagecoach from Billings travels this road, and those drivers can get real nasty if something is blocking their way. They're all about keeping to their schedules. But the coach stirs up a big cloud of dust, so we'll see it coming from a distance and be able to get off the road." And then his eyes came back to hers and his conversational tone turned abruptly cold. "Sullivan should have known I wouldn't escort you to my mine no matter who you pretend to be. What excuse were you going to use to get me to take you there?"

"Deputy Barnes said your mine is close to my father's and you are quite likely the only one who can guide me to it."

"How the hell would he know that?"

His sudden snarling tone decided her against mentioning that the town was rife with rumors about him, none of them flattering. So she merely said, "Because you brought my father to the doctor after the accident in his mine." He just scowled at her. She worked up the courage to say, "Thank you for doing that. *Are* you taking me to his mine?"

He stared at her for a long moment. In the bright morning light, she stared back, but she still couldn't discern what was under all that shaggy hair. But she soon became uncomfortably aware that he seemed to be cataloging her attributes. And she didn't get an answer to her question. She was asked one instead: "What made you think you could convince me to? Because you're pretty? I reckon Shawn would have picked his spy carefully. You're either an actress—or a harlot. Which is it?"

Oh, good Lord, what he was implying was beyond mortifying. And provoking. Did he want her to yell at him? To give him an excuse to abandon her there on that dusty road?

She didn't yell, but there was no way she couldn't sound as insulted as she felt. "I was looking for you before I even met Mr. Sullivan because I am exactly who I said I am and I have a legitimate claim to my father's mine and its proceeds. But to answer your question, no reason had occurred to me why you *wouldn't* be my guide."

"No? I can give you a bunch, but none suitable for a lady's ears—if you really are one." Her blush just got much hotter. "I heard there was a fancy harridan screaming in the streets last week. Was that you?"

She sucked in her breath. "Certainly not."

"Can't imagine there's more than one fancy harridan in town," Morgan countered, apparently not believing her about this either.

"I assure you that was *not* me. I would never yell in public. It would be beyond the pale."

"Beyond what?"

"The bounds of acceptable behavior."

"Then why didn't you just say that?"

She gritted her teeth. The man was intolerable and his disbelief even worse. "Why are you so sure I'm not Charles Mitchell's daughter?"

"He never mentioned a daughter, just sons."

It hurt that her father had forgotten about her. She shouldn't be surprised—out of sight, out of mind—but it still hurt.

"Are you going to cry?"

She blinked, then snapped her brows together. "Absolutely not. I've had two weeks to shed my tears. And grieving is done

MARRY ME BY SUNDOWN   63

in private or with relatives, certainly not with strangers like you."

"Were you fed your lines by Sullivan, or are you just making them up as needed?"

"You don't think I would be grieving for a father I dearly loved?"

"Lady, I told you I don't believe you're a Mitchell," he replied. "You don't even talk right. Can't believe Shawn couldn't afford a better actress."

"I am no such thing, and I talk perfectly fine for someone who grew up in England these last—"

He cut in sharply, "If you persist in the pretense, then we're done talking."

Good. Talking to him was far too infuriating. He obviously wasn't going to tell her anything that she wanted to know and certainly nothing about his mine and its location, so what was the point?

Then he said, "We can pick up the pace now."

Music to her ears, until he mounted again and the entire string of mules began trotting to keep up with his horse. She nearly screamed, she was so sure she was about to fall off. This wasn't anything like urging one's mount to trot while sitting on a comfortable saddle. This sort of bouncing on the hard back of a mule was more than just jarring, it was becoming painful.

And the bustle of her jacket and the blanket under it that she was sitting on had afforded her some cushioning at the slower pace, but not now. It had already been uncomfortable sitting this way without the anchor of a pommel. Her back was already aching from it. Now her arse would be aching, too.

There was no help for it now. She abandoned propriety and swung one leg over the mule's head to sit astride. She felt warm air on her bare legs just above her boots. She didn't dare lean over to push the sides of her skirt down to cover her legs, if the hem would even stretch that far. Good Lord, she could just imagine what Aunt Elizabeth would say if she could see her now.

"How are you holding up now?" she suddenly heard.

"I'll—manage!" she snarled.

He didn't look back to see if she would. The despicable man was probably laughing and didn't want her to see it.

Chapter Eight

"I'M HUNGRY!" VIOLET SHOUTED.

She'd had no breakfast, thanks to Morgan Callahan's despicable abduction, and lunchtime felt as if it had come and gone. But he didn't appear to want to stop for anything, not even to eat. She assumed there was food among his supplies. Or was he looking for an animal to kill? Did he expect to reach his mine before he ate?

They were still traveling on the road, heading mostly east. They'd passed that lovely mountain range she'd been able to see when they'd left Butte. She'd thought that might be where they were headed, but obviously not. They passed over creek after creek, many of which had dried up, followed a river for a while, got out of the way of the stagecoach he'd predicted would come along. North of the road the land was still verdant with green grass and trees, but to the south there was only dirt, dried grass, and scrub brush as far as the eye could see. She couldn't stop thinking about that beautiful mountain range that had looked so inviting. She'd bet it was cooler up there!

"Did you hear me?!"

"You screech like a harridan, so how could I not?" he answered without looking back.

"So it's your intent to starve me?"

He didn't answer, of course not, because that *was* his intent! Violet had never been this sore in her life. Even that bout she'd had with flu her first year in England when her whole body had ached hadn't been this bad. Morgan had kept up a bouncing pace for a good hour before he'd slowed the animals to a walk for the next few hours. That allowed her to actually lean back a little against the large bundle of hay at her back. Gently. She'd be mortified if she pushed it off of Carla's rump and the bale rolled away.

She was silently crying in pain by then, though the heat dried the tears so fast, they probably didn't leave streaks on her dusty cheeks. A few times, she thought she might faint. More than a few times, she wished she would, anything to end this misery, however briefly. Oh, how she wished she were back in England traveling in her aunt and uncle's comfortable, elegantly appointed coach. There would be a basket of rolls and pastries on the mere chance that they would get hungry. She was hungry!

"If you don't tell me when we will eat, I'm dismounting right here," she threatened.

She wanted to, but she hesitated long enough to realize that he wouldn't care, would probably be glad that she'd made the choice to leave herself there in the middle of nowhere. To die. She growled to herself, refusing to give him the satisfaction of having his problem solved so easily. She'd never disliked anyone this much in her life. She disliked him so much, it felt more like hate.

And then he turned directly north into a hilly area. A few

minutes later, she screamed when he fired his gun. She hadn't expected him to do that, and the sound was so loud and close to her. He dismounted and picked up a long, fat snake near his feet. It had orange, white, and black stripes. And he took out a knife and cut off its head.

She winced, disgusted, and heard him say, "It was going to slither past my gals. They would have started bucking to kill it, and you would have landed on your ass. They don't like snakes."

So he'd saved her from falling? Ha! More likely he enjoyed the fright he'd just given her. But instead of tossing the dead reptile aside, he moved to stuff it into one of his baskets. Taking the trophy home? She grimaced at the thought.

Passing Carla again, he handed Violet a strip of dried jerky. She didn't thank him. He could have done that hours ago! And it certainly wouldn't satisfy her hunger for very long, but the first bite she ripped off the strip did take the edge off. And then they continued on.

It was much greener as they rode north, long grass, a few pine trees, more wildflowers, but the day was still sweltering. She had no idea what time it was, late in the afternoon? The last time she'd glanced at the sun to gauge the time, she'd been blinded for the longest time, so she didn't do that again. But her sore body might be making it seem like they'd ridden longer than they had. Where the devil was his mine? And then they were trotting again! But not for long this time.

"We'll rest the animals for a while," Morgan said, stopping beneath the shade of a large tree.

Violet stared blissfully at the lake they'd come to. Carla had already moved to the water to drink and Morgan was walking toward her. "Let me help—"

Not waiting for him to finish, Violet slid off the mule by herself and immediately dropped to her knees, which was not her intention, but her legs just gave out. He shook his head and offered her a hand up, but as long as she was down, she sat to remove her boots.

"I wouldn't recommend—" he began, but didn't finish the warning.

Her legs still shaky, she stumbled to the water's edge, sat down on the grass, and stuck her feet in it. It felt sublime, even if the water wasn't as cold as she'd hoped it would be. She wanted to swim in the lake, which was what he must have assumed she was going to do, but she didn't want her clothes to get wet and she certainly couldn't remove them, not with the bear lurking behind her. Her upbringing forbade it. Her legs probably wouldn't cooperate anyway if she tried to swim. Sitting astride might have kept her from bouncing off Carla's back when the mule was trotting, but constantly gripping Carla's sides with her thighs and calves to keep her balance had worsened the aches in her legs.

She leaned forward to splash water on her face, getting the ends of her hair wet in the process. Then she tried to discreetly knead some of the soreness from her upper thighs, but that hurt too much, so she stopped.

She realized that she undoubtedly looked a fright. The rest of her braid had unraveled and her long golden hair spilled down her back and over her shoulders. Without her usual coiffure, her lovely little hat probably did look ridiculous now, perched atop her wildly disarrayed mane. But she was beyond caring, too sore, too tired, too miserable—and still a little afraid of her abductor escort. What if he wasn't Morgan Callahan? He never had confirmed that he was. But even if he was, that didn't mean she was safe with him.

A splash to her right made her glance to the side. She was arrested, watching the man dip his head in the water then flip his head back to get the wet hair out of his face. Beads of water reached her, though she barely noticed.

It was the first time she was seeing him without his hat on. She'd been able to tell that his black hair was beyond shoulder-length. Slicked back with water as it was now, and with his long beard wet, too, his face was a little more defined, could even be called ruggedly handsome, she supposed. It also allowed her to see that he wasn't really that old, maybe less than twenty-five years. Not that either made any difference. He was still a detestable bear.

He'd been kneeling to dunk his head but stood up now and, once again, hooked both thumbs on his belt—his actual belt, not the gun belt that slanted across his hips. "I appreciate that you've been mostly silent during the ride."

That "mostly" nettled her. "It's been too hot to make an effort to tell you what I think of the despicable way you are treating me," she said indignantly. "And it wouldn't have served any purpose, would it?"

He chuckled and walked away without answering, but then his amusement was answer enough. She huffed to herself and didn't follow him with her eyes. She was content just to sit there in the shade with her feet in the water and ignore the odious man. But she did glance back when she heard the crackling of a fire. He was roasting something above it, had positioned four stakes around it to hold the meat out of the flames. Her eyes flared when she realized he was cooking the snake! Good

Lord, did he expect her to eat that? Even as hungry as she was, she simply couldn't.

She closed her eyes tight, trying to hold back tears. She might have enjoyed the outdoors when she was a child, but she could never have imagined anyone roughing it like this. Or being so poorly prepared that they had to eat snake meat!

A while later he said, "I've let it cool enough for you to hold."

She glanced down to see a long slice of the cooked meat being offered to her over her shoulder. Oh, God, no plate, skin still on it, though he'd at least split it open.

She turned her head aside. "No thank you."

"I thought you said you were hungry? Damn well yelled it, too."

"I am, but only savages eat snake."

"You see a restaurant nearby? Out here, we eat what's available, and while snake meat is tough, it has very little flavor."

"It's certainly not considered fit for human consumption in England."

"Do you see England nearby?"

Was he making a joke? She remembered an exhibit at a London museum about people in some distant land who ate snake meat. Sophie had whispered that the male savages ate it to increase their virility. This man certainly didn't need help in that regard—he was virile enough as he was!

She ignored her growling stomach and repeated, "No thank you."

She squeezed her eyes shut so she wouldn't see him eating. But a while later he tapped her shoulder again, and she turned to see him offering her a piece of bread.

She took it before saying, "So the snake was just to prove what a savage you are?"

"So savage I tried to feed you something that would hold you till the next meal? You need meat."

Not that kind of meat, she didn't, but it was pointless to argue with him. She gazed at the lake as she chewed the dry bread. The less she had to look at the man and his strapping body, the better. His very size still frightened her. He was bearish in appearance and manner. He was rough, uncouth, lacking in refinement, lacking in charm, everything she would find objectionable in a man.

And then her eyes flared wide when she saw a very large bear, a bloody real one, lumbering toward the water on the other side of the lake. Horrified, ignoring her screaming muscles, she jumped up and hurried to hide behind Morgan. Why wasn't he getting his rifle?! She peered around his shoulder and saw the bear stand up to sniff the air before it dropped to all four feet again to drink from the lake. Fascinated, she couldn't take her eyes off it.

"It's not coming over here," Morgan said.

"But if it does?"

"Then I'll be taking home bear meat."

"So you're a hunter, too?"

"Every man's a hunter when it's necessary, but I don't pass up free food, though I admit I'm not partial to bear unless it's only been eating nuts and berries."

Bear meat, snake meat. Did people in this uncivilized land really eat anything that became available? God, they probably did. As he'd pointed out, the nearest restaurant she knew of was half a day's ride away.

Ignoring the bear, Morgan moved to another one of his baskets. When he turned, she was amazed to see him offering her a puffy pastry coated in sugar. She was so pleased that she said thank you this time before she sat down by the water again to enjoy the pastry, glad to see the bear wandering off in the opposite direction. A few minutes later, feeling replete, she wished she could lie down and nap for the remainder of the time they would be there, but was afraid she wouldn't get back up if she did.

She peered up at the cloudless sky. "Does it ever rain in this territory? Or does the rain dry up in this heat and disappear before it can reach the ground?"

He laughed. "I've never thought of that possibility, though I wouldn't be surprised if it happens. But sure, it rains, just not that often. Snows a lot come winter, though."

She didn't care because, thankfully, she wouldn't be here then. She was already dreading having to get back on her feet, much less on the mule. "How much farther to the mines?" she asked.

"Depends." She assumed it depended on whether the animals walked or trotted. But then he added, "But it won't be today."

She was aghast. Was he serious? And if they wouldn't reach his mining camp by nightfall . . . "But where will we sleep?"

"On the ground, of course."

She was utterly appalled by the notion. "I've never slept anywhere but on a bed. I simply won't be able to sleep."

She thought she heard a chuckle. "You will."

She probably would, but she had to point out, "It would be most improper for me to sleep near you."

"Well, if you don't want me nearby to protect you, I can sleep somewhere else."

Her eyes flared, her mind filling with possibilities of what he would need to protect her from. Did he have to be agreeable about this when herds of bears and snakes could converge on them? "Perhaps near but not too close?" she amended.

"I wasn't planning on sharing your blanket, lady. I'll wait for you to invite me."

She gasped and looked away from him again to hide her blush. She heard him walk toward the mules again and glanced to the side to watch him rummage through the baskets until he had a handful of carrots. He proceeded to snap them in two and give each mule half of one, then a whole one to his horse. Feeding his animals lunch—no, she'd seen them eating grass. He was giving them a treat. He definitely had a fondness for them.

She supposed that might be considered a good trait in a man. His sense of humor was another one. He didn't hesitate to laugh when he was amused. So far that humor had all been at her expense, but two good traits were better than none, she supposed. Still, it was quite surprising that an abductor of women had any.

Her boots suddenly landed next to her. She sighed and tugged them back on before she noticed him standing in front of her with an extended hand. She groaned loudly when he helped her to her feet.

"It's probably going to feel worse tomorrow," he warned.

"Impossible."

"Meant to stay here longer and sleep off some of this heat, but we can't with that bear in the area. We'll stop again at the next water."

She nodded, but gasped when she took the first step toward Carla. She couldn't bring herself to take another, which might have been why Morgan swooped her up in his arms and deposited her—on his horse.

"No—" she began.

"I wasn't asking," he said very firmly as he mounted the animal in front of her. "It's either this or you're going to be in bed for the next week crying in pain, and I'd just as soon not hear it. So ignore that I'm on the horse with you and try to forget that you're touching me."

Her abhorrence of their proximity had nothing to do with propriety at that point. It simply concerned who he was. Her torturer! Her abductor! The man who'd tried to force her to eat snake!

But then he added, "Use my back if you want to take a nap. I promise I won't mind."

She sputtered. He took off—at a bloody trot!

Chapter Nine

VIOLET HAD NEVER BEEN this close to a man before. She was actually touching Morgan. Her thighs were touching the sides of his hips. And when he'd taken off at a trot, she'd instinctively grabbed his waist. She was thoroughly embarrassed by this physical proximity, but there was no way around it. After a while, she let go of his waist and just clutched the material of his long vest until he slowed the horse to a walk. That didn't happen soon enough for her.

Even after she could safely remove her hands from his person, she still didn't like riding so close to this frightful beast of a man. He was too big, too masculine, and everything about him made her nervous, but he'd been correct in one regard. She didn't need to use her already screaming leg muscles to stay on the back of his horse. She was perfectly balanced now and firmly seated.

Another disadvantage of riding with Morgan was being unable to see ahead of them because of the width and height of his back. She couldn't tell where he was going anymore. He seemed to meander for a while in different directions, probably to avoid the steeper slopes of the hills they were crossing over.

After perhaps two hours of riding, they crossed a river. She glanced down to see if her boots were going to get wet, but the river was shallow enough at that point for her feet to stay dry. Were they stopping? He had said they would when they reached water again. But he kept going, following the river until they reached a lone tree on its bank. There were forests on all sides of them, most of them in the distance, and mountains on three sides, also in the distance.

Dismounting, he slipped his hands under her waist-length hair to lift her down from his horse without asking permission. "You can sleep until dusk."

If she could move. It hurt so much just standing there, she wasn't sure she could. But at least her legs hadn't buckled this time. And getting to sleep through the remainder of this awful heat sounded heavenly to her—if only there were a bed to do it in.

"I told you I can't sleep on the ground. I'd like to talk to you about my father instead."

"I don't know your father. If you mean Charley, then say so."

She gritted her teeth, but persisted. "What was his life like out here? Did he get used to these wilderness hardships?"

"Charley had help."

"You?"

"And he's none of your business."

"Please."

He gave her a hard look. "I can't see what interest Shawn would have in these questions. You improvising, lady? Think this will make your tall tale more believable? So it's actress after all? Too bad, I was hoping for the harlot."

She gasped. "I've had quite enough of your insults."

"And I've had enough of your jabbering. Sleep or don't sleep, doesn't matter to me, but the animals need rest, so we'll stay here till dusk."

Then what? "Does that mean you intend to ride at night?" He only nodded, which brought the alarmed question, "But isn't that dangerous?"

"Shouldn't be, as long as the sky remains as cloudless as it's been today. Moonlight can be pretty bright out here."

His lack of concern should have been reassuring, but it wasn't. She kept her eyes on him as he went to get her blanket from Carla and spread it out under the tree for her before he unsaddled his horse.

At least she wasn't hungry. The last meal had been quite filling and palatable—minus the snake. But she shuddered to think what the next one would be like, so she wasn't looking forward to it. And then she saw the deer at about the same time Morgan did, some hundred or so yards away.

He reached for his rifle. Violet let go of her parasol to clap both hands over her ears before he could fire. She was watching him, not their soon-to-be dinner, and frowned when he put his rifle away without shooting. She figured the deer must have fled. But when she glanced around, she saw it was still there and so indifferent to their presence that it actually lay down near the river's edge.

"You're letting it live?" she said in surprise.

"Takes time to bleed it so it doesn't taste so gamy. I don't like gamy."

She was surprised that a man who ate snake could be so picky. But she didn't share that thought with him, or how much she abhorred being dependent on him for every morsel of food she got. She wanted to get some rest while she could, even if she couldn't sleep. Dusk came late in summer, but that might be only a few hours away, for all she knew. In Butte she was usually done with dinner long before it started to get dark.

She proceeded to ignore Morgan and inch her way to the blanket. Each little step she took was painful, but she managed not to cringe. Finally sitting down on the blanket in the shade, she continued to watch Morgan because she didn't trust him one little bit. When he walked away, she lay down to rest her back, planning to sit up when she heard him returning. She never heard him. Despite her sore muscles and the lack of a bed, she fell asleep instantaneously.

She awoke to the crackling of a campfire, surprised that she'd fallen asleep on the hard ground after all. And it wasn't dusk, but full dark. That was disappointing. She had counted on seeing the sun setting so she could get her bearings. She was also facing her parasol now, but didn't remember opening it and positioning it on the blanket with her. Had Morgan done that to give her extra shade? She doubted he could be so considerate. She must have done it.

The day's heat was gone. She had no idea how long she'd slept, but she felt refreshed. And hungry again. And cold. But when she sat up, all the pain came rushing back. How on earth had she managed to sleep at all when the slightest turn would have hurt like this?

She didn't think she could make it to Carla to fetch her jacket, but detested the idea of asking Morgan to get it for her. She was *not* helpless. And her abused muscles would never get better if she didn't use them. And then she felt her jacket slide down from her shoulders to her lap. Thank God for small favors. Morgan had probably just tossed it toward her and it had ended up covering her. She didn't, couldn't, credit him with actually placing it carefully over her, but she slipped her arms into it.

He was sitting on the other side of the fire watching her. He was wearing a cream-colored jacket now, made of some sort of smooth animal skin. She saw the vest beneath it, but still no shirt.

He'd built the fire at the foot of her blanket. She started to get up but was brutally reminded by the pain in her legs that she couldn't. He'd predicted that she'd be crying from it. She fought back the tears by getting angry—at herself. Why did she have to be so bloody stubborn? She could have ridden on his horse from the start and avoided the worst of these aches and pains. He'd offered, but she'd been too furious to accept.

She managed to roll toward the fire without leaving her blanket. And saw two fish resting on some twigs next to it, already cooked, as well as another chunk of bread and an apple.

She didn't try to sit up again, just lay there on her stomach resting on her elbows within reach of the food. "Have you changed your mind about continuing on in the dark?" she asked.

"No."

"Then why didn't you wake me before dusk?"

"Maybe I like watching you sleep."

That was absurd when she had to look a fright, her face dirty and dusty, her hair a wild mess, so she put him on the spot, asking, "Why?"

"Why not? For all your lies, you're still a damn fine-looking woman. 'Sides, look at my choices."

She followed his gaze as it turned to his mules and almost laughed, since only their rumps were within view. A joke. Who would have thought a bear could joke?

Glancing at the food again, she asked, "Is half of this repast for me?"

"All of it is," he said. "I'll store whatever you don't eat."

Then he'd already eaten? And caught the fish. Which had her ask, "You didn't sleep a'tall?"

"I will, later," he said, and got up to resaddle his horse. "Just hurry it up, lady. Time's wasting."

She picked apart just one of the fish, then ate all the bread and the apple, but now her fingers were utterly sticky from eating without utensils. She glanced toward the river longingly, before he said, "Here," and turned back to see that he was tipping his canteen toward her. She quickly stuck out her hands, and he poured the last of the water over them before he went to the river to refill his canteen. Then he did the same with hers while she flicked her hands to dry them.

Then she became uncomfortably aware that she couldn't leave yet, and started looking around for a bush. And she had to do this on her own. She couldn't very well mention it to the bear.

But she was scooped up in his arms. "Wait! I'm not ready to leave yet. Put me down!"

She started to struggle when he didn't, until she saw he wasn't taking her to his horse yet. He set her down, taking a moment to steady her, then simply walked away.

Grateful for the bush between them and yet so utterly embarrassed, she found it hard to reconcile the two strong feelings. Her only consolation was that it was dark and he wouldn't notice how red her cheeks were. And then she chided herself for being so silly. Clinging to her civilized mantle was ridiculous when she was smack in the middle of the wilderness. But the conventions of polite behavior were ingrained in her! She wasn't sure she could shed them.

Morgan came back to carry her to his horse. She knew he only did it because he was impatient to leave. So even though she was nestled against his chest and had one arm around his neck, she was compelled to admonish him, "Your helping me this way doesn't improve my opinion of you one bit. You shouldn't have stolen me away from my hotel. You should have given me a chance to buy a horse and hire servants so I could travel to my father's mine in a more civilized fashion. Which, I should add, would have caused less trouble and work for you."

"You're no trouble—well, let me rephrase that: you're no trouble when your mouth is shut. How about you thank me by shutting it now? Or do you need help with that, too?"

He'd stopped and was glancing down at her. His face was awfully close to hers. Was he talking about a gag or a kiss? She wanted neither from him, so she kept quiet and shook her head vigorously. She was done complaining for the moment and back to blushing.

When she was seated on the horse, she saw that he'd already put out the fire and repacked. Before mounting, he handed her the hotel blanket. She didn't need it yet, but probably would as the night wore on since her jacket was designed to look pretty, not to keep her warm. But she didn't expect this ride through the darkness to last very long, not when he hadn't gotten any sleep at the last campsite.

The sky was filled with stars and the moon was indeed bright. The crickets were loud, but a roar in the distance prompted her to put her arms around Morgan. He made no comment, so she kept them there since it made for a steadier seat.

They continued east, at least she assumed so because he didn't recross the river they'd camped by. But the shadowed landscape became barren again, so she gave up trying to find some sort of landmark in the dark.

Two or three hours later, Morgan finally stopped and said, "I need some sleep," and abruptly dismounted.

Before he lifted her down, she had a brief unobstructed view of the dark shape of a mountain rather close by in front of them and another in the far distance to her left. Then his hands were around her waist again, only this time he set her down more slowly and she felt her body brush against his. He was standing too close to the horse. Was the man half-asleep already, not extending his arms fully this time to prevent them colliding?

He made no apology, probably wasn't even aware that their bodies had touched so intimately. The moment her feet were on the ground he moved away from her, so she didn't give it another thought. She didn't move, and wouldn't until she saw where he was going to place the campfire. She assumed he was going to make one, if only for warmth. It was much chillier now. She felt it even with the blanket wrapped about her like a cloak.

Following him with her eyes, she saw that he'd apparently gathered a large armful of dried branches at their last camp while she was sleeping and had tied them to one of the mules. She was glad that he'd thought ahead, since there were no trees anywhere in sight, just a few scraggly bushes and a lot of dead grass. And she didn't see any water nearby.

Once he got a fire started, she slowly moved over to it and

sat down. He tossed her another blanket before unsaddling his horse and spreading out his horse blanket on the other side of the fire. He immediately lay down, using his saddlebag for a pillow.

He did all this without saying a word to her. Was he not talking because he believed she was an impostor, or was this how he behaved with everyone? It was probably true that he'd become a hermit. He was simply accustomed to silence. Or was he just too tired to talk?

She wasn't, and stated emphatically, "I need to reiterate that I am who I say I am. And I know you knew my father."

"I knew Charley, which ain't the same thing."

"Then tell me about Charley. You worked with him, you must even have liked him because you took him to the doctor in town when he was hurt. Was he happy out here? Please, I only had two visits with him in the last nine years. Tell me something about his—his last days."

He sat up. The look he gave her across the fire sent chills down her spine. "What I'm gonna tell you is I'm tired, otherwise I might applaud. How long did it take you to study for this role?"

The question infuriated her. "Eighteen years, that's how long I've been Violet Mitchell!"

"Yet you only show up after Charley dies, 'cause he would've called you a liar same as I am. Nice try, lady, but if I don't get some sleep, you won't like me tomorrow."

A distinct threat, yet she still mumbled loud enough for him to hear, "I don't like you now."

She regretted it immediately, even if it was true. It was still rude, which wasn't like her at all. And turning him even further against her wasn't going to get her any answers. So she raised the proverbial white flag with the neutral remark, "There was water not far from here. Why didn't we camp by it?"

He lay down again and turned on his side facing away from her. "Water draws animals."

And he wouldn't be awake to deal with them? She started imagining all sorts of creatures lumbering or slithering past them on the way to that last water they'd passed. Those animals had to come from somewhere!

She gripped her closed parasol like a weapon and glanced around her. Then heard: "I'm not going to tie you. Disturb my gals and I'll wake up. Run off and I won't care. You might last a few hours on foot, but I doubt it."

Speechless, she glared at his back. The man was utterly coldhearted. She decided she preferred his silence to nasty warnings like that one.

Chapter Ten

VIOLET DIDN'T GET ANY more sleep. She just sat there huddled in her blanket for the remainder of the night. Morgan's proximity didn't help one bit to ease her fear when she knew she could be bitten by a snake or dragged off by a wolf or eaten by a bear before she could wake him up to kill it. There were just too many wild animals in this land, not enough people, and the towns were too far apart. Every little sound, even the swish of a mule's tail, startled her, making her gasp.

It seemed incredible that only a few months ago she was being fitted for beautiful ball gowns. She'd been so excited with the Season approaching, had such hopes and wonderful possibilities before her. Thanks to her aunt and uncle's sponsorship, she, an American, was going to have her debut in London. And she'd found the husband she wanted before the Season had even started, only to have to sail away the next day—to this.

All of her dreams had been coming true, but she couldn't return to that upper-class world if her father's mining venture wasn't successful. That future, the one she wanted, hinged on finding his mine and it being a lucrative endeavor.

She kept feeding the fire with the extra branches. As the night wore on, she got hungry, but after Morgan's warning, she wasn't about to go looking through the mule packs for food. But she was going to wake him the very moment she saw the break of dawn, and kept watching the sky in all directions for it.

"Still here?"

She gasped and glanced back toward the fire to see him standing up. She wondered what had awoken him. It wasn't dawn yet. But then he walked about ten feet away—to relieve himself. She rolled her eyes and pushed herself to her feet to head to the closest bush to do the same. She felt no embarrassment this time, and after massaging her legs all night, it wasn't as painful to walk as it had been yesterday. Her leg muscles still hurt. It would probably be days yet before they returned to normal. Or before she was back in Butte.

She actually looked forward to that, which was amazing because she didn't consider it a civilized town, but at least she could get a bath there, and a proper meal, and a laundress. And a new hat! Hers must have fallen off yesterday during all that trotting, and she hadn't even noticed until last night. Morgan had already ruined it, so she'd only sighed a little over losing it. Two days in the same clothes, however, was scandalous and worth crying over, but she couldn't very well change without taking a bath first, and she wasn't going to get one out here. She felt so dirty after yesterday's ride!

When she returned to the campfire, she saw Morgan saddling his horse. She had a feeling there wouldn't be any breakfast before they departed, at least nothing that she couldn't eat while riding. He confirmed that thought when he handed her two strips of hard jerky before stamping out the fire. She retrieved her canteen and parasol, slipping her hand through each strap to keep them on her wrist, then tried to gnaw off a piece of jerky. It wasn't easy. If it didn't have a salty taste, she would have suspected he'd given her leather to chew on.

"Put this on."

She scowled when she saw him holding out a small empty sack. "Put it on what?"

"Your head. The rest of the way, you don't get to see."

She was mortified. But there was a bright side. If he didn't want her to see how he reached his mine from here, it was because he intended to release her eventually. So he didn't plan on killing her after all. But she couldn't bring herself to put a sack on her head and refused to take it from him.

"I'll faint with that covering my face if it gets as hot as it was yesterday," she warned. "And a blindfold will do just as well, won't it?"

He said nothing. He didn't move either. If he insisted, she was going to balk and fight tooth and nail. Of course she'd fail. He was too bloody big. But he finally pulled the bandanna off his neck and tied it over her eyes. A concession! So he was capable of reason?

He picked her up again and placed her on his horse, but this time he mounted behind her. She even guessed why: so he could easily see if she tried to remove her blindfold. This extreme tactic smacked of fanaticism about keeping the location of his mine a secret from her, or perhaps anyone. Which made her wonder why he hadn't shot her father for showing up near his mine. Or were the two mines not really that close together? Maybe it was only Shawn Sullivan that Morgan didn't want in the area. But the man had seemed nice, his daughter even nicer. What exactly would happen if Sullivan learned of the location?

She really didn't like being seated in front of Morgan. She felt too much of him behind her, and every time he did something with the reins he was holding, his forearms brushed against her waist. But she held her tongue, afraid he might turn around and refuse to take her to the mines if she fussed too much. Good grief, it was abhorrent that her future depended on this particular man!

As the morning grew warmer, she shrugged the blanket off her shoulders and opened her parasol, not realizing it would block Morgan's view. But she found that out quick enough when he snatched it from her hand. He didn't close it, simply placed it on her head as if it were a hat!

"Don't lift it any higher or I'll toss it away," he growled as he put the handle back in her hand.

Violet sighed, aware that, once again, she must look ridiculous. Not that she cared. After all, for whom did she need to keep up appearances out here?

"How much longer before this nightmare ride ends and we reach your mine?"

"Depends."

She snorted. "I'm beginning to think you don't know."

He laughed. Again, the sound of genuine humor coming from him surprised her. It made her wonder if he wasn't always a rude, bearish brute. He used to be a rancher, from a family of ranchers to the east. What would they think if they could see him now? And why had he left home? Kicked out for being the black sheep? One dastardly deed too many?

After her nervous, wakeful night, the lack of sleep caught up to her as soon as the trotting ended. With Morgan's arms on either side of her holding the reins, the horse's slow, steady motion was making her drowsy. She drifted off, unaware that she was leaning back against the man behind her.

The shot from a rifle was a very rude awakening. Another snake? She lowered one side of her blindfold, but didn't see anything dead nearby, so she put the cloth back in place before he noticed.

"What did you shoot this time?" she asked curiously as he dismounted.

"The cougar loping toward us. Got him just as he pounced. He thought he'd found dinner."

Pounced? Had she almost died? She shivered slightly, glad that she hadn't seen that coming. She might have gotten hysterical, then he might have missed his shot. What a horrid thought! God, she hated being out here in the wilderness where death lurked all around them and she had only this man to protect her. She wished she knew how to shoot, wished she had the courage to if she did know, but mostly wished she didn't feel so grateful that she didn't have to—because of him.

"Will you make camp to cook it?" she asked when he didn't get back on the horse right away.

"No, it's one of the bigger wild cats. Some people out here consider it a delicacy since it tastes like pork, but I'm guessing you'd turn up your nose at it as you did with the snake."

"You guessed right."

"I still need to take it home to dispose of," he added.

"Why?"

"Because it will draw vultures that can be seen from far away. And most men would investigate what the birds are after."

She figured they must be near his camp if he was worried

about that. She peeked out of her blindfold again and saw him tying the cougar to one of the mules. Apparently they didn't like the smell of blood, because several of them were making a ruckus. Morgan mumbled something that might have passed for soothing. He really did value his animals, and from the way he talked about them, calling them his gals, she guessed they were more like pets to him.

When he mounted up again, he placed an apple in her hand. She smiled, well aware that he didn't have to feed her. She wasn't going to die from missing a few meals. She had complained when she was hungry and, of course, would continue to do so, but still, he didn't have to oblige.

He also didn't have to allow her to lean against him and fall asleep in his arms. But that's what she'd been doing when he'd shot the wild cat. Maybe he hadn't noticed or didn't care as long as she kept quiet, so she didn't give it another thought and refused to feel the least bit embarrassed by it.

The horse did a lot of zigzagging and climbing. She even heard its hooves striking rock. She could vaguely hear running water in the distance, so she assumed they were following the course of a stream or creek. But it definitely wasn't an ideal path, and she kept getting rocked backward as the horse continued to climb, making it difficult to maintain her erect posture.

She was tempted to take another peek, but Morgan definitely noticed her raising her hand to her face and sharply said, "No."

She growled to herself and called him all sorts of nasty names—silently.

Chapter Eleven

WHEN MORGAN FINALLY REMOVED her blindfold a while later, Violet was sure they'd arrived at his mine, but she was wrong. He took back his bandanna because they were surrounded by pine trees now and she couldn't see anything beyond them. They continued climbing slowly upward. She could still hear water trickling somewhere nearby; she just couldn't see it yet.

With so many hills surrounding Butte, when she'd been in town it had been easy to spot a number of mining camps in the distance because of the workers' tents. There were so many of them, they made the camps look like little tent cities. She'd thought Morgan's mine would be on a hill, too, but they'd been riding uphill for so long she realized they were actually on the side of a mountain.

Eventually the trees on their left thinned and she could see a very steep rock slope that gradually grew steeper and steeper until it looked like a cliff face. A lower slope had formed some distance to their right. Now she realized that they were riding through a narrow valley or ravine.

The trees thinned out further, and soon they came to a western-style fence that blocked their way, just two horizontal planks between posts. Morgan dismounted but didn't help her down from his horse. She was transfixed for a moment when she saw the cabin farther up the slope. It even had a front porch with a roof. She hadn't imagined him living in a wooden structure up here, when all the miners near Butte slept in tents—well, except for well-to-do mine owners like Shawn Sullivan. She'd walked past his big house.

Morgan was unlocking a gate. A sign was posted next to it that read: TRESPASSERS WILL BE SHOT. If she weren't so tired and uncomfortable, she might have laughed, since they hadn't seen another soul in the day and a half it had taken to get here.

"Does anyone besides you ever come up this way to trespass?" she called down to him.

"Charley Mitchell did. He followed me here. Had a damn spyglass so he stayed far enough back that I didn't notice him."

That was clearly a complaint, yet it made her chuckle. "That was rather clever of him."

"More like suicidal."

She gasped, thinking of the warning on the sign. "Did you shoot him?!"

He scowled at her. "Of course not. I gave him time to get off my hill."

He obviously didn't like the fact that her father had started a mine somewhere in these hills, yet eventually he must have accepted him as a neighbor. Her father always had been a charmer. If anyone could tame and talk his way around this bear, Charles could. She smiled at the thought.

She noticed the chimes and cowbells all along the fence when she heard them jingling and ringing as he opened the gate. The chimes were melodious; the bells weren't.

"Bells?"

He picked up his reins to lead her and the mule team into the fenced area, then turned to lock the gate again, before he deigned to answer her. "A couple claim jumpers sneaked up on me and took a few potshots last year. They aren't getting another chance to come in here without making some noise. It's the one disadvantage of mining in such isolation. Something happens to me here, no one will know it."

Disturbed to hear that dangerous men roamed this seemingly deserted wilderness, she pointed out, "The law in Butte knows you live in the area. Wouldn't they search for you if after a few weeks you don't return to town?"

"Why? Miners often move on or go home. No one looks for them."

"But you're a notable person, Mr. Callahan. Just about everyone I spoke to recognized your name and mentioned a different rumor about you. You've apparently been quite a subject of gossip in Butte."

She was rather pleased to see him frown. His having the upper hand all the time was a difficult pill to swallow, so being able to nettle him with something, even as minor as this, evened the score a tiny bit for her.

Which was why she continued, "Aside from the fact that the good deputy knew you brought my father to town when he was injured—which, by the by, was surprisingly decent of you—I assume you mentioned to someone else that your mine is close to my father's. Or did my father tell someone when he was in town?"

"*Charley* did," he grumbled, stressing the name, "when I took him to Butte to file his claim. He was tickled pink that I allowed him to stay."

"Allowed?"

"Don't open that can of worms, lady," he said.

"I insist you explain that remark. Do you somehow own this entire mountain?"

"You're in no position to insist on anything. Or is the lady going to start yelling in public?"

"Your answer is going to make me yell?"

"Your tone suggests you're about to show your true colors, which is no lady at all."

Was it that obvious that she was exhausted and aching in every limb? They had traveled half the day, to go by the sun directly overhead. But the man was so bloody frustrating. He seemed willing to talk about anything—except the two mines. Because he thought she was an impostor. Yet one of the mines was hers now. But until he actually showed her where it was, she couldn't do anything with it. So she couldn't afford to alienate him in a shouting match or tell him how ridiculous he was being. Not yet.

He led them into the yard. The land leveled out inside the fence and was actually flat farther back by the cabin. They passed a large, dark hole in the cliff on the left that she assumed was Morgan's mine. A large pile of wooden beams was stacked outside it. Closer to the cabin she saw an iron or steel door in the cliff. She guessed it secured another hole where he stored his supplies. Not far from the steel door stood a narrow structure about six feet tall with a brick dome and some sort of pulley apparatus next to it.

Before they reached the cabin, she asked, "Why on earth

would you mine here, so far from town, so far from the other mines in Butte?"

"Because I wanted to mine in peace, and if I didn't find ore right away, move on to another spot. I traveled through this mountain range for nearly a month last summer before I settled on this location."

"But why so high up the mountain?"

"This isn't high up at all. This range has an elevation of ten thousand feet. We're still in the foothills here."

She supposed they were, since he'd been able to get this far on horseback. Still curious, she asked, "And why exactly here? Did you know you would find ore here?"

"I ran across a retired army scout on the way here. He was of Crow descent, the Indians who used to live in this region. He said all the mountains in this territory are rich in ore. His people had always known that, they just had no use for shiny metals. He suggested this particular range instead of the ones by the overcrowded mining camps near Butte and Helena. He said I'd know why once I got here."

"Does that mean gold was just lying around up here?" she asked.

"I found a little evidence of it in the creeks and streams around here, but I didn't come this way to pan for gold."

"Why not? Wouldn't that be easier?"

"Sure, but not as profitable as a mine full of it would be. And right here, there was evidence of gold in the cliff face. I also liked this spot because it is reasonably flat and wide enough for a camp, the stream runs next to it, and there's even a water hole in case the stream dries up by the end of summer. And the rock face is high enough to tunnel through without having to worry about cave-ins."

As she looked around for the stream, she noticed all the flowers growing along the right side of the camp. She couldn't see the water, but guessed the flowers were hiding it from view. The colorful blooms made the area he'd carved out rather pretty.

"Well, you obviously didn't need to move on," she commented as she glanced back at him.

"No, I definitely got lucky. There was a smattering of gold for a few feet in, then some silver. I kept digging, hoping for more gold, but five more feet in I crossed a damn mother lode of silver that hasn't let up yet."

She was impressed. If he'd been up here mining since last summer, he must be rich by now. You certainly couldn't tell it by the way he dressed, or lived, for that matter. But his cabin wasn't made of logs, despite there being so many trees up this way. Somehow he'd brought lumber up this hill, and even glass for a couple of windows. But the cabin looked small from out front, which made her wonder about sleeping arrangements. She hoped it had more than one room. Sharing one with him would be scandalous and ruin her reputation! All the more reason for her to quickly find her father's mine and money and persuade Morgan to take her back to Butte.

Other than the gray rock cliff face, it was quite green up here, and the air was cooler even with the sun shining down on them. There were even a few shade trees inside the fence, which continued on the right all the way beyond his cabin. If he hadn't mentioned claim jumpers, she would have thought the purpose of the fence was to provide a corral for his animals.

They hadn't passed her father's mine on the way up here, or perhaps they had while she'd been blindfolded. But it could as likely be in another gorge nearby. And the sooner she found out if her father had stored his money there, the sooner she could go home.

So she asked Morgan, "Will you take me to my father's mine now?"

"No."

"But—"

"Lady—"

"Stop calling me that," she cut in. "The way you say it, it sounds like a bloody insult. If you won't call me Miss Mitchell, then you have my permission to use my given name, Violet."

"Why?" he countered. "We aren't friends, you aren't who you claim to be, and I might have to resort to unusual measures to find out what you're really up to."

Her eyes flared briefly then narrowed on him. "You'll do nothing of the sort, and we both know it. You've fed me. You've even let me sleep against your chest, which I apologize for, but you still allowed it. You wouldn't resort to torture no matter who you think I am, so do *not* make pointless threats."

He turned to her, his light-blue eyes roaming over her for a moment before a lazy smile formed. "Who said anything about torture?"

He took a step toward her, his arms extended. She'd gone too far! He was going to disprove everything she'd just said in a horribly physical manner!

Chapter Twelve

CONSIDERING WHAT WAS RAMPAGING through her mind, Violet gasped and slid down the other side of Morgan's horse to escape him, then groaned as pain shot up her legs from such an abrupt landing. She would have fallen to the ground if she wasn't still grasping the pommel of his saddle.

But he came around the horse and pried her hands loose from the pommel. "Why'd you dismount like that? You in some kind of hurry?"

"No, I—"

She stopped when he swept her into his arms and started walking toward the cabin. She realized he probably only intended to help her up to his porch, since it was about two feet off the ground and the one step that led to it had been built for his long legs, not a woman's. And there was no hand railing to help her manage the steep climb. Her legs probably would balk if she tried to do it herself.

Still, she was utterly flustered by what she'd thought he was about to do and snapped, "I don't want to hear any more threats from you, real or not. I'm at the end of my tether, tired, and hungry, and I need a bloody bath!"

He sniffed. Twice! "Yes, you do."

She gasped at that insult and immediately returned it: "So do you!"

"Are you suggesting we bathe together?"

That infuriated her even more. "I meant nothing of the kind."

She noticed the twinkle in his eyes. Was he trying not to laugh? The beast! Yet as he finally set her down on the porch, he said, "You'll get your bath as soon as I unload the mules."

He left her on the porch and started doing just that. The door to the house was closed, and without his permission, she wasn't going to open it. She sat on one of the two rough chairs on the porch, hoping her brocade skirt wouldn't get splinters from it. She wondered why there were two of them when he'd implied no one else ever came up here, but she supposed her father must have visited him from time to time. It was difficult to picture her debonair father, who socialized at Philadelphia's finest homes and gentlemen's clubs, sitting on the porch of this cabin in the middle of nowhere. She found it hard to believe she was there herself.

The day was still so hot, which made her appreciate the shade on the porch as she watched Morgan. He was leaving everything he took off the mules right there on the ground, his goal apparently to unburden them and set them loose before he put anything away. The unencumbered mules gravitated to the stream, which meandered inside and outside the fence.

He was close enough to talk to her. After his flat refusal to show her her father's mine, she decided to ask him about his cabin, and then steer the conversation to the topic she was most interested in. Aunt Elizabeth had told her she was an adroit conversationalist.

"Why did you build this cabin several feet off the ground?"

"I got up here last summer, long after the spring thaw. So I didn't know if the runoff from the icecaps would come pouring down here this spring."

She thought he might be grinning, but it was so hard to tell with that bushy mustache of his, so she merely asked, "Did it?"

"No, not this year at least, but water did erode this gorge at some point in the history of this range. And the stream did flood this spring about four feet on this side, more on the other side. But last year I didn't know how bad it would be and pictured my cabin being washed down the hill, so I decided to take the precaution of elevating it when I got tired of sleeping in a tent."

"It must have taken you months to build."

"No, just a few days."

"That's impossible."

"Not with friends helping."

She would have said that was also impossible, his having any friends, but it would have been quite an insult; she wanted to disarm him with harmless talk before she mentioned Charles's mine again, so she asked, "Friends from Butte?"

"No, I sent for some friends I grew up with in Nashart, men I knew I could trust not to reveal the location of my mine. I ordered all the lumber, pipes, flues, bricks, and everything else needed and stored it in town before I asked them to ride over. By then I would have been followed if I'd been seen leaving town with building materials, but they weren't."

"By then?"

"Most of the miners in town work for a few big mine

owners. And they're a greedy bunch. But most of their mines started pulling more copper than silver or gold, so they concentrate on copper now—all except for your friend Sullivan. His silver hasn't run out yet."

"He's not my friend. And besides, why would Shawn Sullivan or anyone go to so much trouble to find out where your mine is located? From what I've heard, there's lots of gold and silver in these hills and mountains."

"Sure there is, but Sullivan doesn't want anyone else selling silver. He was getting high prices for his when he was the last supplier in this area. He didn't like it when those prices dropped and his buyers told him to find another market if he wasn't satisfied with what they were paying him. He couldn't figure out where all the other silver was coming from and sent spies all around the area to find out. And came up with nothing. Then one of his men got curious about me. No one had paid me any mind before those prices dropped. They thought I came in, sold a few hides, then left again."

His tone remained calm but had turned a little derogatory when he'd mentioned Shawn Sullivan. Now she understood a bit better why he might be suspicious of her and jump to the wrong conclusion that she was colluding with his worst enemy. But she wanted to know more.

"How did Mr. Sullivan find out you were the mysterious silver miner?"

"Because he was still demanding answers from his men, and they broke into my crates at the station before they were loaded on the train. Sullivan approached me after that and offered a fair price for my mine. He wasn't expecting me to tell him to go to hell. After that, he had his men follow me when I left town. It was beyond annoying. Took me twice as long to get back here since I had to throw them off the scent. The second time his men followed me, I jumped them and left them hog-tied in the middle of the road with *Go to hell* notes pinned to their chests."

Quite an aggressive response, Violet thought; but wanting him to think she was on his side, she remarked mildly, "I don't imagine that went over too well."

"No, the townsfolk didn't like me after that—well, they never did, but they started giving me a wide berth. And Sheriff Gibson gave me a scolding the next time I went to town. He wasn't serious about it. He's had to investigate countless complaints from small mine owners about threats, beatings, even some killings after they refused to sell their operations to rich owners like Sullivan."

He had to be exaggerating or was simply mistaken. But she didn't want to antagonize him by defending Shawn Sullivan, which might reinforce his suspicions that she was working for his enemy, so she only said, "Well, you certainly made your feelings clear to Mr. Sullivan."

"He doesn't take no for an answer. I even changed markets and made a deal directly with a pair of silversmith brothers in New York. And I started leaving Butte by different routes after that, but Sullivan still tracked me down each time I came to town and made a higher offer for my mine. So I stopped going so often, even started sneaking into town in the dead of night, and I stopped picking up the notes he leaves for me at the hotel. He still wants my mine, but that's not all. He wants to know where both mines are, mine and Charley's. He'd be happy with either one to start, because he knows he'll wind up with both in the end."

Sullivan wanted her father's mine, too? That would solve

everything! As soon as she located it, she could sell it to him for a lot of money, then return to London and slip back into the social whirl and win Lord Elliott before some other debutante did. Thrilled to have such a perfect solution to her problems, she had to cover her mouth so Morgan wouldn't see that she was smiling. But would a sale provide enough money for her and her brothers? Or might it be more profitable for them to hire men to work the mine? She wouldn't know until she actually saw it, but at least she had two good options now.

Done with his task, Morgan slapped the rump of the last mule, then started shoving crates and baskets onto the porch under the railing.

"But you already knew all that about Shawn Sullivan, didn't you?" He paused after setting a crate on the porch and looked up at her.

She sighed in irritation. "I barely said two words to the man the night I met him. His daughter, Katie, invited me to join them for dinner. He was there to meet his future son-in-law for the first time, not me."

"Sure."

His skepticism lit the flame. It might be ingrained in her to keep unpleasant emotions under wraps and put on a good face for all occasions, but she'd never been tested like this! She was tired, hungry, dirty, and totally exasperated with this man.

With a smoldering glare, she pointed out, "You snatched me out of a perfectly comfortable hotel room, accused me of being a liar, made me ride a horse in the hot sun for a day and a half, tried to feed me snake meat! And you made me sleep on the bloody ground! The least you can do now is take me to my father's mine!"

"You're not going to like your stay here if you keep asking for something that's not going to happen."

His tone was quite sharp, but she was beyond caring or caution. She leapt to her feet, her hands gripping the porch railing. "*You* aren't going to like my stay here if you don't answer me! It's *my* bloody mine you are refusing to tell me about. It belongs to me and my brothers now. I demand you take me to it right this instant!"

"Make-believe daughters don't get to demand anything."

Another evasion? One too many! In a fury, she reached into the basket at her feet and threw a handful of the contents at him, then screamed in frustration when she saw it was just carrots.

She ran into the house to find something heavier to hit him with, shouting back, "You've stolen our mine! Claim-jumped it, or whatever you call it out here. That's why you want to hide it from me!"

He followed her inside, growling, "You're out of your mind!"

"You're right and it's your bloody fault!"

She grabbed cans off a shelf and started throwing them at him. She didn't pause to see if any hit him before reaching for more. But when strong arms clamped tightly around her middle and her feet left the floor, she burst into tears at being thwarted.

"So much for the lady story," he said as he put her down on a bed.

"Go to the devil!" she yelled, and turned over to face the wall. And cried a lot more.

Chapter Thirteen

"We're so happy you're home, Violet." Sophie sat beside her on the blanket. They were on an outing in the park, a few of the younger girls picking wildflowers. But their favorite park didn't have wildflowers. She tried to tell them that, but no one was listening to her. One of her cousins reached into a picnic hamper and asked her, "D'you want crumpets or cat meat?" Appalled, Violet looked around, expecting to see a cougar, but saw Lord Elliott approaching instead. He looked so handsome in riding jodhpurs and holding a crop. All the girls gathered around him excitedly. He kissed Sophie's hand, patted each of the younger girls on the head, then glanced at Violet and raised his nose a little higher in the air and walked on. He was snubbing her?! Sophie stopped giggling long enough to say, "He heard you're a pauper now. Shame on you, Vi, for letting that happen." Violet burst into tears and started throwing carrots at Elliott's retreating back. But Elliott must have forgiven her, because suddenly she was dancing with him in a beautiful ballroom, laughing at his clever quips. Everything was right with the world again until he *pulled away from her, looking horrified: "A snake is slithering out of your reticule!"*

It was the snake that woke her. She looked around frantically for a moment to make sure there wasn't one with her in the bed that had wormed its way into her dream—nightmare was more like it. She shuddered briefly once she was sure there wasn't a snake in the cabin, as far as she could see.

She took note of her surroundings. There were just the two windows in the front wall to let in light, the glass so thick she could barely see through it. There was next to no furniture. Instead of a cabinet, Morgan had a wall of deep shelves, one for folded clothes and bedding, one for dishes and pans, the rest for supplies, some of which were stored in baskets. Several crates were now stacked against a wall, too. Three chairs surrounded a rectangular table in the center of the room. Apparently, he did get visitors. There was no kitchen, just a fireplace with two raised griddles over it. A Dutch oven sat on the higher one, two pots on the lower one, a low fire burning beneath them. It was a decent fireplace, though, built of stone with a mantel on which a lantern and a few knickknacks sat. She was disappointed by the spartan accommodations. No sofa, not even one comfortable chair, just two narrow beds in opposite corners. Two?

Morgan walked in with a large sack of grain over his shoulder. She could see that he'd bathed. A long towel was still hanging about his neck, but he hadn't fully dressed. His chest was bare and wet, his hair wet, too. It was too much when she wasn't fully awake yet, all that bare brawn utterly transfixing her, not letting her thoughts through, not letting her breathe. . . .

"I built most of the furniture, so it's as rough as you might expect, since I'm not a carpenter. The table wobbles. Ignore it, I do."

She breathed deeply, and tore her eyes off him. He must have noticed her looking about the room to say that. She'd rather ignore him and his comments about his living quarters. Was he trying to soothe her with trivial conversation? That wasn't happening.

She glanced between the two beds, one crumpled with bedding, the one she was sitting on made up neatly. "Who else lives here with you?"

He put the grain sack on a shelf before he turned and said, "No one now."

"Was it my father? Is his mine actually that close to yours?"

"Should I brace myself for another conniption?"

Normally she would be mortified that she'd let him see her at her worst. Good Lord, she'd actually thrown things at him. But he'd deserved it. And then she realized he'd just evaded again!

"I think if I had a gun right now, I'd shoot you," she said tonelessly.

"And miss."

"Probably," she agreed. "Though it would be satisfying to try. You really can't keep doing this to me. That mine is too important to my family."

"Well, that's the thing, Violet Mitchell pretender, it's not. It's important to Sullivan, and what's really important to you is his agenda. Now, I might have thrown a wrinkle into your plan by figuring that out, but you apparently had a fallback plan ready in case I did. Bottom line, Charley's mine is still none of your business, so do us both a favor and stop nagging me about it."

"This is bloody absurd. You assumed this impostor non-sense simply because Katie Sullivan befriended me in town, but it's simply not true. I am exactly who I said I am."

"I spent enough time with Charley to know he was from the East, Philadelphia, I think he said. You, however, aren't from there. Sullivan was pretty dumb to hire a foreigner to play the part of Charley's daughter."

She sighed. It was suddenly clear why he refused to believe her—he'd even brought it up before. Her accent. Even her brothers had mentioned it.

"I tried to tell you on the trail that I've been living with my aunt and uncle in England for the last nine years, which may be why my father never mentioned me to you, and is why I speak with an English accent. Even my brothers teased me about sounding like a Brit now."

"Are they children?"

"What difference does that make?"

"Then they are?"

"No, they are two years older than I."

"Then they wouldn't have let their younger sister come out here alone. You're just providing more proof that you aren't a Mitchell."

She growled under her breath in frustration. "On the trail you implied that once we reached your mine, the truth would be revealed. Well? What kind of proof do you have that what you say and not what I say is the truth?"

"You won't be leaving here until you admit the truth," he replied. "That's all I implied, and I don't give a damn how long it takes."

She was dismayed. Her brothers needed help immediately! "That's unacceptable. My visit to this territory is a matter of the greatest urgency, and besides, I can prove who I am. You need only send a telegram to my brothers. Time is of the essence. I can give you the address, but you might think that's prearranged. I can also give you their names, but again, you might think they are coconspirators. So just send it to Charles Mitchell's sons. Our family is well known in Philadelphia. It will be delivered to them and they will confirm that I came here to find our father. And one of them intended to come with me, but he was detained. He was supposed to follow, but sent word that he couldn't. They are depending on me to find Father's money. D'you have it?"

"You're too interested in that money," he remarked. "Why is that?"

"Because my brothers and I need it."

That got her a long stare before he said, "The brothers who aren't actually yours? When it's more likely that Sullivan has promised you that you can keep any money of Charley's you find out here?"

"D'you realize how exasperating you are? I told you exactly how you can prove who I am. I demand you take me back to town to do so!"

"Well, that's not happening, not until I'm ready for another trip, and maybe not even then. You don't get to lead anyone back here, and letting you loose back in town will just have you running to Sullivan to do that."

Her brief burst of anger petered out, leaving her with a sigh. "I have no intention of parting company with you when you are the only one who can help me. My brothers are counting on me to fix the dilemma our father left us in."

"You mentioned you're on a tight schedule. What's the hurry, other than Shawn's damn impatience?"

"I don't know anything about that man, but my brothers and I are going to lose our family home if you don't turn over our father's money immediately. The loan Papa left them with used the house as collateral, and the payments have escalated. If you won't take me to town so I can get you proof of my identity, then you go. I'll wait here. You can cover the distance in half the time if you travel alone."

"No."

"Why are you being so bloody stubborn about this?!"

He straightened. "Maybe I'm going to enjoy having you around. Maybe I think you're so good at your job that you planned for all contingencies, including paying a visit to Philadelphia first to find out what you could about Charley. Lady, there's all sorts of ways you could have prepared in advance to pull off this scam."

Chapter Fourteen

VIOLET GLARED AT MORGAN. He had to be an idiot if he thought his comment about enjoying having her there could disarm her into telling him what he was convinced was the truth. It occurred to her that he might have been taking what he could from her father's mine before relatives arrived to claim it. And that was why he didn't want to show her where it was and why he might insist to the bitter end that she wasn't a Mitchell.

"What are you going to do when you find out you're wrong and I'm not working for Shawn Sullivan?" she asked.

"I'd rather hear you admit the truth and give me a reason to shoot the son of a bitch."

"Men don't seem to need much reason to do that out here," she replied, remembering that frightful duel she'd witnessed in Butte. "Are you a thief? Have you been working my father's mine all this time since he died? Is that why you're being so evasive?"

"If you want to see me angry, you're sure working in the right direction."

He didn't sound angry. Actually, the bear sounded amused. "*Do* you have his money?"

"No."

An actual answer, but not the one she'd hoped for. "If you're not a thief, why won't you talk about my father or his mine? I have a right—"

He cut in, "That's just it, you don't. D'you think I don't know that you'll take anything I say right to Sullivan's ears? So give it a rest, 'cause I'm damn tired of reminding you that it's simply not your business."

She sighed. Her belly rumbled, but he hadn't mentioned eating yet, and she'd rather bathe first, so she asked, "Where is that bath you mentioned? You said there's a water hole."

He laughed. "Oh, hell no, that's for drinking and cooking in case the stream dries up. There's a spot in the stream that's backed up a little and has formed a small pool. It's where I bathe when I feel like it."

That implied he didn't bathe often. She grimaced as she carefully stood up. Her legs still hurt, but she hoped soaking in cold water would ease her thigh muscles. She reached for the valise he'd set next to the bed and pulled out some clean clothes. Very wrinkled clean clothes. She might have asked if he had an iron, but it would no doubt make him laugh again.

"You're determined?" he asked, watching her.

"Of course."

"The pool is outside the fence, so it's not safe for you to go alone."

"I'll brave it."

"You'd still need a gun—if you know how to use one." When she frowned, he sighed, adding, "I'll take you, as long as you're quick about it. And don't worry, the only thing you'll see of me is my back. Come on, the sun will be setting soon."

"Then take a lantern."

"I said quick, but should have added, or not at all. Take your pick."

She was beginning to think disagreeability was ingrained in him, but before he got out the door, she asked, "Do you have soap?"

He turned about and went to his wall of shelves to rummage through a basket, then tossed her a very large bar. The coarsest type of soap—it would probably rub the skin right off her hands. "A washcloth?"

"Lady, does this look like a hotel to you?" Yet he tossed a small towel at her, then, as an afterthought, the longer one around his neck. She started to ask for a clean one, but he read her mind: "That's the only one, take it or leave it."

She closed her eyes for the briefest moment, wondering what Sophie would think if she could see her now. Her cousin would either faint or laugh, most likely the latter. She was fond of saying that when situations became absurd, they turned comical. But Violet, in the thick of absurd situations and such primitive choices, hadn't reached that point yet.

She followed her host outside. He was waiting at the top step, she assumed to help her down them. She noticed a wheelbarrow full of rocks that hadn't been there before.

"You were mining?" she asked in surprise.

"Why not?" he replied. "I make use of daylight even if you don't."

Sure, remind her that she'd slept a good portion of the day away when she hadn't meant to. And that was definitely humor in his tone. "I assumed you would spend the rest of the day unpacking your supplies."

"I don't unpack anything until I need it." Nor had he been waiting there to help her, and the complaint he made as he went down the steps confounded her: "Waste of two good support beams."

She didn't have a clue—then she did. He'd built railings for the steps while she slept! He didn't need those handholds or they would already have been attached to the steps. He'd built them just for her—and was complaining about it. She was amazed that he'd done it.

She couldn't help smiling and saying, "Thank you."

He stopped to wait for her and, seeing her hand on the railing, just nodded curtly. She saw mules grazing on both sides of the stream, then noticed an extension of the fence that ran through the trees on the other side of the stream. "More bells on that fence, I suppose?" He nodded, and she wondered aloud, "I would think bells could be cut off and a fence hopped in silence, so wouldn't a dog prove more useful to let you know if anyone approaches?"

His answer was to whistle, very loudly. Nothing happened; he was just facetiously implying he had a dog. But he continued down the hill toward the gate they'd passed through when they arrived.

Following him, she passed his horse, the only animal left in the front yard. "Why isn't he with the mules? Or is he a stallion?"

"He'd be a terror around here if he was. No, I just don't take chances with my only way out of here. I lock Caesar in the mine at night. But I dug out a section to make room for my gals, too, during the worst of winter. It's not an ideal stable, but it keeps them from freezing."

Now she understood why he'd brought bales of hay from Butte when there was already so much grass around here. And then she heard barking in the distance. "So you do have a dog?"

The animal hadn't appeared yet, but Morgan said, "I was out hunting after the spring thaw and cooking a rabbit for my lunch when Bo approached my camp snarling at me. Don't know how long he was lost out there, but he was skin and bones by then. There was no doubt he was going to attack, he was that hungry. Rather than shoot him, I tossed him the rest of my meat. It was funny as hell. He wolfed that down in one chomp, then gave me an expectant look with his tail wagging. I'd won him over that easily. So I let him follow me home. He comes in handy, cleaning up scraps. But he wanders pretty far when I'm not here."

"The fences don't keep him in?"

"Now that he's healthy, he has no trouble jumping them," he said.

That was proven a moment later when a large black-haired dog leapt over the nearest fence and jumped up on Morgan in greeting, and then almost immediately started growling at Violet.

She didn't back away. "You could have warned me he's not tame."

"But he is, tame as a pussycat."

"That, sir, is not a good comparison. I had a cat, the meanest feline ever. She hissed and scratched at anyone who came near her."

"Except you?"

"Especially me," she corrected, her eyes still on the growling dog. "I think she knew I preferred dogs and hated me for it. My brothers got dogs, I got the mean cat." And then to the dog, she said firmly, "You, stop that. We're going to be friends."

Morgan chuckled and only had to pet the top of the dog's head to get it to stop growling. "Bo's just protective of his yard. But tell me, why didn't you run into the house screaming? Isn't that what you ladies do when threatened?"

She gave him an indignant look. "I told you I like dogs. Yours will sense that soon enough."

She followed Morgan out of the yard and about twenty feet down the hill. The little pool he'd described was in the thicker part of the forest, but he hadn't mentioned how inviting he'd made it. Smooth rock lined each side to make it easy to get in and out, and there were even a few flowers like those near his cabin.

True to his word, Morgan leaned against a tree, facing away from her. She still kept her eyes mostly on his back as she disrobed down to her underclothes and got in the water. She washed quickly, not wanting to give him another reason to complain.

She noticed another bar of soap next to the stream and almost laughed. Did he think she wouldn't want to use his? She dried herself and dressed behind another tree in dry undergarments, a clean white blouse, and a lavender skirt. After rolling her soap and wet smallclothes in the washcloth, she wrapped Morgan's larger towel around her wet hair, already imagining how painful it was going to be when she took her brush to what was now a wildly tangled mane.

Gathering up her things, she walked over to Morgan so they could head back to the cabin. He pushed away from the tree trunk he was leaning against and loomed over her. It did feel that way, he was so tall.

"This is when you might want to seduce me. If that's one of your options, no point in wasting time."

She was speechless. Strong arms drew her close to him, and he kissed her. Tickled by his mustache, teased by his tongue, she was startled by the fervent sensations that ran through her. It was all too fast and too much. She instinctively shoved him away from her and stumbled on a tree root behind her, toppling backward toward the water.

Chapter Fifteen

HE STOPPED THE FALL. Violet wished he hadn't. She could have used another dunking, she felt so flustered from that kiss. She certainly didn't thank him for keeping her dry when his effrontery deserved a dressing-down.

She glowered at him with high indignation. "I am a proper young lady. Such liberties as you just took I find scandalous! And you will *not* insinuate again that I'm a harlot when I most certainly am not!"

"I know. You're an actress, and a damn good one. Women don't usually react that way when I kiss them."

What arrogance! At least he hadn't been able to tell that she'd rather liked the kiss, found it quite intriguing. That would have been too embarrassing. But he was still insulting her with that actress nonsense, so she stressed, "I'm not an act—"

He cut in, "A little too much protesting, or are you regretting the role you got stuck with? You do know you can improvise, right? So don't kick yourself too hard over the lost opportunity. I'm sure you'll get another."

Opportunity? "That will not happen again," she insisted.

"Does that mean I have to shove you away next time?"

She gasped. She sputtered. He added, "That's a yes, I take it? Fine, since you obviously spent a lot of time rehearsing, I won't interfere with your role again."

Was that an assurance that there would be no more kissing? She wasn't exactly sure, but he'd already walked away, so she followed. But she couldn't help wondering how she might have reacted if he hadn't insulted her before he'd kissed her. Would she have pushed him away? Yes—no—maybe. She didn't know! But for a first kiss, it had certainly been memorable, even if she wouldn't have picked the bear for such an experience.

Back in the yard she hung her wet clothes to dry on the fence at the side of the cabin where they would be out of view of anyone entering or leaving the cabin. Coming back around the porch, she saw Morgan leading his horse into his storeroom. She frowned when he came out alone, closed the large steel door, and locked it. But he'd told her that he stabled his horse in his mine. . . .

Her eyes immediately moved to the other big hole in the cliff, which she'd wrongly assumed was his mine, just as she'd wrongly assumed the steel door led to a storeroom. Her father's mine was this close to Morgan's?! Yes, of course it was, verified by two chairs on the porch and two beds inside the cabin.

Hands on hips, she demanded, "Why didn't you admit my father's mine is right here in your yard?"

He was approaching her but didn't stop, just growled in passing, "I'm pretty sure I warned you not to open that can of worms. Not another word about it, lady."

Oh, they would most definitely discuss it, but maybe after

dinner. When he wasn't growling. But why was it such a bone of contention with him?

She followed him inside to return the bar of soap to the basket and was amazed to see shaving tools in it, razors, strops, a fancy lather mug, little scissors. It was a miracle that they hadn't all rusted from disuse. When she turned around, she saw Morgan slipping his arms into a white shirt. After lighting a lantern, he picked up both pots from the fire and carried them to the table. The wooden table. And there was no metal pot holder to set them on.

"Wait!" She quickly grabbed a small towel from the shelf, folded it, and laid it on the table. "There. So you don't warp the wood."

She heard his snort, but didn't wait for his sarcastic reply. She fetched her brush instead and sat down on the bed to tackle the tangles in her hair. They were as bad as she figured, and her hair was still damp, which didn't help.

But Morgan was suddenly sitting down next to her and taking the brush from her hand. She leaned away with a gasp. "What are you doing? I don't need your help."

"Instead of getting all prissy, why don't you just wait and say thank you later?"

She closed her mouth on what she'd been about to say. Did she really come across as prissy to him? Well, what did he expect when everything she'd experienced with him was new and utterly foreign to her? Including this, a man brushing her hair. Only her maid or Aunt Elizabeth or Sophie had ever done this for her.

She expected to cry from his yanking her hair out by the roots as he brushed through the tangles, but instead she kept feeling his fingers brush against her neck as he divided the locks and held them tight by her nape so he didn't pull any. She was amazed that someone like him could be so gentle, but she wasn't about to share that thought with him. By the time the last of the tangles were gone and he was running the brush through the entire length of her hair, she was close to sighing in pleasure!

When he stood and moved back to the table, she said softly, "Thank you."

His eyes met hers before he replied, "My pleasure. No different from grooming a mule's tail."

He was comparing her to his mules? She decided not to reply and joined him at the table as he ladled out two large bowls, then two small ones. A thick stew with carrots was in the large bowl and beans in the smaller one.

"This isn't the cougar you shot, is it?" she asked hesitantly before she picked up her spoon.

"No, this meat isn't as tender. Dried venison never is. Too bad you're so finicky."

He broke off a chunk of bread for her, but there was no butter for it on the table. It was possibly the last of the fresh loaf he'd brought from town, not so fresh now two days later. Would he make more? Did he know how? The stew was evidence that he had some knowledge of cooking.

She watched him dip his bread in the stew to coat it with gravy before taking a bite of it. She tried that and was surprised by how good it tasted.

"Are you good at map drawing?" he asked after a while. "Or are you just supposed to dazzle me with your beauty?"

These backhanded compliments didn't impress her, but they

did disconcert her a little. He had been watching her while they ate, so she had a feeling he was leading up to discussing that kiss, or getting ready to insult her again.

Violet had kept her own eyes averted—the man still hadn't buttoned up his shirt! But she glanced up at him now to abruptly change the subject. "I want to view my father's mine after dinner."

"There's nothing for an impostor in Charley's mine," he replied.

"His money?"

"With no mine door to secure it?"

That was a good point, but Morgan's mine was about as secure as a bank vault. And if he and her father had been friendly, Charles might have asked Morgan to lock his money up for him. No—he'd already said he didn't have Charles's money. Good grief, this was so frustrating, and he was beyond infuriating with his flat refusals to do as she asked.

He stood up, saying he was going to wash his empty bowls in the stream. She followed him to do the same, annoyed that her legs still hurt so much, annoyed with Morgan, annoyed with the world—and tripped and fell face-first into the bed of flowers.

"What the devil!" she cried out, pushing herself back to her feet.

He glanced back at her. "You didn't notice the fence?"

"You could have warned me."

"Didn't think you'd go walking through my flowers."

"Yes, you did!" she accused.

"Yeah, but I know enough to step over a fence."

"What bloody fence?"

"Use those violet eyes of yours—Violet."

She squinted behind her until she saw a rope strung between stakes barely a foot high. And it didn't exactly contain the flowers. They were already growing on the other side of it.

"It's good enough to keep the animals out," he added. "That and a few good yells taught them pretty quick."

Glimpsing bright orange through the trees down below, she realized it was the setting sun and was pleased to have this confirmation of which way was west. She just didn't know if this mountain range was north or south of the road they'd traveled on so long yesterday, or even east if the road had curved around the range.

Glancing around at the flowers, she realized they were nothing like the wild ones she'd seen yesterday. "These don't grow here naturally, do they?"

"I had a dream one night that my mother paid me a visit. Which is never going to happen, but I still ordered some seeds and tossed them around this spring. New ones keep sprouting, and the garden's a bit messy, but I think Ma would approve."

This was the first time he'd talked about his family. She wanted to ask him about them, but he was already walking away, so obviously he didn't want to continue the conversation. Still, it surprised her that he'd plant flowers just because his mother liked them. Unless he'd used that as an excuse so he wouldn't have to admit that *he* liked them. Did he think that would make him appear less manly? Ha! Nothing could make *him* appear less manly.

Back in the cabin, he lit several lanterns that hung on the walls, then split an apple for them for dessert and sat down to eat his half. She wondered if he would try to stop her if she went down to view what was now her mine. She didn't need his permission—except he didn't agree that it was hers.

And then she was incredulous when he said, "I know that Charley hid his earnings somewhere up here. He heard too much about the money not being recovered from that recent bank robbery in town. That was why Charley refused to use the bank and hid his money up here."

"Did you lose everything in that robbery?"

"No, nothing worth mentioning. I use banks in New York and Nashart. I haven't bothered to look for Charley's stash. You can if you've a mind to, but you don't get to keep it. Find it and I'll send it on to his sons."

That would actually work out perfectly—if it was enough. "How much did he have?"

"Now you're being ridiculous. Have you run out of ammunition?"

"I beg your pardon?"

"The proof of your identity you offered earlier involves sending a telegram, which I can't do immediately. So what else do you have to support your claim?"

She hadn't thought he would accept personal information about her father as proof that she was Charles Mitchell's daughter, and he still might not, but she was invigorated from the bath and her long nap, and ready to do battle again. "You're quite right. The proof I offered you earlier is days away, not here right now. But I have more up here." She pointed to her head. "I can tell you more about my father than you can tell me. His hair was a lighter shade of blond than mine, his eyes dark blue, and he favored a handlebar mustache—at least, he did the last time I saw him. He was a tad over six feet tall. He broke his right leg when he was a young man and was left with a very slight limp that wasn't noticeable unless he was overly tired, so hardly anyone knew about it. He had a good sense of humor and liked to tell jokes. I could recount some he might have told you, but I'm bad at remembering jokes even if I've heard them a dozen times. But there was one about two sailors, and another one about a princess and her watchmaker, something about her constantly summoning the poor man to her palace to repair her watch that wasn't broken. And Charles's birthday was May fourteenth. Oh, and my brothers are twins. If he mentioned that, he might have admitted that he could never tell them apart."

"Could you?"

"When we were children I could, but when I saw them for the first time in five years just three weeks ago, both fully grown, no, I couldn't." She was pleased that he no longer looked skeptical. "You finally believe me, don't you?"

"It was the jokes. They were horrible."

She laughed. "We loved them—when we were children."

Chapter Sixteen

THE BURDEN OF MORGAN'S disbelief that she was Charles Mitchell's daughter had been more harrowing than Violet had realized. Now that it was gone, Morgan no longer made her quite so nervous. He might still look like a shaggy bear, but she'd had brief glimpses of his gentle side, and he no longer seemed ferociously unreasonable. He also no longer had any excuse not to answer her questions.

"What did you mean when you said you allowed my father to stay?" she asked first.

"The answer might not be good for the digestion," he warned.

"I assure you I have an excellent constitution."

"I meant mine."

"Oh, the answer makes you angry," she said, then reminded him, "But I've weathered your storms so far, haven't I?"

He chuckled. "Yeah, I suppose you have. Well, I woke up one morning to find your pa picking at the cliff only a few feet from my claim. I wasn't happy about it."

"You were furious, weren't you?" she guessed.

"You could say a little more'n that. I yelled at him to get the hell off my hill. He just waved at me and smiled, as if he didn't hear me, which just made me angrier. I went down there and saw that he'd hammered in a stake that was literally touching mine. But he hadn't made a dent in the rock yet. So I told him that his claim was invalid and he had to be gone by the end of the day."

She paled. "Was that true?"

"Yeah, two mines can't be placed that close together unless the owner of one buys out the other or the two miners partner up. Your father should have known that. Then I took a good look at him. He was already sweating and the sun hadn't even come over the range yet. It was cold as hell that early—"

She interrupted, "You realize that 'cold as hell' is an oxymoron?"

"You realize you got my drift anyway?"

She blushed a little. "Continue, please."

"It was obvious he wasn't going to last more than a few hours, if even that, so I went back to the house to make coffee and sat on the porch to wait until he figured out he was no miner. He might not have been too old to mine, but he was certainly in no condition to do hard labor. And I was right. Within the hour, he collapsed."

Her eyes flared. "What do you mean by that?"

"Exactly what I said. Charley grabbed his chest and fell over. By the time I got down there, he wasn't conscious. So I carried him inside the house and put him on my bed and waited for him to wake up and explain."

"What was there to explain? He had a bad heart. Dr. Cantry mentioned that when I spoke with him."

"I didn't know that—yet. And there are other reasons why someone might pass out like that. Some people can't tolerate the altitude up here, have trouble breathing. But, yeah, Charley mentioned his heart problem when he woke up. He'd only just found out about it himself, and that it was bad. But he assured me that he had no choice, that he had to mine even if it killed him, and he explained why. Your mentioning that loan that he left your brothers with was my first clue that you might be telling the truth. He told me the same thing that morning, and that his boys were depending on him to make the family rich again."

She winced. It sounded so fanciful when he said it, a lost cause. And yet her father had a mine that now belonged to her and her brothers. An invalid mine? Obviously not, since it was dug, staked, and recorded in town—with Morgan's permission. He'd allowed it. Why would he do that when he'd admitted how angry he was at her father that day?

But she still had so many things to worry about: how to get her silver out of here, how to pay off the loan immediately, claim jumpers, how to hire workers to mine for her. Or she and her brothers could sell it. Morgan had told her Mr. Sullivan was interested in buying it, but she had a feeling Morgan might raise hell about that option, so she decided not to mention it yet.

Instead she asked, "Do I need to worry about those claim jumpers? Did they ever bother you again?"

"There were signs of someone stealing my silver ore last year while I was in town, leaving picked-out pockets in the walls. After that, I ordered the steel door when I bought the building materials for the house. And there was one other time, end of last winter, when I saw evidence of trespassers in my camp, but

I can't say for sure if it was those two claim jumpers who shot at me."

"Do the claim jumpers work for Mr. Sullivan?"

"That's a dumb question. I'd probably be dead by now if they did. No, they showed up early on, when the people in town thought I was a trapper selling hides every so often. They were either already roaming these hills and happened upon me, or they followed me up here before I grew cautious after learning how cutthroat mining can be around here, even this far out."

She felt a twinge of unease now that she knew for sure she was a mine owner. Morgan had already told her about the sheriff investigating small miners' complaints that big mine owners had threatened them, and he'd just implied again that Sullivan wanted to harm him. Having met Shawn Sullivan and his daughter, she just couldn't imagine him doing anything like that. Morgan was wrong about Mr. Sullivan, but she wasn't about to try to convince him of that when that particular subject was what he'd call a "can of worms."

So she moved on to the question that confused her most. "Why did you let my father stay?"

"He said I'd have to shoot him to get him to stop mining here."

"No, he didn't," she replied indignantly on her father's behalf.

"Yeah, he did. But I was already feeling sorry for him after hearing why he was so desperate. He was willing to die to help his family. Caring about kin that much is something I can understand." He suddenly stood up. "More dessert?"

"After a visit to the mine."

"You don't want to wait until morning?"

"Does daylight reach into the mine?"

"Not very far," he admitted. "Grab a lantern, then."

She picked up the one on the table and he reached for one on the wall, then led the way across the yard to the large hole in the cliff.

Inside the tunnel, she noticed that the support beams were as tall as Morgan. Anyone taller than him would have to duck.

"Why is the floor so smooth?" she asked.

"Because I chiseled it smooth."

She gasped. Lowering her lantern and looking at the floor more closely, she saw brighter streaks in the rock. "Is that silver we're walking on?"

"The tunnel runs straight through the lode, which was reached after six days of digging. It's not pure silver, it never is. It needs to be processed, which is what the smelter outside is for. But it's a rich lode, eighty percent silver with a sprinkling of copper and gold."

Eyes wide, she realized all her problems were solved! Those bright streaks in the rock weren't just on the floor, but on the walls and the ceiling, too.

"Your pa's stuff is here," Morgan said when he stopped, not quite at the end of the tunnel, though close enough for her to see the back wall in the lantern light. "I used his horse to carry him to the doctor and I didn't bother to retrieve it after I was told he died, so the stable has probably sold it by now. This is everything else Charley had with him when he came up here."

She moved around him and saw a bedroll, a rifle, two saddlebags filled with mining tools and cooking gear, everything he would need to survive up here alone. But he hadn't ended up alone, he'd ended up making friends with a bear. Her father's valise was there, too. She dropped to her knees to open it.

Behind her, Morgan said, "He never talked much about home. He seemed ashamed to admit that he'd been rich at some point and wasn't now, but it was obvious from his manners and the way he talked that he was a gentleman. I would have got around to hiring someone to take this stuff to his boys—he never mentioned their names—I just didn't see any reason to hurry when there's nothing of value here."

"My brothers are Daniel and Evan. You could at least have let them know he'd died."

"It'll be a cold day in hell before I want to deliver news like that. They'll hear from me soon. I was taking their address to Doc Cantry this trip so he could send them a telegram, but I found you there instead."

Violet was only half-listening to Morgan as she looked inside her father's valise. The lantern she'd set down didn't offer much light in the dark tunnel, so she couldn't see much of what was in it, but she reached in to pull out a few things. A small handful of letters rested atop the pile of clothes, letters tied with twine, all of them from her brothers, which was where Morgan must have found their address.

She pulled out one of her father's jackets and held it up to her face. The smell of it brought tears to her eyes. She was surprised she even remembered that scent after all these years, but it had been his favorite cologne. *Oh, Papa, why were you so careless with your inheritance that you had to resort to these drastic measures?*

"Are you crying?"

She dabbed the cuff of the jacket against her eyes before saying, "Of course not. Thank you for leading me to Papa's belongings. It's incredible that he was able to dig all this out at his age."

"He didn't—I did."

She glanced around. "I don't understand. This *is* his mine, correct?"

"Not exactly."

She was too excited about all the silver in the mine to want to argue with him, so she merely pointed out the obvious. "He staked the claim—you let him—so now it belongs to his heirs. And you don't need to help with the mining anymore, I can get workers up here to do—"

"Stop right there," he growled furiously. "I dug this tunnel for Charley only because I felt sorry for him. I sure as hell don't feel sorry for you. And you damn well aren't deciding anything about what I dug out. Your pa didn't find the silver here, I did. He broke every rule putting a claim down this close to mine. If I hadn't agreed to partner with him, he would have had to move on somewhere else. If you try to bring workers up here, I'll damn well close the book on that partnership and go to the claim office and get his claim invalidated."

"You're a horrible man!"

"No, I've got a heart of gold, just not for you!"

She'd never seen him this angry. It terrified her because she barely knew the man or what he was capable of in this state. He'd been doing all the work for someone else when he had his own mine? No one could be that generous. He had to be lying, everything he'd told her had to be lies. He'd even admitted that the only way he could get rid of Charles was to kill him!

Without thinking it through, she reached for her father's rifle and pointed it at Morgan's chest. "You killed him, didn't you? I only have your word that you found him unconscious. Everything you've said could be lies to cover up what really happened."

"Lady, if I was going to kill him, I would've done it when he first showed up, and I would have finished the job, not hauled him to town unconscious. No one, not even the doc, knew that he wasn't going to wake up and talk again before he passed on. And now you've pissed me off. Point a rifle at me again and you damn well better pull the trigger. You're on your own."

Now she'd made him angry? He'd already been furious, she'd just tipped the scale. She let the rifle slip from her fingers as she watched the lantern light move down the short tunnel. Then it was gone—and the cabin door slammed shut in the distance, like a bell tolling her doom. She was horrified by what she'd just done after he'd admitted he and her father had been partners. Her panic at seeing him so angry was no excuse. She'd just enraged a bear, and he wasn't forgiving.

She had a lantern, but that wouldn't give her any warmth tonight. She untied her father's bedroll and spread it out, then curled up on it, hugging her father's jacket to her chest. Tears were running down her cheeks again, but for herself this time. Morgan really was abandoning her in this cold, dark mine.

Chapter Seventeen

MORGAN LAY ON HIS bed, glowering at the ceiling. He was still livid. Stupid woman. She just didn't get it, that no one could find out about this location or else Sullivan would use underhanded methods, even resort to violence, to commandeer his highly productive mine. He didn't want to have to kill anyone to protect his property. No, she just didn't care about the hell it would put him through, was only interested in what she could get from a mine she thought was now hers. It wasn't. His partnership agreement had been with Charley, made with a handshake. There was no document to prove it. It sure as hell didn't mean he was going to partner with Charley's heirs or a woman who'd just tried to kill him!

If he hadn't known Charley's rifle was empty, he would have had to grab it from her and risk getting shot. But she didn't know it was empty. Her threat had been valid in her mind, but her reason was ridiculous.

The woman was cunning, smart, too beautiful, and she'd used it all to get under his skin and lull him into trusting her.

He'd been a sucker for that pretty face, and had been feeling guilty ever since she mentioned the loan that Charley also had mentioned. Actually, even before that he had started thinking he might be wrong about her. She was stubborn like her father and had a natural refinement that went deeper than any role-playing. He wished he still thought she was an impostor. It would be so much easier to deal with her now if he did, but he didn't.

But he sure as hell wasn't going to partner with a viper, Mitchell or not, who now had a very good reason to want him dead, so she'd have both mines and could do whatever she wanted with them. That wasn't happening.

He sat up and stared at the closed door. She wasn't even going to ask to come back in? She was going to deliberately spend the night in that cold tunnel just to make him feel more guilt! Like hell. . . .

He went outside and entered the mine, following the light to the end of the tunnel where he'd left her. She sat up.

"I'm—" she started.

"Shut up," he snarled.

He swiped up the lantern, grabbed her hand, and dragged her back to the house, then slammed the door shut behind them. "Not one damn word if you know what's good for you," he warned before he got back in his own bed and glared up at the ceiling as she settled on hers.

She was silent. *Finally she listens?* He snorted to himself. And still fumed. And couldn't sleep. It was small consolation that he knew she couldn't either after she'd slept the day away.

An hour later, he said coldly, "The agreement I had with Charley was only temporary to help him out of his bind. It ended the day he died. And without a new partnership, which I am in no way inclined to make, that mine is useless where it sits, so there's nothing for you to exploit or sell here. You and your brothers are welcome to the money Charley made from the mine if you can find it, but under no circumstances will I allow you to tell anyone where these mines are located. Got that?"

"I'm sorry I drew a gun on you. I don't really think you killed Papa. It's just that your anger frightened me and I reacted badly."

Was that tearful voice real or just an act? Damnit, she was doing it again, trying to make him feel sorry for her. "You come west without knowing the difference between a gun and a rifle?"

"I do know the difference, but it was a traumatic moment and I misspoke. Must we discuss this? I have apologized, and it was quite sincere."

"Words don't cut it after the fact, so drop it and go to sleep."

He shouldn't have even been here to meet this woman. He'd meant to return to Nashart in the spring. He had more than enough money now to do what he wanted. But he'd bought those damn flower seeds, and Charley had showed up the day after he'd returned from town with them. And when Charley died, he still didn't leave. He kept coming up with excuses not to go home, because the simple fact was he was in no hurry to be browbeaten by his father to go back to ranching.

That wasn't going to happen. He had other plans for the fortune he'd dug out of these hills that had nothing to do with cattle, and nothing Zachary could say would make him change them. He'd been thinking about it too long. And it was going to make his mother happy. But he would face one hell of a fight when he did get home. Arguing with his pa was never easy. It simply went against the grain not to do what Zachary Callahan wanted.

His brothers felt the same way. Hell, even his oldest brother, Hunter, was going to marry a woman this summer that he'd never met, just because their father said so. The marriage was supposed to end a feud that should have ended long ago but hadn't. Hunter hated the idea of an arranged marriage, but he'd still go along with it. Heck, it might have happened already, though the letter his mother had written him early last month had said the girl was delayed in arriving. And he hadn't gotten around to checking the post on his last trip to town—because of prissy Miss Violet Mitchell.

Anger still gnawed at him. He didn't hear any movement in the bed across the room. He knew she tossed in her sleep. He'd watched her do it when she'd slept on the trail, and again today when he came in to start dinner. Not one toss yet tonight, which told him she was lying there plotting her next move. He didn't for a moment think she'd give up on that mine. She was stubborn like her father. He'd never imagined Charley had a daughter, let alone such an exasperating one—who was far too attractive.

He got up and started opening crates until he found the one full of whiskey bottles. He winced at the fumes that rose up. At least one bottle hadn't survived the trip despite the careful packing.

He took a bottle back to his bed, drank a quarter of it before remarking, "You said they're older than you?"

"Who?"

"Who else? Your brothers. Fact is, I'm not sure I would have felt sorry for Charley if I hadn't pictured two young boys, destitute, helpless, waiting for him to come home with some money. I should have pressed him about his family, asked him how old his sons were—then you wouldn't be here, and he might not be dead."

"So he's dead because you didn't ask a very obvious question? You admit it was your fault?"

He glanced over to see that she was leaning up on an elbow, staring at him, looking as huffy as she'd just sounded. He should have turned out the lanterns. Seeing her in bed again, even if she was fully clothed, still had an effect on him. There was no getting around the fact that she was a beautiful, desirable woman, even if she was the most stubborn, exasperating female he'd ever met.

"That's not what I said. As it happens, if I hadn't dug for him for the month he was up here, Charley would have fallen over dead within a week doing it himself. So you could say that I gave him a few more weeks of life. But I sure as hell wouldn't have helped him if I knew his boys were full-grown men who can take care of themselves. And you, a fancy dresser, obviously don't need money."

"I do, for a dowry."

"A dowry?" He snorted. "Who the hell comes with a dowry these days?"

"It's expected if you marry an English lord, which I plan to do. I even met the perfect one right before I sailed home—and found out I'm no longer an heiress. So don't tell me what I don't need when you know nothing about my plans for the future."

"So that's what this is about? You're out here driving me crazy for a damn dowry?"

"Not just that. Our family home is my priority. Papa came

out here to recover his fortune. You gave him hope that he could do that."

"So Charley died with hope. That's not a bad way to go."

She gasped. "You're just as insufferable foxed as you are otherwise, and if you don't know what 'foxed' means, it means you, sir, are drunk. And will you please stop referring to my father that way. His name was Charles. None of his friends and acquaintances ever called him Charley."

"I did, and he never seemed to mind, so how about you stop complaining about nonsense that has absolutely nothing to do with you. And I'm not drunk."

"Of course you are, but you're too thickheaded to realize it!"

He sat up. She wisely turned over and showed him her back. At least the scared little girl who could tug on his emotions was gone.

Chapter Eighteen

VIOLET WOKE AT DAWN, surprised she'd slept at all. Morgan was still in his bed, his back turned to her. Only one lantern was still flickering, almost out of fuel. The fireplace was cold as well, leaving the room quite chilly.

She grabbed the blanket from her bed, wrapped it around her shoulders, and went outside, heading down the slope to climb the fence, not caring if the racket she made woke Morgan. She'd looked for a chamber pot in the cabin yesterday, not really expecting to find one, nor had she. And she'd already climbed this fence after seeing Morgan hop it, then hop over the stream and disappear into the trees, only to return a few minutes later. She was glad she hadn't asked about the chamber pot. She was sure it would have made him laugh.

He'd made getting over the fence seem so easy, but it was quite awkward for her. His camp was so primitive she had no other choice. At least she found the narrow part of the stream he had hopped over, although when she tried it, the heels of her boots got wet because her legs weren't as long as his.

It was hard not to think of last night. She'd gone from elation over how rich her mine was and how it was going to solve all her problems to anger and suspicion when Morgan had told her the mine didn't belong to her and her brothers to utter despair when he'd abandoned her in that cold tunnel. She'd been crushed. But he'd come back. Even as furious as he was, he had some sort of protective instinct that wouldn't let him leave her there all night. Her opinion of him had risen a notch.

But she still had trouble believing that she and her brothers had no right to the mine, that her father didn't really own it just because of its proximity to Morgan's. After all, she'd verified that his claim was recorded. Didn't that make it official? Could the position of the mine really invalidate that if there was no partnership? Morgan had been generous in doing most of the work for her father, but she had doubts that he'd told her the whole story. She wished she could consult a solicitor.

She did feel bad, however, about calling him foxed last night when he probably hadn't been. She also felt bad about thinking, even for a moment, that he'd killed Charles. If everything he'd said about his working relationship with her father was true, the man really was generous beyond words. He'd said he had a heart of gold, but that didn't even half describe his doing all the work in the mine and then sharing the fruits of his labor with someone else when he didn't have to.

On her way back to the cabin, she stopped at the stream to wash her face, then turned about before lifting her skirt to dry her face. The skirt she'd donned yesterday. She was dismayed that she'd had to sleep in her clothes again, as if they were still camping outdoors. She hoped tonight would be more peaceful because she simply had to rectify the sleeping situation so she could resume her civilized habits, which included sleeping in a nightgown. But first she needed to create some privacy for herself in the cabin.

As she climbed over the fence again and headed for the porch, her eyes were drawn to the top of the cliff. The dawn light was brighter up there, making the silhouette of a man with a rifle cradled in his arms stand out starkly. She screamed.

The door to the cabin burst open and Morgan rushed down the steps, gun in hand, demanding, "What?"

Frozen, Violet just pointed. Then she heard Morgan say, "Don't worry about him. That's Texas, a good buddy of mine." He lowered his gun. "He came with my other friends to help throw up the cabin and agreed to stick around."

"So he's a guard?"

"Yeah, he stands watch at night, then sleeps during the day when I'm working."

She recalled his previous remark about the disadvantage of mining in such isolation. "You said no one would know if something happened to you here. That was a lie."

He just shrugged. "You weren't supposed to notice Tex, and he hasn't always been here. We alternate making trips to town for supplies, so one of us is always here to guard the mine. When Charley was here, he did the guarding and Tex flanked me to make sure no one was trying to follow at a distance."

So many crazy precautions—he really was fanatic about keeping this location a secret.

And then he yelled up to Texas, "Come on down for breakfast so you can meet my unwelcome guest."

"That was rude," Violet remarked.

"No, it wasn't. Rude would have been using words that made you blush." He looked down at her as if waiting for something, and finally demanded, "No retort?"

"Do you want another fight?"

"Honey, what we do isn't fighting, it's just you doing your best to infuriate me."

"That isn't—" she started to deny, but he was already walking back to the cabin, so she hurried after him to point out, "Don't you need to unlock the gate for him if he's coming for breakfast?"

"No. I usually leave it open when I'm here. I must have been distracted by you yesterday when I relocked it, but I corrected that while you were taking your long nap."

He could have told her that before she'd climbed over the bloody fence! She didn't say so. She really didn't want to keep fighting with him. What she needed was to come to an arrangement with him. He might have given her leave to search for her father's money, but what if she couldn't find it? And even if she did and there was enough money to pay off the loan, that wouldn't solve her and her brothers' entire dilemma. They needed a lot more money to maintain their lifestyles. She had to persuade Morgan to turn the partnership he'd had with her father into a partnership with her.

She groaned, realizing what a challenge that would be. She'd have to make him like her, want to help her. Of course, she remembered that he'd seemed to like her last night when he'd kissed her—but had he thought he was kissing Violet Mitchell or an actress? And using his attraction to her could be a dangerous road to take, considering that they were sleeping in the same room. She wouldn't be blatant about it; she'd simply be more like her usual self, charming. Aunt Elizabeth had often told her she was charming. And her aunt had given her and Sophie pointers on how a lady could wrap a man around her finger. Violet would just have to see if an opportunity arose to tame a bear. . . .

He'd already disappeared inside the cabin, so she sat on the porch. It was still cold, the sun still behind the range, but the yard was a little lighter and the scent of pine in the air was pleasant.

Before long Morgan came out and handed her a cup of coffee, which meant he'd made a fire. She was tempted to go back in the cabin, but didn't. There was something nice about this porch so early in the morning with wilderness all around them and the mules grazing across the stream. She wondered if this was what his family's ranch in Nashart was like.

She took a sip from the cup to find he'd sweetened the coffee with something that made it quite tasty. "No tea?" she teased. He just raised a brow at her, so she added, "That was a joke."

"Could have fooled me."

When she set the cup down on the floor, he went back inside, but came right back out carrying a crate; he set it down next to her chair, then reached down to put her cup on it. How could such an ornery man manage to be so thoughtful— occasionally?

"How much time do I have to look for Papa's money before you take me back to town?"

"Two weeks at least."

"What if I find it today?"

"Ask me after you get that lucky. But you can't go looking for it outside the fence without some protection."

She was sure he wasn't offering to escort her. "I can take my father's rifle."

"It's not loaded. Charley ran out of shells trying to hunt and asked me to pick up more for him, but I didn't see the point. He wasn't a good shot."

"Then why did you get so mad last—"

He interrupted, his voice surly. "You didn't know that rifle wasn't loaded, and we're not discussing your intent again. Flapjacks will be ready shortly."

He turned and went back inside, done talking. She sighed, once more regretting making him so angry last night that she'd lost all headway with him. If she could just stop thinking of him as a bear and stop detesting her surroundings, she was sure her natural charm would resurface.

There was no sign of his friend coming up the hill yet. It probably would take a while since he would have to ride all the way down from the cliff top to where the rocky slope started before he could then come up Morgan's hill.

Before going in for breakfast, Violet decided to fetch her father's valise. It felt wrong to just leave it in the mine, and she wanted to go through it more thoroughly later. Now that there was daylight, she didn't need a lantern to enter the mine, since it wasn't very deep.

Mission accomplished, she entered the cabin cautiously, hoping Morgan had calmed down. He was putting an open jar of preserves on the table, as well as a crock of butter. Their eyes met for a moment. His were inscrutable, and his beard and mustache hid most of the lower part of his face so it was impossible to tell if he was still angry.

She pushed her father's valise under the bed, then sat on the edge of it as she braided her hair, aware that he'd paused to watch her. And then she heard him snort and turn about to get their food. Had she merely distracted him, or was he fascinated by her hair?

He'd begun piling a plate with flapjacks. He'd rigged a metal shelf over the fire, high enough not to be touched by the flames, and had cooked the flapjacks on it. Rather ingenious, she thought.

He turned to set the plate on the table. She quickly sat down. He filled two more plates before he sat down to start eating, apparently not waiting for Texas to arrive.

She tested his mood by asking, "Was your friend using the second bed in here?"

"No, I built that for Charley. Tex has his own camp up on the hill. We share the hunting and he comes down occasionally for dinner, but otherwise, he likes being alone up there where he can do his composing without me interrupting him all the time or complaining about the racket."

"Composing?"

"He plays the harmonica and loves creating his own music. He's damn good at playing, but it's not at all harmonic when he starts composing, no pun intended. 'Course, every other week he'll head to town to play poker and get drunk."

She realized that might cut in half the two weeks Morgan had said she'd be at his camp, since Texas could take her to town. But she didn't need to mention that yet, since Morgan had already told her to ask him again if she got lucky. "That long ride just for that?"

"Habit. Cowboys are used to hitting the saloons for some hell-raising every weekend. It took some arguing to get him to go only twice a month."

"Were you a cowboy, or did you consider yourself a rancher because your family owns a ranch?"

"I herded cattle until the day I left home, so, yeah, either name applies."

"Do you have a big family?"

"Felt like it, growing up with three brothers."

One of Aunt Elizabeth's pointers was that men liked to talk about themselves, so a lady could get in their good graces by asking them about themselves, but Morgan was providing only terse answers to her questions. Was he the exception that Elizabeth had never run into?

She tried again to find a subject he might want to talk about. "Why didn't you like being a cowboy?"

"Never said I didn't like it. Fact is, I loved ranching with my family. But there are other things I want to do now that I consider more important."

He didn't elaborate, and despite her curiosity, she recalled another of her aunt's adages: never pry or become a nuisance when you ask a man about himself. So she referred back to his mention of poker. "You don't get the urge to hit the saloons, as you say, like your friend?"

"I did until Sullivan found out about my silver and started hounding me to sell my mine. I stopped going places where he'd find me. I do my drinking here now, and if I feel like a game of poker, I'll head up the hill. But it's no fun playing with Tex. He loves the game, but he's no good at bluffing or recognizing a bluff, so it's like stealing money from him."

"It's complicated, that game?"

"No, but there are some nuances that make it more interesting. You play?"

He raised his brows, waiting for her answer, looking hopeful. She almost wished she could say yes. "Is it anything like whist?"

"Like what?"

"Never mind. Perhaps I'll ask your friend to teach me how to play poker during his visit."

He snorted. "If you really want to learn, you'll ask me."

She felt like smiling but didn't. Was that a bit of jealousy, his not wanting anyone else teaching her something he could teach her? Or did he just want her to be good enough at the game to make it interesting for him? She almost laughed, guessing it was the latter.

"Maybe I will when you aren't busy," she said. "By the by, where is Bo? You don't let him sleep in the house?"

Since the matter of her being protected while she searched for her father's money hadn't been resolved, she planned to search inside the fences today. Charles could have buried his money close to the house while Morgan was in one of the mines. And Bo might be able to help her find it if he knew how to follow a scent.

"He wanders a lot and is still young enough to want to chase anything that moves, even birds. He prefers sleeping under the house where he hides his bones. But he's usually nearby at mealtime."

"Would you mind if I invite him in?"

"Why?"

"Didn't I mention I love dogs?"

"Pretty sure you only said you liked them. And it's my turn for a question."

"We're taking turns?"

He ignored that and asked, "Why haven't you demanded that a screen be put up between the beds?"

"D'you have one?"

"No."

"I didn't think so. I can be pragmatic, you know, and not complain about what can't be fixed—no matter how uncomfortable I might find it. Actually, sometimes I complain due to frustration, though with you, maybe a little more often."

"Trying to make me feel special?"

She laughed, caught herself doing it, and stopped. When had he become amusing? "However," she continued in a determined tone, "I've decided this *can* be fixed, and since you mentioned it before I could, I'm going to hazard a guess that you have a solution?"

"I'm to produce a screen out of thin air for you?"

"No, you're going to improvise!"

Chapter Nineteen

VIOLET KNEW SHE SHOULD be sitting with Texas Weaver on the porch where he was eating breakfast. Good manners demanded it, since Morgan had already left to start his workday. But finding her father's money was more important. She went through his valise more carefully, hoping to discover a clue about his hiding place, but found nothing. He'd brought so little with him, nothing of sentimental value, not even the pocket watch he loved so much. Would he really have left it at home?

She finally lured Bo in from the porch—at least *he* was keeping Texas company—to sniff her father's jacket. But when she stepped out on the porch with Bo following, the dog stopped when she did. So much for his interest in chasing scents.

She saw that Texas was done eating, so she suggested, "Join me for a tour of the yard, Mr. Weaver?"

"You mean walk with you a spell?"

"Yes, while we talk." He followed her down the steps. He struck her as a nice sort of fellow, handsome with dark hair and a mustache, and well-mannered. He had only raised a brow when Morgan introduced her as Miss Mitchell, which made her guess they'd spoken at some point yesterday when Morgan had still doubted her true identity.

"I was wondering if Morgan ever deviates from his schedule of going to Butte every two weeks?" she asked as she led him toward the mule pasture.

"It's for fresh supplies, ma'am, so either he goes or I go."

That didn't exactly answer her question. "But you also go to play poker, don't you? Will you do that sooner than two weeks from now?"

He opened the gate to the mule pasture. "I reckon so, but if you're hankering for a ride, I can't oblige without Morgan's say-so. But he's hell-bent on getting rich, downright obsessed with his mine. It's all he cares about. So he sees you as a pretty big thorn, and thorns need to be pulled out sooner rather than later."

Violet frowned. "I don't appreciate being called a thorn, but I assume by 'pulled out' you mean 'taken back' sooner than later?"

He grinned slightly. "Yes, ma'am."

That was the answer she was hoping for, though he could have said so in a less insulting way. But she didn't want to push Morgan into deviating from his schedule by continuing to be a thorn in his side. She needed a lot more from him than an opportunity to search for the money her father had hidden. She really couldn't leave here without an agreement to continue the partnership he'd had with Charles.

"We got along briefly last night," she felt compelled to mention.

"Briefly? Does that even count?"

She sighed, wondering if all cowboys were this frustrating to talk to. When Morgan had introduced Texas to her, she'd politely guessed, "So you're from Texas?"

He'd merely said, "No, ma'am." And he hadn't seemed inclined to explain further, but Morgan had added, "But his ma is."

Texas continued now with a warning: "Morgan's not a man to mess with. You can only push him so far before he'll push back. So you might want to stop riling him."

That wasn't exactly true. She'd pushed and gotten her screen. She was quite pleased about that. After breakfast, Morgan had stacked crates at one end of her bed and nailed a corner of an extra blanket to the top one, then stretched it along the side of the bed and fashioned a hook with another nail to attach the other corner of the blanket to the wall. She'd be boxed in, but she would definitely have some privacy at night.

But that wasn't what Texas was referring to, so she replied, "I have stopped riling him—now that he believes I'm a Mitchell."

"Then I reckon he'll take you to town when he's ready. He'll just make sure you can't find your way back here."

No, of course not. Protect the location of the mine at all costs.

Texas didn't appear to be in any hurry to get back up to his camp on the cliff top, so Violet headed toward the back of the cabin after they left the mule pasture. She was glad of the company as she started her search, though she wasn't very hopeful of finding the money near the cabin. Morgan would have noticed anything out of the ordinary close by.

"Did Morgan get along well with my father?" she asked.

"I didn't spend that much time with the two of them

because my schedule was different, sleeping during the day, guarding the mine at night, but I enjoyed Charley's good-natured company and I think he enjoyed my harmonica playing. And I can tell you they laughed a lot, those two. Could hear it from up the hill. It always made me smile. I'm sorry about your pa's passing. He was good for Morgan the short time he was here."

Violet glanced aside before his words made her cry. They'd rounded the cabin. The water hole was there. It was not as deep as she'd imagined, but the water in it was very clear. She pointed at the long pile of small stones that was blocking most of the gorge.

"What's that?" she asked.

"Morgan calls it slag. It's the by-product of the smelting process. It actually has value because it's used as gravel in making glass and concrete, but Morgan doesn't have time to lug it to town. He makes more focusing on his silver."

The very length of Morgan's disposal area attested to how much work he'd done here. It was piled six feet high where it touched the cliff, sloping down some ten feet into the pathway. Beyond the slag pile the gully narrowed further. She could see little flat land, so she couldn't imagine her father wanting to go that way to hide his money. And she didn't think he'd go north either, since Texas was up that way. But she still had the rest of the mountain to search.

Heading back to the front yard, she asked, "Will you be returning to Nashart when, or rather if, Morgan does?"

"There's no if about it," he said with a slight blush. "My sweetheart, Emma, is there."

"She didn't mind that you took this job so far away from her?"

"It's not that far, and I go home to visit every other month. But Emma did mind, until I told her how much I was earning here. We never thought I'd make enough money to buy us a house. I worked for Zachary, Morgan's pa, and he would've let us use one of the cabins he had built in the hills for his married ranch hands, but Emma is a town gal. Thanks to Morgan, who pays me more in one month guarding the camp than I earned in a year herding cattle, we'll have our own place in town when we get hitched."

"You didn't want to help him mine?"

"Hell no, I'm a cowboy, won't even touch a pick. He offered me a share in his mine, even tempted me by mentioning that Emma might appreciate the extra muscles I'd gain mining." He snorted softly. "Emma likes me just fine as I am, so I refused."

Violet smiled, but couldn't help wondering how many muscles Morgan had gained here doing all the work himself. "When is the wedding to be?"

"When Morgan's ready to go home."

"What if he is never ready?"

"Then when Emma gets tired of waiting. But Morgan's going home. He misses his brothers and his folks too much not to. He never intended to dig out every bit of silver up here, just enough for what he wants."

"What's that?"

"Not for me to say."

Apparently she'd broached a subject he wasn't allowed to discuss, because he tipped his hat to her in good-bye and went on to open the pasture gate again. When he whistled, his horse came immediately, but so did Caesar and one of the mules. She ought to find out where Morgan kept the carrots. Caesar didn't look too pleased that he wasn't being offered one, even butted his nose against Texas.

But she wasn't going to get sidetracked when it was imperative that she spend her time looking for the money that could save her and her brothers from penury. Morgan never had told her how much money was hidden, but she would bet he knew the exact amount, since he'd done the mining and the selling of the silver. She wondered what else he wasn't telling her. But she supposed she ought to let him know she was going outside the fence to continue her search, so it was time for another confrontation. Oddly, she felt a sense of anticipation, as if she were looking forward to it. . . .

Chapter Twenty

Violet changed into her prettier pink blouse and found a matching ribbon for her braid, determined to look a little more presentable before approaching Morgan. But she was actually out of breath by the time she reached him in his mine. It was a good thing she'd brought a lantern, because when she'd entered the tunnel she could barely make out the light at the end. Her father's tunnel was barely a scratch compared to this one.

"Good Lord, this is hundreds of feet long!" she exclaimed. "Why don't you dig side tunnels closer to the entrance, instead of just this long one?"

"I plan to. But first I wanted to find out how far in this lode goes. Expected to reach the end of it long ago, but haven't yet."

He didn't turn around to talk to her, just kept swinging his pick at the wall of rock in front of him. He wasn't wearing a shirt, and his back glistened in the light of the two lanterns hanging on the support beams behind him. She was fascinated by the rippling of the muscles in his arms and back. He was a primal vision of man carving the land to his whim.

He broke the spell he'd cast when he asked, "Did you come in here for a reason other than to annoy me?"

"Don't be nasty. I wanted to ask your advice on where else to look for Papa's hidden money—or, more precisely, what to look for other than disturbed dirt. I checked your yard, even the mule pasture, and found nothing."

"He definitely wouldn't hide it there. My gals made him nervous."

The remark brought a smile to her face as she recalled that her father didn't like to ride horses, either. She and her brothers did, but their father did all his gadding about in a carriage or coach. He must have hated having to ride a horse out here in the West.

"Anything else I should know before I venture beyond the fence?"

"It's sure not going to be lying out in the open. It might be buried under a large rock or stuffed inside a hole in a tree trunk."

"Up a tree?"

"No, a hole in the tree that's close to the ground. Charley wasn't agile enough to climb trees. But figure on anywhere that's a few minutes' to a few hours' walk from here in any direction. I was in the mine about four hours the day he told me he'd hidden the money. So you'll need to learn how to shoot a rifle and take it with you. Go get Charley's."

He finally turned around. She couldn't help noticing that his chest was glistening with sweat, too. She knew she shouldn't be staring at his naked upper body, but she couldn't help it.

"Shouldn't you be on your way?"

Her eyes snapped up to his. "You said the rifle isn't loaded."

"I'll meet you in the yard with a crate of ammunition and show you how to load it and shoot it. You're not leaving here till you hit what you aim at."

She groaned. Learning how to shoot could take the rest of the day. Was it really necessary if she didn't go beyond shouting distance? But she left to do as he said. A shooting lesson might give her an opportunity to bring up forming a new partnership with him.

By the time she'd retrieved the rifle from the other tunnel, Morgan was already in the yard with a crate at his feet. Taking the weapon from her, he said, "This is a Spencer repeating rifle. The magazine holds seven bullets, and this lever needs to be pulled after each shot. After the seventh, you will need to reload."

He demonstrated as he spoke, but he was still shirtless and her eyes kept drifting away from the rifle in his hands to that thin mat of hair across his upper chest.

Then she heard, "You try," and gave him a blank look. He actually chuckled.

She said, "It's not funny. You could have dressed more appropriately for this lesson."

"When I'm going right back into the mine? Do I need to repeat myself?"

She sighed. "Once more, please."

He did, and she paid better attention this time, so when he said, "Your turn," she was able to load the magazine. "Now, positioning is very important."

He started to move behind her, but she turned so she was still facing him and quickly said, "I'd like to discuss the partnership you mentioned last night."

"I told you it's over and done with, so, no."

"Humor me, please. At least tell me the particulars of it."

"There's no point."

"Please."

He stared at her so long she almost said, "Forget it," but then he said, "Charley suggested an eighty-twenty split in my favor, since he knew he wasn't going to be able to contribute much. But I was feeling generous the day we came to terms, so I lowered it to seventy-thirty."

She frowned. "Thirty percent instead of half doesn't strike me as a fair partnership."

"When he did so little digging? You really want to take that stand?"

She pointed out, "Would you have been able to mine the silver on his claim without his agreement?"

"No, I can't lawfully mine beyond my stake in the yard. If there weren't restrictions, one person could claim everything."

"So this was all extra silver for you, even if you did have to split it. That's quite a contribution from him, if you ask me."

"No one's asking you. And I did consider that, but the fact is, I didn't need to dig another mine. There's more silver on my claim than I'll ever dig out, and it's a hundred percent mine. So the extra silver was just a minor incentive for me to accept Charley's deal."

"It was his idea?"

"Yeah." He nodded. "Like I said, he was pretty desperate that day."

"What about the money you said he hid? Is it worth the effort to search for it?"

"He had around thirteen hundred left after our first joint-venture load paid off. It was eighteen hundred, but he insisted on giving me a quarter of that for his share of the supplies and the use of my smelter. It was too much, but I couldn't talk him out of it. I think his pride got in the way."

She was incredulous that her father's 30 percent share amounted to so much money. "That thirteen hundred will at least let my brothers stave off the banker for a few months, if I can find it. But what I don't understand is why my father didn't send that money to my brothers right away. Or write them when he went to town again."

Morgan looked like he might be frowning, but she couldn't be sure because of his mustache. "Because he didn't go back to Butte after he filed his claim. He got accosted the day he filed it. I found him roughed up in an alley struggling to his feet and got him out of town fast. He was bruised up pretty bad, but otherwise okay. He didn't know who did it, but before the men attacked him they asked him where his mine was located and he refused to tell them. I don't doubt it was a couple of Sullivan's men."

"But how did they even know about it?"

"Your father stopped in a saloon to wait for me to finish my business and apparently bragged that he had a silver mine near my claim. I'd warned him not to mention the mine to anyone, but he was so happy he got himself drunk and spilled the beans. So that's why he didn't go back to town until a month later when I took him after the accident. He was guarding the place while Texas and I went to Butte. I suspected the claim jumpers might have killed him when I found him, but there were no fresh tracks outside the mine and there was blood on the support beam next to where he fell."

"What was he doing in the mine while you weren't here?" she asked.

"He still tried to dig through the tunnel a couple hours a day off and on. I told him he didn't have to, but he was stubborn, wanted to contribute. Unfortunately, he never made much progress."

"But you and Texas went to town after my father was roughed up. You could have mailed a letter for him."

"Yeah, I could have, but he never asked me to. Maybe he was waiting until he had enough to pay off the loan in full."

"I don't suppose you continued to mine on his claim after the accident?"

"No, I went back to working my own mine."

She sighed. "About this shooting lesson . . . ?"

" 'Bout time," he said, and stepped behind her again.

She gasped softly the moment his arms came around her, but she knew he only did it to position her hands on the rifle and lift her arms to the appropriate height. "The butt of the rifle needs to be pressed against your shoulder or the recoil could knock you on your as—uh, backside and hurt like hell, so don't fire unless the butt is firmly seated like this. Now, let's see if you can hit something before the ammunition crate is empty. Try one of those cowbells on the fence."

She would have huffed at his sarcasm if his chest wasn't still pressed to her back, causing a flurry of agitation inside her.

"Did I need to mention you have to pull the trigger?"

More sarcasm, but he stepped back this time, letting her breathe normally again so she could point out, "Wild animals that can hurt me aren't as small as that bell. At least give me a target the size of a small animal."

"All right, follow me."

He picked up the crate and moved to open the gate, continuing another twenty feet before putting the crate down. She followed and even closed the gate for him—and noticed that the rifle was already starting to feel a little heavy. Was he really going to make her carry it as she searched for the money?

Before she brought that up, she looked at the gun on his hip. She was surprised he wore it even when he was mining. "Wouldn't a pistol be easier for me to handle?"

"Not if you want to hit what you're aiming at," he said, putting his hands on her shoulders and turning her around so he could help her position the rifle again. "The rifle you hold high so you can look down its barrel at your target. I have an extra Colt, but you shoot from your waist with that type of gun and hitting your target requires a lot more practice."

He aimed the rifle for her, placed her left hand under the barrel to support it. Tipping her head and looking down the long length, she saw it was pointing at his trespassing sign. She was about to pull the trigger when she felt his breath against her ear. A delicious shiver ran down her spine, and she nearly dropped the weapon. She lowered it before it slipped out of her hands. She turned slowly as he stepped back, and only then realized that he'd merely been leaning close to see if her aim was accurate.

"Have you changed your mind about learning to shoot?" he asked.

"No, I—" Good grief, where had her bloody thoughts gone! "You just described how you shoot a Colt, but I'm a woman. Wouldn't it be just as effective if I raised the pistol to the same height as the rifle and looked down the length of my arm?"

He stared at her a moment before chuckling. "You could be right. Wait here while I fetch it."

What was it about Morgan Callahan that enabled him to make her nervous and breathlessly stirred up at the same time?

She set the rifle down and fanned her cheeks with both hands until she saw him heading back to her. Still shirtless. Still flaunting a physique that had to be the pinnacle of masculine beauty and temptation. Did he know what a fine figure of a man he was? Maybe he did and that's why he hid an ugly face under that horribly shaggy beard, so it wouldn't detract from his magnificent body—and she still wasn't thinking clearly!

"I don't have an extra gun belt for this," he said as he reached her, "so you'll have to figure out how you're going to carry it."

"Couldn't I borrow yours?"

"No."

The weapon was nearly a foot in length, making it too long to fit in her purse or the pocket of her skirt, but she supposed she could tie it to her waist with a long ribbon. She would just have to make sure Morgan didn't see her carrying the gun that way. She caused him enough amusement as it was. But when he put the weapon in her hand, she realized that it was so light compared to the rifle, she could probably just carry it in her hand.

"All of this is to protect me from animals that will probably run away from me before I run away from them, right?" she asked.

"You never know," he said as he showed her how to load the Colt by demonstrating with his own. "Encounters with people in these hills are rare, but in addition to claim jumpers, I've heard of outlaws out this way and seen the marshals and bounty hunters searching for them. There are also other prospectors traveling through these hills. The greatest danger to you will come from wild animals, but you still need to be able to protect yourself from any strangers you come across."

She was more concerned about wild animals. "What about bears? Do they come up here?"

"Ran across one fishing at the river below here last year. Made a coat out of him. But haven't seen any this far up. Now, let's see if your idea has merit. Shoot the sign."

She lifted the gun, looked down the length of her arm, and pulled the trigger. The weapon seemed to jump in her hand, pointing upward as if it had a mind of its own. Texas yelled from the cliff, "I'm trying to sleep up here!" And Morgan started laughing.

But then he was standing behind her again, his chest pressed to her back, and he rasped by her ear, "You forgot the support." He raised her left hand and placed it under her forearm. "Grip firmly the way you did with the rifle barrel to hold your arm steady. Try now."

His breath crossed her cheek this time. He was doing it again, trying to see for himself if her aim was accurate. Did he really think she could concentrate when it felt like she was utterly surrounded by him and all she could think about was kissing him?

"What are you waiting for?" he asked.

She lowered the gun, pointing it at the ground, and turned about in his arms. He'd already straightened, so she had to glance up to meet his eyes. She was going to make it clear that he was far too distracting for this to work and suggest that his friend teach her instead. The words didn't happen.

The kiss began softly. As she'd guessed, his mustache tickled her upper lip, and she couldn't help the giggle that started, but it was cut off almost instantly when his hand at the back of her neck pressed her closer to him and his lips spread hers apart, or her gasp did; in either case, the kiss was now deep and amazing and so very stirring, with so many wonderful sensations show-ing up all at once. There was a fluttering in her belly, her pulse racing, a tingling up her back, and a shocking urge to put her arms around him when his tongue slid next to hers.

She moaned in delight. Unfortunately, he didn't recognize it as a sound of pleasure and stepped back. And for once, she could tell that he was frowning. But for once, she didn't want him to.

"That was—" she began.

He cut in, "Necessary to clear your head. You were getting distracted. Now, concentrate and keep practicing. I'll check on your progress in a few hours." He walked away, but tossed back, "And no cheating by getting closer to the sign."

She would have admitted the kiss was nice, but maybe it was better that she didn't let him know that she'd liked it quite so much. That might bring him back for more when she supposed they ought not to be doing that, considering they didn't even like each other. But without the insult preceding it this time, she couldn't deny being kissed by the bear had been thrilling.

Feeling a bit full of herself because of it, she raised the weapon she was still holding, supported her arm, and fired off several shots. She stared incredulously at the sign she'd just damaged, then yelled to Morgan before he disappeared inside his mine, "I've mastered this!"

"The hell you have."

"Three shots, three holes in the sign. It would appear shoot-ing is my forte."

He snorted and continued on, yelling back, "Return before dinner or you go without."

She wasn't displeased with his sour reaction. She smiled, guessing that his anger wasn't directed at her. He was mad at himself because he'd wanted to kiss her, and he had.

Chapter Twenty-One

V**IOLET RETURNED TO THE** camp at precisely five o'clock. She'd dug her pocket watch out of her valise before she left to make sure she would return long before the sun set. But spending most of the day walking over uneven terrain had left her tired and thinking about taking a short nap before dinner.

She forgot about the nap when she found Morgan in the yard pouring large rocks from a wheelbarrow into some kind of device. He turned a handle to raise a large square of metal covered in netting, then let it drop into the container below. When she saw him pouring small stones from the container into crates, which were stacked nearby, she realized the device was a rock crusher.

"You're saving rocks?" she asked as she approached.

"That's silver ore," he corrected. "I'm getting it ready for smelting."

Since he nodded toward the big brick dome, she guessed, "So that's what you call a smelter?"

"I light it about every four days, and only at night, since it makes a lot of smoke, which could be seen from far off during the day. The wind usually comes up the gully or over the lower slope and blows the smoke away from the cabin. Stinks like hell and can even make you sick if you inhale too much of it, so I don't smelt unless there's a good breeze."

"You built that?"

He nodded. "It's just made of clay bricks. Couldn't very well get a ready-made metal one up this hill, those things are huge. So are rock crushers, so I made one of those, too, just had to order a block of steel and the nets to hold it. You'll need to go into the cabin when I do the burn, just in case the smoke drifts into the yard."

"It seems like a lot of extra work. Wouldn't it be simpler to sell the ore as it is?"

"Simpler, but not as convenient. I did that the first few months I was here, which is why I bought so many mules to carry it to town. It's easier to transport silver bricks than bulky raw ore."

"Do you make more money if you smelt it first?"

"A lot more. It's still not pure silver, but it averages eighty percent, which is considered high, and if the silversmiths back east want sterling, then they can process it further. That requires a lot more chemicals than I have here and huge machines that generate more heat than a small smelter like mine." He finally glanced around at her. "I didn't hear any shots while you were gone. No animals today?"

"Only small ones, but Bo chased them off before I got near them."

"I don't like you going off like that."

His protective instincts were rearing again? She felt like smiling. Maybe Aunt Elizabeth's pointers were working. She wanted to hear him say that he'd been worried about her, so she asked, "Why?"

"If something happens to you, then I have to waste time looking for your body." And then he stared at the ribbon around her hips. "That's a cute gun belt you've got there."

Her cheeks lit up angrily on both counts—she *knew* he'd say something snide about her ribbon, but that remark about wasting time was the last straw. She marched off to the cabin, but she was too agitated—and dirty—to take a nap, and a few minutes later she came out with the bar of brown soap and her last set of clean clothes. Crossing the yard to the gate, she yelled, "I have the gun, so I do *not* need your escort for this bath!"

All he did was yell back, "You're bathing again already? You just did that yesterday."

She growled under her breath. Had she really thought he might worry about her, the thorn in his side? Of course he wouldn't. If anything, he'd probably hoped she'd get lost and not return.

She was laughing at herself by the time she left the little pool. Nothing like a cold dunking to put things in perspective. She didn't need the man to like her; she just needed him to admit that the partnership he'd made with Charles should and would continue with the Mitchell heirs. The reasons he'd partnered with Charles were still valid and hadn't been satisfied yet.

Good grief, for that very short time after he'd finally accepted that she was Violet Mitchell, they'd laughed and gotten along fine. She wanted that back. Then she could broach a plan to save her family's home immediately. She needed Morgan to pay off the loan so she and her brothers could repay him instead of the bank. It would require coaxing the bear into being generous again. How hard could that be? Hadn't he admitted he had a heart of gold? But she couldn't ask him until he was in a more agreeable state of mind, and he wouldn't get there if she kept arguing with him. What was wrong with her to keep deviating from Aunt Elizabeth's advice?

Returning to the cabin, she unhooked the improvised screen so she could sit on the bed to redo her braid without the blanket getting in her way. She was longing to sleep in a nightgown tonight. Should she dare to do so with Morgan in the cabin? Or was he going to smelt tonight after dark? He hadn't exactly said.

It was the first thing she asked when he returned to start dinner.

"No, I told you, only every four days. I'll crush rocks every day, but I need enough ore to make it worthwhile to light the smelter. You didn't wash your hair?"

She blushed a little. She hadn't washed it because she didn't want Morgan stirring her up again, as he'd done during the shooting lesson, by insisting he help her brush out the tangles. So she said, "I prefer not to wash it this late in the day, because if I braid it before it's dry it will be all wavy tomorrow."

"So don't braid it."

"It's my habit to braid it before I go to bed, to keep it out of the way."

"That's a good idea, considering all the tossing and turning you do when you sleep."

She was taken aback by his intimate observations of her. Had he watched her sleep? "How do you know that?"

"Couldn't help noticing when we were on the trail."

Oh, that. She was relieved until he added, "You talk in your sleep, too."

She gasped. She did nothing of the sort! But she really didn't want to get into another argument with him, which his observations were priming her for, so she clamped her mouth shut and looked away from his still naked chest. Why couldn't he put on a shirt after he left the mine? But she figured maybe he wanted to bathe first, which he left to do as soon as he'd gotten the meal started.

She stared at the fire while he was gone, trying to calm herself. She shouldn't let the man and his habits agitate her so. It seemed to work, because she was able to smile at him when he walked in, mostly because he was wearing his shirt now.

He brought the food to the table. She smirked to herself when he grabbed a towel and laid it on the table before setting down the hot pots. One contained some sort of meat in gravy, the other buttered carrots. The bread he put on the table smelled fresh, so she guessed he must have made it while she'd napped yesterday.

Once they started eating, he asked, "Who's Elliott?"

She almost choked. She did talk in her sleep? She must have been beyond exhausted for that to happen—well, she had been yesterday. There was simply no way that Sophie, with whom she had shared a room all those years, wouldn't have mentioned something like that if Violet did it regularly.

Morgan was looking at her expectantly, so she cleared her throat and said, "He's the English lord I told you about, the man I plan to marry when I return to London."

"He's already asked for you?"

"No, but the London Season of endless parties was about to begin just as I had to leave to come home. I've been looking forward to the Season for years. I still can't believe I'm missing it. And the balls—I do love dancing. Lord Elliott was immediately interested in me when we met, broke quite a few rules because he wouldn't leave my side! So charming and debonair. He even told me he was looking for a wife, so I know he would have asked to marry me if I were there to enjoy the Season with him—instead of here sorting out this mess Papa left us with."

"You blame Charley for dying?"

"No, of course not!"

"Sounds like it to me," he said with a shrug. "And this Elliott you're going to pay to marry you sounds like an idiot."

"I told you, dowries are expected among the aristocracy, something you obviously know nothing about. So do us both a favor and finish your meal in silence, as I intend to do."

She ended that with a glare. Why did that make him grin? Had he deliberately provoked her and was pleased he'd succeeded? But she refused to say another word to him while she was so hotly smarting, or she would certainly say something she would regret.

She finished her dinner quickly and retreated behind the screen so she wouldn't have to look at Morgan for another minute. The new arrangement really did afford her some privacy. Much better. But they were still in the same room, even if she couldn't see him now, so she couldn't quite bring herself to undress and put on her nightgown. Sometimes she wished proper behavior wasn't so bloody uncomfortable.

Chapter Twenty-Two

"WHAT IS IT, BO?" Violet yelled as the dog started barking up ahead.

She ran toward him, hoping he'd finally figured out that she wanted him to find her father's scent. She'd continued to let him sniff her father's jacket before she began her search each day. But when she reached him, she saw that he'd just found a family of rabbits and couldn't figure out which one to chase.

Assuring herself that the dog just wanted to play with his find rather than eat it, she continued walking. She was becoming frustrated after four days of searching up and down these hills and finding nothing. She'd gone west down the hill yesterday, all the way down, and was utterly disappointed by the view beyond the trees, just another open vista of endless golden and green grassland. She'd walked around every pine tree on the way down, annoyed that none had any exposed roots or hidey-holes to speak of, so she considered that a wasted day.

And the queasiness she'd been feeling wouldn't go away. She was so dreading asking Morgan for that loan to save her family home. But how else would her brothers be able to come west to work their father's mine? Even if she found the money and sent it to them so they could make the next loan payment, Mr. Perry would surely seize the house when he found out both of her brothers had left town without paying back the entire loan.

Violet had to make a deal with Morgan on their behalf without being able to consult them first. What if her brothers balked at the idea of working in the mine? After all, it would be very hard labor. They might want to find some other way to pay Morgan back once the house was safe, and then he might get mad and have them jailed if they didn't pay up or start working toward that end right away.

So many negative possibilities kept filling her head that she'd accomplished nothing over the last three days other than not getting mad at Morgan or arguing with him. But being afraid to broach such an important subject just increased her nervousness. A flat-out no from him would wreck all her hopes and dreams for the future.

And although she'd been maintaining peace with Morgan, she hadn't gotten the sense that he would be receptive to her loan proposal. In fact, his movements and actions such as banging plates on the table and stomping out to go work suggested he was still brooding. His mood seemed to have worsened since their dinner three nights ago when he'd asked her who Elliott was. Perhaps she'd gone on too long singing Elliott's praises and complained too much about missing all the lovely parties during the London Season. She'd broken one of Aunt Elizabeth's rules about charming a man: she'd talked too much about herself. And last night she'd annoyed him so much that he'd stomped out of the cabin and slept on the porch.

But that hadn't been her fault! She'd been unable to sleep

because her legs hurt from so much walking and her calf muscles had cramped. She'd lifted her nightgown to rub her leg, having given in to sleeping more comfortably in the gown the previous night.

He must have heard her groan and asked, "What's wrong?"

When she told him, the next thing she knew the bare-chested bear had swiped aside her screen and tossed a bottle of liniment on her bed. She'd gasped because her nightgown was still hiked up, giving him a clear view of her aching legs. But all he did was scowl, drop her blanket-screen back down, and go back to his bed.

The cooking fire was still burning low, throwing off some light in the cabin, but it was too dark in her enclosure to read the label on the bottle. "What is this for?"

"All sorts of things, one of them sore muscles."

Her eyes flared. "You had this and didn't offer it to me when we arrived and I could barely walk?"

"My friends from Nashart left a few things behind when they went home. I forgot about it. Just found it yesterday when I was looking for the fresh salt."

Appeased, she'd immediately started rubbing the liniment on her calves and sighed in relief, mumbling, "This works rather quickly. I'll try it on my thighs, too." A few moments later she was sighing in relief and pleasure again, then was startled when she heard Morgan stomp out of the cabin.

Violet didn't like remembering any of that, when all it did was assure her that Morgan still wasn't ready for The Talk. How frustrating! Her father had found exactly what he'd come west for, a new fortune, but it was up to her to secure it for her family.

Returning to camp later than usual, around six in the evening, she found Texas in the cabin instead of Morgan. He'd just made himself a cup of coffee and remarked, "Morgan's mining late again. He's been working like a demon these last few days."

She wouldn't know, because she'd been out searching like a demon herself. "I've had no luck finding my father's money, and I still seem to be annoying Morgan."

"Sounds like you could both use a break. You'd surely be less of a thorn in his side if you played poker with him. He loves that game." And then he laughed. "He's not as good at it as he claims to be. You might end up winning some money from him!"

She thanked Texas for the advice before he left, thrilled that she had a new way to continue her charm offensive against the bear. So that night, her fifth in Morgan's camp, she waited until they'd finished dinner before suggesting, "Teach me to play poker? Or are you too tired?"

In answer, he took a small box off one of the shelves and set it on the table in front of her, saying, "Divide the nuggets while I clean up."

Violet opened the lid and lifted out a deck of cards, then stared in amazement at the layer of gold at the bottom of the box. Carefully dumping the nuggets on the table, she divided them into two piles of thirty each, putting the odd one back in the box.

When he came back inside with the clean dishes, she guessed, "This is the gold you found in the creeks when you first got to this range, isn't it?"

"What's left of it, yeah."

"What is it worth?"

He shrugged as he sat down across from her. "Maybe twelve hundred or so."

She gasped. "But why haven't you sold them?"

"Because I told my family I was coming here to find gold, and I'll take home whatever's left of those nuggets to prove I did. In the meantime, when Tex and I feel like playing poker, I give him a couple nuggets in exchange for forty bucks since I don't keep cash up here, while he does. 'Sides, he loves playing with nuggets in town games. It never fails to cause a ruckus and get him a pretty gal for the night—were you named for the color of your eyes?"

She blinked at the question he'd tossed in, grateful that it kept her from blushing over his "gal for the night" remark. "No, I was told my eyes were baby blue when I was born. But violets were in bloom and my father brought a bouquet of them to my mother, and the name just occurred to her when she saw them. My eyes didn't turn violet until I was about six months old, according to my father, and my parents laughed when it happened. Then again, my mother also had violet eyes, so she might have been expecting mine to change color. I don't know. She died before I was old enough to ask her."

"I'm sorry."

"So am I. But her absence was why I took on the mantle of being a mother to my brothers."

"When?"

"When I was five."

He laughed. "No, you didn't."

"I did, and they humored me, though it probably would have been in their best interests if they hadn't, because I got better at it."

"Being a mother?"

"Keeping them in line. They were so rambunctious at that age. Now, about this poker game?"

He explained the rules. He even laid out hands to show her the different ways she could win, from a mere highest card to a royal flush and everything in between. Then he shuffled the deck and dealt five cards to each of them.

"What about the bluffing you mentioned?"

"Say you've got three aces. Odds are that's going to be the winning hand. But you don't want anyone to know that, so instead of betting three aces, you pass on the bet and hope someone else will think you'll drop out if they bet. So when they do bet, you can be nice and just call, or go for blood and raise. Now they have to put in more money to see your winning hand, or they'll fold and you get the pot."

"I've got three aces."

"No, you don't, and saying so isn't bluffing. You bluff with the way you bet, high or low, not by saying what you have or with the expression on your face. And it isn't mandatory to bluff, it just makes the game more interesting."

Which was apparently what he was hoping for, so she smiled sweetly and asked, "But is it against the rules to say what's in your hand?"

"No, it's just not a smart way to play the game, and it isn't considered a bluff."

"Why not? You still need to decide whether I'm telling the truth, which by your poker definition would be am I bluffing or not. Besides, I really do have three aces, and you need to pay to see them, right?"

He raised his brow at her and called her bet, but raised her two more nuggets. She called him and upped that three more, but asked, "Could I have raised with all my nuggets?"

He rolled his eyes. "Yes, but this is a practice game, and you running out of nuggets on the first hand would end it. Besides, I'm calling without raising further, so that ends it."

She smugly laid down her cards. He burst out laughing, seeing her three aces along with a pair of nines. She was delighted, not about winning but because she'd managed to amuse him.

They played for another hour, with Violet losing all of her nuggets. It seemed to leave him in a good mood, but it was late now and, he'd yawned a few times, so she decided that tomorrow, come what may, she would ask him for the loan and present her partnership proposal.

Chapter Twenty-Three

F ILLED WITH DETERMINATION, VIOLET started walking south right after breakfast the next morning, vowing to find the money. She would insist that Morgan immediately send it to her brothers. Two days ago she'd searched in this direction, but she'd covered only the slopes that were easy to navigate. Today, feeling more comfortable in the wilderness, she would venture into the rougher terrain where high, rocky ledges abounded.

She got excited when she found some disturbed dirt. She pushed the dirt away with a sharp stone. Bo's whining should have been a clue, but she was terribly disappointed when all she uncovered was one of the bones he'd buried. He quickly swiped it up and trotted off. She sighed and sat in the grass for a few minutes, looking around. The ledge she'd come across, which was only about five feet high, started a few hundred feet back, and up ahead she could see a black hole at the base of it. Thrilled to have found a potential hiding spot, she leapt to her feet and ran to it, then stared wide-eyed at what was crawling out of it.

"Oh, aren't you just too adorable!" she gushed as she picked up the puppy and cuddled it in her arms. It had a cream-colored belly, but its coat was mostly brown hair tipped with black. The lower part of its face was white. "We're going to be best friends, you and I, and Lord Elliott will love you after I marry him, I will insist."

Delighted to finally have a dog of her own that she could raise and train herself, she didn't give the hole another glance, turning to rush back to camp to show Morgan what she'd found. She shouted for him to come out of his mine. He came tearing out, gun in hand, and with a big grin on her face, she held the puppy up for him to see. But he barely glanced at it; he was looking behind her instead.

"You shouldn't have brought that here."

Her chin rose a notch. "I'm keeping it."

"If you want to stay here and live with it till it dies, fine, I'll kill its mother for you when she shows up, and she will. But you can't take it wherever you're going from here. Most folks have a strong aversion to wolves, even small ones."

"A *wolf*?"

"Did you really think it was a dog?"

"It's a baby!"

"Which has a mother who will be looking for it. Damn, when the hell did wolves move onto my slopes? Have you seen any others while you've been wandering?"

"No," she said miserably.

She was crushed, so much so that she felt tears welling in her eyes. Obviously she couldn't keep it or have its mother killed.

"Come on, we need to put it back exactly where you found it, and douse it in water to remove your scent. Go dunk it, I'll get a sack to put it in."

She knew he was right, she just didn't like it at all, and promised herself that as soon as she got back to England she was buying a dog, though she supposed she ought to discuss it with Elliott first. Maybe he already had lots of dogs. Maybe he didn't like dogs. If he didn't, she might have to reconsider him as her primary choice of husband.

Morgan took Caesar for the short journey, pulling Violet up behind him. He didn't waste time saddling the horse. Thanks to Carla, she was already used to riding without one. Reaching the hole, he dismounted and carefully rolled the pup out of the sack onto the ground. It immediately pounced on his boot, but Morgan didn't notice, had already glanced up at her to warn, "You'll need to stay away from here."

"But I haven't finished searching this area. I thought I had gotten lucky when I saw this hole, but I got distracted by the puppy and forgot to look."

He glanced inside it for her. "It's not deep, looks freshly dug out, too, probably for the birthing. The female could already have been in the process of moving her litter if she noticed you around here in the last day or so. That could be why there was only one pup here, when she-wolves tend to birth four or five. If this one is gone later today"—he paused to shake the pup off his boot—"then she's likely moved on with the lot of them. They tend to avoid people. I'll check again before dinner."

Back at camp, he lifted her down from Caesar, but didn't remove his hands from her waist once her feet were on the ground. She glanced up to see why and found his blue eyes studying her.

She waited with bated breath, only to hear him say, "You'll feel better after lunch. You can eat while you're fishing."

She stared at him as he headed inside the cabin. What the deuce had just happened? Fishing?!

She followed him to demand, "When did I decide to go fishing?"

"You need a distraction from the pup you had to part with. You can get it fishing. Charley fished twice a week for us to contribute to our store of food, so I don't see why you shouldn't as well. I would advise you to hold a pole in one hand and a revolver in the other, but I'll make it easier for you and go with you instead. Your father's pole is on the other side of the house, along with his box of lures. He fashioned a bunch from the smaller slag stones and tied a few around his hook, since slag turns shiny in water. I suppose you need me to teach you how to fish first?"

"No, Papa taught my brothers and me when we were children. He would take us fishing at least once a month during spring and summer."

"If you tell me you dug for worms, too, I won't believe it."

She smiled at him. "I did actually join my brothers at night for the worm hunts and turned over my share of stones looking for them, but I always called one of my brothers over to gather them up. And they didn't need to be asked to attach them to the hook for me the next day. There are some things a girl just isn't meant to do, touching worms being one of them," she ended primly.

He chuckled. She went out to find the pole. His improved mood was promising. Had he forgiven her for threatening to kill him? If so, it was going to make asking for that loan and partnership a little easier. Maybe she wouldn't wait until tonight.

Chapter Twenty-Four

"**D**'YOU KNOW WHAT HAPPENED to my father's pocket watch? Did he break it or lose it? I checked his valise, but it wasn't there."

Violet was sitting on the riverbank a few miles from Morgan's mountain; he was lying back next to her in the grass, his hat mostly covering his face. She had a pole in one hand and her parasol in the other, and a good thing she'd brought it, since there were no trees in either direction along this section of the river to offer shade. But she was having trouble keeping her eyes off of that long stretch of body. At least he was wearing a shirt, and had started doing so whenever he wasn't in his mine.

When he didn't answer, she wondered if he'd fallen asleep, so she added a little louder, "I meant to mention it sooner, but I kept forgetting. It has sentimental value, or I wouldn't ask. My mother gave it to him and there was an inscription on it: *So you don't forget to come home.* Papa said it was a joke between them because he was often late getting home for dinner."

"I saw him use it only a couple days before he had the heart attack and fell, so he didn't lose it. If you didn't find it among his belongings, then he probably had it on him when I took him to town—and he would've been buried in what he was wearing."

"That's—that's actually comforting. He would have liked that."

He sat up. "You aren't going to cry again, are you?"

She glanced aside and gave him a weak smile, but his hat was still tilted so low that all she could really see was that ridiculous beard. Which had her blurt out, "Why don't you shave? You have the tools for it at your camp."

"Waste of time," he said, and lay back down to completely cover his face again with the hat.

"D'you even have a mirror here to see how—how shaggy you look?"

"So my shaving would be for you, not me?"

She blushed. "I was just curious. Did you herd cattle with that beard, or did it scare the cows into running away?"

"Hell, no, my ma would skin me alive if I came in the house looking like this." She started to chuckle, but he added, "And I have shaved here—twice, I think."

She laughed this time, and guessed, "One of your disguises for town? Mountain man, hermit, cowboy, just never miner?"

"Something like that."

An hour later, with still no bites, she stood up to recast the line farther out. Sitting again, she complained, "You can't protect me if you're sleeping."

"Was I snoring?"

"No."

"Then figure I'm not sleeping." He sat up to open the

basket between them. "Eat up, just don't let go of that pole. It's the only one we've got."

She took the sandwich he handed her. "Are you sure there are fish in this river?"

"Pike and trout. Charley always came back with a basket-ful."

She groaned. They'd be there all day if he expected that many fish. But he didn't seem impatient to get back to work, and she couldn't get back to the south slope until that wolf and her pups were gone. But more importantly, they were talking, without rancor, without accusations. She was surprised by how nice it felt.

She wondered aloud, "If my father fished here often, might he have hidden his money here?"

"Yeah, but I doubt he did. People passing through this area follow this river north and south, and Charley knew that. Seems to me he would've looked for a more private spot where it would be less likely someone would stumble upon his money." And then, as he dug out a handful of cherries from the basket for her, he asked, "Why'd you get shipped off to England?"

"You make it sound like I was sent away as a punishment. I assure you I wasn't. Aunt Elizabeth is my mother's sister and is married to an English lord. When she came to visit us in Philadelphia, she was appalled to find me running wild—her words. I merely liked the outdoors, but I admit I had been skipping some of my studies. But she also upbraided Papa for allowing me to act like an adult when I wasn't even ten yet. She was concerned that I was missing my childhood. I think Papa was a bit cowed by her. She can be quite formidable. He didn't argue with her about taking me to England, where I would have a woman's guidance and be raised properly."

"You don't think it's odd that Charley didn't tell me about you?"

"Odd for you, but maybe not for him. He probably didn't think losing his inheritance would affect me, since I was still in England in the care of my aunt and uncle. Or maybe he just didn't think it appropriate to mention his daughter to a shaggy bear."

"A bear, huh?"

"I heard more than one person liken you to one when I was in town."

"But is that also your opinion of me?"

"Well, I won't say if the shoe fits . . ."

He laughed, making her smile.

Finished with lunch and seeing him lie back down, she stood up to get more serious about catching a few fish. And standing on the edge of the river, she was able to cast the line out even farther. Ten minutes later she pulled in her first catch and let it plop down on Morgan's chest, then laughed at how fast he sat up.

"That's one," she said, grinning. "One to go."

"Or three to go, if you want to be nice and catch a couple for Tex. He was tickled pink over that cougar meat you didn't want. Told me to thank you for turning your nose up at it."

She chuckled. "No, he didn't."

So Texas had been reciprocating over the last few days with two rabbits and a turkey that he'd simply tossed down the cliff for Morgan to find when he came out of the mine. When she'd asked Morgan why she never heard the shots from those kills, he'd told her, "Tex actually prefers a bow and arrows when none of his buddies are around to tease him about it."

Morgan removed the hook from the fish for her. She returned to the spot on the river's edge where she'd got lucky and cast the line out again, then looked back at him to ask, "Why did you leave ranching to mine instead? Does your family need money?"

"No, we own a rich spread. But more'n once growing up, I had this idea that Nashart should have a store that stocked all the fancy eastern stuff that my ma, Mary, had to order and then wait weeks or even months for it to be delivered. I can't count how many times she asked me and my brothers to ride to town to see if the merchandise had arrived. And how many times she looked disappointed when we had to tell her it hadn't come yet. So I finally decided to build her that store right in our own town, but I couldn't tell the family about it. Callahans are ranchers, always have been, always will be, and my pa would've flat-out balked at my idea, even though my ma is going to be tickled pink."

"So you came out here to make the money to do it, thereby skipping the argument?"

"Oh, there will still be an argument, and a damn big one, but since I won't be asking my father for the money, that store is still going to be built."

"I just can't picture you as an emporium owner," she teased. "You'll scare everyone out of your shop!"

He snorted. She grinned. But his reasons for wanting to do this were commendable. For his mother. To make her happy. To bring fine clothes and furnishings to the people in this wild, remote territory. If she didn't dislike him so much, she might like him—wait, that made no sense.

"What will you do with your mine when you go home?"

"I've considered turning it into a big production when I'm ready to leave, hiring a manager. But I've also considered blowing it up when I go."

She gasped. "And just bury all that wealth? You could sell it instead."

"That's the thing—I might've, if Sullivan hadn't pissed me off, but now I won't."

He didn't actually growl those words, which was promising; unexpectedly, this gave her a perfect opening to discuss business with him, so she said, "There's one other option. My brothers and I can continue to mine here if you form a new partnership with us."

"You're going to swing a pick?"

She would probably be as pathetic at it as Charles had been, but she stubbornly lifted her chin. "I will if I have to. I should already be your partner. The laws of inheritance should have applied, making me a mine owner. And need I point out that the terms of your agreement with Papa haven't been fulfilled yet? Didn't you say you formed the partnership to help my father and his family out of their financial bind? So we need to renegotiate to see this through."

"Is that so?"

He lay back down and covered his face with his hat. She reprimanded herself for approaching this the wrong way. Demands weren't going to work with this man, hadn't she already learned that?

"Let me start over—"

"Maybe—after you catch another fish."

Her brows snapped together in a frown. Stipulations? Or had she caught him off guard, and he needed a few minutes to do his own fishing—for an excuse to tell her no? But, according to him, he didn't need an excuse, didn't need to deal with her about anything since, as he'd pointed out, he no longer had a partner in her family. And he could easily invalidate her father's claim the next time he was in town. So maybe he was only making sure that she caught enough fish for their dinner before he told her no, guessing she'd stomp off angry when he did. Infuriating man!

She stared at the water again, in time to see two fish swimming past, completely ignoring the lures. She stepped back to pull her line into that pathway, and a few minutes later got the second tug.

It was an even bigger fish, and she resisted the impulse to drop it in the center of Morgan's chest again. She just held it next to him and said, "The hook, please?"

He sat up and smiled. "Now, that's a big one. One more should do it."

She cast the line again and, keeping her eyes on the water, took a deep breath and blurted out, "I need a loan for three thousand dollars. The next payment on the loan Papa took out against our family home is due soon, and it won't even make a dent in the balance still owed, even if my brothers had the money to make the payment, which they don't. There is not enough time to get my brothers here to start mining, when the trip to Butte took me nearly a week. But if you could send them the money now to pay off the loan in full, they could come here immediately to mine and pay you back."

"So you want a loan from me to pay off a loan?"

"Yes—please," she said sweetly. "You did agree to help with this very thing."

"When did I do that?"

"When you partnered with my father. He was desperate to

get rid of this loan and make a fortune so he could give us back the life we were accustomed to, you said it yourself, and that's why you helped him. The reason still exists. The loan is still looming. The goal that started this hasn't been met yet."

"There's no tearing hurry, Violet."

She swung around to stare at him. "How can you say that? My brothers are almost out of time!"

"No, they aren't. I sent off a second load of silver from Charley's mine the day before his accident. After I took your father to the doctor, I sent a telegram to my buyers, the silversmith brothers, and told them to deposit Charley's money with mine until he recovered. The next two times I checked on him that month, he was still unconscious. And then Tex went to town to play poker and brought me the bad news that he'd died. That was about a month after the accident. Charley never did find out that he'd netted another eighteen hundred."

"You have that money?"

"Not anymore. The last time I went to Butte, I arranged to have that eighteen hundred sent to your brothers. That was the same day I heard about you. In any case, they should have gotten that money this week."

That was such a relief! Daniel or maybe both of her brothers might already be on their way here because of it. "Why didn't you tell me this sooner?"

"I did, the night you convinced me you are Violet Mitchell, in the mine. I told you your brothers would hear from me soon."

"No, you didn't."

"I did, actually, but I guess you could have been too distracted looking through your pa's belongings to hear me. Now, I suppose I could reverse the seventy-thirty arrangement to thirty-seventy, but only long enough for you and your brothers to pay back the loan."

She was incredulous. Had she just gotten two yeses? But then she groaned—no, only one yes. That "only long enough" wasn't going to get her a dowry or enough money for her brothers to live comfortably.

Upset, she said, "Or you could make it a real partnership with them and a fifty-fifty split. They are both strong men, and with both of them digging, they can mine double what you do."

"You're offering me more'n I just said I was willing to accept? Why?"

"Because it's a viable mine that can produce more silver than is required to pay you back. It can secure my brothers' future."

"And get you a dowry." He suddenly sounded annoyed, which she didn't want until after he agreed to this business arrangement! But then he added, "You don't need to dangle a carrot in front of a man to get married. A man is going to want you just for yourself."

She blushed at his flattering opinion of her, but pointed out, "It's different among the English aristocracy. A dowry is expected, it is a tradition. A lord can't marry a pauper, it would be scandalous."

"But you're an American."

"And I was an heiress, which made all the difference over there."

"So if they don't see money when they look at you, they look at someone else? You really want a man like that?"

He was poking holes in her plans for her future. Why would he do that when it didn't concern him? But in a way, it did. Her plans were dependent on his agreeing to her full proposal, which he hadn't done yet.

She quickly got back to that. "I was just saying that everyone wins if you maintain a partnership with the Mitchell family even after we repay the money I hope you will loan us. And consider this: it would allow you to leave, to go home and still earn fifty percent from the partnership, without any work crews coming up here. I swear we'll continue to take all the precautions that you do to keep this location a secret."

"Let me think about it."

That wasn't a no! She nodded, delighted. But her delight soon waned as another hour passed without him saying anything more about it. The next fish she caught was too small to count, but they returned to camp after she landed another big one.

Waiting for his answer was agonizing. She couldn't push him about it, he didn't like that. She couldn't nag either—he definitely didn't like that. She had to be patient when it wasn't in her nature to be. But too much depended on her not disturbing the peace.

He didn't take the extra fish up to Texas when they got back to camp, but she knew his friend slept during the afternoons and that he would usually just lower a basket down the cliff whenever Morgan called up that he had something for him. After all, it was a long ride around that cliff.

"Stay off the south slope if you do any more searching today," he reminded her as he lifted her down from Caesar. "Or you can give the animals a brushing if you want to wait until tomorrow—that's if the wolf is gone. I'll check before dinner."

While that thirteen hundred dollars would still be helpful, the urgency to find it would be alleviated if he'd just give her his answer. He didn't. Instead, he went mining for the rest of the day.

Chapter Twenty-Five

Violet tried to keep in mind how nice that little fishing trip had been. And she kept reminding herself that Morgan hadn't said no to her partnership proposal. But how bloody long did he need to think about it? Any way he examined it, he had to conclude that the arrangement she was offering would be highly lucrative for him.

She didn't bring it up that night at dinner as they ate the fish she'd caught. Morgan told her the little wolf had moved on so she carried on as usual the next day, searching the south slope for her father's money, counseling herself to be patient. Morgan didn't seem to be in a good enough mood at dinner for her to ask him if he'd made a decision, so she'd suggested another game of poker. Aside from criticizing her bluffing again, he didn't say much and went straight to bed afterward.

The next morning while she was drinking her coffee on the porch as usual, she decided to make a greater effort to put Morgan in a good mood, including showing him how helpful she could be as a partner. So when he came out of the cabin to head to work, she told him she was taking the day off from her search.

"You'll get bored," was all he said.

"No, I'll brush the animals and perhaps even make dinner tonight."

"So you *can* cook?"

She hadn't thought that far ahead. "Well, how hard can it be?"

"You can look in my ma's cookbook for a recipe if you're determined to burn down the cabin, or you can just peel a few carrots and potatoes and I'll do the rest."

He was half teasing, at least about the destruction of his cabin, but that was a good sign. So she smiled. "Perhaps you're right. You are an excellent cook, after all."

Did he blush a little at the compliment? She smiled to herself and watched him enter the mine. A few minutes later, he brought Caesar out into the yard as he did every morning, and once he was in the mine again she got busy.

She fetched a bucket and the horse brush and tackled the grooming of the animals first, coaxing each one to the stream for a dousing and then a thorough brushing. The mares cooperated, but Caesar didn't. She ended up going to find the carrots; seeing that there were plenty left in the crate, she chopped one up. She put the pieces in her pocket and gave the large horse a piece every time he tried to move away from her. It worked. She briefly thought about braiding their tails, but grooming seven animals properly took up the entire morning, which was verified when Morgan returned to prepare lunch. Well, she did want the rest of her plan to be a surprise, and now it would be, since it would have to wait until he was back in the mine again.

When he went back to work, she tried to get Texas's attention without being too loud about it, hoping he wasn't already sleeping. When he poked his head over the cliff edge, she called up, "Join us for dinner? And bring your harmonica. I would love to hear some music tonight."

"I'll bring the rabbits," he replied.

Oh no, Bo's playmates! But he added, "Just caught a pair north of here."

Pleased that Texas would be joining them for dinner, Violet returned to the cabin to do what she'd never done before: clean the house. Fortunately, it was a small house. She swept the cabin and the porch, and aired out the bedding. She even gathered some of Morgan's pretty flowers and, finding an empty jar, set them at the center of his table. She then peeled the vegetables and left them in a bowl. Finally she made up both beds neatly, then went for her bath, hoping she still had enough time to make an extra effort with her appearance. She couldn't manage her usual coiffure, but she dug out her hairpins and twisted her braid to form a bun, then pinned it at her nape. The last touch was tying a pink ribbon about her neck to match her pretty pink blouse.

Morgan arrived first to get his bath towel. He stopped in the doorway, looking surprised. "You cleaned?"

"You said that I would get bored," she reminded him. "So I made sure I wouldn't. And I invited Texas to join us for dinner. He's bringing the meat."

"But you actually cleaned?"

She didn't blush, she threw his towel at him instead and pointed in the direction of the bathing pool. He laughed as he left, confirming he'd been teasing again by exaggerating his surprise. Texas arrived next with the two skinned rabbits.

"Place looks nice for a change," he remarked. "So do you—not that you don't always, but—"

He was blushing so much she cut in, "Thank you, I understand. I didn't leave camp today and needed to keep myself busy."

"I'll just get these started," he offered, and moved over to light the fire.

"Can I help?"

"Appears you already have," he said, noticing the bowl of peeled vegetables. "I'll just chop up everything so it will roast quicker. Morgan will probably want to make some gravy to top it all off. That boy does like his gravy."

She went out on the porch to wait for Morgan. When she saw him approaching, she noted that he was carrying just the towel because he'd already donned his shirt, which was wet in spots because he'd washed his hair and beard. Had he made an extra effort because he'd noticed that she looked a little more elegant tonight? It would be nice to hear him say so, but she doubted that he would compliment her.

When he stood next to her on the porch, she whispered, "He started the meal. I hope he cooks as well as you do."

"Better. He learned from Jakes, our bunkhouse cook back home."

"He still expects you to make the gravy."

He grinned. "He loves my gravy."

She almost laughed, wondering which one of them was the real gravy lover.

Later, while they ate the hearty meal, Texas asked her how she spent her days in London. Her cleaning the cabin today might have given him the wrong impression about an English lady's daily routine, so she said, "Walks in the park with my cousins, reading, calling on other ladies of leisure with my aunt. There were a few social gatherings even prior to the start of the official Season this summer, which is a whirlwind of balls and parties I was looking forward to attending."

"Did you have servants?"

"Oh, my, yes. There are more than a dozen in my uncle's house—footmen, upstairs and downstairs maids, the cook and her helpers, several ladies' maids, and my uncle's valet."

He seemed incredulous. "All in one house?"

She smiled. "It is a big house."

"And the men over there of your acquaintance, what sort of work do they do?"

"The rich don't work over there, do they?" Morgan answered Texas's question by asking her one.

"Lords don't, it would be considered scandalous, but rich tradesmen do, the same as here in America." She paused before pointing out, "You're rich, yet you intend to keep on working. It's all a matter of preference, wouldn't you say?"

"And what country you live in. In ours—yeah, it's yours, too—people don't look down on a man for working even if he's rich enough not to need to."

It was beginning to sound as if they were heading for an argument, which was the last thing she wanted, so she smiled and said, "Quite right," then to Texas, "I'm hoping that when you finish eating, you will play us one of the songs you've composed. Perhaps one with a waltz tempo so Morgan and I can dance."

Morgan put in, "He's going to be eating until he walks out the door, aren't you, Tex?"

Texas glanced at Morgan, then at her, then back at Morgan, then down at his plate, which still had a few bites of food on it.

"I don't know, I may be laughing too hard to play anything, if I have to watch you dancing. A waltz?" He started laughing early.

Violet grinned at Morgan. "It will be fun. I'll teach you if you don't know how." She stood up and held out her hand to him. "Come, I'll show you the steps while Texas finishes his dinner."

For a moment she didn't think he'd leave his chair, but then he rose and she was reminded of how tall he was, of his magnificent physique. Forcing herself to focus on the dance, she positioned his right hand on her waist and clasped her right hand with his left. Lightly resting her other hand on his upper arm, she said, "The waltz is a lively formal dance in triple time. Follow my footsteps. One, two, three, then backward, one, two, three. We will turn rhythmically around as we progress around the dance—er, cabin floor. Now again."

Texas had started playing his harmonica by then, a lovely tune she didn't recognize. But when she demonstrated the rise and fall part of the dance, where they needed to briefly go up on their toes, Texas started laughing again and the music stopped.

He complained, "She should be teaching me. After all, I'm the one getting married soon and will have to dance at the wedding shindig."

Morgan's hand tightened a little on hers as he told his friend, "I'll teach you once I learn. I'm already getting the hang of it. Stick to your harmonica playing."

Violet laughed as the music started again, but Morgan did in fact seem to know what he was doing now. She liked the feeling of his hand on her waist, and he was surprisingly light on his feet for a big man. Smiling at her, he twirled her out onto the porch, lifted her down the stairs, and danced with her in the yard under the stars, where they had more room and didn't have to worry about bumping into the table. His blue eyes gazed at her intently as they moved in time to the music. She was enchanted. It was almost what she'd imagined her first ball would be like—well, not the venue, but certainly the thrill of dancing with a tall, strapping, exciting man who was giving her his undivided attention.

"So this is how they dance at the balls you mentioned?" he asked. "It's a lot different from our boisterous western dancing, though both seem to involve twirling about."

"Maybe you can teach me a western dance later?"

"Maybe I will. But tell me more about your balls. What does a lady do if she's asked to dance but doesn't like the fella? Or does that proper etiquette you've mentioned require her to accept all offers?"

"No, she can simply say her dance card is full."

"And what would she do if her partner holds her too close?"

He pulled her closer to him to demonstrate. Violet was startled to feel her breasts brushing against his chest. Giving him an admonishing look, she said, "A lady would tap his shoulder with her fan and remind him of proper decorum." And she pretended to tap his shoulder, but he didn't loosen his hold on her so she could step back.

Instead he lowered his head and said close to ear, "And what does a lady do if her partner does this?"

A little shiver ran down her spine, and all of a sudden he was kissing her. She'd expected it when he'd brought her outside, remembering all those warnings about gentlemen who might suggest a stroll on the terrace just so they could steal a kiss. But she hadn't expected to want this particular kiss so much—yet she did, and responded with all the pent-up passion she felt for him. He'd lifted her off her feet with one arm tight around her waist and was still dancing with her held so close to him, not as quickly, yet they still seemed to be twirling. But one kiss turned into another more intense one that stirred her even more deeply. She'd already let go of his hand and put her arms around his neck, while his free hand now moved slowly up and down her back, exciting her further, until his fingers moved to the back of her neck to caress her there.

One moment she was sighing in pleasure, and then she was gasping as Morgan tripped over the flower fence, losing his footing, but quickly turning their bodies to cushion her fall as they tumbled into the bed of flowers. Breathless, Violet found herself lying on top of him, powerfully aware of the hard, masculine body beneath her. Impulsively, she turned her head to kiss him—but she couldn't be that bold! So she immediately rolled off him, but he rolled as well toward her; thinking he meant to put himself on top of her, she rolled again, and landed smack in the stream.

She came up sputtering, wiping water from her eyes and face, and burst out laughing. She couldn't stop, not when he started laughing, too. She didn't think she'd ever laughed so hard in her life.

When he grabbed her hand to pull her out of the water, she grinned. "By the by, the lady would have slapped his face."

"Is mine in danger?"

That just started another round of laughter.

Chapter Twenty-Six

V IOLET AWOKE EARLY THE next morning and was surprised to see that she was alone in the cabin. Dressing quickly, she opened the door to let in more light and was even more surprised to find Morgan sleeping on the porch again. It couldn't be comfortable, and she had her screen now. But after last night, maybe it was a good thing he had. Her charm offensive had certainly backfired. He'd ended up charming her!

What a fun night it had turned out to be, one she wasn't likely to ever forget. Surely it had left him in a good mood, too. "Did you intend to sleep this late?" she asked loud enough to wake him.

He stirred, mumbled something as he stood, then walked into the cabin to start breakfast. She didn't consider that mumble a setback, merely an expression of annoyance that he wasn't the first one awake as usual. She expected him to tell her any moment now that he accepted her partnership proposal. He did realize she was still waiting for his answer, didn't he?

But he didn't get around to mentioning it while they ate.

When he started to walk out the door still without addressing the issue, she was done waiting. "What's your answer to the proposals I presented the other day?"

He turned, leaned casually against the doorframe, and asked, "Do you still want to borrow three thousand, or do you want to subtract the eighteen hundred from it and just borrow twelve hundred instead?"

He was going to give her the loan! She was thrilled and couldn't help beaming at him before she answered, "My brothers have other creditors they need to pay. Daniel was even detained by one of them at the train station the day we were to come here together. I don't want to take any chances that they might come up short and not be able to pay off the house loan completely. I'd still like them to get another three thousand."

"Then I'll send it."

"When?"

"Soon."

"But—"

"No buts. I said I'll see they get it. You know, you're pretty good at saying please when you want something, but you're lousy at saying thank you when you get it. You might want to think on that before you yell at me anymore."

He left. She ran to the door to yell, "Thank you!"

"You ain't welcome, Mitchell," he growled back.

She sighed and watched him remove his shirt before he disappeared into his mine. What the deuce had just happened? He'd made her sound so ungrateful, which wasn't the case at all. And then she realized, he *still* hadn't answered her completely. He was lending her and her brothers the money, which implied he agreed to let her brothers come here and work to pay him back. But he hadn't said anything about forming a real partnership with them. She couldn't press him about it now when she'd somehow annoyed him again.

She'd meant to borrow Carla for the day, but decided against it. She couldn't just take the mule without asking, and she'd already asked Morgan for too much. She would just walk faster today. She was determined to try to reach the next gorge on the south slope, if it was actually reachable in a day.

A few hundred yards beyond the now empty wolf hole, the slopes got a little too steep for her to traverse easily. But she hadn't searched down this side section yet because, like the path up to Morgan's camp, it was too thick with trees, and she'd gotten frustrated with her last attempt to search around the pines. But it occurred to her that her father might have considered the forest an ideal hiding place because the pine needles would have completely covered any hole he'd dug, and even he wouldn't be able to find his own money again without marking the tree near it.

Excited by her new idea, but daunted by how big this forest was, she gathered up a bunch of loose rocks and made a little pile of them before she started straight down the slope, picking up pinecones on the ground and making another mound about two hundred feet down, then another two hundred feet north, marking a square section to search. But by the time she made one sweep back to the top edge of the forest, her legs were getting tired from the climb, so she scratched the idea of making sections and decided to just search the two-hundred-foot-wide area all the way down to the bottom of the forest, then rest before returning to camp for lunch.

Another good idea—or it would have been if she hadn't seen the man leading a horse through the trees toward her. He wore a wide-brimmed hat, a gun belt, and a vest over a blue shirt. Was he a cowboy? He didn't look like a miner. She ducked behind the nearest pine tree before he could see her, but the trunk wasn't as wide as her skirt!

"Lost, missy?" he called out.

What had Morgan said? To shoot any strangers she encountered? But this was just one man, not the two claim jumpers he'd mentioned, and this man might be a lawman out looking for those two thieves. In any case, she couldn't very well shoot anyone without reason. Morgan should have known she wouldn't. Still, she raised her Colt to eye level and supported her arm before she stepped around the tree to point the weapon at the stranger.

Now he was maybe only thirty feet away, close enough for her to note his curly brown shoulder-length hair, dark eyes, and mustache. He continued to approach her.

"Stay back," she warned nervously. "I have a couple partners nearby."

He reined in. "Careful with that gun. Don't want to shoot yourself."

"If I do, the shot will be heard. If I shoot you instead, the shot will be heard. Either way, help will be here in minutes, so why don't you just head back down the hill, then no one will get hurt."

"You sure do talk funny, but you're not being very friendly. I could use some grub if you have a camp close by."

She didn't lower the Colt, kept it aimed directly at his chest. If she screamed, would Morgan hear it, as far south as she'd gone? But the man might draw his own gun if she did. Oh, God, a shooting match here in the forest? She started to tremble with fear and gripped her arm and the Colt tighter so he wouldn't notice.

"I can't take you there," she said.

" 'Cause you're alone up here?"

"No, I'm not, but my partner doesn't like visitors. He tends to shoot them on sight."

He laughed. "I reckon I know who that is. So he's still here after all this time?"

"Who?"

"The miner. Not surprised he got himself a pretty little gal up here to keep him company—and it took you long enough."

She didn't understand what he meant until a gloved hand clamped down over her mouth and the Colt was pulled out of her hand. There were two of them. And now it was too late to scream.

Chapter Twenty-Seven

"HAVEN'T SEEN YOU LOOKING like that in a while," Texas remarked, and dug an extra mug out of his supplies when Morgan came up the cliff slope to his camp. "You trying to make me homesick?"

Morgan fingered his freshly shaven cheeks before he sat on one of the crates Texas used for chairs. "Figured it was time to get back in the habit, since I don't reckon we'll be here much longer."

"What'd she say about the new you?"

"What's she got to do with it?"

Texas grinned and teased, "After last night, I'd say everything. But she won't recognize you, that's for sure. You might even get a scream or two. So make sure she ain't holding that gun you gave her first."

Morgan snorted and poured himself some coffee. He wasn't sure why he'd waited until Violet left camp this morning to shave off his beard and most of his mustache. He wasn't sure why he'd gotten the urge to anyway. Just because she'd called him shaggy the other day at the river? It was a bad idea he was already regretting, since he anticipated her teasing him about it, thinking he'd done it just for her.

He tried to put that annoying female from his mind and drank from his mug, staring at the panoramic view of the mountain range stretching to the south. "If it wouldn't have been a pain in the ass making stairs long enough to get to the bottom of the cliff, I might've put my cabin up here. Damn fine view you got."

"As if you're ever out of the mine long enough to notice a view."

"Yeah, well, that's probably why I didn't. Got something that needs to be done, and I'd appreciate you doing it today. That loan Charley was so worried about, it's been burning money in bank interest instead of getting paid off. Violet talked me into a loan so she and her brothers can get rid of it."

"Was the bargain too good to resist?"

Morgan chuckled. "Ladies don't make bargains like that. She tossed out logic instead, reminding me that I'd been helping Charley to that same end. It was a good point. And she promised that her brothers would show up to work it off."

"Without asking them first?"

"I have a feeling that won't be an issue. You didn't notice how bossy she is?"

"Can't say that I did."

"Well, she doesn't ask, she demands. Probably a habit she developed when she mothered her brothers."

Which prompted the question, "Are those boys old enough to mine?"

"Older than her."

Texas laughed. "Yeah, that's bossy."

Morgan handed his friend a piece of paper. Texas glanced at it and said, "That's mighty generous of you."

"That's how much I liked Charley."

He wasn't even sure how that had happened, and so quickly. It wasn't because Charley reminded him of his own father. They were nothing alike. But he'd admired his gumption, his determination to do right by his sons at any cost; and the fact was, the man was a sweet-talker. In that, he'd reminded him of his brother Hunter who could sweet-talk his way around anything. And Morgan had simply enjoyed Charley's company.

"The instructions and both addresses are on that," Morgan said. "Send the first telegram to the Mellings, the silversmith brothers I deal with. Have them send three thousand from my account to the Mitchells, and sign that one from me. Send the second telegram to Violet's brothers, telling them to expect to receive the money to pay off their loan from the Melling brothers, and to come to Butte as soon as it's done. Sign that one from her."

"You want me to take the little lady back to town to wait for her brothers?"

"No, I'll take her to Butte next week. It'll take at least that long for them to get here. But once I show them how to use the smelter, it'll be time for me to pull up stakes and go home."

"Well, hot damn," Texas said with a big grin.

"Yeah, it's time." Morgan grinned back.

Texas got up to start saddling his horse. "I'll be spending the night in Butte after I finish your business, so don't expect me back until tomorrow."

"I figured," Morgan said, and headed back down the hill to get lunch started.

There was no sign of Violet yet, but she'd been consistent

about returning around noon to eat before she headed out again. He hoped she did find that money Charley had hidden before it was time to leave. It would make her happy, something she could remember when he explained why he wouldn't partner with her brothers permanently. He wasn't looking forward to that conversation.

Like Charley, Violet's brothers were eastern-bred gentlemen who wouldn't want to dig in a mine for very long. They would grow tired and dissatisfied and would want to bring men up here to do the work for them. But as long as Shawn Sullivan was around, they wouldn't be safe doing that. However, if he allowed them to mine for a limited time, perhaps two months, they would make enough money to last them a lifetime. They could leave as rich men before they got fed up—or, worse, got careless and led Sullivan here.

Morgan finished making lunch and sat on the porch waiting. To go by the sun inching onto the boards above the steps, Violet was about an hour late. Bo lay in the open doorway, as if he, too, were waiting for Violet.

"This is going to look silly if she opens the gate just as I saddle Caesar to go look for her," he said as he stepped over Bo to get his rifle. Coming back to lean against the doorframe, he glanced down at the dog. "She'll think I got worried. Can't have that. Ten more minutes? Wag your tail if you agree. Wag your tail if you disagree—yeah, that's what I thought. You're too accommodating, Bo."

"Hello in the cabin!"

Morgan straightened immediately and raised his rifle, his eyes scanning the area until he spotted the hat close to the ground on the other side of the fence by the gate. Since he'd been watching for Violet in that direction, whoever was out there had to have slithered up from the stream. Without a horse. No doubt it was tied farther down the slope out of sight.

"How many are you?" he called out.

"Just me, and I've come to talk."

"We've met, haven't we?"

"You could say that."

"Figured you two had left the area."

"We did, but we keep checking on you from time to time. And today was our lucky day. We've got your woman. Give us your mine and we'll give her back."

His answer was to shoot the hat. It flew backward, but there was no head under it. He heard a laugh, likely from behind one of the trees down there.

Rifle pointed between the two closest trees, Morgan said, "She owns the other mine here and you already got her. One of you marry her and you're all set." If they were stupid enough to go looking for a preacher, he could easily ambush them on the way.

"She is a fine-looking filly. My brother might go for that."

"But he's not here to say. Course, if you intend to mine next to me, I'll shoot your ass."

He fired off two rounds, hitting each of the two closest trees. That caused a nervous yell. "You can't kill me, dumb-ass! She's tucked away where you won't find her. And if I don't come back, she dies."

"You should have moved on last year. Now you've pissed me off." Morgan fired off two more rounds.

"Cut it out! He really will kill her if I don't come back with a deal."

Morgan took a deep breath to calm his fury. That didn't

work. He tried it three more times, but this kind of rage wasn't going away. But it wasn't in his voice when he said, "All right, I'm lowering my rifle. If you want to come to terms, show yourself."

The blond man who stepped out from behind the tree was hefty. Good, a nice target. And a gun was in his hand, but he'd spread both arms wide, so the weapon wasn't pointed toward the house.

"I'm planning to leave this camp pretty soon," Morgan said. "I'll give you two thousand for the woman. It would take you a year to make that much mining without a smelter." That wasn't even close to true, but he had a feeling these two wannabe miners didn't have a clue.

"You got one of those."

Morgan nodded. "I do, but the smelter goes with me, and I'm blowing up these mines when I leave. You should accept my offer. It's going down in value as we speak. One thousand for the woman. In fact"—he raised his rifle and fired—"I'll fetch her myself."

The man had fallen to the ground with a bullet in his leg. He was still in view and easy enough to finish off, but Morgan didn't want him dead, so he let the claim jumper crawl back behind a tree for cover while he stepped into the cabin.

He waited for about five minutes before he yelled out the door, "You know it would be easy to finish you off. I advise you to toss your gun over the fence before I finish my lunch and agree to take me to the woman. Think carefully. You and your brother have been a pain in my ass for too long."

"You don't really want her back, do you?" was growled angrily.

He wanted her back too much, but he answered, "I'd rather kill you and your brother, so the only way you get to live is to take me to her. Ten minutes to make up your mind."

He didn't expect the man to surrender. He just wanted to give him enough time to get to his horse and flee. Then he could follow the blood trail straight to Violet.

Chapter Twenty-Eight

VIOLET HAD JUST LEARNED from firsthand experience that hindsight was useless. She realized now that she should have fired her weapon immediately when she'd had the chance, even if she'd only taken a warning shot. Morgan would have heard the shot and come to investigate, and her heart wouldn't be pounding with fear.

But Morgan would know by now that she had been captured. The man who had gagged her had ridden off to tell him so, while the other one had ridden with her down the hill, then south along the base of the mountain range until he finally came to a temporary-looking camp. They seemed to think they could get Morgan to abandon his mine in exchange for her return. They were in for a nasty surprise.

She really wished she didn't know who these men were, but she did, the claim jumpers who had tried to kill Morgan last year, the two he'd looked for but never found. She'd gleaned as much from what the men had said to each other.

As soon as she was set on the ground and her gag was

removed, the curly-haired man asked, "What's your name, honey?" When she didn't answer, he grinned and pointed at his hair, volunteering, "Family calls me Curly, enemies aren't so nice. Real name is well-known. Tell me yours and I'll tell you mine."

She ignored his humor, but wanted to talk to him so he wouldn't think she was afraid of him. "You don't actually live on this range, do you?" Her mouth was so dry after being gagged that her voice sounded scratchy.

"Live outdoors? Why would we? We've been living in comfort in Helena for a few years now. Roughing it out here is for loners like your friend, though even he finally built himself a house. Did he do that for you?"

It didn't sound as if they knew about Texas. And they certainly didn't know much about Morgan.

"No, he didn't," she said. "He doesn't like me, considers me a thorn, which you've managed to rid him of. I'm sure it wasn't your intention, but you've done him a favor."

His dark brown eyes moved over her in an insulting manner before he laughed. "Then we win either way, 'cause I sure as hell wouldn't mind keeping you for a spell. Would you like that?"

Her stomach turned in repugnance. She glanced away so he wouldn't see the fear in her eyes. Her feet weren't tied, but her wrists were still bound in front of her; however, she didn't think about running. That would just give him an excuse to put his hands on her. She hoped Curly wouldn't try to assault her, at least not before they had Morgan's answer. Would Morgan give up his mine for her? Stupid question—of course he wouldn't. But she imagined he would get angry when he heard the claim jumpers' demand. That would be like poking a bear. . . .

He handed her a canteen. "Sit. Striking a bargain with the miner might take a while."

As thirsty as she was, it was frustrating that he'd given her a canteen without removing the cap for her, and he wasn't offering to untie her so she could open it herself. Did he want her to ask him for help? Or was he making it clear she was completely at their mercy? He'd already turned his back on her to watch the path below. So she sat, placing the canteen in her lap long enough to get the cap off so she could bring it to her lips with both hands—and loudly spewed the liquid out of her mouth. Whiskey?!

He heard the spewing. "Damn, wrong one. That weren't intentional."

As if she would believe that, but he did fetch a different canteen. She smelled its contents this time before she drank, then watched him go to his horse again. He came back with three strips of jerky for her. She wasn't hungry, although she ought to be, as late in the afternoon as it was, but there was a deep queasiness in her belly instead. Fear. She thought she was doing pretty well at hiding it. She wasn't sure if she feared just for herself, or for Morgan, too.

Morgan might shoot before he was even told that they had her. He had a bloody sign on his gate proclaiming that's exactly what he would do. Then he wouldn't be able to find her. But he would look. He was an honorable man who wouldn't stand by and do nothing when he knew a woman was in danger. And he'd shown her in too many ways that he cared about her welfare—also that he was attracted to her. But what if he got hurt in a shoot-out with the claim jumper? It could already have happened. Would shots from the mine be heard this far away? She had to get out of this herself.

She stared at the horse, which was still saddled. She could escape if she could get on it before the claim jumper yanked her off. She couldn't try it yet. They were both the same distance from it.

"Do I need to tie your feet, too?"

She glanced at him and saw that he'd been watching her calculating her options. She tried distracting him. "If you live in Helena, why do you come to this mountain?"

"Never would've if we didn't see the miner heading up it last year on our way to Billings. It was my brother's idea to make the detour to see what he was up to."

"And steal his mine?"

He grinned. "Seemed like a good idea at the time, though it didn't work out too well. He's pretty good with a gun for a miner. But we've checked back a few times to see if he's moved on, since we pass this range no matter which route we take to Wyoming to sneak in and visit our ma. Thought we got lucky last year when we found his camp empty, but it didn't really look deserted, so we hid till night to see if he was only out hunting. When he didn't show, we got enough ore out of there to fill our bags. That was a nice payday and got my brother determined to take over that mine eventually. Since then he's put up a damn steel door. Not so easy now to help ourselves to his silver. But we've been waiting patiently for another chance, and today on our way to Butte, patience surely has paid off."

"Butte?"

"Yeah, that town over yonder," he said, pointing his thumb behind him.

"Butte is northeast of here?"

"You've never been? It's only a half day's ride from here."

Good grief, had Morgan really taken her on such a round-about route that he'd wasted a full extra day getting her to his camp? Yes, of course he had. At the time, he'd been sure she worked for his enemy.

How ironic that she had a claim jumper to thank for telling her exactly where they were, on that lovely mountain she'd seen in the distance—and passed right by—the day Morgan took her out of Butte. But considering everything the claim jumper had just said, she asked, "If you want to mine, why not just make your own?"

"'Cause this one is already dug and beamed, has a smelter, even a house now, and water right there. And we don't mind killing him for it."

She gasped. He chuckled, adding, "Who's gonna know if we take over his mine?"

"I'll know what you've done."

"Not if you're dead, too. Lawmen ain't hunting for us up here, and we aim to keep it that way. Just have to be real careful down in Wyoming when we visit Ma, or we'll end up getting strung up again. My brother didn't like being kicked out of Laramie and shot the ornery deputy doing it. There were a few witnesses. The posse found us pretty quick, four of them. They hanged us out in the middle of nowhere from the only tree around. But our ma heard about what happened and she followed the posse. She got there in time to shoot them all and our ropes. We thought Bert was dead, he weren't breathing. Ma was mighty steamed up about it and started beating the living daylights out of him, and damned if it didn't wake him up."

"So you've never done anything to deserve a hanging?" she asked. "Just your brother—and your mother?"

He laughed. "Didn't say that. We had to eat and put some money in our pockets before we found a new place to live. But I won't kill you if you can be accommodating. Can you?"

"I thought you were negotiating with the miner!"

He shrugged. "If that works, sure, but you said it wouldn't work. Or were you lying about him not liking you? You were, huh? Course you were, pretty thing like you."

She looked away, closed her eyes. She was going to have to beat him to that horse. But she heard another horse approaching. She glanced around to see his brother riding up to them and dismounting—or attempting to. He fell halfway to the ground, groaning. Blood was pouring down one of his legs.

"You're bleeding, Bert?" Curly said. It sounded like an accusation.

"He shot me. This is the second damn time he's shot me! I want him dead."

"Idiot, you've left a blood trail that will lead him here."

"He won't find it." Bert smirked. "I rode down the stream until I was out of the mountains, then galloped on the flats straight here."

"That skinny-ass stream that flows by his camp? Your horse would've still left some tracks around it."

"Good, then we wait till he shows and shoot him, and her, too."

"I'm not shooting her," Curly said, giving Violet another glance. "She's too pretty."

"Can't leave witnesses. Bad enough we can never live in Wyoming again with all those wanted posters hung in every town down there. Up in this territory, they don't know us. We're keeping it that way."

There was no hiding her trembling now when she saw

Curly grudgingly nod his agreement. And Bert managed to get to his feet to draw the gun from his holster, and then her Colt, which he'd stuck in his pants. But it was obvious that he'd been weakened by blood loss. The man hadn't even stopped long enough to tie off the wound to try to lessen the flow. He seemed somewhat dazed from it, wobbling on his feet. She might be able to leap at him, knock him over and grab one of those Colts. But she'd never done anything so daring or aggressive in her life! It certainly wouldn't be easy with her wrists tied together. She'd have to get the gun even as he fell, before she got shot for the effort. So grab, roll, shoot. What other choice—?

The bullet went right through Bert's neck, blood splattering in every direction. Both of his Colts fell to the ground as he tried to cover one side of his neck. He fell over, face-first.

With blood on her face, her hands, her dress, and a dead man lying only feet away, Violet was screaming hysterically. She couldn't stop, not even when the brother who wasn't dead yanked her up and held her in front of him, his gun pressed to her cheek. He slowly turned in a circle as if he couldn't find the shooter, had no idea from which direction the shot that had killed his brother had come.

"Show yourself or she dies!" he yelled. And then he hissed by her ear, "Shut the hell up. He can't hear me with you yelling. Shut up or I'll smash your head!"

She vaguely heard another shot as she fainted.

Chapter Twenty-Nine

SHE WAS BEING CARRIED, she guessed by Morgan. But when Violet opened her eyes she screamed and struggled, not recognizing whoever was taking her away.

"Wasn't exactly expecting this reaction to my shaving. It's still me, Morgan, you know."

It was his voice, even if it wasn't his face. She stopped struggling to gaze up at him, trying to process the change in his appearance. It truly wasn't easy.

"You look so different," she said as she clung to him. "But you rescued me. I knew you would. I was so scared!"

He held her tighter. "You're safe now."

"Are they both . . . ? "

"Yeah. Faked or not, your fainting got you out of the way so I could take a clean shot at the last one. Smart thinking if you planned it, good timing otherwise."

She wasn't sure how to fake a faint, but now there were two fewer killers on the loose, so she should be glad. She should thank him for rescuing her, too. She would have died if he hadn't.

He set her on the ground when he reached Caesar and wrapped a blanket around her, probably because she was still trembling. But when he tied the two horses he'd been leading behind them to Caesar's saddle, she asked haltingly, "What are you doing? Are you taking the bodies with us, too?"

"No. Texas will retrieve them when he returns from Butte. They were both wanted in Wyoming, dead or alive, so there's a reward."

"How do you know?"

He picked her up and set her on Caesar before mounting behind her. "Because they were dumb enough to carry their own wanted posters on them."

So Texas hadn't been in the camp to help him? Morgan had come after her alone? But no one else had been needed. Just two shots, and he'd killed both men. He was more dangerous than she'd realized, like that gunslinger she'd seen in Butte. Was everyone in the West like that? Ready to kill if necessary—or, like those two outlaws, ready to kill for any reason? She couldn't stay in this barbaric land any longer. She had to leave, with or without a partnership agreement, and return to the civilized world, her world, where men didn't fall dead at her feet. . . .

He'd drawn her across his lap before starting off, his arms tight around her. "You're still trembling," he said after a few minutes. "Did they hurt you?"

"No, they only gagged me and tied my hands, but they would have . . ." She couldn't bring herself to say it.

"Don't think about it. You're safe now. No one's going to hurt you and we'll be home soon."

Home? She could never call this wild, violent land home. But she felt safe in Morgan's arms.

It was nearing dusk when they rode up the hill to his camp. He carried her inside the cabin and set her on her bed. "Will we be safe here? What if other outlaws show up? Texas isn't even here to help guard."

"You know you're safe with me, Violet. And Bo doesn't go far from you. And you have this." He set the Colt that he'd retrieved from the claim jumper on the top crate by her bed. "Don't hesitate to fire it, if only to summon me."

She smiled weakly. She already knew she should have done that today. Next time—God, there couldn't be a next time. She wasn't stepping foot out of this camp again unless the bear was with her.

He knelt to remove her boots, then left. She didn't move, simply stared at the floor by her bare feet. Even after he came back in and began washing the blood from her face and hands with cold water, she still just stared at the floor, letting him remove the signs of what had happened. But what would wash away the fear and terror that were lurking in her mind?

He lit a few lanterns and started the fire before he said, "You need to eat."

She didn't answer. After a moment he stood in front of her again and added, "Maybe you need this instead."

She saw the glass in his hand filled with golden liquid, the stuff he drank, whiskey or rum. "No thank you."

He tipped up her chin and looked at her closely. "How are you feeling?"

"I can't stop thinking about the dead men and all that blood."

"You were brave today. I doubt many London debutantes

would be able to help take down two American outlaws the way you did."

He was trying to make her laugh, but his grin, so easily seen now, just pointed out that this wasn't her Morgan. His voice, his eyes were familiar to her, but the rest of his face wasn't. It was too bloody handsome. Why'd he have to shave? The bear had been somewhat safe.

"They were bad men, Violet," he added. "Now they won't be able to hurt people anymore."

But she'd watched them die! She began to shake uncontrollably. And cry, great wrenching sobs. She couldn't stop either reaction. She'd been so sure she was going to die today.

"Sometimes a good cry helps, according to my ma. I'm sorry you went through this, but I promise it will get better."

She covered her face with her hands and felt him sit on the bed next to her and draw her onto his lap to try to soothe her. She remembered that her aunt had said something similar about tears being beneficial, so she didn't try to stop crying, but she did try to stop thinking. The tears finally wound down to sniffles. She didn't feel better yet, but maybe she could more easily lock those memories away now. And thinking about the new Morgan helped. He was still safe, still protecting her. Even if he was too handsome, she sensed that deep down he was still the bear.

"You want some of that whiskey now?"

"No, I think your mother was right about a good cry," she said with a smile to assure him the flood was over.

He wiped her cheeks gently. "We should probably get rid of your dirty clothes and brush your hair."

She gave him a curious look. "You do like doing that, don't you?"

He grinned, abashed. "Can't help it, with beautiful hair like yours."

It was nice of him to just call her clothes dirty instead of mentioning the blood splatters, and she did want to get rid of them, so she helped him get them off her, saying, "They need to be burned."

"We don't need a room full of smoke. I'll deal with them later."

He found her brush and had her sit between his legs on the edge of the bed. He unwound her braid first, then began the long, gentle strokes that felt so good. "Picture my flower garden," he said softly. "If I were to stay here longer, what would you recommend adding to it? I was thinking violets, but would roses be better? Are they popular in England?"

She laughed, aware that he was trying to make her feel better; it was certainly working. "Everyone knows English roses are the most beautiful."

She turned halfway to face him, arrested again by his handsome face, but it was suddenly very important that he know how grateful she was. "Thank you for rescuing me and taking care of me."

She leaned over to kiss his newly smooth cheek, but didn't lean all the way back, still staring at him. He'd done so much for her today, but she suddenly wanted more, and before she could stop them, the words came out: "Kiss me."

He didn't hesitate, put his mouth to hers gently at first, and then more passionately. Had he already been thinking about this and only resisted for her sake? It only took moments for her to wrap an arm about his neck and kiss him back with equal passion.

A different realm, this, sensual, feelings so new they were

yet to be explored, so far removed from what she was escaping. She delved deeper, quickened at the touch of his palm to her cheek, her neck, her breast. When a hand moved ever so slowly up her leg, it was hot skin she felt, making her realize she was only wearing her underclothes now. But propriety didn't intrude, not even a little. There was just him and what he was doing.

He laid her back on the bed and joined her, half lying on top of her because there was so little room—or because he wanted to. She liked the position, liked feeling so much of him against her. His body, so long, so strong, was her shield from harm. He was her guardian knight, but tonight he was much more than that. He'd saved her life today, rescued her from danger and darkness. And now he was showing her the sweeter side of life—the tenderness! The exquisite pleasures she'd never imagined.

She wanted to say thank you, but even more she didn't want to distract him, not when he was still kissing her, still moving one hand up and down her body in such an exciting way. He raised one of her legs over his shoulder, then bent down to kiss her breast, but he also slid an arm beneath her between her legs to lift her even closer to him. It felt unusual and yet thrilling, the heat of his mouth over her nipple, that hard arm rubbing between her legs, igniting little fires that coursed through her. Little moans escaped from her in gasps as he continued to kiss her breasts.

She almost cried out when his warmth left her as he rose to his knees to take off his shirt, but she was arrested by his new appearance, by how handsome he was. Good God, he was tantalizing, and all those muscles, flexed as he tossed the shirt away, flexed again as he removed his gun belt and then started on his belt. Her aunt had been so right when they'd had "that talk" and Elizabeth had warned, "Some men don't want to be naked in bed, but some do. Hope for one that does." She hadn't really understood, but now she did—because this man was a feast for the eyes, Adonis in the flesh. Just looking at him set her pulse racing!

He'd already untied her chemise, those silk ties, a mere decoration, never used because it was easier to slip the garment over her head. It lay open now, both of her breasts exposed, so she didn't even think of protesting when he removed her drawers, too, longer to watch him, longer to be fascinated by his own undressing.

She was fully embracing the unknown, but she still felt a moment of apprehension when he discarded his pants and she saw the size of his manhood. It might have been better to cut her curiosity short. She closed her eyes. She didn't have to know everything. And yet the moment he slid up her body, his skin against hers, and kissed her deeply again, the thought was gone and she opened her eyes. She *did* want to know everything, to feel everything sensual he could share with her.

Her arms were around him and she moved a hand into his hair, running her fingers through it. The black mane was still long, but not so shaggy now, even soft to the touch. But his beardless face still fascinated her, and she cupped one of his cheeks to feel stubble already returning. She smiled. She probably wouldn't shave either if the results barely lasted a day.

He put his hand over hers, brought her fingertips to his lips and kissed the pulse under her wrist. He was staring at her now, those lovely powder-blue eyes, warm with passion and . . . concern?

"You've been through a lot today," he said. "I didn't mean

for things to progress this quickly, but I want you so much. I don't want to stop, but I will if you want to wait until you feel better?"

Stop? "No, I want this, want you. Please don't stop."

He groaned and kissed her deeply. Then she felt it, gone in a blink, her maidenhood. And him inside her, foreign but still, waiting. She'd closed her eyes with a gasp but opened them now to see his smile, then felt that amazing length sliding deeper. Divine. There was more to explore, more to feel as he moved steadily inside her, then faster, bringing forth multiple gasps from her. But she sensed something else approaching that widened her eyes, gathering momentum, elusive until she was overwhelmed by a sudden burst of pure, wondrous pleasure.

She cried out with it, held on to Morgan's shoulders tightly, utterly incredulous that something like that even existed. And it left all sorts of unexpected feelings behind, tenderness, caring, gratitude, and an urge to hug him, to simply hug him.

Chapter Thirty

VIOLET RESISTED THE URGE to continue hugging the man on top of her, feeling a little shy now for having behaved so passionately with him. Morgan had felt the same amazing thing she did, had been quite loud about it, but he was still now. Nonetheless, she couldn't resist lightly caressing his shoulder and muscular arm. His face was pressed between her shoulder and her neck, his breathing still labored, his arms keeping most of his weight from her chest. She wondered if they would sleep like that. She didn't think she'd mind. But the bed was so narrow, would it even be possible for two people to sleep on it with any degree of comfort? And once he slept, his arms would relax and she'd end up crushed and have to wake him, and they might end up making love again. . . .

She frowned. They probably shouldn't do that again, no matter how nice—no, how amazing it had been. Being this close to Morgan, feeling surrounded by him, made her feel so safe, so comfortable. But she was hungry, very hungry, noisily so.

He chuckled when he heard her belly growl. "That stew I made for lunch should be hot by now."

He kissed her neck, then her cheek, before he lifted himself off her and headed to the fireplace. Naked. A blush crept up her cheeks.

She got up quickly, grabbed her valise, and rushed outside to the porch to dress, yelling back, "Do put something on!"

"I've only been sleeping with my pants on for your sake, Violet. It's not how I usually sleep."

"Your thoughtfulness was and is appreciated!"

She hoped he got the point. Just because she'd lain naked with him didn't mean she would eat or sleep all night that way.

Dressed, she tied her hair back, too hungry to braid it, and hurried back inside. He'd put his pants back on, even his shirt, though he hadn't buttoned it. That's not what caused her to blush again. She was feeling incredibly embarrassed over what they'd done in that very room.

He put the large bowl of stew in front of her, remarking, "Why'd you tie your hair back?"

"To keep it out of the way."

"It's never in my way. I like it better down." She started to remind him about tangles, but he said, "We can argue about it later." And he tossed her half of the bread loaf with a grin.

He sat down across from her. She wanted to look away but really couldn't. He was too bloody handsome now, and maybe only a few years older than her.

"How old are you?" she asked.

"Twenty-three, second son of four. Hunter's a year older and the charmer in the family. Our brother John is twenty-one and hot-tempered. The runt, Cole, is just nineteen and can't make up his mind who he wants to take after."

"How would you describe yourself?"

"You know me. What would you say?"

"You're still a bear even if you don't look like one now," she replied. "But I suppose if I had to describe you in one word, I would say determined."

He grinned. "Good choice."

He shouldn't do that. His smile almost transfixed her, making him even more handsome. Thank God she hadn't been able to see that before. But how was she going to deal with it now when it was hard to tear her eyes away from him?

She stared at her stew, determined not to look up again. "What was it like, growing up with three brothers?"

"Fun—usually. The old feud we have with the Warrens, neighboring ranchers, led to all sorts of mischief, since they have three boys near our ages."

"What sort of feud? The killing kind?"

He snorted. "No—least, not in our day, though it might've led to that if a truce hadn't been arranged years ago by Mrs. Warren with the offer of a marriage to her only daughter, who was still a baby at the time. The peacekeeping wedding is to happen sometime this summer. It could be over with, for all I know—or called off, if Hunter backed out of it. He sure wasn't happy about our parents volunteering him just because he's the oldest, without his having any say about it, and to a filly he's never met. The Warren daughter was raised back east for some reason. Never did find out why. But if that wedding doesn't happen, then there might end up being bloodshed."

"So you don't really know what you'll be going home to, when you get around to it?"

"I'll likely know. My ma writes me here and keeps me apprised of what's happening at home. There are probably a few letters waiting for me in town that I didn't pick up this last trip."

Because of her. Because he got the wrong idea about her, got mad about it, and arbitrarily abducted her instead of simply knocking on her door at the hotel and asking her why she was looking for him. But she wasn't going to open that can of worms, as he would say.

So she only said primly, "Feuds are archaic. No one in the civilized world has them anymore."

He laughed at the remark. "Want to bet? They might not label them feuds where you come from, but there will always be neighbors who can't get along, grudges that escalate, and the more common revenge motives that can affect whole families. Emotions that start disputes like that can arise anywhere, in any country. In your civilized world, it might even be labeled war."

She blushed slightly, forced to allow, "I cede to your reasoning."

"Well, that's a surprise."

She made a face and stood up to go outside. She wasn't going to embarrass herself by saying why. He followed her out, but when she glanced back she saw him heading to the pasture to check on the horses. Now that there were two extra ones, she supposed she could offer to help him. After all, she did know how to saddle and unsaddle a horse; she'd just never had a reason to tell him that. Would he still lock Caesar in his mine now that the claim jumpers were no longer a threat? Probably.

Drowsy after that filling meal, she was extra careful with her steps on the way back to the cabin, now that it was mostly dark. The moon wasn't up yet, but she could see well enough with the streaks of the sunset in the sky. She wanted a bath, a real one, craved it, but her mind balked at cold stream water tonight, and the thought of going to bed with wet hair was just as abhorrent, so a bath would have to wait until morning.

Returning to the cabin, she found Morgan putting the dinner bowls away, his back to her. And it was close enough to the time they usually went to sleep, so she said, "Good night."

He turned. She was immediately arrested again by the new him, the too-handsome version. She ended up standing there like a bedazzled loon, which allowed him to reach her and put his arms around her before she even thought about retreating out of his way.

The hug was gentle, the kiss somewhat brief, before he said with a smile, "Sweet dreams, Thorny Violet."

But he didn't let go of her, and she felt the urge to hug him back. She resisted, turned away, although she no longer felt the least bit tired. And suddenly she stopped resisting. She turned back, put her arms around his neck, and whispered, "Morgan . . ." Then led him to her bed.

Chapter Thirty-One

VIOLET WAS ALONE IN her bed when she awoke—and naked. The skin on her face felt a little chafed. She recalled Morgan kissing her and her kissing him during the night. But in the cold light of morning, she remembered everything else that had happened last night, and was mortified by what she'd done.

At least he'd hooked up her screen when he left her bed. To save her embarrassment? Nothing could. But she quickly reached for the clothes that had been laid over the crates at the foot of her bed and dressed, hoping he wasn't still in the cabin.

He was. Stepping out from behind the screen, she saw him fully dressed and sitting at the table drinking coffee. She paused to ask, "We slept together all night?" Then she blushed furiously again.

Morgan raised a brow. "The sleeping part is all you remember?"

"We shan't talk about it," she said as she sat down at the table.

"If you say so."

"I do. Nor shall it happen again."

"I thought we weren't going to talk about it."

"I simply don't want to raise expectations."

"Consider them not raised." But then he said, "You know, you don't have to be beyond-the-pale polite with me—did I use that phrase right?"

"Not really, but I caught the drift. However, I will always be polite, no matter whom I'm talking to."

"Always?" He grinned.

Good Lord, was he constantly going to make allusions to what they'd done last night? He'd saved her twice yesterday, first from harm, then from her horrific memories and fear. And the two outlaws had deserved to die, had killed people for no reason and without remorse. By getting rid of those two men, Morgan had likely saved countless other lives they would have taken. Yes, she could deal with that harrowing adventure pragmatically now. But she wasn't sure she could deal with resisting Morgan.

"How are you feeling this morning? You were pretty shaken up yesterday."

"I'm better," she assured him.

"You still ought to rest up today, maybe give up on searching for your father's money, or wait until Texas returns. He doesn't sleep the entire day and could go with you some."

"I'll be fine, and I'll have my gun."

"That gun didn't help you much yesterday," he said pointedly.

"I erred in not using it, but I learn from my mistakes. I'll fire off a shot immediately if I see anything that walks on two feet."

"Well, help yourself to lunch today, since I might be late. There's a lot I want to accomplish in the mine before we return to Butte next week to meet up with your brothers."

"My brothers?"

"I asked Texas to go to town to send that money you wanted delivered to them. They'll receive it in a couple days."

So she'd accomplished her goal? The family home would be saved. She should be jumping for joy, but she had too many other things on her mind now: the way he was looking at her, noticing that he'd shaved again this morning, remembering that he'd buried his face in her hair last night after he spread it across her pillow, the very tender way he'd held her through the night.

She ate her breakfast, but after he left, she remained at the table, wallowing in regret. It didn't matter how much she might like him, she'd ruined her life. She'd behaved recklessly and had given her virginity to a man she was never going to marry. And she might even be pregnant! She could imagine how appalled Aunt Elizabeth and Sophie would be by what she'd done. But after the terrifying run-in with the claim jumpers, who could blame her for seeking comfort in the arms of a man as attractive, strong, and decent as Morgan Callahan?

He'd come to like her, too. And he wanted her as much as she wanted him. There was no way they would be able to resist each other if they lived in this cabin together for another whole week. It would be wrong to allow it because she could never marry him.

She looked around the shabby cabin, saw her bloodstained clothes still on the floor, weapons lying around. This was no life for her. She knew what she had to do. She had to go back where she belonged, where death didn't lurk around every corner. And she had to do it now. It couldn't wait another day. What they'd done last night could never happen again, the risk was far too great: babies, a forced marriage—or, worse, he wouldn't even offer marriage. Her life would be ruined in either case! And she was *not* going to end up pregnant. She refused to give up her dreams because of her sinful fascination with a bear.

She felt a sense of urgency to act, because given how easily she had succumbed *and* initiated what had happened last night, she didn't think she'd have the willpower to resist him, not with the way he looked now. And that name he'd called her, Thorny Violet, the way he said it, it was a bloody endearment! Tears sprang to her eyes, remembering.

THE FIRST THREE HOURS flew by. The outlaw's horse was a surprisingly strong and responsive mount, but she knew better than to push it. But with each mile that passed, Violet felt more confident that she'd done the right thing, leaving without saying good-bye. Morgan wasn't ready to take her to town, and he would have argued against her going alone, leaving her no other option.

So she'd gathered up a few essential personal belongings, a canteen of water, a blanket, her valise and parasol, and the lunch he'd mentioned; then she'd saddled the horse. Following the outlaw's directions, she'd be in Butte by late afternoon, where she'd have a real bath and sleep in a real bed. Thank goodness this strange adventure was almost over. She'd even accomplished what she'd set out to do: she'd claimed her father's mine and secured her own and her brothers' futures. The telegram Morgan had sent to her brothers could serve as a written confirmation of their new partnership. She'd let her brothers do the rest while she returned to London, and Morgan would end up with more of what mattered most to him, silver.

She'd followed the river north for a while until she came to a narrow section and crossed it, stopping only long enough to refill her canteen, then continued north until she found the road, exactly where she expected it to be—now. She couldn't imagine how lost she would have been if she'd gone south as she would have if Curly hadn't told her where Butte was in relation to Morgan's mountain.

The dark clouds were overhead before she saw them coming. She'd been in this wilderness with Morgan for more than a week with not a drop of moisture from the sky. It wouldn't dare rain today of all days. She continued on for another ten minutes before the rain started. Bloody hell. But she didn't let a little rain stop her until a half hour later when it turned torrential and she took shelter under a rocky ledge. Wet, furious at this delay, she hoped the rain wouldn't last too long. It was still early in the day. She could reach Butte before nightfall.

So she ate her lunch, waiting for the rain to stop. But night arrived and the rain kept pouring down. She felt less confident by then about her decision to leave the camp. All she could think about were the wild animals that roamed through the wilderness. She chided herself when she started wishing that Morgan were there. She kept telling herself she'd made the right decision, but she was so tired, wet, and hungry by then; she sat with her gun in hand, listening for cougars, bears, and snakes, trying to stay awake.

The horse nudged her awake the next morning. She was glad to see the sun shining. Her muscles aching, somehow she managed to mount the horse and continued riding. An hour later she panicked when she heard hoofbeats behind her. Morgan had caught up to her. Would he be furious? But when she glanced back, she saw a group of men. Had he sent a posse after her? No, of course not. He couldn't have gotten ahead of her to arrange one, not in that downpour yesterday.

She continued on, hoping they would just ride past her, since they were moving faster than she was; instead, they pulled in abreast of her. One of them politely said, "Hold up, ma'am. Where are you headed? Are you lost? Do you need help?"

They were cleanly dressed and respectful. The one who spoke even tipped his hat to her. But away from Morgan, Violet was back to being prim and proper. She said, "I'm going to Butte, which I know isn't far now. With whom am I speaking?"

"We were doing some surveying in the area for a mining outfit and are heading back to Butte, too. We'd be happy to ride with you and make sure you get there safely."

She nodded her consent, pleased to have come upon decent men who merely wanted to help. They surrounded her on the ride, one in front, one on either side of her, and two behind. Soon she was sneezing from the dust being kicked up by the horse in front.

"Here, you can use this to keep the dust out of your face."

She glanced to the side. One of the men was offering her a bandanna. "Thank you," she said, reaching for it.

"Stop for a moment and let me tie it on for you," he added. "Your hands are full with the reins and that pretty parasol."

He was right, so she reined in while he leaned closer to reach her. But she smelled something funny as soon as the bandanna covered her nose. It made her light-headed, and a moment later she felt herself passing out.

Chapter Thirty-Two

"MAYBE YOU SHOULD FETCH your doctor to make sure she's all right. Is this really who you've been searching for? She doesn't look at all well."

A female voice made that observation. No one replied to it, but footsteps walked away. Violet fought to open her eyes. The only person who might have searched for her was Morgan. Had he just left the room? Unless the law had noticed her sudden disappearance from Butte. The woman could have been speaking to the sheriff or the deputy.

Violet was in a pretty bedroom, lying in a large bed, her head slightly propped up on a pillow. The woman standing next to her was on the high side of middle age, with tightly coiffured red hair, blue eyes, a somewhat fashionable day dress.

"Awake finally?"

Violet could barely concentrate, she felt so fuzzy-headed. "Where am I?"

"You're in my brother's house. I'm Kayleigh Sullivan. You

know my brother, Shawn. I was told you dined with him and my niece at the hotel."

Katie's aunt? Violet relaxed a little and gave the woman a weak smile. "I'm Violet Mitchell."

"Yes, we know, dear. Are you feeling better?"

"What happened to me?"

"You were riding with some of my brother's men when you fainted. You were lucky to have run into them so they could get you back to Butte safely. Now, would you like me to have this food warmed up? I may have brought it too soon."

Food? "No! Cold is fine, burned is fine, anything is fine. Really."

She didn't blush at how desperate she sounded, just tried to sit up, too eager to find the food before it was taken away. But she groaned and fell back against the pillow. Her back hurt; so did her arse. Had she fallen when she fainted, or was she still feeling the effects of sleeping on rock under that ledge? She didn't remember falling, just that odd smell before she fainted. But if she'd broken something, she was going to cry. To have gotten so close to town without injury . . .

The woman tsked and leaned over her. "Just a prop-up for now, shall we?"

"Yes, and thank you," Violet said as the other pillow on the bed was added to hers so she could sit up halfway; the tray was set on her lap.

"Of course, dear. How long were you starving out there in the wilderness?"

Violet brought the bowl to just under her chin. Soup? She wasn't sick, she was hungry. But there were buttered buns on the tray, too, and a small bowl of strawberries.

"Since yesterday afternoon," she said, and started spooning the soup into her mouth.

"I wouldn't have thought your mine was so far away—that is, we assumed when you left town you did so with young Callahan, that he showed you the way. He wouldn't bring you back to town?"

Violet managed not to frown, but the mention of her mine was too unexpected. How did this woman know about it and that she'd been with Morgan? And why would Shawn Sullivan's men bring her here instead of to Dr. Cantry? Unless, as his sister had remarked, he'd organized a search for her. Because the law wasn't doing enough to find her? Why not? Mr. Sullivan did know her, after all, and knew she was his daughter's friend.

So she wasn't sure if she should be worried about it or not, given that her view of Shawn Sullivan differed from Morgan's. And nothing Morgan had said about the man had changed that, since it was all supposition, every bit of it, just part of his obsession with keeping the location of his mine secret. He'd even admitted that Mr. Sullivan kept offering a higher price for his mine. That alone should have assured him that Sullivan wanted to acquire it legally.

But she still asked, "Why was your brother searching for me?"

"Shawn went to your hotel to invite you to dinner again, only to be told that you'd left rather mysteriously. He assumed you'd found Callahan to guide you to your father's mine, which Katie mentioned you were hoping to do. But when you didn't return to town soon, Shawn became concerned, considering everything that we know about that ornery Callahan. It must have been awful having to deal with someone so rude and surly. I heard he doesn't even wash!"

Violet choked back a laugh. If only they could see Morgan now. But she certainly didn't feel comfortable talking about him or their mines with a stranger, even if Kayleigh was Katie's aunt and Violet felt safe here, so she asked, "Whose room is this?"

"Katie's. She won't mind your using it. She rarely visits us anymore. I can't say I blame her. This town is taking forever to shake off its primitive beginnings."

"Did Katie get married?"

"Yes, and Shawn was so disappointed that business kept him from attending the wedding, but we received a telegram that everything went off perfectly. But do stop eating so fast, dear, or you'll get stomach upset. I assure you I'll bring another tray if that one isn't enough."

Violet didn't pause in eating, just nodded. But Kayleigh was staring at her skirt and the bed beneath it. Violet followed her gaze and saw just how dusty she was.

"Yes, that spread will have to be cleaned now," Kayleigh said with yet another tsk. "I tried to get them to pull it down before you were laid there, but they were in such a hurry, no one listened. I do have water heating for your bath. I think you even have blood in your hair. Goodness, how did that happen? Did you kill him? Is that why you came back to town alone?"

"I haven't killed anyone!" she said indignantly.

The very idea that she would hurt Morgan was ridiculous. But she'd just gotten too many questions all at once! And blood in her hair? It couldn't be from the shoot-out with the claim jumpers two days ago, because Morgan had brushed her hair and would have noticed it. She must have scratched her head last night or today if she did in fact have a fall. Why couldn't she remember?

"Of course not, dear," Kayleigh was agreeing with her. "Now, if you don't have clean clothes in that tattered valise, I can bring you some of mine."

Her valise wasn't tattered, it was just dirty like her. But she was out of clean clothes, so she said, "Thank you, mine do need washing."

"I'll send the housekeeper for them, but I expect the doctor to be here soon, so we might want to postpone the bath until after he examines you. You should probably stay in bed until he does. If you have suffered an injury, you don't want to make it worse."

"You're very kind."

"Why wouldn't I be? You're one of us."

What did that mean? Or was Kayleigh being snobbish, because they were both ladies and there were so few of them in Butte? She had denigrated the town, and Morgan, for that matter, though everyone in Butte did the latter. When the woman finally left, Violet got to eat the rest of the meal in peace. But it wasn't enough.

The door had been left open, so the man with the doctor's bag didn't need to knock and simply entered. "You aren't Dr. Cantry," Violet said.

"No, I'm not, nor are we affiliated, though we are on good terms," he said. "I'm Dr. Wilson. The mine owners hired me to tend to their workers, while Cantry sees to the townsfolk. But I deal with his patients when he has to leave town, and he returns the favor when I visit my son in Helena. It works out well."

"So he's currently out of town?"

"Not that I know of. Mr. Sullivan sent for me. Now, please be at ease, miss. I'm not going to ask you to undress."

She hadn't thought he would. After listening to her heart, gently touching the sore areas on her back, and cleaning the cut on the side of her head, he gave her an encouraging diagnosis. The abrasion on her head was superficial and would heal quickly. Her soreness was due to too much time in the saddle, and he attributed her fainting to the heat and lack of adequate food and water. He recommended a few days of rest. Her body agreed. But she still needed to get a telegram off to her brothers before she could think about convalescing quietly.

At least Morgan wouldn't look for her in this house—unless she left it. Maybe she could ask Kayleigh to send the telegram for her. She just wanted to make sure her brothers didn't set out for Montana because she would soon be home in Philadelphia.

Tomorrow or the day after, she intended to buy a train ticket home. She couldn't impose on the Sullivans for more than a day or two, and she was afraid to check into any of the hotels where Morgan could find her. She did *not* want to be abducted in the middle of the night again. But she couldn't stop thinking about him. She hoped he would understand why she'd left and not be hurt that she did so without saying good-bye. She could leave a note at his hotel. She knew he ignored notes there, but if he was looking for her, he might check. She didn't want him to worry or keep looking for her after she left the territory. . . . Bloody hell, she missed him. She had to stop it! He wasn't the man for her, and she didn't want any part of his way of life.

Chapter Thirty-Three

"YOU'RE A MESS, CHILD. Were you really out in that wilderness on your own?"

A different woman had entered the room, a basket on one arm, a dress draped over the other. She was middle-aged and her brown hair was pulled back into a simple bun. Was she the housekeeper? Two boys followed her in with buckets of water that they carried behind a screen in the corner of the room, then left to get more. The basket the woman set on the nightstand had little meat pies in it. Bless her, Violet thought, at least someone knew soup wouldn't be enough.

"Yes," Violet replied. "Foolish, I know. I just got in a bit of a panic after some outlaws absconded with me; then they died—at my feet. It was suddenly paramount that I get back to civilization immediately."

"Oh, you poor dear. I can't imagine witnessing such violence." The woman shook her head and walked to the wardrobe to hang the dress she was carrying.

Mentioning those outlaws brought that gruesome scene

into her mind, so she quickly did what she'd done during her ride to Butte when those images had plagued her—she thought of Morgan and his lovemaking, her real reason for fleeing. She had some very real regret that she would never see him again. He'd protected her, treated her well, was the bravest man she'd ever known. He was smart, even funny, and he'd given her such an amazing romantic experience. But there was a hard, dangerous side to him that enabled him to thrive in this rough, wild land and that she didn't completely understand or feel comfortable with. But she really must have been in a panic to set out for Butte without a care for her own safety. In hindsight, it had been a stupid thing to do.

"I'm Mrs. Hall," the woman said, returning to Violet's bedside. "Abigail Hall, the housekeeper here, though someone's been calling me Abby recently and I rather like it, so it's fine if you do, too, Miss Violet. Do you need help getting to the tub?"

Violet smiled. "I'm not sure, but if there is hot water in it, I'll definitely manage to get into it somehow. I need to send a telegram today, too. I was going to ask Mr. Sullivan's sister to do me that favor."

"Don't bother her about it. She can be . . . forgetful. But I'll bring you some paper and send it for you myself. The doctor mentioned that you need rest."

"Thank you."

"Mr. Sullivan expects you to join him and Miss Kayleigh for dinner tonight," Abigail said. "But I can delay that for a day, if you're not up to it. He might be in an all-fired hurry to talk to you, but I think the doctor's recommendation should be taken into account."

"Why is he in a hurry to speak with me?"

"That man is always in a hurry, but in your case, I expect

he'll make you an offer for your mine, now that you've found it. It can be dirt-poor and he won't care, not if it's near Callahan's mine."

Violet frowned, bothered by the fact that both Kayleigh and Abigail knew she'd been with Morgan and had located her father's mine when she hadn't told either of them that, or mentioned it to Sullivan's men, as far as she could remember. It was beginning to feel a little odd; then again, she hadn't disabused them of their assumptions, had just evaded confirming them, and she would rather not lie about it if she didn't have to.

So she simply said, "I can't sell either mine."

"Well, then, that's that. Perhaps for once he'll take no for an answer."

That sounded somewhat ominous. Nonsense. She was letting Morgan's rants about Sullivan get to her. But Morgan wasn't a liar. Had his obsession with his mine colored his thinking about Sullivan's efforts to acquire it? He had said that Sullivan had left a pile of notes for him at his hotel that he'd never even read. She supposed there was nothing wrong with persistence like that—as long as it didn't turn into coercion. But she wouldn't be in this town long enough to get badgered into selling a mine she wasn't sure she had the right to sell. Even if she did have the right, she couldn't do that to Morgan.

She spent close to an hour in the porcelain tub and didn't care that the water got tepid, not when she'd longed for a real bath for more than a week. Abigail brought her dinner, which served as confirmation that dining with her hosts had been put off, but the housekeeper warned Violet that she would be carried to the dining room tomorrow evening if necessary. There was that Sullivan impatience again.

Of course, that wouldn't be necessary. She was feeling

better, more like herself already. But she was relieved by the delay. Once she turned down Sullivan's offer for the mine, whatever it was, she'd probably have to leave his house immediately. She didn't think he'd actually kick her out, but she'd feel uncomfortable remaining. It was too bad he hadn't invited her to breakfast instead. Then she could go straight to the train station afterward.

She spent most of the next day in bed, getting as much rest as she could before her train journey home. Abigail confirmed that she'd sent the telegram to her brothers. With all of her clothes out of her valise for washing, she'd been able to find all of her hairpins and put her hair up properly. Her clothes had been returned clean and pressed, so she felt quite presentable for dinner. Abigail led her to the dining room.

The interior of the Sullivan house was as grand as its handsomely designed brick façade, which had so impressed her the day she'd come to see where he lived. She walked through well-lit, carpeted hallways past beautifully appointed rooms with fine furniture, tasteful fabrics, and gleaming silver bowls, vases, and mirror frames. She wasn't the first to arrive in the dining room.

Kayleigh, who was standing by a chair at one end of the long table, smiled and greeted her. "Feeling better today, Miss Mitchell?"

"Still a little sore," Violet replied. "But yes, much better and somewhat civilized again."

"Callahan's camp is primitive, is it?"

She didn't confirm that she'd been there, saying instead, "Everything outside of town is."

She glanced about the room at furnishings and luxury goods that couldn't possibly have been bought in this town:

fine china, silver cutlery, a crystal chandelier, a long dining table with ornate legs. It reminded her of Morgan's dream to bring fine things to the people in the territory. She hoped he attained his goal—and she really ought to stop thinking about him.

"Do sit, Miss Mitchell," Shawn Sullivan said as he entered the room.

She swung around to see the man she'd met at dinner with Katie and her fiancé. Sullivan had brown hair sprinkled with gray, but Katie had gotten her green eyes from her father. Wearing a well-cut charcoal-gray business suit, he was smiling and appeared as gregarious as he'd been that night in the hotel dining room. The man couldn't possibly be as nefarious as Morgan had depicted him. He came forward to pull out a chair for her, one that placed her halfway between him and his sister, who took the seats at either end of the table.

"You have been most kind to offer me your hospitality, Mr. Sullivan."

"Of course, of course, how could we not? I'm glad my men encountered you and were able to help you. We were concerned when you left so suddenly with Morgan Callahan after he was spotted in town. I know Katie said you hoped he would guide you to your father's mine; I was just surprised that he agreed to. It couldn't have been pleasant dealing with someone that stubborn and rough around the edges. But I expect you're on good terms with him now?"

An actual direct question to get their assumptions confirmed. There was no point in denying it or trying to evade it this time, when she had in fact told Katie that. And she didn't have an alternate excuse ready for where she'd been all this time.

"Somewhat," she said. "At least when he's not accusing me of working for you."

Shawn laughed. "Did he?"

There was nothing funny about the frustration that Morgan's misunderstanding had caused her, but she wasn't going to be rude, so just said, "For a few days, yes. But we sorted that out."

"My men didn't see him when you rode toward town. Did he really leave you to get back on your own?"

He was asking far too many questions about Morgan. "Is dinner going to be late?" she asked politely with a smile, trying to mitigate her rudeness at evading his question.

He nodded at a servant standing silently by the door. Moments later, the first course arrived. She hoped eating would get his mind off Morgan, because his interest was making her distinctly uncomfortable. She didn't want to reveal any information that might hurt Morgan or her family's interest in the mine. If Sullivan was leading up to asking her where Morgan's mine was, she was going to have to get up and leave.

She tried to distract him further by asking, "Will Katie be living in Chicago with her husband? I thought I might visit her briefly before I return to England."

"Her husband has his own house in Chicago, yes," Shawn answered, but then gave her a pointed look. "Do I need to let our sheriff know that Callahan left you out in the wilderness to die? Is that what you're trying to avoid mentioning?"

She gasped. "He did nothing of the sort! He merely wasn't ready to come to town, but I was, so I left to return to Philadelphia. My brothers will deal with our mine from now on."

"But they aren't here, are they?"

"No, they're still in the East."

"You would go home and then come all the way back here just to take them to the mine?" he said a bit incredulously. "When I could have one of my men do that for you?"

Coming back to Montana wasn't an appealing thought, but she'd known when she slipped away from Morgan that she might have to. Waiting for her brothers to arrive in Butte was an even less appealing solution. Actually, she could probably give them directions, draw them a rough map. She knew the exact mountain range now, just not which exact gorge to climb; but there were only a few gorges, so they would find the right one in a matter of hours. Relief flooded her with that realization. She could catch the train in the morning!

As for Shawn's offer, she merely reminded him, "You don't know where it is, so how could you?"

"Because you will show me before you leave town—then you won't have to return merely to be your brothers' guide."

"After all you've been through, I'm sure you're hoping to see the last of Butte when you go," Kayleigh added.

The man's persistence was becoming annoying. But she wasn't about to admit that she could provide directions to the mines. And she had a solution for the problem he was predicting, without admitting that there was no problem.

"That is very kind of you, but Morgan can—"

He cut in, "Morgan is in the habit of making sure he isn't seen when he comes to town, nor does he pick up messages. Your kin will end up stuck in this town waiting for a man who never shows up."

She was even more annoyed that what he was saying could well be true. Morgan might not accept the notes her brothers would leave for him. He might be too angry at her to deal with Daniel and Evan, although he had to want her brothers to work at the mine long enough to repay the three thousand dollars they'd borrowed from him. Still, she simply couldn't be sure of how he would react at this point. But he'd never forgive her if she led Shawn Sullivan to his mine. That she was positive of.

She wished Sullivan didn't sound so sincere, which made it difficult for her to refuse his offer. But she simply didn't need his help, nor did she believe he had her best interests in mind. She just couldn't let him know that. So she reiterated, "I just want to go home and forget about this horrible ordeal."

"Certainly, and you can do just that as soon as you show me to my new mine. I will pay you a hundred thousand dollars for it. You won't be going home empty-handed, and you'll never have to venture west again."

She was astonished by the offer. A sane person would accept it immediately. But Violet suspected that Sullivan had made such a high offer because the mine was worth more than that. Or he figured he'd be getting another mine for free—Morgan's. *My new mine?* Was he that positive she wouldn't turn him down? Or would it even matter once he knew the mine's location? She needed to stall.

"You are generous, but it's not a decision I can make without first discussing it with my brothers. I assure you I will the moment I arrive home. They will likely want to accept your offer. They are gentlemen, not miners. But I truly can't make this decision on my own."

"Then you can telegraph them in the morning."

He was bullying her, she realized, maneuvering her into a corner. The man really didn't take no for an answer. "No," she said bluntly. "This is far too important a matter to entrust to telegrams. The decision will be made, sir, when I get home."

"Then we will leave first thing in the morning. You can still show me to the mine tomorrow, so when you and your brothers accept my offer, none of you will need to come back here ever again. I am being magnanimous, Miss Mitchell. Keep that in mind."

He stood and left the room before she could reply to his warning. Hadn't she just refused him? Had he somehow not heard her? Regardless, the only thing she'd be doing in the morning was catching a train.

Chapter Thirty-Four

WHAT A HORRIBLE DINNER this had turned out to be, Violet thought as she was left alone in the dining room with Sullivan's sister, who didn't even try to hide her disapproval of Violet's response to her brother's offer. Although she felt most uncomfortable, she finished eating as if nothing untoward had happened. The memory of starving for a day and a half kept her from abandoning the food in front of her.

At least Kayleigh was silent. Violet waited until the servants had cleared the dishes before carefully pointing out, "There is absolutely no reason to pressure me this way."

"Except he's waited long enough."

For something he had no right to? Why was that being laid at her door? But she didn't want to antagonize Kayleigh further, so merely pointed out, "He'll have our answer in a week's time."

"There is only one answer to such generosity, or do you not have the sense to know that my brother offered you too much?"

Had he? The woman couldn't know if it was too much or

too little. Morgan had called the silver in his and her father's mines a mother lode. She'd seen it with her own eyes on the walls, floors, and ceilings of both mines. But none of that mattered, since she didn't own the mine outright and didn't think she could sell her share of an informal partnership. Not that she would. She just wasn't going to explain any of that to these people.

Forcing herself to be polite, she thanked Kayleigh for dinner and returned to her room. Should she leave tonight? Obviously she was no longer welcome there. But to get a hotel room this late . . . no, one more night here wouldn't hurt, and maybe she wouldn't even see the Sullivans again if she left early enough in the morning.

IN THE MIDDLE OF the night, something hard poked her in the side, awakening her. Her first thought was that Morgan had found her and was absconding with her again. But she'd left one lamp lit, turned low, and saw the gun the moment she turned over, and who was holding it.

"Abigail?"

"Shhh," the woman whispered. "No talking yet. Follow me."

Violet was frozen in place, shocked. The woman had seemed nice these last two days, but she didn't really know her, and Abigail worked in what was now a hostile household. But the gun was no longer pointed in her direction. She glanced toward the open window—

"There's no need for that. I'm on your side. You'll find out why in a minute."

Violet didn't believe her. There would be no need for a gun if Abigail were telling the truth. She tried to stall. "I need to dress."

"Shhhhh," the woman hissed more sharply, pointing the gun at her again. "Come as you are."

She got out of bed warily, wondering if she could grab the gun from Abigail without getting shot. Reaching the door, Abigail told her to open it, and then pushed her to the right, away from the main staircase that descended to the first floor. Still being nudged from behind, Violet went around a corner and came to another, narrower staircase that spiraled upward to the third floor or an attic.

She would have balked right then and there if Abigail weren't pushing her from behind and pressing the gun to her back, forcing her up those stairs. And she'd thought Abigail was a kindly woman. What a bad judge of character she was! Sullivan must have ordered this. But why send a woman to do nasty work like this?

When they reached the door at the top of the stairs, Abigail whispered, "Open it!"

A lamp was lit in there, dimly illuminating an attic with a slanted roof. All sorts of boxes and furniture were stored there, pushed to one side, leaving a cleared area for a narrow bed. The person in it sat up as they walked in.

Violet stopped short, unable to take another step, horrified, thrilled, utterly confused. Her whisper was timorous: "Is—is that really you?"

"Come closer, Vi."

Oh, God, it was Charles's voice, his face. She burst into joyful tears. "Papa!" She ran to the bed to wrap her arms around her father. She clung to him tightly, afraid that if she didn't he would disappear. He wasn't dead, he wasn't dead! Please don't let this be a dream!

"Let me look at you, sweetheart."

"Not yet. I don't want to wake up yet. Just hold me like you used to."

He tried to wipe the tears from her cheeks. She felt his touch. She wasn't dreaming. "How is this possible? You were buried!"

"Whoever or whatever was buried, it wasn't me."

She leaned back to look at his face, his wonderful face, thinner, a little older, but still the face of her dear father. "You're alive. This is—you can't imagine."

"I'm glad to see you, too, darling. But what are you doing here? You shouldn't have found out about any of this nasty business."

"Daniel wrote to me in London, asking me to come home to deal with an urgent matter. I was shocked to find my brothers in dire straits and in danger of losing the house."

"Why? I left them enough money."

"No, they spent it all trying to keep up appearances as you instructed. So I came to find you."

He sighed. "It should have been enough, and it would have been if I hadn't had that accident. Where are your brothers now?"

"They're still in Philadelphia—"

"I have three children, two of whom are strapping young men, and it's my daughter who came to this wild territory alone to find me?!"

He sounded quite annoyed with the boys, so she quickly said, "They were trying to hold everything together at home and deal with the banker, who has already come close to seizing the house. Evan is even desperately courting an heiress, whom I hope he won't have to marry now, because he didn't sound smitten with her."

Charles shook his head sadly. "This is my fault. I was foolish with my inheritance. I'm the one who didn't do well by my children. I'm so sorry, sweetheart."

"It doesn't matter," she assured him. "I don't care if I ever have my debut in London, I'm just so happy you're alive!"

"How long have you been in Montana?"

"A few weeks," she said evasively. "When I was told that horrible news about you, well, I tried to find your mine to see if it could save the house, and I met Morgan—"

"What did you think of him?" he cut in.

"Oh, don't get me started!"

He laughed, hugging her closer. "He does take getting used to."

"But he definitely likes you. He's lent us the money to pay off the house loan, so you don't have to worry about that anymore. Now, what are you doing in this attic?"

"He was carried in unconscious," Abigail said behind her.

The housekeeper! She'd forgotten Abigail was even in the room and glanced around to her. "Why didn't you just tell me my father is alive?"

"And get this noisy reaction downstairs where Kayleigh or Mr. Sullivan might've heard you? They can't know that your father is awake, or that you know he's here, or I'll never get him safely out of here. I'm sorry I startled you with the gun, but it was necessary to get you to come along quietly."

"Don't blame Abby," Charles said. "She was very nervous about bringing you up here without being seen."

"As for your question," Abigail continued, "they pulled their scam as soon as Dr. Cantry left town and the miners' doctor took over for him as he usually does. A few of Mr. Sullivan's men sneaked Charles out of the doctor's house and carried him here at night. And they had him buried, supposedly, the very next morning, and merely informed Dr. Cantry about it when he got back to town. Your father has been a prisoner here ever since."

Violet shook her head, finding it hard to grasp all of this. "Wilson seemed like a real doctor."

"He is," Abigail said scornfully. "But he's in the mine owners' pockets, will do whatever they tell him to do and probably asks no questions."

"But why is Father a prisoner?"

"The better question is, how did you come to be in Sullivan's house?" Charles asked.

Violet hesitated for a moment, seeking an explanation that was truthful but held no whiff of scandal. "Once Morgan agreed to pay off your loan, I had to get back to civilization and didn't want to wait until next week for him to escort me back. I sort of sneaked off without telling him—don't say it! I know that was unwise. But I was almost to Butte when I ran into Sullivan's men and fainted, and they brought me here."

"No, dear," Abigail said. "I overheard the men talking to Mr. Sullivan. They knew they'd met up with Violet Mitchell when they heard your British accent. They put chloroform on the bandanna they gave you so they could knock you out and bring you here."

Violet shivered, saw the anger on her father's face. "So that's why the bandanna smelled funny. I have no memory of what happened after that until I woke up in this house."

"Despicable!" Charles said, shaking his head. "Well, I've been in this attic for close to six weeks. I'm actually grateful I was unconscious for most of that time. I only woke up a few days ago. Sullivan doesn't know that yet, and we're keeping it that way." He gave Abigail an adoring smile before he added, "This woman has been my guardian angel. She's the only person in this mansion with a strong and unerring moral compass."

Abigail blushed. "I refuse to be a party to the Sullivans' wickedness, even though Kayleigh threatened to put me in prison for supposedly stealing from them if I told anyone they were hiding Charles up here. It's unconscionable what they're doing to this fine man!"

"Thank you for taking such good care of him," Violet said sincerely. Glancing at her father again, she reminded him, "You still haven't said why you're a prisoner here."

"Abigail overheard Sullivan giving orders to his men. He's waiting for me to regain consciousness so I can tell him where my mine is located." Charles suddenly looked fierce. "But I'm not telling him no matter what happens. I'm not selling out my partner. And the money made from my mine is for my children!"

Violet was horrified, imagining what Sullivan and his men would do to him to gain that information, and glanced frantically at the housekeeper. "Why is Sullivan going to such lengths to take over Morgan's and Papa's mines when he already has one? Is his here in Butte running out of silver?"

"Not yet, but it's only a matter of time. He's greedy for money and power, no amount of either of those things will ever be enough, and he doesn't want anyone challenging his position as the last of the silver kings. He was furious when he found out that Callahan was taking that title away from him. As rich and powerful as he is, no one ever tells him no, except Morgan Callahan. All that did was make Mr. Sullivan mad and more determined than ever. He's one of those men who just don't care who they step on to get what they want."

Violet had told Sullivan no, which made her distinctly uneasy now. "Can't you bring the sheriff here?"

Abigail sighed. "If only it were that simple. Sheriff Gibson is a good man, but he would never believe me, a nobody-housekeeper, if I told him my employer, one of the richest and most powerful mine owners in the territory, was holding your father prisoner in his attic. It's an incredible accusation. The sheriff would never insult Mr. Sullivan by asking to search his house without good cause. And who knows what Mr. Sullivan would do to me if he found out I'd gone to the sheriff? I fear, though, that he would kill Charles rather than let him be found here to incriminate him."

"What about the empty grave? That would be proof, wouldn't it?"

"But it's not empty. They actually had a body, a miner who'd just died and hadn't been buried yet. But Charles shouldn't have been here this long. Mr. Sullivan had intended to deal with him when he regained consciousness, instead of with Callahan. Exchanging him for Callahan's mine was his alternate plan, but the boy never picked up the messages Mr. Sullivan left for him at his hotel."

"Ransom notes? There's our proof."

Abigail shook her head. "I saw one of them on his desk before he had it delivered. It didn't mention ransom. He's too smart to implicate himself like that. His demands will be made in person, without witnesses."

"But it won't work. There's nothing that could make Morgan give up his mine."

"Have you misjudged him?" Charles asked in concern. "He's been nothing but good to me, Violet, when he didn't have to help me. And he pretty much gave me all that silver when he didn't have to do that either."

"But his mine for ransom? He's obsessed with the bloody thing."

"Even if he didn't just hand it over to Sullivan, he would have gotten me out of this if he knew about it. I have no doubt of that."

She blushed, because she didn't doubt it either, not really. Morgan had rescued her, hadn't he? Risked his life to do so. And he'd been right about Shawn Sullivan after all. The man really would resort to any means to get what he wanted, including abduction and murder. She was just so afraid of what would happen to her father if Morgan didn't agree immediately to Sullivan's demands.

She was beginning to feel—trapped. "We should leave now while they're all asleep."

"We can't," Abigail said. "As long as Sullivan is in the house, his guards surround it. We can't even sneak out a window without one of them noticing—not that your father is up to something like that. He's still very weak."

"I can't leave without him," Violet insisted.

"You aren't listening, dear. You're as much a prisoner as he is. They just haven't made that clear yet because you haven't tried to leave."

"Abby isn't being melodramatic, Violet," Charles put in. "Sullivan and his sister came up to the attic the other day. They thought I was still unconscious and were arguing about getting rid of me. They're losing patience, waiting for me to wake up.

I'm surprised I didn't give myself away, with them standing there talking about killing me in a few more weeks."

"It's going to happen sooner now that they have you, child," Abigail warned her. "They will use him as leverage against you if you don't pretend to cooperate and take them to the mines. But once they have what they want, they can't just let you go, either. So this needs to be resolved before that happens."

"How?!" Violet was terrified for both her father and herself.

"He plans to leave with you and his men in the morning. He's certain you can lead him right to Callahan's camp because you've been there. Can you?"

"Yes, I can now. But when Morgan took me there, he went by a circuitous route that took a full extra day, and he blind-folded me for the last six hours of that trip, just so I couldn't lead anyone back there."

Charles grinned. "That's perfect—you can honestly say that it took you nearly two days to reach it, when it's only a half day's ride from town. Try to stay on the east road as long as you can, so the sheriff can easily find you."

She glanced between them. "You two have already planned this?"

Abigail nodded. "And for it to work, you will have to go with Sullivan willingly. If he has to force you by revealing that your father is alive and threatening to kill him if you don't take him to the mine, he'll leave too many men behind to guard the house, and I won't be able to help Charles escape."

"Aren't there a lot of servants here who could stop you?" Violet asked.

"They won't, but Kayleigh will try to. However, she leaves the house every day for one reason or another, usually before noon. We will leave as soon as she does and go straight to the sheriff. And I'll count how many men Sullivan rides out with to make sure the sheriff takes more than that number with him. So just cooperate as long as you can. You can do so grudgingly if you think that will help—yes, I was listening outside the dining room door tonight and heard your protests against taking him to the mine. Just get as far from town as you can before you admit you're not sure where the mines are. We need half a day at least to sneak your father out of the house and get him to the sheriff, and the sheriff may need a few more hours to round up a big enough posse."

Violet nodded, trying not to reveal how worried and scared she was. She wished Morgan were here to deal with all of this for her.

Her father must have sensed her unease, because he said, "I'm sorry for putting you in this dangerous situation, Violet. But I'm so proud of the brave, capable woman you've become. I have faith that you will keep a level head and lead Sullivan and his men astray until the sheriff can apprehend them."

She smiled weakly, but to put her father at ease, she joked, "It sounds like I'll be sleeping outdoors again tomorrow night."

"You just need to buy us time tomorrow until the sheriff catches up with you," he stressed. "Can you do that?"

"Of course," Violet said. Well, what choice did she have?

Chapter Thirty-Five

FOUR DAYS. MORGAN THOUGHT that by now he would have found Violet—one way or another. He'd searched all the hotels and lodgings in Butte, checked the train station each day to make sure she hadn't bought a ticket, spent half a day watching Shawn Sullivan's house, though that had been a waste of time. And each day he returned to the wilderness to continue the search, south, north, even a day farther east.

His anger kept him going, refused to let him stop. It had been with him from the moment he'd realized she'd sneaked off while he was working in the mine. The one day he didn't come out for lunch, damnit! And she'd done it after they'd made love, after he'd felt a closeness to her that he'd never felt with another woman. And she'd started it by asking him to kiss her and telling him not to stop. Had that been her way of thanking him because she'd already known she was leaving? Yet he recalled how upset she'd been that day after being captured by the claim jumpers and witnessing their deaths.

She was a young lady out of her element who'd been scared

that night and needed someone to comfort and protect her, and while she had desired him at the time, she might have regretted what she'd done. Of course she would. She was used to sophisticated, wealthy noblemen, even talked about marrying one. She'd never settle for a mountain-man miner like him. One more thing to infuriate him, that she didn't think he was good enough for her.

No matter what came to mind to explain her taking off like that, it didn't diminish his anger. It was a fact that she'd left the moment she'd gotten what she wanted from him, the money to pay off that loan on her family's home and a mining partnership that would last long enough for her to pay it back. Would she have stayed if he'd agreed to a permanent partnership? Possibly, but he'd never know now.

He couldn't even guess which way she'd gone. That was why he hadn't found her yet. The rain had washed away her horse's hoof marks, and he'd done too good a job confusing her about the location of the mines. He'd even ridden to Dillon, the last town before Butte on the train line, to see if she'd bought her train ticket there. If she'd ridden directly west and run into the train tracks, and remembered that town from when she'd arrived, she might think she was closer to Dillon and head south to it. But she hadn't been there either, and his anger had turned into fear. Four damn days. Could she really still be alive out here in this heat, without food?

He'd returned to his cabin late last night for a few hours of sleep and to check if Texas had left another note. His friend was out searching for Violet, too, but his latest note was no more encouraging than the others. Morgan had ended up sleeping till noon, a waste of good daylight, but he wasn't surprised, with as little sleep as he'd been getting since she'd left him. Left him? It did feel personal when it shouldn't.

He had planned to check Butte again and then Helena today, though with this late start, Helena might have to wait until tomorrow. She might have gone there just to hide while she waited for her brothers to arrive.

He rode north to the east road. Halfway there he saw the dust cloud, not big like the ones stagecoaches made because of their speed, but big enough to indicate more than a couple of riders. He stopped and pulled out Charley's spyglass. Eight horses riding at a slow trot—and he spotted Violet on one almost immediately. How could he miss that silly parasol?

His relief was tremendous, until he saw who was riding next to her, and then his rage surged back, worse than ever, because he'd been right from the start—she really was in cahoots with Shawn Sullivan. Had the man promised her a fortune for her mine that night he met her at the hotel? She'd just had to find her way there first, and she'd done that and was now leading him right to both mines for her big payday. Sullivan wouldn't care that she wasn't in a position to sell Charley's mine; he'd pay just as much for the location.

And they were almost there. They would notice him soon after they left the road to ride south. He was so furious he couldn't even think how to keep them away from his mountain. They were too close, and besides, she was leading them right to it. He really had misjudged her. *This* was what she'd apologized for with the gift of her body. She'd known all along that she would betray him.

He headed back to the mountain to take cover in the first copse of trees, a mile or so before Texas's camp. He pulled out the spyglass again; Sullivan's party hadn't come into view yet. He waited, still not sure how he was going to handle this. Fire the first shot? He'd have cover, they wouldn't. Or maybe he should just go blow up both mines before they reached them. Now, *that* sounded like a plan he could live with. And he'd beat them to town and have Charley's mine invalidated to boot. Revenge at its finest. So why did it give him a sick feeling in his gut?

He trained the spyglass again, then frowned when there was still no sign of a dust cloud. Cautiously he rode, back toward the road, but still didn't see it. What the hell? He kept going, and when he finally reached the road, he saw the tail end of their cloud—beyond his mountain.

He started to laugh. She didn't know where the mines were. Had she found her way back to Butte by sheer luck, or had she encountered someone who had shown her the way?

He began to follow them, staying far enough back that he could only see that dust cloud with the spyglass. When they made camp for the night and settled down to sleep, he was going to steal her away from them. He wasn't going to leave her out here with Sullivan long enough for her to eventually figure out where the mines were. He was going to take her straight to the claims office in Butte and have her watch as he invalidated Charley's claim. Just desserts, as far as he was concerned.

Chapter Thirty-Six

VIOLET'S GUN WAS IN her valise. No one had searched it to see if she had a weapon, probably because she was a woman. She'd been told to leave the valise behind, that she wouldn't need it, but she'd refused, so one of the men had tied it to her saddle. Having her own gun close at hand was the only thing that kept her from panicking during that long day of riding surrounded by guards who had the look of hardened men.

They definitely weren't Shawn's miners, each with a gun on their hip and a rifle on their saddle; they wore vests, their coats already removed—it was going to be another hot day. These were likely the men that Morgan had told her had broken into his crates at the train station and beaten her father in an alley. Irish easterners, probably from Chicago where Shawn was from and who obviously didn't mind breaking the law any more than their employer did.

Kayleigh had awakened her at six o'clock that morning, telling her to be dressed to travel, as if she'd already agreed to this trip, so she'd replied, "An excellent idea, in case my brothers do agree to sell the mine."

"Oh?"

"Obviously, none of us will have to come back this way if your brother knows where the mine is located."

"Of course." Kayleigh smiled. "Smart of you to finally realize that, lass."

They had been a little late in leaving, due to some emergency at Sullivan's mine that he'd had to deal with, so they hadn't departed until nine o'clock. She'd had to mention when they left that it was going to take a day and a half to get to the mine. She'd expected that acquiring more provisions might delay them further, but they'd apparently already prepared for being gone several days.

It was another sweltering day on the road. And she couldn't stop worrying. This plan had sounded fine when she'd discussed it last night with Abigail and her father, but what if Abigail was a part of Sullivan's plan and was just pretending to be on their side? Had the housekeeper really gotten Charles out of the house today? Would the sheriff show up to rescue her?

At least she was pleased when they passed Morgan's mountain. She made sure not to even glance at it. But when they made camp that night, Shawn Sullivan didn't hide his impatience.

He joined her at the campfire where she was sitting. It was one of three his men had started, and they were close enough to the road for the sheriff to see the firelight if he hadn't stopped for the night, too.

Sullivan looked frustrated and tired, but his tone was sharp when he said, "If you've lied about how long this trip is going to take—"

"I haven't lied," she cut in. "It took a full day and a half to get there, plus a few extra hours of Morgan riding at night. The last thing I saw before he blindfolded me was three mountains pretty far away in different directions, north, south, and east, similar to where we are now. I don't know which one he headed to after that."

"But you managed to get back to Butte. You can't even remember that route?"

"What I did was get horribly lost for a day and a half until I had the good fortune to run across your surveyors. My only guess is that the mines are north of this road, because he did turn north at one point before I got blindfolded."

He moved away, but her trembling set in as soon as he did. She didn't know what she was going to do if the sheriff didn't arrive soon, at least before dawn. She could only keep them on that road for about three more hours, because she'd already told Sullivan that they'd turned north. She was going to have to pick a spot to do that while the three mountains were still within view. Would the sheriff notice their tracks leaving the road tomorrow if he had halted his search for the night? Bloody hell, where was he? He should have arrived by now.

She'd been allowed to sleep by herself beside one of the campfires, a little distance away from the men. But she couldn't sleep, was attuned to every little sound around her, a cough, a snore, the crackle of the fires, crickets that chirped too loudly, everything but the sound she most wanted to hear—the posse arriving. She felt like crying again, but didn't. She wanted to escape, and gave that some thought. But that would give away her plan, reveal that she wasn't really cooperating, so she forced herself to have faith in Abigail and the sheriff. She couldn't lose her nerve at this point!

A hand went over her mouth. She hadn't heard him coming but could see him clearly in the firelight, Morgan leaning over her. He'd come to rescue her again! He really did care for her. She tried to sit up. The hand on her mouth tightened. Did he think she'd give him away?

Before she realized what was happening, he picked her up, threw her over his shoulder, and moved silently away from Sullivan's camp. Then he started running. She bounced painfully against his shoulder and back, gasping for breath. How long could he run and carry her this way? When he finally set her down on her feet, she leaned over, drawing air into her lungs. Morgan loomed over her, and she saw Caesar hobbled nearby. She straightened up and whispered, "Thank you for rescuing me again. This situation isn't what it appears to be. I wasn't taking Sullivan to your—"

"Shut up."

He looked so furious she couldn't keep silent. "I didn't betray you!"

He grabbed her by the shoulders. "I don't want to hear your lies." His mouth covered hers abruptly in a kiss that was rough, passionate, and deeply satisfying. She slipped her hands around his neck and pressed her body against his, responding with equal fervor, so relieved he'd come for her, thrilled by the intensity of his desire and the way his hand was caressing her backside, pushing her closer to him. But . . . he'd said she was lying? She had to make him understand.

Pressing her hands against his shoulders, she shoved, and he stopped kissing her. When she looked up at his face, she was startled by the fierce anger in his eyes. She'd only seen it once before—the night she'd pointed the shotgun at him. "You're mistaken—"

"No, *you* made a mistake. You should have shown your true colors earlier. We could have had a lot more fun in the sack before you sold me out to Sullivan."

"That's not true!" She struggled to put some distance between them, but Morgan held on to her. "I'm here to help—"

They both froze at the sound of pistols cocking.

"Let the lady go, or you'll get more than one bullet in your back."

Violet gasped. Oh, God, three men were pointing pistols at them. Sullivan's guards.

Morgan released her. One guard immediately confiscated his Colt. Another approached her to ask, "Are you all right, miss?" She just nodded. The third man took the hobbles off Caesar before they began the trek back to Sullivan's campsite, two of the guards flanking Morgan, holding their guns ready.

As she walked, Violet couldn't tell if she was shivering from the cold or trembling with fear for herself and Morgan. But she felt no relief when she saw the glow of the three campfires. Sullivan was standing by one of them. A guard ran ahead and spoke with him.

"Well, well, Callahan, finally we meet again." Sullivan was smiling. "But you show up in the middle of the night and try to abduct Miss Mitchell and do who knows what else? I'll have to turn you over to the sheriff. You should be thrown in jail for attempting something that low."

"No, Sullivan, I just hate to see my dead partner's daughter with scum like you. She doesn't know anything. Let her go. You can deal with me now."

Sullivan laughed. "Too late. I don't need you anymore. Miss Mitchell is going to show me where her father's mine is located, and yours too, as I understand they're right close to each other. In fact, I offered her a hundred thousand dollars for her mine, and she's going to get her brothers' approval to sell it to me."

Morgan snorted. "She might look like a lady, but she's a viper and a liar. She doesn't own that mine; it's an invalid claim. She can't sell it to you or anyone else. Besides, she doesn't know where it is. She's led you on a wild goose chase."

"I think you might be the one who's lying."

Sullivan turned to Violet expectantly. She was horrified that she had to lie and act like the viper Morgan had just labeled her in order to preserve the rescue plan.

"I *do* own the mine and I know exactly where it is," she insisted. "He's the one lying to you!"

Morgan glowered at her before turning back to his nemesis. "Don't get taken in, Sullivan. She might have spent some time in my camp driving me crazy, but she doesn't know the exact location."

Sullivan smiled. "But you do." And then he told his men, "Tie him up, and it better be as tight as if he were in a prison cell. He gets away and you're all fired." Yet he was smiling again at Morgan when he added, as if giving Morgan a choice, "Why don't you spend the night with us and show us to the mine tomorrow morning?"

"I saw you coming. There's no way you'll ever get your hands on those mines. I planted dynamite charges in them. You go near them and step in the wrong places, half the mountain will come down on you."

The guards looked a little worried, hearing that, but Sullivan didn't. "Nice bluffing, Callahan. But you'll take me there, and you'll step in the right spots, otherwise Miss Mitchell could have a fatal accident. No one would be surprised if a gently reared lady fell off her horse and broke her neck riding up these rocky slopes."

Violet blanched. Morgan was gagged before he could respond. She stared at him, but he didn't seem to notice because he was glaring daggers at Sullivan as the man walked away. One of the guards nudged Morgan pretty hard in the side with his boot, sneering, "There's no need to wait till the morn."

"What do you think you're doing, O'Donnell?" Shawn demanded as he walked back to the group.

The guard stepped back, but wasn't contrite. "I was thinking to get the answers you want."

"Beating him isn't necessary, not when we have her. We can't leave now in any case, no matter what he says, so he's got the night to decide if the lass lives or not. That's all the torture he needs. Miss Mitchell or his mine."

Oh, good Lord, what a choice to give Morgan when he was so angry at her! Violet did the only sensible thing she could think of at that point—she started screaming as loudly as she could and wasn't going to stop. She ran around the camp, trying to evade Sullivan's guards, who definitely wanted her to stop it. But the sound would travel far, especially in the stillness at night. If the sheriff was close enough to save them, he'd hear it. If not, she and Morgan would both die tomorrow.

Chapter Thirty-Seven

VIOLET WAS TACKLED BY two of the guards, who gagged her and tied her up for the night. They put her on a bedroll and tossed a blanket over her. She craned her neck to try to catch a glimpse of Morgan, who lay behind her, which was a little too difficult to attempt more than a few times, and he wasn't looking at her anyway. She so regretted not getting a chance to convince him that she hadn't betrayed him. He obviously hadn't believed her when she'd said it. And now she might never get another chance.

When she awoke, dawn had come and gone. The sun hadn't topped the ranges to the east yet, but the sky was bright with early morning light. Just one campfire was burning and a pot of coffee was boiling on a rack that had been placed over it. By rolling her body, she managed to sit up, and glanced over to where Morgan lay, but couldn't tell if his eyes were open yet. Her hands, which were tied behind her back, tingled uncomfortably.

One of the guards poured cups of coffee for Sullivan and

himself, but didn't offer her one, so she had a feeling she wasn't going to be untied today. Why would they bother when it was likely she'd have an "accident" later and end up in a shallow grave before day's end?

Violet was startled by the thunderous sound of hoofbeats. Sullivan looked alarmed as at least twenty men on horseback surrounded his camp.

He grabbed the arm of one of his men and shoved him toward Violet. "Untie her immediately, and take off that gag!"

But when the man took a step toward Violet, a bullet hit the dirt between them, changing his mind. Rifles were already aimed at Sullivan and his men.

As the posse dismounted and started handcuffing Sullivan's guards and collecting their weapons, Sullivan walked confidently over to a big, barrel-chested man who looked older than the others and remained seated on his horse. "You're just the man I wanted to see, Sheriff Gibson. Callahan over here"—he gestured toward Morgan, who was still bound and gagged—"showed up last night and abducted Miss Mitchell. If my men hadn't rescued her, good Lord, who knows what would have happened to her. Arrest that scoundrel immediately!"

The sheriff tipped his wide-brimmed hat back and smiled down at Shawn. It wasn't a friendly smile. "Save it for the judge, Mr. Sullivan. Imagine my surprise, if you can, when a dead man walked into my office yesterday, and quite a tale Charles Mitchell had to tell. Oh, and even better, your own housekeeper confirmed every word of it."

As one of the men in the posse helped Violet to her feet and took off her gag and untied her, she saw that Sullivan no longer looked so self-righteous. In fact, he was scowling. "I just took the burden off Dr. Cantry by letting Mitchell convalesce in my house. He should be thanking me, not accusing me of wrong-doing."

Sheriff Gibson laughed. "Is that so? Then I'm guessing you don't know that he regained consciousness sooner than you thought and was awake to hear you and your sister discussing when and how to kill him?"

Sullivan's face turned red. Gibson continued, "So here's the thing, Mr. Sullivan. Abduction and confinement of good law-abiding folks doesn't sit well with our circuit judge. Falsifying a man's death and causing his family untold grief, when all along you've got the fella imprisoned in your attic, won't either. And here you are giving me even more evidence against you, out here trying to steal a couple of mines, hog-tying the two owners of those mines. The judge really won't like that charge, not when he's a mine owner himself, you know. But I do thank you, Mr. Sullivan. Been a long while that I've been hankering to tell you that you're under arrest, and that's what I'm telling you now."

"You're making a mistake, Sheriff Gibson," Sullivan said furiously. "I warn you—"

The sheriff interrupted sharply, "Like I said, save it for the judge. You know they hang horse thieves out here. Won't be long before they start hanging mine thieves, too. You better hope the judge hasn't reached that point yet. And don't think I won't be presenting my earlier suspicions alongside all these new facts, like those two mines on either side of yours that you miraculously managed to buy right before the owners had very odd accidents. But you were careful then not to leave a trail of crumbs. Weren't so careful this time, now, were you?"

"I haven't killed anyone."

"That anyone knows about. But I have not one but two

signed statements that you intended to commit murder. And I reckon I'll have two more before we leave here." He paused to look at Morgan, who'd been freed from his bonds, and asked him, "Did he threaten to kill you in so many words?"

"He was very clear that he'd kill Miss Mitchell if I didn't show him the way to my mine."

The sheriff glanced at Violet. "Did you hear Mr. Sullivan say that?"

"I can repeat every word exactly," she assured him.

Gibson grinned. "Then I reckon it's a good thing I brought some paper with me so you both can write it all down. No need for you two to wait until the court convenes. Signed statements are just as good around here." And then his eyes pinned Sullivan again. "The judge just might think that's enough to warrant a hanging. Stew on that on the way back to town."

"After my lawyer gets through with you, you'll never work in this territory again, Gibson!" Sullivan snarled.

"Someone gag him." The sheriff's response drew a few chuckles from the posse.

Violet rubbed her wrists and took a step toward Morgan, but the nasty look he gave her stopped her cold. That hurt, his not wanting to talk to her or share this moment of relief with her. She remembered the angry, possessive way he'd kissed her last night, and also the beautiful, passionate night they'd shared when he was so loving and irresistible, the many caring things he'd done for her. She would never forget any of that, but it was just as well that they keep their distance from each other, because she would be leaving soon. Yet she hoped she would have a chance to explain to him why she'd run off.

"Are you all right, Miss Mitchell?" Sheriff Gibson was approaching her.

"I am now, thanks to you, Sheriff. I was so scared that you wouldn't arrive in time."

"We caught up to you last night, but didn't want to attempt to capture Sullivan while it was dark, which could have turned messy with men dying needlessly. But you weren't in any more danger. I left a couple men to watch your camp. This bunch wasn't going anywhere without my knowing about it. You were very brave to go along with Sullivan and lead him on a wild goose chase so Miss Hall could get your father out of Sullivan's house. They're safe at my office with Deputy Barnes. I reckon you and Miss Hall are the heroines of the day. Without you, Sullivan's ruthlessness and perfidy wouldn't have been exposed so thoroughly."

She blushed a little, glancing at Morgan to see if he'd heard the sheriff's praise and understood now that she hadn't betrayed him. He was within earshot of the sheriff's voice, but he wasn't looking her way.

Sheriff Gibson had followed her gaze, and addressed Morgan: "Didn't recognize you at first without your beard, Callahan. Isn't this little lady amazing?"

Morgan *still* didn't look at her when he replied, "She's the bravest debutante I've ever met."

Violet blushed further with the realization that he'd never met any other debutantes, so he wasn't really agreeing with the sheriff.

Once the prisoners were secured and the posse was ready to depart, Gibson told Violet and Morgan, "I won't be returning to Butte with you. I'm going to take half the posse and the prisoners and veer off to Helena where the territory judge is holding court this week. I don't want to wait for the trial to be held in Butte. That's just asking for a riot, and I don't doubt it will happen if Sullivan's miners get wind that's he's under arrest and they might lose their jobs if their employer gets convicted."

"But what about Sullivan's sister, Kayleigh?" Violet asked. "She knew my father was a prisoner in that house and was in on the plot to steal our mine."

"I went to their house to see for myself where your father had been kept and to confront Miss Sullivan for her part in it. She started crying and confessed that she's had to do whatever her brother ordered because she is utterly dependent on him, so she had no choice. Whether that's true or not, I don't know, but I'm not partial to arresting women, so I told her to catch the next train out of town. The judge will decide if that family gets to keep their holdings here."

Violet immediately thought of Katie. She didn't think the daughter should be punished for the father's sins. "Other than Kayleigh, who knew exactly what her brother had been doing and seemed as rapacious as he was, I doubt the rest of his family knew how ruthless he could be."

"That family is rich as sin. I wouldn't worry about the rest of them."

Morgan didn't look happy that any Sullivan was escaping justice, but then he'd come very near to dying today. But maybe his disgruntled look was just for her. She was still getting the cold shoulder from him. Even after she'd told him last night that she hadn't betrayed him. Even after he'd just heard about the part she'd played in their rescue. He had heard it, hadn't he? How could he not?

Nine men escorted them to Butte, but they were widely spread out along the road since Violet and Morgan didn't need protection now. Violet wasn't sure how she ended up riding next to Morgan a few hours later, but it was just after they passed his mountain, which was the perfect time to break the ice with him.

She glanced his way and asked, "You aren't going. . . . ?" She didn't say "to your mine," just nodded back toward his mountain range.

He shook his head. "And miss seeing Charley alive and kicking?"

"I don't think he'll be kicking for a while. The ordeal has left him very weak. But you can't imagine how happy I was to find him alive."

"That must have been an incredible surprise."

"I confess, at first sight I was afraid he was a ghost! But of course that was silly, and yes, it was unbelievably amazing that he isn't dead after all."

"You're fortunate that someone in that house knew what Sullivan was up to and didn't like it."

"Yes, today would have turned out quite differently without Abigail Hall's help."

He still looked so unapproachable, reminding her of the bear she'd first met. She regretted thinking the worst of him, not that he'd been the best company those first few days she'd known him, but she'd been at her worst, too. While he'd protected her again and again, from wild animals, from muscle pain—well, he'd tried to—from outlaws. He'd even taught her to shoot so she could protect herself. And he'd danced with her under the stars! Yet she'd repaid him by disappearing without a word. She was afraid she might have hurt his feelings or his pride. And he'd obviously looked for her. All those days since she'd left his camp? No wonder he was so mad!

She'd been trying to speak normally, as if it didn't feel like they were complete strangers again, but she had to explain.

"You may not have guessed, but I was terribly distraught by the violent encounter with those two outlaws. When you went to work the next day as if none of it had happened, the horror of it all came back to me and I sort of panicked. I simply had to get back to civilization immediately, but you'd said you wouldn't take me until the following week."

"You could have said so, instead of taking off on your own when you didn't know where you were."

"But I did know. One of those outlaws mentioned Butte and gave me rough directions to town before you arrived to rescue me. He said it was only a half day's ride away, so I thought I could get there before dark." She wasn't going to mention that that hadn't happened, but did admit, "Yes, it was beyond reckless, and I walked right into Sullivan's plot when his men found me before I got to town. But I was never a party to any of Shawn Sullivan's illegal machinations."

"Doesn't matter. You made your choice," he said, and spurred his horse forward, ending the conversation.

What the bloody hell did that mean? But she was afraid she knew. He wasn't talking about trusting him to change his plans and take her to town if he knew she couldn't bear to stay at his camp another minute. Her "choice" had been to leave him instead of pursuing a relationship with him. With everything this man could make her feel, she wasn't sure she'd made the right choice.

Chapter Thirty-Eight

T HEY ARRIVED BACK IN Butte by dusk. Violet went straight
to the sheriff's office. Morgan followed her. Deputy Barnes immediately stood up from behind the desk. "Been expecting you
after one of the posse rode ahead to give us the good news.
Heard congratulations are in order, that you were quite the
heroine, Miss Mitchell." And then he glanced at Morgan and
laughed. "What happened to you? Misplace your beard somewhere?" And then he laughed harder.

"Not funny, Deputy." Morgan glowered at him. "Where's
Charley Mitchell?"

Morgan left as soon as they were told which hotel Charles
was in. Violet ended up following him now. All without a word
to each other. And she was annoyed that the hotel happened to
be the very one she'd been kicked out of—Morgan's hotel. Yes,
of course it would be. The one time Charles had come to town
with Morgan, they'd probably both stayed there.

She wasn't happy about it. She even glared at the desk clerk, daring him not to speak to her when she asked for her father's room number and requested a room for herself for the night. The bloody fool actually looked at Morgan first to get his permission. And Morgan gave it with a nod.

Her annoyance mounted over that ridiculous byplay. While Morgan asked for his messages, she marched upstairs and knocked on her father's door. She had to knock several times before he answered. She entered to find him lying in bed, looking as if he'd just awakened from a nap. Her anger was replaced by a burst of happiness. She was never going to get over this joy that he was alive.

She gave him a brilliant smile. "It's done, Papa. Shawn Sullivan has been arrested and taken to Helena to be tried in a court of law."

"That's wonderful news," Abigail said from a chair by the window.

"Abigail! I didn't see you there."

Charles chuckled. "I keep telling her to stop watching me sleep."

The housekeeper stood up with a slight blush and approached Violet. "I was just making sure he didn't need anything while we waited for you to get back. I'm very pleased you've returned safely."

"It all went as planned." Violet hugged the older woman. "Thank you so much for everything you've done to help us. We couldn't have come through this without you."

"I'm just glad it all worked out. But now you're here, I could do with a nap myself. I was falling asleep in that chair. We'll see each other later, dear."

Violet nodded and turned to her father again with another wide smile. "We can go home now and—"

"Hell, Charley, you're skin and bones," Morgan interrupted as he came into the room moments after Abigail left.

"Not quite, though it feels like it," Charles admitted with a grin as he sat up. "Good to see you again, partner."

"Not nearly as good as it is to see you," Morgan said with a chuckle. "I'm sorry you had to go through that hell, but as your daughter told you, it's over."

"I slept through most of it, and you never knew it happened. We were both spared that, at least."

"Don't forget about the grief," Violet put in, but immediately regretted saying it. She joined her father, sitting on the edge of the bed. "I'm sorry. It's going to take a while for me to let go of all the emotional upset Sullivan caused. Did you send word to Daniel and Evan that you're alive?"

He extended an arm, and Violet moved closer to him so he could put it around her. "Not yet. I will in the morning."

"No, I will. You're not getting out of that bed until you're ready."

"I'm not sick, dearest, just weak. Dr. Cantry was summoned to examine me and spent most of his visit apologizing for what happened. Needless to say, he won't be asking Dr. Wilson for any more favors. That fellow actually skipped town. The deputy checked. And Cantry's prescription was simply food and more food to get my strength back, but I can't seem to eat very much at one sitting yet."

"Abigail didn't go back to that house, did she?" Violet asked.

"No, we got her a room here," Charles said. "She's done with that family and mentioned returning to Chicago to live with her brother. I think I'm going to miss her. She cared for me the whole while and fussed over me like a mother hen once I woke up."

Violet grinned. "I'm good at fussing."

"You're good at bossing, sweetness," Charles corrected gently. "Even in your letters!"

She laughed. "Let's call it fussing, shall we? But you don't have to part ways with Abigail Hall. Our home in Philadelphia is currently without a housekeeper, so you could offer her the job. And she can help you shop for furniture. I wouldn't trust that task to my brothers."

"What happened to—?" Charles started, but then sighed. "This damned heart. If it hadn't caused me to hit my head that day, I would have paid off that loan in just one more week, thanks to Morgan. The situation was never supposed to turn so dire that your brothers would summon you back from London, but I'm so fortunate that you came."

"And now it's not dire, thanks to Morgan," she said.

Charles smiled at Morgan. "I understand you've been incredibly generous again in loaning my daughter enough money to stop her immediate worries. We'll need to discuss how to pay that back—"

"I've already done that, Papa," Violet cut in. "Morgan and I struck up a new partnership agreement whereby Evan and Daniel will come west to work in the mine until they earn enough money to pay Morgan back, and then maybe"—she glanced at Morgan questioningly—"Morgan will agree to a fifty-fifty arrangement for the boys to continue mining."

"Your daughter needs a dowry for her English lord," Morgan said scornfully.

Charles looked puzzled. Violet blushed and told her father, "We can discuss England later."

"Any arrangement we made was discussed before we knew Charley is alive," Morgan said. "He and I will discuss a mutually satisfactory arrangement when you aren't around."

"He's right, sweetness, you no longer need to concern yourself with business matters."

Feeling a little hurt, she offered, "Should I leave so you can do that now?"

"No, of course not," Charles said, and hugged her more tightly to him. "Morgan and I will find time to talk later. We're not going anywhere yet, and I'm certainly not leaving Montana until I hear the results of Sullivan's trial."

"That could take a few more days, at the very least," Morgan pointed out.

"I've already concluded that," Charles replied. "And as long as there is going to be a delay, I intend to return to the mines tomorrow."

"Tomorrow?!" Violet and Morgan said almost at the same time, but Violet added, "Out of the question. It's too soon for you to ride a horse."

"Nonsense, my dear. I might have to ride slowly, but I assure you that I can ride."

He wanted to retrieve his hidden money, she realized. And, while she was dying of curiosity to know where he'd hidden it, she was more concerned about his health.

Charles added, "I promise I'll stop at the slightest twinge, and I can rest up there at a camp for a few days. By the time we return, the sheriff should be back in town. And besides, I have a few things to pick up there before we go home. Mainly I left my pocket watch in the cabin. You know that watch is very

dear to me. It's a symbol of love and the happy marriage I enjoyed with your mother, something I want to leave to you to
ensure you're blessed with a marriage that is as happy as mine
was. I'm not leaving the territory without it."

Touched by her father's words, Violet hated having to tell
him the bad news. "It's not there. I checked your valise as soon
as I thought about that memento."

"That's not where I kept it. I shaved every morning and
kept my shaving tools in a bag on the shelf. I would put the
watch in it every night to remind me to put it back in my
pocket in the morning. Otherwise I forgot it. Dreadful habit of
mine to forget about trinkets if they're not right under my
nose."

"I forgot about that little bag of yours," Morgan confessed.

"No reason for you to remember it when you were always
in the mine by the time I performed my morning ablutions.
But the day I had the accident, I didn't shave. I'd already had a
few twinges in my chest and didn't feel up to it. By noon I was
feeling better and hurried out to the mine. You know the rest.
Besides, I'm also going back to dig out my money. It appears I
need to refurnish the house as soon as I get home, and that
money will come in handy."

Dig it out, not up? "Where did you hide it? I searched
everywhere," Violet said.

He grinned playfully. "You'll see."

She'd rather not. She'd rather talk him out of going back
there. Morgan could gather her father's belongings and money
and send them to him in Philadelphia. If he would. If he
stopped being mad at her long enough to do them a favor.

She waited for him to suggest it, but instead Morgan said,
"I'll see if I can borrow a wagon tomorrow and get it fitted with

a mattress for you. If you insist on going up to the mines, you can at least do it with a care for your health."

"You know that a wagon will make the trip even longer," Charles pointed out.

"Yeah, I know," Morgan said on his way out the door.

Violet's mouth had dropped open, so she snapped it shut. Then she couldn't help saying in a grouchy tone, "He always gets his way, doesn't he?"

"That's been my experience, but it's usually all to the good, so it doesn't trouble me in the slightest."

She wished she could say the same.

Chapter Thirty-Nine

Violet felt nostalgic as they approached Morgan's mountain and crossed the river near the spot where Morgan had taken her fishing. It felt so long ago, yet only a little more than a week had passed since then. It had been such a fun, idyllic day. They'd laughed, they'd talked, really talked, and without rancor for a change. She even smiled at the memory of dropping the fish on his chest and his reaction to it. Should she suggest another round of fishing tomorrow? Would he offer to go with her this time? Would he even remember how much fun they'd had that day?

She sighed. He'd refuse, of course, and then she'd be embarrassed for even asking. That wall of ice still stood between them, and that cold shoulder definitely kept her from indulging in fantasies that he could be more than a business partner to her.

Texas rode in not long after they reached the cabin. He greeted Charles warmly. He merely looked at Violet and grunted, which caused her cheeks to go scarlet and Morgan to tell her, "He searched for you, too," before he and Texas left the room.

"Is there something I should know about?" Charles asked.

"Other than Morgan and I are back to being enemies, or at least he thinks so?" she said drily, but immediately wished she'd kept that to herself.

"That sounds . . . extreme."

"It's not," she replied. "It was extreme at the beginning when he didn't believe I was your daughter. Then when he did believe it, we got along. Now we don't again."

"Because?"

"He hasn't said so in so many words, but I have to assume it's because I left the camp without telling him and he felt obliged to look for me—and didn't expect to find me with his worst enemy."

"That wasn't your fault."

"No, it wasn't."

"I understand why he's angry that you ran off and put yourself in danger. But who can quibble with the results of your impulsive decision? I was rescued and Sullivan is in jail."

She couldn't tell her father about the other consequences of her impulsive decision, so she just smiled, then said, "As for Morgan's still being in a snit about it, I don't see that it matters. He's your friend. He doesn't need to be mine, does he?"

"The atmosphere would be more congenial if he were, but I suppose not."

Morgan came back in, just long enough to hand Violet a stack of money. "Your half of the reward Texas got for taking those bodies to town. I don't want it. You can put it toward your dowry."

He made the last word sound like a curse; it wasn't the first time that word had seemed to annoy him. She glared at his back as he left the room again.

"The atmosphere—" Charles began.

Violet interrupted, "Yes, I know, it's bloody chilly in here."

"What bodies was he talking about?"

She groaned and joined her father at the table to tell him about the outlaws, the wolves, even her almost shooting Morgan for killing him—might as well make a clean breast of it. Of course, there was one thing she couldn't mention. Her fall from grace.

When she was done, he said the last thing she expected. "Is he in love with you?"

"Of course not." Nonetheless, her heart leapt.

"It would explain his 'snit,' as you called it."

"So would a hundred other things," she exaggerated. "Believe me, love I would recognize."

"These westerners are different from the people you've grown up with. They're quiet, restrained. When a man wears a gun, he pretty much needs to keep his emotions in check, so what he is feeling might not be so obvious to other people."

She smiled at him. "I understand what you're getting at, but Morgan has been far from restrained. But I'll talk to him and see if I can muster up a truce at least for the duration of our visit here."

She just had to get up the nerve first, because it wouldn't be easy, would likely be most uncomfortable. Maybe tomorrow. In the meantime, at least he was amiable to her father.

She pushed that topic aside in order to appease her own curiosity. "So where did you hide your money up here? I searched for it for days before Morgan loaned us the money to pay off the bank."

He grinned and stood up, leading her down the porch steps and around to the back of the house, then about ten feet beyond the little water hole. She watched as he slowly reached into the slag pile and pulled out a little sack. She laughed. Of course it would be in the one place she had decided wasn't worth checking. He showed her the tiny mark he'd made on the cliff face a foot above the top edge of the slag to indicate where he'd hidden his money. It wasn't big enough to notice unless you were looking for it.

After a hearty dinner that evening, she took a quick bath in the stream. There was a tent set up in the yard when she returned. Morgan had already said she and Charles could have the cabin to themselves for the two nights they would be there. Bo seemed delighted with the arrangement. He was already lying in front of the tent, his tail wagging as she passed by. But Morgan wasn't in it yet, as she found out when she entered the cabin and saw him sitting at the table with her father.

He stood up immediately. "I'll see you in the morning, then."

He wasn't saying that to her. He didn't even glance at her as he left. She gazed after him wistfully, missing the Morgan who at least talked to her. Her father rose too and crossed over to give her a warm hug good night.

"You can't imagine how glad I am to have you home again," Charles said.

She knew he meant back in America, so she didn't mention that they weren't home yet—or that she wouldn't be staying once they were. That was another conversation she wasn't looking forward to. The few times she'd tried to broach it in the wagon on the way here today, he'd distracted her with another topic, so she had a feeling he'd guessed that she wanted to return to England and was avoiding the subject.

The next morning Violet woke up before her father and took her coffee out to the porch, as had been her habit during her stay at the camp. Morgan had come in while they were asleep to make the coffee. He'd left a basket of pastries on the table, too, and an assortment of fruit.

She stared at the entrance to Morgan's mine. The steel door was open, indicating he was in it. Once again, she thought about asking him if he wanted to take her fishing today. It would be such a perfect opportunity to mend that fence, as it were. Should she wait until he joined her and her father for lunch?

Bo caught her eye when he came out of the tent and trotted toward the stream. She started to call him to her, but stopped when she saw him reach his target. So Morgan wasn't mining after all, but sitting in the bed of flowers?

Recalling how they'd tumbled into those flowers the night they'd danced, she left the porch to join him at the edge of the stream. She brought her coffee with her. He'd done the same. Because he'd known she'd come out on the porch as soon as she woke up and he didn't want to be there with her? She sat down next to him anyway.

"I thought you would be mining as usual," she said.

He glanced at her briefly. "I always knew when I was ready to go home, I wouldn't give two hoots about this mine anymore. But I didn't expect to meet Charley and like him as much as I do. So your pa and I came to a new agreement last night, and the only reason I'm telling you this is because it cancels the one you and I had."

"I assured you that you would be paid back!"

"Settle down, we're not rival miners now. We might have more to dispute, but your father and I don't, and I'd prefer you hear this from me. I've swung my pick for the last time. With Sullivan out of the way, I no longer have a reason not to let crews in here to deplete the rest of the silver from both mines or to form a real partnership, including an even fifty-fifty split with your family. One or both of your brothers can oversee the place until we can hire an experienced manager to run the operation. But the location no longer needs to be kept secret."

And then it seemed to just fall out of his mouth as an afterthought: "Why did you really leave?"

She'd been waiting for him to look at her again, but even for that question he didn't, so she glanced down at the stream as well before saying, "What I told you wasn't a lie, but there is more. Yes, I was still distraught because of the violence, but I was also appalled at myself for what happened afterward and beyond embarrassed about it. I simply couldn't stay any longer, but you weren't willing to take me back to Butte yet. You wouldn't even take me to town to pay off the loan. You sent Texas instead. So I took matters into my own hands."

"That's it?"

He was looking at her now! She felt like groaning. "If you must know, you were being too familiar."

"*I* was?"

She blushed at the reminder that she'd started it. "Afterward, you were."

"You would have preferred that I ignore you after we made love? Really? That wouldn't have made you spitting angry?"

Bloody hell, she thought, of course it would have. She gave him a pointed stare. "I'm going to speak plainly this once, then we will never mention it again. What we did can't ever happen again, and I was afraid you'd expect more of the same if I stayed." There. That was *almost* all of it.

"Probably," he said grudgingly.

"Then you understand!"

"No."

She looked away so he wouldn't notice her gritting her teeth. She was not going to tell him how much she wanted him, that even now it was hard to resist putting her hands all over him. It would be beyond the pale to admit how much he tempted her to sin again.

But it was also a sin to lie, so she cleared her throat and said softly, "I was also afraid I'd want more."

Morgan turned to her and gave her the most amazing smile, one filled with happiness, pleasure—an invitation? "So why can't it happen again?"

Violet gritted her teeth again. "Because this isn't my world. I don't belong here. I'm going back to London where there's civilization, polite society, servants, indoor plumbing, fashionably dressed people . . ." She couldn't finish because she started to choke up, realizing how much she was going to miss him when she left Montana.

So he finished the list for her. "The fancy parties, the dancing, and all those dukes and earls, and, of course, Elliott. I see." He nodded as if he understood perfectly now. He smiled at her. "Want to go fishing today?"

Violet jumped at the invitation. "Yes!" Then she smiled shyly. "I was hoping you'd ask."

Chapter Forty

THE LAST TWO DAYS at the mining camp had been idyllic for Morgan—once he'd put his anger to rest. He was surprised at how easily Violet had managed to defuse it. The truth was, he didn't like being angry with her. And her reasons for running out on him had been valid. He'd had no intention of taking her back to town for at least another week. His usual two-week mining schedule was the excuse he'd given her, and he'd been glad to have one, because the simple fact was that he liked having her here and hadn't wanted to give her up yet.

Which was why when he'd had that long talk with Charley about a new partnership, he'd convinced his friend to come to Nashart with him to finish recuperating there. They just hadn't told Violet yet. Of course, that idea could backfire on him. She might just catch the train in Butte by herself to return to Philadelphia and then sail to England and that damned lord she wanted to marry, instead of staying with her father. Could she be that heartless? No. Thorny, yes, but not heartless. But she might insist on taking Charley straight home with her.

But while his anger was gone, there were still annoyances nagging at him. Violet's damn dowry, for one, and what it signified. After the intimacy they'd shared, he'd really thought she'd hand him back the money he'd given her for her dowry. Stupid of him to test her like that. But despite what'd they'd done, despite her confession that she'd feared she'd want more—it brought a smile every time he remembered that—she obviously still intended to marry her English lord.

He was also annoyed by how serious she'd sounded when she told him, "What we did can't happen ever again." She'd closed the door before he could even try to open it again. But unlike anger, annoyances he could keep to himself, and he did. And she wasn't gone yet. . . .

They got back to town late because they'd left the mines at noon. He didn't have much to bring with him, just his personal gear and Bo, since he was leaving all the supplies, including his mules, for her brothers to use. After getting rooms at the hotel, he went to see if the sheriff was back in town yet with news about Sullivan. He wasn't, so he sent off a telegram to Sheriff Gibson in Helena and another to the Mitchell twins to tell them to meet their father in Nashart.

And he finally picked up his mail. There were three letters from his mother and one from his father. He read Mary's first, in the order in which they'd arrived, and laughed at the last one. All this time he'd thought his brother was trying to get out of his arranged marriage, only to find out it had happened over a month ago. And Degan Grant had been there to keep the peace. Morgan had even been invited to the wedding in the second letter, although Mary had tried to make it a surprise for him by telling him only, *You'll want to come home for a brief visit by the twenty-third.* But that had been last month. His father's letter wasn't a surprise, but it also made him laugh. Zachary had been unable to order him home, but now he tried luring him with the news that copper had been found on their property—a great deal of it. What made him laugh was the line *If you have to mine, do it at home!* His pa would be glad that he was done with mining, but he wouldn't be happy about his next business venture. And he still wasn't looking forward to that argument.

The next day dragged by waiting to hear from the sheriff about Sullivan's sentencing. Violet had tsked about the delay, but Morgan had heard her assure Charley that she agreed with them, they couldn't leave without learning the outcome of the trial.

Morgan left the two Mitchells alone, hoping Charley would get around to telling Violet he was going to Nashart if they had some time to themselves. And then he heard the rumor raging through town. Degan Grant was getting married right there in Butte. Morgan had to see that for himself, and all he had to do was follow the crowds. It appeared half the town wanted to witness the gunslinger's wedding.

He'd missed the wedding ceremony, but heard the sounds of merriment behind the church. He spotted the Grants immediately. Degan had that aura about him that screamed gunfighter and had even worn his gun to the altar. The little wife was unusual, too. She had the shortest hair he'd ever seen on a woman, ash-blond in color, and very dark eyes.

As he approached them, he caught Degan's eye and heard him say, "Well, I'll be damned."

The pretty blonde whispered something to her new husband that Morgan didn't catch, but he extended his hand and introduced himself. "I'm Morgan Callahan."

"I guessed as much," Degan replied, shaking his hand.

"Yeah, Hunter and I hear that a lot, how much we look alike. Congratulations on your wedding—but please tell me you're not here because of me."

"I'm not, but why would you think so?"

"I heard from some miners here that you were working for my father. I know he hates that I prefer mining to working with my family on the ranch."

"That's between you and Zachary—and it's not why he hired me."

"So it's true? You actually brought about my brother's marriage to the Warren girl?"

"I'd say Hunter managed that on his own," Degan said.

"I'm surprised. He really hated having that arranged marriage hanging over his head. I figured it wasn't going to happen unless he was dragged kicking and screaming to the altar."

"Believe me, nothing would have kept Hunter away from that wedding. You'll understand why when you meet his wife."

Morgan smiled. "I'm sorry I missed all the fun, but I struck it rich and will be going home for a visit as soon as I settle a dispute with a rival lady miner. And, no, I'm not asking if I can hire you! But maybe I can kiss this bride, since I missed kissing my brother's new wife?"

"Not a chance." Degan put his arm around his wife's waist.

Morgan laughed, insisting, "I'm not like Hunter, who charms every woman in sight! But I'm not going to argue with the notorious Degan Grant, either. Have a happy marriage, you two."

He left and made his way back to the telegraph office. Still no reply from the sheriff, but he took the time to send word to his family. He didn't tell them that he was coming home—he wanted that to be a surprise—but he told them that he'd finally struck it rich. He also mentioned Violet vaguely. She was still a thorn he hadn't yet figured out how to extract from his life—or if he even wanted to. And he mentioned that Degan Grant had got hitched. They would probably get a kick out of that.

Just in case they heard from the sheriff before the end of the day, he went to the stage office and bought tickets for tomorrow, warning the man that he'd expect a refund in the morning if they decided to stay in Butte longer. As he returned to the hotel, a boy caught up with him and handed him a telegram. Morgan read it, then stuffed it in his pocket and went to find the Mitchells.

Before going upstairs, he checked the hotel dining room to make sure they weren't already there. They were. And it was uncanny how in a room full of people, his eyes went immediately to Violet. Cheeks still porcelain, thanks to her parasol; golden hair prettily coiffured tonight. She never had worn that silly hat again. He supposed he owed her a new one.

She was so damn beautiful, his violet with thorns. He wasn't sure he could let her leave the territory. He wasn't sure he could stop her. He wasn't sure he should try. She was a fish out of water here. She didn't belong in the West. She belonged in a fancy house full of fancy servants with a fancy English lord. . . .

He growled under his breath and turned to leave.

Chapter Forty-One

"GOOD GRIEF, HE DIDN'T see us," Violet said to her father, and stood up to wave and call out to Morgan before he left the doorway. When he reached them, she asked, "You aren't hungry yet?"

"I can eat." He caught the attention of the passing waiter, saying, "Steak, and a lot of it." As he sat down, he said to Violet, "You'll never guess who just got married."

"You are correct, since I don't really know anyone in this town."

"You'll remember this man. I heard he was in a gunfight near here while you were in town, that notorious gunfighter, Degan Grant. Half the town turned out to witness his wedding today."

She shuddered delicately. Charles noticed and put a hand over hers, forcing her to explain. "I witnessed him shooting another man my first week here. So utterly barbaric. Dueling has been outlawed all over the world—everywhere except here."

"It used to be a lot wilder here," Morgan said. "Gunfights

are not nearly as common as they were ten, fifteen years ago. You could say the West is growing up."

How utterly absurd. That would make the odds astronomical that she would see one in the street and then get dragged into another near the mines in just one month in the West, yet it had happened to her. But she didn't want to argue the point with Morgan. They'd been getting along well the last few days and she didn't want to ruin it.

And she was managing to ignore how bloody handsome he was now—well, not really ignore, that was impossible, but keep a tight rein on her prurient reactions to him. Her father's presence helped. He'd even joined them on that second fishing trip, though he ended up napping in the grass for most of it, so she hadn't been alone with Morgan. But Morgan had made that day fun again. Every single fish he unhooked for her he then tossed at her until she was throwing them back at him, and at one point she was chasing him to do so. And he talked a lot about his home, telling her about his friends, his family, what it was like growing up on a ranch with such a big family. She was going to have some nice memories of Montana mixed in with the bad when she left. When she . . . left. Good Lord, she felt tears starting! What the devil?

"We don't have them in Nashart," Morgan added with a pointed stare at Charles. "It's a peaceful town."

Violet blinked rapidly before she glanced up. She almost asked, "Have what?" until she recalled the argument she'd avoided. He was still talking about outlaws and gunfights, or the lack thereof.

"Which is why I'm looking forward to recuperating there," Charles said.

She frowned. "In Nashart?"

Morgan answered, "We can reach Billings in just under two days since the stagecoach travels day and night at top speeds, stopping only to swap out horses and drivers and to allow passengers a quick bite to eat. Then it's another day by train to Nashart. Texas will be bringing the horses, since traveling by horse takes two to three times longer. He's also agreed to show your brothers to the mines, but he insists on getting married to Emma first."

She tried not to show her conflicted feelings at hearing this surprising news. Another delay in getting back to England, but it would give her more time with her father—and she wouldn't have to say good-bye to Morgan yet. She wished that didn't please her so much.

But she kept her tone neutral when she commented, "I thought these stagecoaches were crowded."

"They usually are, which is why I bought all the seats on the one leaving first thing tomorrow, so Charley can lie down. Can't do that on the train. I want to see him get better just as much as you do."

He was right, of course. There would be three train changes on the way back to Philadelphia, even if she and her father took the express, and Morgan wouldn't be there to help with her father if assistance was needed. Another week or so of rest and Charles might be able to make the long journey home without difficulty, but not yet.

But then it occurred to her. "Aren't we waiting to hear from Sheriff Gibson?"

"I just got Gibson's telegram. There wasn't a jury trial. There rarely is with a circuit judge, especially when a lawman is present to testify to witnessing the crime. Sullivan got fifteen years for the abductions and planned murders that would have happened if he hadn't been caught, and another ten were added because he committed and plotted those crimes in an effort to steal a mine. Gibson was right, the judge really didn't like that charge."

"It's not enough," Violet said tersely. "Not when his intentions were so clear. Had he succeeded, he would have killed all three of us to cover up the theft of the mines. And he falsified your death, Papa! The grief that caused me and Evan and Daniel is unforgivable."

"Of course it is," Charles said. "But twenty-five years for a man his age pretty much amounts to a life sentence. It's certainly more than I was expecting, so I'm satisfied with the verdict."

"So am I," Morgan said. "A ruling like this will send a clear message to other unscrupulous miners and businessmen in the territory." Then he asked Violet, "So we're in agreement then? We catch the stage in the morning?"

He'd been in doubt? But then her father added, "Morgan has already telegraphed the boys for me, to tell them to meet us in Nashart."

Hearing that, she stood up immediately. "Then I need to tell them to bring one of my trunks with them. I'm suffering from an appalling lack of clothes because I never expected to be here so long. Don't wait on me to eat." Violet hurried out of the room.

CHARLES GRINNED. "THAT WAS easier than I expected. Are you sure she's in a hurry to return to England?"

"She's mentioned more than once that she intends to marry a particular English lord in London. Has she really not told you yet?"

"I'm not surprised she hasn't. She would consider it a

delicate matter, because she knows it will disappoint me. When I let her go to London with her Aunt Elizabeth nine years ago, I never intended for her to live there permanently. I thought she had come home to Philadelphia to stay until you mentioned she has plans to marry in England."

"Could you forbid her to go?"

"Not if it's what she really wants. That particular child of mine has been known to—dig in her heels? Is that how you say it out here?"

Morgan chuckled. "To say she's stubborn? It sure is, and I already knew that. But she's your only daughter. Her place is with you right now, at least until you're fully recovered."

"I don't doubt she intends to make sure of that before she goes anywhere. She may have tried a few times to broach the subject of her plans for the future, but I interrupted her before she could. I don't want her to go or to turn insistent about it. But I do owe her a full and honest discussion about what she wants to do." And then Charles gave him a curious look. "You know, I've seen how carefree and happy you two can be when you think no one is watching. You get along exceptionally well, considering that you haven't known each other for very long. It's almost as if you've already formed a bond with Violet. So tell me, is her helping me to recuperate the only reason you think she should stay? Just for me?"

Morgan grinned, only slightly abashed. "I can't deny I enjoy her company, when we aren't fighting—hell, even when we are. I surely wouldn't mind exploring that more fully. So, no, I won't be happy if she leaves the country."

"Does she know that?"

Chapter Forty-Two

As she prepared for bed that night, Violet couldn't stop smiling. She realized that, like her father, she was looking forward to seeing Morgan's "peaceful" town. Could it really be so different from bustling, overcrowded, and dangerous Butte? And she would be able to regale her cousins with a description of an authentic American cattle town when she returned to England.

With this unexpected detour to Nashart, it felt as if another weight had been lifted from her shoulders. The misgivings she'd been having about getting on the train with her father weren't only about his health; they were also about saying good-bye to Morgan. She was dreading that. It had nearly brought her to tears in the dining room tonight.

Yet it wasn't as if she could marry a man like him, even though he didn't look like a bear anymore. Before leaving London, she'd picked out the perfect husband. She'd been planning on marrying someone like Lord Elliott Palmer for at least six years, ever since she started talking and dreaming about love and marriage with her cousins. Morgan simply wouldn't do. He was excitement, passion, wicked pleasures, while Elliott was refined, sophisticated, and everything proper. There was just no comparison—and besides, she was sure Elliott could be exciting, too. There hadn't been time for her to find out.

She was getting into bed when a knock came at the door, and she pulled the spread off the bed and wrapped it around herself like a robe. It must be her father—hotel employees wouldn't knock at that hour. So she opened the door wide instead of just a crack.

Morgan must have considered that permission to enter her room, because he did. She stood there with one hand still on the doorknob and the other making sure the spread was covering all of her nightgown. It didn't help her composure that she'd just been thinking about him.

Before he even turned around to face her, he said, "Your pa pointed out to me that you might not know that I'm partial to you."

Partial? What a tepid word! He favored her? Was fond of her? Or he just wanted her? But she'd already surmised the latter, because she had those exact same feelings about him. But just because they wanted each other . . .

He turned, their eyes met, and she sucked in her breath. There it was again, that overwhelming attraction that flamed up between them. She forced herself to keep still. She wasn't going to run to him no matter how much she wanted to. She didn't have to. In the blink of an eye, he was beside her, his hands on her shoulders, his body pressing in closer, then his mouth. Her back was shoved up against the wall and part of the still-open door, which slammed shut. As he kissed her, he slipped one arm around her waist, lifting her and guiding her right leg up around his hips. She raised her left leg and didn't hesitate to wrap both around him, or wrap her arms tightly around his neck.

She couldn't count how many times she'd let such an encounter play through her mind since that momentous night in his cabin, but now that it was actually happening again, she knew her imaginings had lacked the real passion, the explosion of feelings, the want, the need, the heat that were overwhelming her now. She even felt a little frustration that their lovemaking wasn't happening fast enough, yet at the same time such delight that it was happening at all, despite her warnings and proper disclaimers that it couldn't.

Her nightgown was hiked to her waist. Having been alone in her room, she had nothing on underneath it. Incredibly, the friction of the rough fabric of his pants pressing between her legs brought her first orgasm while she was still pressed to the wall. She dissolved, her head dropping back, his lips scalding her neck as little gasps escaped her. He carried her like that to the bed, both of them falling down on it in unison so her hold on him didn't break.

But he was kissing her deeply again, so she didn't pay much attention to his unbuckling his belt and taking off his pants, or lifting her nightgown, until he stopped kissing her and pulled the thin cotton garment over her head. Her loose hair fanned out behind her. His lips were back on hers, and then he was inside her, thrusting exquisitely, causing gasp after gasp and then no breath at all as the second orgasm rose up and washed over her. He joined her in that one. Sharing it gave her the most sublime feeling.

She didn't want to move, probably should, but didn't want to. The bubbly warmth she was feeling inside was worth savoring. He rolled to her side and pulled the sheet up over them. He even gently lifted her long hair and draped it over the top of her pillow for her, then lay down next to her. But when his arm went around her as if he meant to spend the night there, her eyes widened and she rolled out of bed. Fell out would better describe it, but she didn't hit the floor because she straightened in time. But, realizing she didn't have a stitch on, she dropped down below the edge of the bed and pulled the sheet her way. When she finally stood up, somewhat covered, she saw he was lying on his side, his head propped up with a hand, and completely naked because she'd just swiped the sheet from him!

She'd done it again, tossed out all thoughts of propriety and rectitude. She was appalled by her behavior once again. She swung around so she couldn't see him before saying, "Get dressed!"

She heard vague sounds that assured her he was at least putting something on; then he said, "I know that wasn't supposed to happen again, but it was a mutual impulse, we both loved it. Think about that before you run back to England."

All she got out of that statement was that he *did* want to treat her like a wife without offering to make her one. Of course she would refuse, but he could at least ask!

She could hear him walking away. She turned to see he'd only put his pants on and was carrying his shirt and boots. Before he reached the door, she had to make him understand why they couldn't keep doing this.

In a stiff tone that mimicked the one her aunt used when she gave one of her scolding lectures, she said, "A lady always has a chaperone with her to guard her virtue for this very reason—so things like this don't happen. Due to unexpected circumstances, mainly my maid's quitting as soon as we reached America and my brother's being detained at the train station in Philadelphia, I was forced to travel alone. I thought I could manage, and I was managing—until I met you."

He didn't look the least bit contrite when he turned around with a grin. "I can do that. You want me to?"

Her virtue was gone, and she wasn't sure what he was suggesting, unless . . ."*You* can't chaperone me when you are the very thing from which a chaperone is supposed to protect me!"

"Sure I can. I can beat myself up if I have to."

Now he was just teasing, and amazingly enough, she burst out laughing. Good Lord, exquisite sex and then he made her laugh? There was something good to say about a man like him, after all. But she still pointed a finger toward the door.

"No hugs or cuddles?" he asked with a raised brow.

"Go."

"At least a kiss good night?"

She rolled her eyes, repeating, "Go!"

But she grinned the moment the door closed behind him. Incorrigible bear.

Chapter Forty-Three

M ORGAN HAD TOLD HER to bring a pillow, had yelled it from the other side of her door early that morning. She'd told him not to be absurd. When she had to sleep sitting up in a moving stagecoach that night, she kept leaning in his direction, waking, and apologizing. She realized then why he'd suggested a pillow.

The fourth time she fell toward him, he pulled her closer, put her head on his shoulder, and said, "I can't sleep if you keep crashing into me. Stay put."

Violet would have argued if he hadn't made it seem like she'd be doing him a favor. But when she woke again in the daylight, her head was on his chest instead of his shoulder, and her hand rested on it, too. His arm was around her back, holding her close to him. She leaned away slowly in case he was still sleeping. And caught her father watching her. She wasn't fully awake yet, or else she would have blushed.

She whispered across the aisle to him, "Did you get a good night's rest?"

"Better than you two did, I imagine," Charles said in a normal tone of voice, adding, "And he's awake."

Now she really was embarrassed, but Morgan straightened up in his seat and said, "We'll have our own beds tonight in Billings, and get you settled in at the ranch tomorrow."

The ranch? She hadn't imagined they would be staying with his family in Nashart, though she probably should have after her father had said he was looking forward to his stay there. And it might be nice. Morgan had told her enough about his family to make her feel like she already knew them. She wondered how he would behave around them.

He didn't come knocking that night at the Billings hotel. She kept listening for it, not that she would have opened the door. Maybe he'd been serious about appointing himself her chaperone. The thought was silly enough to make her smile.

After riding in a stagecoach for two full days and all of one night, Violet found the train ride on the third day quite comfortable. Bo seemed to prefer it, too. They pulled into the Nashart station late in the afternoon.

"Well, hell, so much for surprises," Morgan said when he looked out the window and saw the crowd on the station platform.

He immediately got up and jumped off the train. Violet heard hoots and hollers, whistles and voices raised in excitement, and when she looked out the window, she saw Morgan being overwhelmed with bear hugs and pats on his back, and some kisses, too.

His whole family was there, apparently. The older couple were obviously his parents, the three young men also obviously his brothers, but the beautiful copper-haired woman who greeted him so warmly, even kissing his cheek—who the bloody hell was she?

Violet stood up and put her bustled jacket back on. It had been too warm to wear it on the train, but with Morgan's family outside, she wanted to look her best and was glad she'd worn her fancy rose traveling ensemble today. Parasol in hand, she offered her arm to her father.

"How do you think they found out he was on this train?" she said as they headed to the exit together.

"Texas, probably," Charles guessed. "He would have sent word to his fiancée that he was coming home for good, and Emma could have told the others."

"That's a shame. I was looking forward to seeing the surprise on their faces, but instead it's Morgan who got surprised."

Violet stepped off the train first and turned to help her father down to the platform. She wished she hadn't heard the whisper behind her: "You think he brought the thorn home with him?"

She didn't blush, but she did purse her lips in disapproval of that ridiculous name Morgan had called her more than once. And he'd obviously referred to her that way in a letter to his family, since one of them had just used the silly name. She swung around to see who had made that remark, but found they were *all* looking at her.

Morgan took that moment to make introductions. "Ma, Pa, I'd like to introduce my partner, Charles Mitchell, and his daughter, Miss Violet Mitchell."

Mary Callahan stepped forward to shake their hands, saying, "I'm Mary, my husband is Zachary. Any friend of Morgan's is a friend of ours, so y'all are welcome to stay at our ranch."

"You are most kind, Mrs. Callahan," Violet said.

But Zachary wanted to know, "What kind of part—?"

Morgan cut in, "Pardon me, Pa, I'd like to finish the introductions first."

He went on to do that, ignoring his father's frown. Zachary Callahan appeared to be in his fifties, with coal-black hair and dark-brown eyes fanned with laugh lines, hinting at a good-natured temperament. He didn't look like a man who could intimidate the bear, yet she knew Morgan was dreading the fight he expected when he got around to sharing his plans.

As for Zachary's sons, John—the hot-tempered one, according to Morgan—had black hair and brown eyes and a look all his own, darkly brooding, one might say. Cole, the youngest, had brown hair and eyes, and was shorter than his brothers by a few inches. He had boyish good looks, sort of like a younger version of all of them. They did all resemble each other in certain ways—except that Hunter and Morgan looked very much alike. If she didn't know they were a year apart in age, Violet would have thought they were twins.

Mary Callahan was the most surprising member of the family. She was petite but she didn't look delicate. She wore her long brown hair in a single braid lying over her shoulder and had keen blue eyes. Morgan's eyes—Hunter's, too. She was wearing a skirt made out of rough material that might actually be rawhide. When she moved to say something to her husband, Violet saw it wasn't a skirt at all, but very wide pants. A female cowboy! She even had the wide-brimmed hat, which she held in her hand, a red bandanna around her neck, scuffed boots, and, most intriguing of all, a gun belt around her hips.

As for the copper-haired beauty with emerald-green eyes who had caused Violet a brief moment of pique, she turned out to be Hunter's new wife, Tiffany, the feud-ender. Violet was glad to meet her now that she knew she was married. They were the same age and might become friends. It would be so nice to have a friend here, someone with whom she could share confidences as she'd done with Sophie.

"You're from England, aren't you?" Tiffany asked Violet.

"London," Violet replied.

"You have a lovely accent. I look forward to hearing about all the latest fashions and social events."

Hunter chimed in, "My wife used to be a fancy easterner, now she's a fancy westerner, but she'll still talk your ear off about fashions."

But with the introductions over, Zachary was quick to seek the answer to his earlier question. "Mr. Mitchell is your partner in what?"

Morgan ignored it and asked, "How in blazes did you know I was on this train?"

Zachary raised a brow, not missing his son's evasion, but he let it go and answered, "That's a mite funny. We got a telegram this morning from Abe Danton, who moved to Billings last year. He thought he was doing us a favor letting us know that Hunter had just boarded the eastbound train and should be home soon. Hunter had a good laugh about it, since he was out front with his brothers waiting for me and your ma before heading out to the range."

Morgan snorted, insisting, "Hunter and I don't look that much alike."

Hunter elbowed him. "From a distance we do, and stop complaining. You should be thankful you share my devastatingly good looks—"

"Devastatingly good—"

"So my wife tells me. Too bad our other brothers, the runts, missed out and resemble the mules in the south pasture."

"Hey, now," Cole mumbled.

But John actually took a swing at Hunter, who apparently expected such a response from him and stepped out of the way, allowing the punch to catch Morgan's shoulder, which prompted Morgan to put his brother in a headlock. But John managed to trip him and they both went down, sprawled at Violet's feet.

She jumped back to avoid getting knocked down herself and brandished her parasol at them, scolding, "Children have better manners!"

Zachary nodded, Mary looked at her in surprise, and John blushed furiously as he scrambled to his feet. Charles protectively put his arm around Violet's waist. But Hunter was bent over laughing. It must have been infectious, because now the other Callahan men were laughing, too.

Mary didn't find it funny and admonished sternly, "She's right, you're no better than wild broncos. Keep those fists in your pockets, John. And stop teasing your brothers, Hunter. All of my boys are beautiful."

Hunter grinned. "Only a mother would say that."

"Well, I'll say this, if no one else will," Zachary began, his eyes on Morgan. "It's about damn time you came to your senses and got yourself home, Son."

Violet noticed Morgan stiffen, even if no one else did. "I never lost my senses, Pa. But if you want to have this argument right here and now—"

Mary cut in, "You'll do no such thing. We're tickled pink you're home, Morg, all of us are. Now, let's get you home and settled, then you can regale us with your exploits and explain how you came to have a partner, and why on earth you would call this beautiful lady a thorn."

Morgan actually grinned. "She's named after a flower."

"Violets don't have thorns, boy," Zachary pointed out.

"Don't they?"

Mary snorted. Violet felt a blush creeping up her cheeks, and she knew the others would notice it because all eyes were on her after those ridiculous remarks. And when she saw Morgan still grinning over that offensive name he'd given her, she pressed the point of her parasol to his chest and said, as politely as possible, "I may have thorns, but you, sir, have the manners and temperament of a bloody bear."

The Callahans looked stunned. Mary broke the silence, saying, "Well, then, shall we go?"

As Mary led Violet to a buckboard wagon, she whispered, "So, how did my son behave like a bloody bear?"

Chapter Forty-Four

VIOLET BLAMED HER REACTIONS at the train station on how unusual Morgan's family had turned out to be. She hadn't expected his mother to be a cowboy—well, cow*girl*, but still . . . She hadn't expected his father to be so testy, though she should have, considering what Morgan had told her. She hadn't expected one of his brothers to throw punches. But it was obvious that Morgan was glad to be home, despite that tense moment with his father. This was the Morgan she liked, relaxed, quick to laugh, not so much carefree but definitely tolerant—or at least, hard to provoke, which was definitely a good thing for a man as big as he was.

Mary insisted that Violet ride with her on the perch of the two-seater buckboard, while Tiffany rode in the back with Charles. A horse had been brought from the ranch for Morgan and he rode with the rest of the men, fanned out on both sides of the buckboard, not close enough to hear the uncomfortable conversation Violet was having with his mother.

In low tones Violet tried to reassure Mary that she'd been

exaggerating when she called Morgan a bear, but admitted he'd had quite a shaggy beard when they first met, that he used it to disguise himself as a mountain-man trapper to hide the fact that he was mining. Which led to a whole different topic about keeping the location of his mine secret. She finally eased out of the subject, since it was Morgan who should be telling his mother about his mine, not her. She simply commented on the beautiful landscape they rode through—green, grassy fields and magnificent snowcapped mountains in the distance.

It didn't take long to reach the Callahans' home, and on the way Tiffany pointed out her own home, a pretty house surrounded by trees and fronted by a lovely lake. And then the ranch loomed ahead, with so many buildings that it looked like a little village. Violet was impressed by the size of the ranch, and was relieved it wasn't as primitive as she'd imagined.

Morgan let out a whoop. "It's good to be back at the Triple C!" And he raced his brothers to the house.

Two stories high and built of smoothly cut boards, the house was big and spread-out, with a long, covered porch in front. There was nothing rustic about it. The moment Violet stepped inside, she loved the ambience, half western, half eastern, a very homey balance.

This was where Morgan had grown up. The front room alone could have been his playground, it was so big and open, with no walls separating the parlor, hall, and foyer. She could picture him and his brothers playing here, running through the house, riding horses outside. What a wonderful place for boys to be raised.

Mary took her straight upstairs to the large bedroom that would be hers, saying, "There's a bathing room downstairs off the kitchen that's got its own pump. You're welcome to first dibs on it before dinner."

Violet smiled. Well, the house was a bit rustic after all, with one shared bath downstairs. But she would make do. She wasn't there to be critical, and in fact, she already liked this house and would probably enjoy her stay there for a week or two.

After her bath, she changed into her only other skirt and blouse that weren't stained, then went to find her father. She found him asleep in bed. A tray holding an empty plate sat on the night table. She smiled. Of course her father was tired after their long journey. How thoughtful of the Callahans to bring dinner to his room.

Downstairs she found most of the Callahans in the large room. They were standing as they talked and laughed, all of them holding drinks, even Mary. She saw them all vaguely because her eyes went straight to Morgan and stayed on him. He hadn't shaved yet and his cheeks were shadowed with stubble, but he was wearing a string tie and a light-blue shirt that matched his eyes—and he was still too bloody handsome. She felt a little giddy just being in the same room with him.

And then the two missing Callahans walked through the front door, Hunter and his wife, Tiffany, who was wearing a sparkling evening dress. Violet felt like groaning. She hoped her brothers would arrive soon so she'd have more clothes to choose from.

Mary raised a brow at her daughter-in-law. "I hope you didn't ride over in that getup."

"I did," Tiffany said, but pointed her thumb at Hunter. "In his lap on his horse."

That got a few chuckles, but Mary teased, "You didn't need to dress up, gal. I'm not breaking out the good china tonight."

Tiffany grinned. "Don't begrudge me. How often do I get the opportunity? And your houseguests are as eastern as I am. They will appreciate that we're not all cowpunchers here in Nashart."

Violet certainly did. Mary urged everyone into the dining room then, and Violet ended up sitting directly across from Morgan—not by choice; it just worked out that way after Tiffany insisted Violet sit next to her. Platters and large bowls were already being passed around the table, so she didn't think it would be too difficult to keep her eyes off Morgan long enough to eat.

There was a lot of noise, with many people talking all at once, but that quieted down once everyone started eating. So Mary's voice was quite clear when she said to Morgan, "I hope you brought your shaving razor home with you."

Violet smiled. So Morgan and his brothers got their penchant for teasing from their mother. Morgan glanced at Violet before he laughed at Mary. "It was the bear remark, huh? She explained it to you?"

"Barely any skin visible on your face, Morgan? Really?"

"I wouldn't know. Didn't have a mirror, didn't care. I wasn't there to look pretty."

Hunter was laughing, but still got in, "So you really got rich?"

Morgan nodded. "I accomplished what I set out to do—well, half of it."

"And the other half?"

"None of your damn business, Brother."

So he'd told no one yet about his plans for an emporium, not even his brothers? Or was he just making sure that his father found out first? It could get uncomfortable around here once they learned he hadn't come home to join them on the range again. She hoped not.

And then she heard next to her, "Have you heard yet how Hunter and I met?"

She glanced at Tiffany. "To end a feud?"

Tiffany huffed, "That silly old thing should have ended long before I was born, but no one got around to saying enough is enough, so poor Hunter was sacrificed to end it by joining our two families through marriage."

"I only viewed it as a sacrifice before I met you, Red," Hunter clarified.

"And that's what I was getting to, how we met." Tiffany proceeded to regale Violet with how she'd assumed the identity of the housekeeper her father, a neighboring rancher, had hired, only to get snatched up by the Callahans as a practical joke on her father, though they did actually need a housekeeper, too. "And I'd promised my mother that I would stay in Nashart for at least a month to give Hunter a chance to woo me, so it was a perfect opportunity for me to get to know him while he didn't know who I really was. Then I could honestly tell my mother that I'd met him and he wouldn't do. Trouble was, he most certainly did do—he's a little bit irresistible once you get to know him."

"Only a little?" Hunter complained.

"You know exactly what you are, darling," Tiffany said, and blew a kiss to her husband before grinning at Violet. "Now, tell me how you met Morgan."

"He abducted me out of my hotel room and dragged me into the wilderness."

There was silence; then the laughter started. Violet would never have said it if she wasn't sure they would think she was joking, and they did. She smiled to confirm it, then looked at Morgan for help. "You tell them."

She thought he'd give them a modified version, but she failed to notice his wicked grin. "I thought she was a con artist working for a ruthless mining company owner who was trying to steal my mine."

There wasn't any laughter now, and Zachary demanded, "Did you abduct her, Son?"

Appalled, Violet jumped in to rescue them both. "It was just a misunderstanding that we quickly sorted out." After explaining the strange circumstances she'd confronted when she arrived in Butte and her need for a guide to take her to her father's mine, she simply said, "So I was pleased that he arranged that trek into the wilderness."

"Walked right into your trap, didn't I?" Morgan grinned.

"You wanted information, I wanted information," she reminded him pertly, then said to Tiffany, "It was a rough few days to begin with, but as I said, we got it all sorted out."

"All the while he looked like a bear," Mary added with a disapproving look at Morgan.

"Well—yes," Violet answered.

Tiffany asked, "A cuddly bear or a grizzly?"

"The latter. Quite frightful, actually."

"Enough about me," Morgan growled.

"Not nearly enough," Mary insisted. "We have a whole year to catch up on, Morgan. You didn't exactly write very often and shared barely anything of note when you did."

"Because there was nothing to tell. I mined for a year and nothing else. I was single-minded about it because the sooner I reached my goal, the sooner I could come home."

"We thought it would've been sooner," Cole put in. "That you would have hired a crew to mine for you."

"I thought so, too, until I found out how cutthroat it is in that area. One mine owner in particular was willing to kill to get my mine, so I had to keep the location of my camp a secret, which meant no crews, and I had to do the mining myself. That routine only got interrupted when Charley's daughter showed up. She reminded me of things I was missing—like family. And the threat has been dealt with, so Charley and I will hire a manager to run the mines now and get crews in there to work them."

"So you're not going back?" Mary asked.

"I'll go back every so often to make sure it's running smoothly and the manager is doing a good job, but it won't be to stay."

She gave him a brilliant smile, then called for the maid to bring in dessert. There was more teasing, more laughter, but thankfully, no more personal questions.

When they stood up to leave the table, Morgan came around to take her arm and whisper, "Come with me. I have two things to show you."

She was surprised when he led her to the back of the house, through the kitchen, and outside toward the cluster of other buildings. She remembered thinking Morgan might be used to gazing at pastures with animals from the front porch of his ranch house, but the only thing out front would be a clear view of the setting sun in another hour or so.

"What are all these buildings for?" she asked.

"There's a stable, there's a barn. Ma likes to say we're half farm, though Pa vehemently objects to that term. But we do keep enough farm animals—chickens, pigs, a few dairy cows—to be self-sufficient when it comes to eating. And, of course, steak is brought in from the range. She even has a vegetable garden that one of our former cooks started a while back. I think the only thing we fetch in town anymore is grain for bread. The long building is the bunkhouse, but there's also a washhouse and a number of storage sheds."

He led her into the barn, where she saw bales of hay, a wagon, Mary's buckboard, and two dairy cows in their own stalls. There were a few other stalls, but they were empty, and it was mostly just a big open space with a loft where more hay was stacked. She didn't miss seeing the cat up there staring down at them as they continued toward the back of the barn.

Then she saw Bo sitting on his haunches, but he barely glanced at them, and she finally noticed why. He was keeping his distance while he avidly watched another dog curled in the corner. Or rather, he was watching all the babies playing around the other dog.

"Oh," she cooed, unable to take her eyes off the puppies.

"They aren't wolves," Morgan remarked with a chuckle. "Cole said they're around two months old now and ready to leave their mother. Take your pick. One of them is yours if you want it."

She couldn't help throwing her arms around his neck and hugging him, then immediately dropped to her knees before he could return that hug. There were four of them in assorted colors—no, five, the smallest was still nursing. The mother was medium-sized and all golden, but had pointed ears, so Violet couldn't imagine what mix of breeds she might be. She started picking them up. Only one was all gold like its mother, and one was mostly gold with black patches; another was gold and brown, the fourth brown and white, and the runt appeared to be all black. When the runt moved away from the dam, she saw that its face was actually golden, the black only starting at its forehead. She picked that one up and fell in love.

"Him," she said.

"Is it?"

She didn't know and held it up for him. "You check."

"Not a him," he said.

She smiled. "Even better. You realize you couldn't have given me a nicer gift."

He grinned. "Yeah, I had a feeling."

"It can come inside the house, correct?" she said on her way out of the barn, the puppy in her arms.

"I'd say it will whether it's allowed to or not," he said, following her.

And then she stopped. "Oh my." She was staring at the beginning of a magnificent sunset.

"That was the other thing I wanted to show you. Let's head to the front porch where you can get an unobstructed view."

She nodded. They made their way to the long swing on the porch that she'd noticed when they arrived; it hung from the ceiling and had room for two. She sat down, and Morgan joined her there and pushed a little with his long legs, making the swing rock slowly. At the mining camp, the sky was obscured by all the trees, but here she could appreciate the beauty of Montana's big sky.

She petted the puppy in her lap. Morgan slipped his arm around her shoulders. He probably thought she didn't notice because she was so amazed at the flaming colors in the sky. She noticed. She noticed everything about him.

"I bet you never saw a sunset like this in London," he remarked.

She laughed. "No, there's too much fog and coal smoke!"

There were other beautiful things in London, but she didn't mention them, because nothing could really compare to this view and how happy she felt sitting here sharing it with him.

She went to sleep that night with her very own puppy curled in the crook of her arm and memories of that lovely little interlude on the porch.

Chapter Forty-Five

THE NEXT MORNING ON her way downstairs to take the puppy outside, she heard Zachary demanding, "Then where the hell did Morgan go?"

As she reached the bottom of the stairs, she could see most of the parlor and the couple in it. Zachary hadn't been talking to her, but both of Morgan's parents looked at her when she came into view, so she shrugged. "I haven't seen him today."

"He didn't mention his plans to you when you sneaked off with him last night?" Zachary asked.

Violet objected to what he was implying, but she didn't blush. Instead she raised Tiny, the name she'd given her precious gift, and said, "He took me to the barn to let me pick out one of the puppies for myself."

"At least it's not a pig," Zachary grumbled, and headed out the front door.

Mary chuckled when she saw Violet's confused look and explained, "Tiffany kept a pet pig in the house while she lived with us. Go ahead and take your pet outside to start its training. Use the side yard. Her ma favors that area, so the pup will recognize the smell and know what to do. And don't let it sleep in your bed yet, or you could wake up to wet sheets."

Violet's eyes flared. The puppy had woken her, licking her cheek. She hadn't even thought to check the sheets.

Mary grinned. "I'll see if I can find some old newspapers and a box for you to put the pup in at night. And the coffee's hot. There's fixings to eat in the kitchen. We're not formal about breakfast, so get a plate and sit wherever you like. I'll take you out for a tour of the range later, if you like. Find me when you're ready."

Violet smiled. "Thank you. I'll take a plate up to my father, too."

A little later Mary took her out to the range to see where the cattle were grazing. There were no fences out there, so cows that wandered had to be brought back to the herd; and because the herd was so big, it needed to be moved to new grazing pastures often. But she hadn't expected the sheer size of that herd, more than a thousand cows. No wonder it took the whole family plus a lot of cowboys to manage it.

Then in the afternoon Tiffany came by to take her for a tour of her house, a short ride away. Violet laughed when she saw how many servants worked there, which caused Tiffany to whisper, "They're all from New York and they may be hard to keep. I've already heard complaints about how isolated they feel here. They miss the bustle and excitement of crowded city streets. But they haven't been here long, so I hope they'll fall in love with Montana as I did."

Violet was impressed by the home. It was built with lumber, but the inside was furnished and decorated as finely as any home in Philadelphia, or London, for that matter. Tiffany explained, "Hunter and I took our wedding trip back east to pick out all the furniture. The house was finished long before the furnishings got here, but it was worth the wait."

Violet could have told her that waits like that would soon be a thing of the past, but again she said nothing about the emporium Morgan planned to open. She hoped he would break the news to his family soon. She was beginning to feel uneasy about their reaction.

After they settled in the parlor with coffee and pastries, Tiffany asked bluntly, "You and Morgan, is there something we should know about?"

"No," Violet replied a little too quickly. "He helped my father when he most needed it, so I'm grateful to him."

"It's probably something he does naturally," Tiffany guessed. "I heard he has the most friends of all the Callahan brothers. Hunter draws women like bees to honey—or he *did*—while Morgan draws lasting friendships. The way Hunter tells it, Morgan can make each of his buddies feel like his best friend. I guess he's charismatic that way."

"So is my father. That would explain why they became friends so fast."

Tiffany nodded. "Morgan hasn't been home since I got here, so I was really looking forward to meeting him. But I sense some sort of tension and, well, I assumed it was because of you."

"No, but the tension should ease up in a few days—or get worse! I'm sorry, I really can't say more about it."

Tiffany laughed. "So mysterious. I love it!"

When Violet returned to the ranch, she found her father sitting on the porch. She laughed at him. "You just aren't going to stay in bed, are you?"

"I'm not supposed to. Rest was defined as doing nothing strenuous other than eating more than I can stomach. I'm also supposed to slowly work in some exercise. Walking about a house got full approval."

"I hadn't realized Dr. Cantry was so specific in his recommendations. We should probably visit the local doctor this week, too, or find out if he'll ride out here."

"I can make the trip to town if we borrow Mary's buckboard. But sit down." He waited for her to do so, then took her hand in his. "It's time we talk about your future. I confess I've been dodging the issue, because I love having you back and don't want to see you go. I think it may have been a mistake to let you stay in England for as long as you did, because you appear to view it as your home now, where you want to marry and have a family. But you need to remember that you have a home with me and your brothers, too, Vi. However, whatever you decide, I will honor your wishes because I love you and want you to be happy."

"I know you do, Papa."

"No matter where you are, soon you will be an heiress again with a dowry that will rival that of a duke's daughter. Just keep in mind that you can have your pick of husbands in this country, too. You needn't choose only from the men available in England."

"I thought I knew what I wanted, but now I'm not so sure," she admitted.

"There's no rush! Take your time and think about what you really want. Just know that I'm on your side no matter what."

She grinned. "Well, if you are up to walking, what I want to do right now is introduce you to my new puppy."

Chapter Forty-Six

VIOLET WAS STILL ON the porch with Tiny asleep in her lap when Morgan returned to the ranch. Her father had already gone in to take a nap before dinner, so no one was there to see how brazenly she stared at Morgan from the moment he came into view. He had dressed up a bit fancy today, wearing an eastern-style coat and a string tie, even polished boots, though the gun belt ruined the effect. Had he visited his friends? Or a woman?

The last thought irked her a little, so she wasn't exactly smiling when he sat down next to her. But he was. Whatever he'd done today had apparently made him happy.

But his first question was about her. "How are you getting on here? Comfortable enough?"

"Yes, your family is very friendly—well, aside from your father. He seems a bit cantankerous."

"He only gets that way when he has a bone to pick and he can't get to it. They're all still on the range?"

"I believe so," she replied. "Your mother took me out there for a tour. I was amazed to see so many cows in one place."

"Cattle," he corrected as he reached into his pocket and handed her a strip of rawhide. She would have dropped the ugly thing if he hadn't nodded at the puppy. "Give her this and maybe she'll leave your shoes alone."

She laughed. "Puppies eat shoes?"

"Dogs will gnaw on them at any age. I laughed like hell when I saw Bo trotting off with one of my boots one day. We always had a dog or two around here when I was young, just never in the house where they could get near the boots."

She set Tiny down on the porch to let her sniff the strip of leather. She latched on to it immediately and plopped down to start chewing it. "It's safe for her to eat?"

"She's not going to eat it, only chew it. Throw it away when it gets soggy."

She nodded, still watching the pup. But Tiny appeared to lose interest in the rawhide and stood up and moved away from them, sniffing at the floorboards. Guessing what would happen next, Violet quickly scooped up her pet and took her to the side yard. She heard Morgan laughing behind her.

When she came back and took her seat again, she said, "Your father was looking for you."

"I'm not surprised. I was scouting the town to figure out where I want to build my emporium. Nashart grew while I was gone. There's one intersection on the main street now that's filled with stores and businesses on all four corners, but there's another partial intersection with only one street coming in perpendicular to the main road, so I bought the property on the other side. It took a while to convince the mayor to sell me what will one day be a whole street and half a block on either side of it. Since he has no plans in the works yet for that section, it was just a matter of haggling. And it's perfect, or will be by the time I'm done with it. I won't need it all, but now I can control what gets built there. Now I can have that talk with my pa."

She raised a brow at him. "You were holding off until you bought the land first? Why?"

"Because Pa could have stopped me cold if he knew my intention. He and Mayor Quade are poker buddies. He could easily have pulled a few strings to get Quade to refuse to sell me any part of town. Quade did in fact ask me a few times if Zachary approved of my buying such a large parcel."

"How did you answer?"

He grinned. "I didn't. I smooth-talked him away from Pa's opinion by stressing how pleased my mother is going to be with the new business."

She chuckled. "So you implied that because your mother was in favor of it, of course your father must be, too?"

"Something like that. But I also assured him that what goes up on that street will be businesses the town doesn't have yet, which will draw a lot more people to Nashart—and a lot more women." He laughed. "Which is what sold him and got me a good deal. Nashart has always been short on women who aren't already married—and the mayor is a widower."

"It sounds like it's really happening. I confess, I find it hard to believe that a cowboy-turned-miner will now be happy working in a shop."

"This is just the beginning. I'll have to do a lot of traveling, to purchase all the things I want to sell. I'll start with the big cities in the East, and eventually I may want to travel to Europe."

So he did have bigger plans than spending every day in a

shop in Nashart. "That sounds exciting. France is known for fine craftsmanship in furniture. And England—"

She stopped, not wanting to remind him of her future plans, but the simple word *England* had done it. He remarked, "Maybe I'll visit you in London on one of my business trips. But in the meantime, would you like a tour of town tomorrow? I can show you where I plan to build. We can make a day of it and have lunch in town."

Spend the whole day with him—alone? But she'd made her stand about that, so she replied, "I'll see if my father is up to it."

"Charley doesn't need another bouncy ride this soon. And you'll have the whole town as chaperones. It's not like I have a bedroom there to lure you into—though I could arrange for one. . . ."

She could tell he wasn't teasing because she saw the desire in his eyes. Her pulse started racing at the thought of being in bed with him again. No, she wouldn't let herself be that reckless. But she did want to go to town with him, so she teased, "I suppose it will be a good time for you to test your chaperoning skills."

He laughed, but then she gestured toward the approaching dust cloud. "Since you're likely to get cornered for that 'talk,' I think I'll take Tiny down for another spin around the side yard, then visit her littermates.

"Good luck," she added as she walked down the stairs.

"If it gets loud, cover your ears!" he called after her with a chuckle.

She didn't think he was teasing. She did expect it to get loud, so she moved toward the back of the house so she wouldn't hear it. But the two men's voices grew loud enough for her to recognize an angry tone, if not the exact words, until there was a really loud yell: "The hell you did! No son of mine is going—"

"Pa, it's a done deal. It's what I spent a year working for. And I'm damn well old enough to make my own bloody decisions!"

Violet's eyes flared when she heard him say "bloody." His use of the Britishism made her grin.

"Not in my house, you don't!" Zachary yelled before a door slammed and it got quiet.

That wasn't the least bit amusing. Had Morgan just been kicked out of his own home? He could probably use a little encouragement.

She headed back to the porch, but slowed her steps when she saw that Zachary was still there, not Morgan. She was put on the spot when the older man pinned her with angry eyes. "Did you put him up to this, gal?"

She slowly continued forward. "I haven't known your son for very long. His decisions have nothing to do with me. However, I do know he's starting a new business. It's for his mother, your wife. He told me about all the times he and his brothers had to ride to town and then return here only to tell Mrs. Callahan that what she'd ordered and was waiting for hadn't arrived yet, and how disappointed she was. He wants to make sure she's never disappointed again. That's why he went searching for gold and silver ore, because he knew you wouldn't finance such a venture. Or would you have loaned him the money?"

He sat back in his chair with a sigh. "You spend your whole life building something to leave to your children, and then they don't want it," he grumbled. "I probably wouldn't have been open to his idea—unless he explained it like you just did. All for his ma, huh? I can't rightly argue with that, much as I love that gal."

"Maybe you should tell Morgan that."

"Maybe you should mind your own business, missy."

What an ornery old cuss, Violet thought. If she'd known him better she might have made a sharp reply, but she said nothing more and left him to stew over what he should or shouldn't have said to his son.

She went upstairs to see if her father was awake. He probably was, considering all the noise she could hear emerging from an open door a few doors down the hall from her room. She set Tiny inside her room, then went to investigate. She stopped in the doorway to see Morgan slamming a bureau drawer shut and throwing a pile of clothes on the bed, where his saddlebags and a valise lay open.

"You probably don't need to do that," she remarked.

He glanced at her but didn't stop what he was doing, and there was anger in his tone—just not for her. "Nothing is changing my mind, certainly not that old coot. I love him, but he's still treating me like a boy. Hell, I crossed that bridge five years ago. I think Pa failed to notice."

She smiled. "I'm sure he noticed. But parents will always treat their children like children and try to do what's best for them. They aren't always right. However, I think he's come around. You probably don't need to take a sword and shield to dinner, either."

He stared at her a moment, then laughed and walked over and pulled her into his arms, hugging her. "So you're my good-luck charm now? What the heck did you tell him?"

Words caught in her throat, being this close to him again.

All she wanted to do was kiss him. She came so close to putting her arms around him and doing it.

But she managed to step back into the hall and say, "Just what you should have told him first: that you got the idea for the emporium from your mother. That's all he needed to hear. He does have a soft spot for her, you know."

She hurried on to her father's room before she changed her mind about kissing Morgan. Good grief, how could she marry Lord What's-his-name when this man tempted her beyond reason? Because it was what she'd always dreamed of—and yet, Morgan was the one filling her dreams now. He seemed to be with her every bloody night!

Chapter Forty-Seven

MORGAN STOPPED THE BUCKBOARD in front of the house to wait for Violet. His mother was leaning against the porch post drinking her coffee. She was dressed for the range, just hadn't left yet, and since they hadn't spoken privately after he'd made his announcement about the emporium last night at dinner, he wasn't really surprised.

She'd been pleased last night. After she got over her amazement, she'd laughed a lot. His brothers had teased and were already calling him "shopkeeper." Hunter had even ribbed, "You'll have to put your gun away, or your customers will think you're there to rob the place!" His father had been mostly silent, but he'd smiled a few times as he'd watched Mary express her delight.

But this morning his mother said, "You're really doing this?"

"Dig out your old catalogs, circle everything that caught your eye, that you ordered, that you thought about buying but didn't, and leave them in my room. Yes, I'm really doing this.

'Buy it, have it in your home the same day,' that's going to be my motto—at least for Nashart. I might even name the emporium East Comes West."

"I love the idea, Morg," she assured him. "Don't think for a minute that I don't. But I loved having you on the range with us, too."

"I'm not leaving the territory, Ma. I may even get back on the range someday. But for now, this is the only thing I want to do. My store may never sell a damn thing out here, but it's going to be fun creating it, and very satisfying to see you shopping in it."

"What about Miss Mitchell?"

"I'll give her a tour of town today and show her my property, if she'll stop primping and get herself down here."

"That's not what I meant. You fancy her?"

He grinned. "Who wouldn't?"

"Have you told her?"

"She's already picked out an English lord to be her husband. She's going back to London. And I'm making sure she has a dowry for it."

Mary laughed. "Now, that's not how you get the girl. You give her a choice—but first you make sure she knows she has a choice. Do I need to tell you how to spill the beans properly?"

Morgan snorted. "You think I can't say it?"

"Have you ever?"

"No, but how hard can it be?"

"Pretty hard when you're not sure of the answer," she replied.

"Well, that's not holding me back. It's because I do care about her that I have to let her go. She doesn't belong here, Ma."

"Neither did Tiffany, but you can't get that gal to leave now.

You don't see it because you grew up here, but Montana has its own charm. Maybe you should ask Miss Mitchell to help you design your store. That might delay her leaving and give her time to start liking the place. Actually, who better than a young lady of London society to advise you on what's fashionable, what women like, and what fancy stores look like in the big cities?"

Morgan laughed. He was sold on his mother's idea as soon as she said the word *delay*, but he also liked the part about asking Violet for advice on décor and what merchandise to stock. But he teased his mother, saying, "I'm not opening a dress shop."

"At least stock some bonnets!"

He rolled his eyes, because now he had to. Anything his mother wanted. That was the point, after all.

THEY HAD ALREADY DRIVEN down every street in Nashart so that Violet could see everything the town offered before Morgan took her to the land he'd bought, just a long stretch of dusty ground with some grass and a few trees that intersected with Nashart's main road. But then she saw the stacks of lumber. "You're ready to start building?"

"I bought up all the lumber in town and ordered a lot more," he explained. "And I'm thinking about offering the owner of the stable on the main road and the owners of the three other buildings next to it an opportunity to relocate to my new street so I can put the entrance to my store right on the main road. What do you think?"

"Visibility from Nashart's main road would be ideal if you can manage it, even if you do have an entire street of your own to work with back here."

He grinned. "Oh, I can manage it, since I'm their landlord now."

"But the size of the building for your store will depend on what you plan to sell. Which is?"

"Furniture and silverware to start with. The Melling brothers who buy my silver make everything you can think of: jewelry, candelabra, knickknacks, dinnerware, picture frames, even fancy mirrors, so I'll be going to New York to visit them soon. Oh, I'll also sell bonnets."

She was delighted. "Really?"

"Ma mentioned it this morning."

"Well, that will certainly draw the women in town. So a silver section combined with jewelry, that you might want up front. The furniture will take up the most room because you will probably want to display full sets of it, and at least two sets each for bedrooms, dining rooms, and parlors. What about a second floor?"

"I was thinking I'd live up there myself."

"But you may end up needing a second floor for the store—and do you really want to climb two flights of stairs to the third floor to go home at the end of the day?"

"I'd still like my own place here in town."

"Why? Your family's ranch isn't far from here."

"And if I get hitched?"

"Hitched to what?"

He laughed; she grinned. She did know what the phrase meant in Montana. But when they left his new property to have lunch, it ended up being all she could think about. He was already planning ahead for when he got married—just not to her. He'd had many opportunities to broach that particular subject with her. The times they'd made love were prime examples of when he should have gotten down on his bloody knee just so she *could* say no. Damnit.

"Why the sour face?" he asked when she set the restaurant menu down. "Nothing on the menu appeals to you?"

She cast off her jealous thoughts and dredged up a smile for him. "No, I was just thinking that you've been talking about a store bigger than any I've ever seen."

"I have the room for it, so why not?"

"Indeed. In big cities, there isn't much land available, so shops are squeezed in wherever there is space. But with your big store, you will need more than a few employees."

"I've already asked around. There're only two men in town willing to work for me who don't already have jobs, and neither of them wants to do any selling."

"There are employment agencies in the big cities that can hire employees for you, but if you do bring people in, you will need to provide them with someplace to live. Perhaps build rooms in the back? Or you could build your own boarding-house for your employees next to the store."

"Another good idea I hadn't thought of."

"And what about a warehouse to store your merchandise, or are you going to make your customers wait, as your mother did, when you need to restock?"

"You're amazing," he said with a wide smile. "I never really thought that far ahead."

"So think about it. When you buy in bulk, you will get discounts, which will raise your profits. You did plan on making money at this, correct?"

He chuckled. "That wasn't the goal, but I suppose it would be a nice bonus."

"And the rest of your street? You'll have room for a boardinghouse, a warehouse, even a house for yourself. You've got both sides of the street to fill."

"Only because the mayor wouldn't agree to prevent any saloons going in, so I took the whole parcel. But it's probably a good investment. I can lease the land to other merchants, or just wait and see what the town needs and put the stores up myself."

She started to laugh. "So not just an entrepreneur, but on your way to being a business tycoon?"

"No, just thinking ahead, mainly making sure this particular street doesn't attract any rowdiness."

She raised a brow. "You promoted your town as peaceful, as I recall."

"Cowboys will still raise hell on a Saturday night."

"Oh, that." But her thoughts had raced ahead, and she suggested, "An ice cream shop! I haven't seen one here. And a bookstore or a library."

Now he laughed. "Let me finish designing my store before I start thinking about others. But by all means, start a list. And maybe think about sticking around to help me bring it all together."

That suggestion sort of fell out there. He wasn't even looking at her when he said it. And she actually wished she *could* be there to see his finished dream. If she didn't have to get back to that lord—what the devil was his name? Staring at Morgan, it simply wouldn't come to her.

And then she realized what he meant. "Are you offering me a job?"

"No, I was thinking more about a partnership."

Her eyes flared. In his store? Or in his life, as his wife? His store, of course. That was not how a man proposed marriage.

And a business partnership would require her staying here and being tempted by him indefinitely. . . .

She assumed he would give her time to think about it, which was good, because she didn't want to dampen his enthusiasm with her answer. His store was an exciting venture—but Morgan was the real excitement, the man she wanted to be partnered with in every way. Oh, good grief, having only half of the partnership she wanted would never be enough for her.

She almost said no immediately. She didn't, but she would have to say it eventually.

Chapter Forty-Eight

"**W**HAT ARE THE ODDS?" Morgan said as they left the restaurant.

Violet glanced at him, about to ask what he meant, but he wasn't looking at her. He was gazing down the boardwalk. She squealed in delight when she saw her brothers hurrying toward them. Indeed, what were the odds of seeing identical twins in town who weren't the Mitchell brothers? She laughed and ran ahead to hug them.

"Why didn't you let us know you were arriving today?" she asked.

"We did," one of them—Daniel?—said. "I sent the telegram to Butte as soon as I bought the train tickets and got the date of our arrival here. You must already have left by then."

"No matter, you're here! And you must be anxious to see Father. We're staying at the Triple C ranch with his partner's family, and"—she turned to make sure Morgan was still behind her—"this is his partner, Morgan Callahan. Introduce yourselves, I'm not even going to try."

He laughed and did—it *was* Daniel—but told her, "I'm making it easy for you. My hair got long while I was detained, and I decided not to cut it. I'll wear this queue for now, until you get used to us again."

Evan was shaking Morgan's hand. "We can't thank you enough, Mr. Callahan, for sending us that money, first to ease the urgency of making the loan payments, then to actually pay off the loan. Vi, you should have seen Mr. Perry's face. He looked so disappointed."

"I wanted to throw the money in his face, but Evan wouldn't let me," Daniel added. "You can't imagine what a relief it was to pay off that loan. Thank you, Mr. Callahan."

"Charley was, is, my friend," Morgan replied, then grinned. "And your sister just had to remind me of that with a bit of nagging."

Violet gasped. "I don't nag!"

"Charley?" Evan asked.

She tsked. "That's what Morgan calls Papa." But she wasn't letting her brothers off the hook. "Daniel, why and where exactly were you detained?"

"My tailor had me thrown in jail for not paying my bills."

Evan quickly added, "With the first money that arrived, there was enough to hold off Perry and pay off Dan's debts to get him out of jail. But that was a hellish month, Vi, grieving for Father, worried sick about you when we didn't hear from you again, all while the clock was ticking down on the house."

"Well, you'll be glad to know that the man responsible for faking Father's death and causing us that grief is on his way to prison, but I'll let Father explain that later. I'm sure you're eager to see him, so shall we?" She pointed them toward the buckboard in front of the restaurant.

Morgan helped her onto the driver's seat to ride next to him again, so she had to turn in the seat to converse with her brothers.

"Papa did exactly what he set out to do: he's found a new fortune, thanks to Morgan's benevolence. You two won't have to work in the mine, but one or both of you will need to oversee the miners who will do the work, at least until a manager is hired and until we've earned enough to pay back the loan Morgan gave us. But Papa and Morgan can explain that in more detail later. So you can both stop worrying—and that means you won't need to marry that heiress now, Evan, unless you want to."

"No!" He laughed. "It was merely an option, and a very unpleasant one. She's rich as sin but doesn't even feign being nice."

"He's politely not saying she's insufferable and arrogant, and he was being overly kind when he told you she was pretty, because she's not," Daniel put in. "But we thought it best not to mention that when we had all that other bad news to tell you the day you got home."

"Good of you to spare me, but next time, don't. Well, there won't be a next time."

"I'm excited to be here," Evan said. "I never dreamed we'd get to see this part of the country."

"I feel the same," Daniel said enthusiastically. "So I volunteer to manage the mine."

But Evan objected. "We may have to fight over it, Brother."

"Mines," Violet corrected. "There are two of them side by side, and we have an equal partnership with Morgan. We can figure out who goes or if you both go later."

They were halfway to the ranch when Evan said, "Vi, I just remembered! You'll need to send someone with a wagon for your trunks."

"Trunks? I just asked for one."

"Yes, but you didn't say which one, so we had to bring all of them to make sure you got the right one."

"I'll take care of it," Morgan told her, then added in a whisper, "You're happy around them, aren't you?"

"Of course I am, they're my brothers."

He smiled. "Another good reason for you not to run back to England."

Was that a subtle way of asking for her answer to his partnership offer? But he wanted her to help run his store here in Nashart, and her brothers would be near Butte—but they wouldn't be an ocean away, either. Was Morgan playing underhanded, or just sweetening the pot?

She might be able to put off answering him until she was ready to leave, so she could continue helping him in the meantime. She wanted to fantasize a little longer about how wonderful it would be working beside this man permanently. She just had to ignore for now the one stumbling block: how inappropriate it would be to partner with a man while she was an unmarried woman. It just wasn't done. She was sure her father would forbid it.

Her brothers' argument about whether they should rent a carriage while they were in Nashart caught her attention. "Stop it," she ordered. "There are no carriages to be had—" She broke off, and gave Morgan an excited glance. "A carriage-maker! For one of the shops on your new street. Or you might even bring in a few carriages yourself and add them to your emporium's inventory."

He grinned. "I like seeing you like this, open, bubbly—bossy."

She laughed. "I'm not bossy."

"She is!" both brothers said in unison.

Chapter Forty-Nine

THE STAY IN NASHART was turning out to be most pleasant. Violet loved advising Morgan about his fancy emporium; in fact, it was nearly all they talked about that week. And soon the mines would be earning an incredible amount of money for both partners. Daniel and Evan had left a few days ago to manage them temporarily since they both found the prospect interesting. Morgan spent hours instructing both of them on everything they needed to know to start mining.

While Morgan could have gotten his friends in Nashart to help him build his store in just a few days once all the lumber had arrived, Violet had reminded him that it wouldn't be grand enough for the distinctive furnishings he intended to sell, so he'd sent off a few more telegrams to the Melling brothers in New York, asking them to find an architect as well as an experienced manager for him.

Texas got married the very day he arrived back in town, too eager to make Emma his wife to wait for a traditional wedding to be arranged, so only Emma's family witnessed the ceremony.

Two days later, he left to take Daniel and Evan to the mines—but Emma went with them. No more separations for those two, a thought that made Violet sad because it reminded her that she would soon be separating herself from her own family—once again. Which had sparked an argument—with herself. But her brothers helped end it by stating a simple truth.

Both were angry with her when she got around to telling them her plans. But it was Daniel who said, "It may take months for Father to regain his usual vigor. Are you really going to leave us before then?"

"I could return with my husband."

"An English lord visiting America? Must you marry him, Vi? Nine years was too long for you to be over there, and you want to make it forever?"

She'd started to cry, and emotion won out. It was that word *forever*. And she'd already been leaning toward not going. It was definite now.

And today—today she was getting married. Well, maybe. She wasn't exactly sure how it all came about, but she was certain it had started with Mary Callahan, who came into the dining room just as she and Morgan were finishing lunch. He had business in town and had just stood up to leave. He kissed his mother in passing. Mary stared after him for a moment before she turned to Violet and remarked, "He's partial to you."

Morgan had used the same word back in Butte, but it hadn't been clear what he meant by it, so Violet asked his mother, "What exactly does that mean around here? Something more than fond?"

"Hell, yeah, a lot more. And it's obvious. How come you don't see it?"

Actually, she did see it when he looked at her, touched her,

354 ~◯ JOHANNA LINDSEY

did nice things for her; it was just that she'd never heard it. But Morgan was a man of action, not a fancy talker. And, as she knew from playing poker with him, he held his cards close to his vest.

With a big smile on her face, she ran upstairs to find her father. Stepping into his room, she said, "What would you think about my staying here and marrying your partner?"

He put down the book he was reading, stared at her for a moment, then laughed. "I think that would make me incredibly happy. He already seems like a son to me. And I must confess that I saw this coming—well, I hoped. So I suppose I should also confess that I haven't needed to convalesce here, sweetness. I was just giving you and Morgan time to realize you never want to part. You can tell him you both have my blessing."

Delighted, she sat in the chair next to his bed to make a few confessions of her own, how her old dreams of marrying an English lord had waned in comparison to being partners with Morgan in his store—yes, he'd asked her to be his business partner—and how love was so very confusing, but temptation wasn't. Yes, she even said that to her father! And she admitted that she'd known for a while now that she wanted to marry Morgan, but now that she was sure of how he felt about her, she didn't want to wait another moment, wanted to be married today.

It was late afternoon when she went downstairs to see if Morgan had returned. He hadn't, so she rode to town to find him. She could wait for Morgan to do the asking, but she couldn't imagine how long that might take. It was a momentous decision for her to do the asking instead, and if she thought about it long enough, she wouldn't. So she rode straight for the church first, then set out to find Morgan. She was impatient by the time she spotted him leaving the telegraph office.

She galloped toward him, reined in abruptly, and said without preamble, "Marry me by sundown. The preacher has been informed. My father has been informed. You can tell your parents." And she rode off just as abruptly with her cheeks scalding from a deep blush.

The trouble was, she felt like her old self in Nashart, especially after being with her brothers this week, so she'd gotten a bit bossy. There was no other excuse for what she'd just done, ordering him to marry her instead of asking as she'd intended. She was mortified! How could she face him again? How could she not?

Those thoughts raced through her mind as she rode back to the ranch. But when she came to Tiffany and Hunter's house, she slowed down. She could hide there for a while. But as soon as Tiffany opened the door to her pounding, she cried, "I ordered him to marry me today!"

"What did he say?"

"I didn't give him a chance to say anything!"

"But you beat him to it?"

"I did what?"

Tiffany couldn't stop laughing long enough to answer, but when she finally did, she said, "It was only a matter of time, honey. Everyone guessed it would happen soon. Morgan is probably *so* relieved that you beat him to it and did the asking. Why wait, after all, when you both know it's what you want? And don't worry about a thing. I'll get you to the church on time. Did you specify a time?"

"I told him by sundown."

Tiffany giggled. "How western of you. I bet that made him laugh."

If she hadn't left him shocked. If he wasn't already riding out of the territory. . . .

But she stood in the church late that day as the sun set, wearing one of her white evening gowns trimmed in lilac satin, more sedate than one of her ball gowns. Tiffany had fetched it for her, since Violet was too afraid to return to the ranch and run into Morgan if he was back there. Tiffany even supplied her own wedding veil for the occasion. And sneaked Violet into town early so they wouldn't run into any of the family. She'd even refused to let Hunter into the house while they were getting ready. Tiffany Callahan was turning out to be a wonderful friend.

Her father, along with Morgan's family, started arriving at the church, followed by most of the people in town. Word had spread fast. She wished the Faulkners could have been there, too. What a long letter she would have to write to Sophie and Aunt Elizabeth! Morgan's brothers tried to talk to her when they arrived, but Mary shushed them, which was a good thing, because the slightest wrong word could make Violet bolt, she was that nervous. Morgan hadn't arrived yet, and the most nerve-racking part was standing at the altar waiting for him. Traditionally the groom waited for the bride. But nothing about this wedding was traditional, including the possibility the groom wouldn't show up for it—although his family must expect him to or they wouldn't be there, which was why she hadn't run yet.

And then he walked down the aisle toward her, her bear, amazingly handsome in his fancy black suit, wearing the biggest grin. He wanted to be there! She was so relieved she thought she might swoon.

When he reached her, he took her hand in his and brought it to his lips, then whispered, "Yes, by the way."

Hunter took that moment to call out teasingly, "Who's holding the shotgun?"

"I am," she and Morgan said in unison.

She gave Morgan a weak smile for shouldering the blame. "I'm sorry about how I broached the subject with you."

"I'm not. I wasn't going to. I love you too much and didn't want to try to keep you here if you really wanted to go."

Hearing that, she threw her arms around him. But someone else yelled, "Get married first!"

They laughed, faced the preacher, and got hitched. Yes, she could definitely think of marriage to Morgan that way. She was going to embrace his way of life, not try to lure him to hers. Well, good intentions . . .

He was kissing her before the preacher said he could, and she got lost in it, reveled in the sweet, hot sensations he evoked, would have stayed that way forever if Morgan hadn't taken her hand and rushed them out of the church amid all the loud congratulations. He helped her get in the buckboard waiting out front, then drove them out of town—but not toward the ranch.

"They're all going to want the traditional bride's kiss," he warned. "Just make sure you slap any men who take too long at it, or I'll have to start throwing punches."

But he'd just absconded with her! She started to laugh again. She had a feeling she was going to do a lot of that this evening, she was so happy. She glanced back to see the whole town following them, in wagons, and buckboards and on horseback. And then she heard the music, and looked ahead once more to see lights strung up in the field they were approaching. There was a large wooden platform there, too, and many benches and tables laden with food.

"This is where the town comes for gatherings and dances and to celebrate special events," he explained. "And today couldn't be more special. We'll leave when you're ready, or if either of us gets too drunk. I booked us a room at the hotel. There's no way we're spending our wedding night with my family down the hall."

She grinned and stroked his face. "Good idea, but we're not getting foxed. You can partake of a few, but I want you sober tonight."

"Bossing me already, Mrs. Callahan?"

She chuckled. "Sorry, it's a habit. And I'm never going to stop being embarrassed about asking you to marry me."

"You didn't ask, as I recall. But let me fix that. Will you do me the honor of being my wife?"

"Too late, I already am!"

"Yes, but now you're not the only one who asked."

That was sweet of him, but she already knew that about him, and that he was kind, thoughtful, and generous, once you got to know him—even before you did, her father being a prime example. She wasn't amazed that she'd fallen in love with this man, only that she hadn't figured it out sooner.

They danced and enjoyed a few drinks, and the men lined up for kisses. And she got to meet the rest of Tiffany's family, the Warrens, who had once been on the other side of that old feud, but were now close friends of the Callahans.

Her father's toast brought tears to her eyes. "To the bride and groom, I wish the happiness I found in my own marriage, the blessing of children who will make me a grandfather"—he paused to wink at Violet—"and the joy of cherishing each other. To Violet, my only daughter, my pride and joy, I know you think this is the happiest day of your life, but love has a way of giving you many such moments. Enjoy them all—and try not to boss your husband too much." He waited for the laughter to quiet down before continuing, "To Morgan, I truly couldn't have asked for a better man to give my daughter to in marriage. I already thought of you as a son, so I couldn't be happier that you're now a member of our family—let your wife boss you a little, she can't help it."

More laughter, especially when Morgan said, "I said I do, now I say I will!"

"To the bride and groom!" Charles finished, raising his glass.

It was such a festive evening she hated to see it end, but she was more eager to have her new husband all to herself, so she was the one who suggested that they slip away quietly, which they did.

On the ride to the hotel in the buckboard, she held up her hand to admire her wedding band, wondering how Morgan had gotten it so quickly. She'd visited every store in Nashart that week, and none had sold rings, as far as she'd noticed.

"Did you borrow these rings for the ceremony?" she asked.

"No, I ordered them before we left Butte, the day you agreed to come to Nashart. I was already hoping you'd never want to leave once you got here." Watching her, he added, "Maybe I shouldn't order jewelry for the store. I'll end up giving it all to you instead of selling it, if it makes you look like that."

"Like what?"

"So delighted."

"But I won't let you give it all to me. I am your partner now and will have a say."

"You are?"

"Most definitely. I'd already decided, but this partnership"—she tapped the ring—"needed to come first. Well, I had to marry someone before I could go into business with a man, you understand. It would have been beyond the pale otherwise. So it was only proper that I ask you to marry me first."

He laughed. "I'm glad you thought of being proper."

She blushed. "That wasn't all I thought about. How I feel about you in particular sort of made it mandatory that you come first."

He let go of the reins to drag her into his lap. She squealed until she realized they were in front of the hotel and he was only lifting her down, yet he didn't let go of her. He carried her inside and straight up the stairs. She recalled how differently she'd felt when he'd carried her *out* of that hotel in Butte, rolled up in a blanket. She couldn't stop smiling. When he set her down, the door to their room was closed behind them and the bed was in sight. She wondered why they weren't kissing already. The last time they'd been alone in a hotel room, the atmosphere had been explosive. But Morgan was slowly taking the pins from her hair, then softly kissing her neck, then removing more pins. He was also gently nudging her backward.

Feeling her temperature rising, she said, "I'm not going to say I'm partial to you, though I am. I prefer to say I love you, because I do, you know." That got her a kiss before he continued that slow nudging toward the bed. With a slight blush, she added, "I was miserable when I left you, and I suppose I can tell you that now."

He confessed as well. "I was hoping for more time to win you by tempting you with being my partner. But if you had said yes, you better believe I would have asked you to marry me then and there."

She chuckled. "You've made it very hard for me to be proper around you and keep my hands off you."

Cupping her cheeks in his hands, he kissed her long and luxuriously before he said against her lips, "No more resisting, so if you've a mind to ravish me, go right ahead. For the first time, I know we have all night."

She grinned at his suggestion about ravishing him, and she definitely liked that she had all night to do it. "That sounds like you'll get to cuddle," she teased.

His grin grew wide. "Every night from now on. God, woman, you make me so bloody happy."

She started laughing; he started kissing her more deeply. So maybe she would lure him just a little bit to her ways, even if only in the phrases he used. Time would tell. But the only thing that really mattered tonight was that the bear was now her husband, and good grief, he made her so bloody happy, too!

HEADLINE
ETERNAL

FIND YOUR HEART'S DESIRE...

VISIT OUR WEBSITE: www.headlineeternal.com
FIND US ON FACEBOOK: facebook.com/eternalromance
CONNECT WITH US ON TWITTER: @eternal_books
FOLLOW US ON INSTAGRAM: @headlineeternal
EMAIL US: eternalromance@headline.co.uk